PRAISE FOR THE
MACHINERIES OF EMPIRE SERIES

'Lee's ability to balance high science fiction concepts—worlds, cultures, and weapons—with a deep examination of character—tragic flaws, noble purpose, and societal ideas—is nigh unprecedented in space opera.'

B&N Sci-Fi & Fantasy Blog

'How do you follow-up a breathtaking, multiple award-nominated debut that combined world-changing technologies, interesting reality-altering mathematics and awesome characters? *Raven Stratagem* is as mind-blowing as its predecessor, but in a completely different way.'

Kirkus Reviews

'Without a doubt, *Raven Stratagem* is proof that Yoon Ha Lee sits next to Ann Leckie atop the podium for thoughtful, intricate, and completely human science fiction.'

Tor.com

'This stunning sequel to the Hugo- and Nebula-nominated *Ninefox Gambit* contains a satisfying mixture of interstellar battles, politics, intrigue, and arcane technology… Readers who don't mind being dropped in the deep end will savor this brilliantly imagined tale.'

Publishers Weekly Starred Review

'Lee has leveraged the adage that "any seemingly advanced science can look like magic" to create truly bizarre technologies; while there is plenty of gripping space opera action, the real pleasure of this series is the inventive worldbuilding.'

Library Journal Starred Review

'The story is dense, the pace intense, and the delicate East Asian flavoring of the math-rich setting might make it seem utterly alien to many readers—yet metaphors for our own world abound. Readers willing to invest in a steep learning curve will be rewarded with a tight-woven, complicated but not convoluted, breathtakingly original space opera. And since this is only the first book of the *Machineries of Empire* trilogy, it's the start of what looks to be a wild ride.'

N. K. Jemisin, *The New York Times*

'I love Yoon's work! *Ninefox Gambit* is solidly and satisfyingly full of battles and political intrigue, in a beautifully built far-future that manages to be human and alien at the same time. It should be a treat for readers already familiar with Yoon's excellent short fiction, and an extra treat for readers finding Yoon's work for the first time.'

Ann Leckie

'Cheris and Jedao are fascinating, multi-faceted entities, filled with contradictions and idiosyncrasies; Lee's prose is clever and opulently detailed; the worldbuilding is jaw-droppingly good. Like the many-eyed Shuos, the book appears to delight in its own game, a tangle of plots and subplots. It almost seems content to never be deciphered, but if you persist, you're in for a fantastic story. Lee's novel is a brilliant way to begin a trilogy.'

Ars Technica

'Yoon Ha Lee recasts Korean legend in a densely rendered, high-tech future universe, with intricate worldbuilding.'

The Guardian

'Rather than aping the generic clipped-and-grim style so often employed by other, less talented writers, Lee leans in the other direction, finding a sumptuous beauty in physical moments and complexity in thought and motivation. *Ninefox* is a book with math in its heart, but also one which understands that even numbers can lie. That it's what you see in the numbers that matters most. And that something—maybe all things—begun with the best, truest of intentions can go terribly wrong once the gears of reality begin to churn.'

NPR

'Beautiful, brutal and full of the kind of off-hand inventiveness that the best SF trades in, *Ninefox Gambit* is an effortlessly accomplished SF novel. Yoon Ha Lee has arrived in spectacular fashion.'

Alastair Reynolds

'*Starship Troopers* meets *Apocalypse Now*—and they've put Kurtz in charge... Mind-blistering military space opera, but with a density of ideas and strangeness that recalls the works of Hannu Rajaniemi, even Cordwainer Smith. An unmissable debut.'

Stephen Baxter

'For those itching for dense worldbuilding, a riproaring plot, complex relationships, and military SF with a deep imagination, it'll do just the trick. Lee's already shown he has the chops for short fiction, and now *Ninefox Gambit* proves that he's a novelist to watch out for. This is military SF with blood, guts, math, and heart.'

Tor.com

'"You know what's going on, right?" *Ninefox Gambit* asks. Often, you have to say, "Uh, yeah, of course," when the real answer is "I have no idea, but I really, really care." And then you keep reading.'

Strange Horizons

'For sixteen years Yoon Ha Lee has been the shadow general of science fiction, the calculating tactician behind victory after victory. Now he launches his great manoeuvre. Origami elegant, fox-sly, defiantly and ferociously *new*, this book will burn your brain. Axiomatically brilliant. Heretically good.'

Seth Dickinson

'A high-octane ride through an endlessly inventive world, where calendars are weapons of war and dead soldiers can assist the living. Bold, fearlessly innovative and just a bit brutal, this is a book that deserves to be on every awards list.'

Aliette de Bodard

'Ambitious. Confusing. Enthralling. Brilliant. These are the words I will use to describe Yoon Ha Lee's utterly immersive, utterly memorable novel. I had heard very high praise for Lee's short fiction—still, even with those moderate expectations I had no idea what I was in for. I haven't felt this blown away by a novel's originality since *Ancillary Justice*. And, since I'm being completely honest, *Ninefox Gambit* is actually more inventive, boundary-breaking, and ambitious than that.'

The Book Smugglers

'Cheris' world feels genuinely alien, with thrillingly unfamiliar social structures and technologies, and the attention to detail is simply stunning. Just don't ever let your concentration slip, or there's a good chance that you will miss something wonderful.'

SciFi Now

'A dizzying composite of military space opera and sheer poetry. Every word, name and concept in Lee's unique world is imbued with a sense of wonder.'

Hannu Rajaniemi

'There's a good chance that this series will be seen as an important addition to the space opera resurgence of recent years. While Lee has developed a singular combination of military SF, mathematical elegance, and futuristic strangeness, readers may note echoes of or similarities to Iain M. Banks, Hannu Rajaniemi, C. J. Cherryh, Ann Leckie and Cordwainer Smith. Admirers of these authors, or anyone interested in state-of-the-art space opera, ought to give *Ninefox Gambit* a try.'

Worlds Without End

'Daring, original and compulsive. As if Cordwainer Smith had written a *Warhammer* novel.'

Gareth L. Powell

'That was a great read; very intriguing world building in particular. I now want to sign all my emails with "Yours in calendrical heresy."'

Tobias Buckell

First published 2019 by Solaris
an imprint of Rebellion Publishing Ltd,
Riverside House, Osney Mead,
Oxford, OX2 0ES, UK

www.solarisbooks.com

ISBN: 978 1 78108 564 6

This is a work of fiction. All the characters and events
portrayed in this book are fictional, and any resemblance to
real people or incidents is purely coincidental.

10 9 8 7 6 5 4 3 2 1

A CIP catalogue record for this book is available from the
British Library.

Designed & typeset by Rebellion Publishing

Printed in Denmark

HEXARCHATE STORIES

YOON HA LEE

SOLARIS

CONTENTS

HEXARCHATE (AND HEPTARCHATE) TIMELINE

PRE-HEPTARCHATE

pre-calendar   "The Chameleon's Gloves" takes place.

HEPTARCHATE

0   Heptarchate founded.

first century   Rahal Ienora creates compromise local remembrance system so people don't get messed up by local day-cycles vs. the high calendar.

342   Hajoret Kujen (later Nirai Kujen) is born.

354   Hajoret Kujen becomes Warlord Halash's concubine.

356   Hajoret Kujen admitted to Nirai Academy Prime.

ca. 370   Modern mothdrives and harnesses introduced, permitting a period of rapid expansion; modern remembrances introduced through the influence of Nirai Kujen.

383   Nirai Kujen enters the black cradle with Heptarch Nirai Esfarel.

804   Garach Rodao is born.

809   Garach Jedao Shkan (later Shuos Jedao) is born.

814   Garach Nidana is born.

826   Cadet Garach Jedao Shkan causes the suicide of Cadet Vestenya Ruo at Shuos Academy.

831   Shuos Jedao is assigned to Heptarch Shuos Khiaz's office as infantry.

832   Shuos Jedao is seconded to Kel army as a senior lieutenant.

839   "Extracurricular Activities" takes place. Shuos Jedao is promoted to tactical group commander.

841   Shuos Jedao is promoted to brigadier general and is raped by Heptarch Shuos Khiaz, then suborned by Heptarch Nirai Kujen.

850   Shuos Jedao is promoted to general.

852   Battle of Candle Arc.

853   The massacre at Hellspin Fortress.

854   General Shuos Jedao is executed and enters the black cradle.

907   General Kel Dessenet uses Wildfire over the Aerie to destroy an invading swarm. The formation is put on the proscribed list by Kel Command.

916   Hafn invasion.

944   Liozh revolt.

ca. 950   Eshpatan (Shuos Jedao's homeworld) is lost to the Hafn in a border flare-up.

HEXARCHATE

952   The heptarchate is officially disbanded and reformed as the hexarchate.

970   Lieutenant General Kel Vrae Tala loses the Fire Grasses campaign.

981   Hexarch Nirai Kujen takes Shuos Jedao and three servitors to the base on Tefos. Jedao leaves with Kujen;

the servitors, including Hemiola, remain to maintain the base.

1081 Hexarch Nirai Kujen checks in at Tefos Base, again accompanied by Shuos Jedao.

1155 Alaikko Inesser (later Kel Inesser) is born.

1175 The Fortress of Spinshot Coins has its defenses upgraded.

1179 Neshte Khiruev (later Kel Khiruev) is born.

1181 Hexarch Nirai Kujen again checks in at Tefos Base, accompanied by Shuos Jedao.

1184 Vauhan Mikodez (later Shuos Mikodez) is born.

1185 Vauhan Istradez is born.

1187 Nirai Mahar is born.

1193 Muyyed (later Kel Muyyed) is born.

1196 Eurikhos Dhanneth (later Kel Dhanneth) is born.

1202 Rhezny Miuzan (later Kel Miuzan) and Rhezny Ganazan (later Kel Ganazan) are born. Nirai Kujen is anchored to Nirai Mahar.

1207 Kel Inesser is promoted to major general.

1208 Rhezny Brezan (later Kel Brezan) is born.

1209 Shuos Mikodez becomes hexarch with Shuos Zehun's support.

1211 Hexarch Shuos Mikodez orders the assassination of two cadets at a Shuos Academy Tertiary.

1221 Nirai Faian ascends to false hexarch.

1222 Ajewen Dzera marries Ajewen Derow; he takes her name per Mwennin custom.

1225 Ajewen Cheris (later Kel Cheris) is born.

1236 Kel Khiruev is promoted to general.

1246 Kel Brezan is promoted to lieutenant colonel.

1251 *Ninefox Gambit* takes place.

1252 *Raven Stratagem* takes place.

1261 *Revenant Gun* takes place.

1263 "Glass Cannon" takes place.

THE CHAMELEON'S GLOVES

RHEHAN HATED MUSEUMS, but their partner Liyeusse had done unmentionable things to the ship's stardrive the last time the two of them had fled the authorities, and the repairs had drained their savings. Which was why Rhehan was on a station too close to the more civilized regions of the dustways, flirting with a tall, pale woman decked in jewels while they feigned interest in pre-Devolutionist art.

In spite of themself, Rhehan was impressed by colonists who had carved pictures into the soles of worn-out space boots: so useless that it had to be art, not that they planned to say that to the woman.

"—wonderful evocation of the Festival of the Vines using that repeated motif," the woman was saying. She brushed a long curl of hair out of her face and toyed with one of her dangling earrings as she looked sideways at Rhehan.

"I was just thinking that myself," Rhehan lied. The Festival of the Vines, with its accompanying cheerful inebriation and sex, would be less agonizing than having to pretend to care about the aesthetics of this piece. Too bad Rhehan and

Liyeusse planned to disappear in the next couple of hours. The woman was pretty enough, despite her obsession with circuitscapes. Rhehan was of the opinion that if you wanted to look at a circuit, nothing beat the real thing.

A tinny voice said in Rhehan's ear, "Are you on location yet?"

Rhehan faked a cough and subvocalized over the link to Liyeusse. "Been in position for the last half-hour. You sure you didn't screw up the prep?"

She snorted disdainfully. "Just hurry it—"

At last the alarms clanged. The jeweled woman jumped, her astonishing blue eyes going wide. Rhehan put out a steadying arm and, in the process, relieved her of a jade ring, slipping it in their pocket. Not high-value stuff, but no one with sense wore expensive items as removables. They weren't wearing gloves on this outing—had avoided wearing gloves since their exile—but the persistent awareness of their naked hands never faded. At least, small consolation, the added sensation made legerdemain easier, even if they had to endure the distastefulness of skin touching skin.

A loud, staticky voice came over the public address system. "All patrons, please proceed to the nearest exit. There is no need for alarm"—exactly the last thing you wanted to say if you didn't want people to panic, or gossip for that matter—"but due to an incident, the museum needs to close for maintenance."

The woman was saying, with charming anxiety, "We'd better do as they say. I wonder what it is."

Come on, Rhehan thought, *what's the delay?* Had they messed up preparing the explosives?

They had turned to smile and pat the woman's hand reassuringly when the first explosives went off at the end of the hall. Fire flowered, flashed; a *boom* reverberated through the halls, with an additional hiss of sparks when a security screen went down. Two stands toppled, spilling a ransom's worth of iridescent black quantum-pearl strands inscribed with algorithmic paeans. The sudden chemical reek of the smoke made Rhehan cough; you'd think they'd be used to it by now. Several startled bystanders shrieked and bolted toward the exit.

The woman leapt back and behind a decorative pillar with commendable reflexes. "Over here," she called out to Rhehan, as if she could rescue them. Rhehan feigned befuddlement although they could easily lip-read what she was saying—they could barely hear her past the ringing in their ears—and sidestepped out of her reach, just in case.

A second blast went off, farther down the hall. A thud suggested that something out of sight had fallen down. Rhehan thought snidely that some of the statues they had seen earlier would be improved by a few creative cracks anyway. The sprinklers finally kicked in, and a torrent of water rained down from above, drenching them.

Rhehan left the woman to fend for herself. "Where are you going?" she shouted after Rhehan, loudly enough to be heard despite the damage to their hearing, as they sprinted toward the second explosion.

"I have to save the painting!" Rhehan said over their shoulder.

To Rhehan's dismay, the woman pivoted on her heel and followed. Rhehan turned their head to lip-read their words, almost crashing into a corner in the process. "You shame me," she said as she ran after them. "Your dedication to the arts is greater than mine."

Another explosion. Liyeusse, whose hearing was unaffected, was wheezing into Rhehan's ear. "Dedication... to... the... arts!" she said between breaths. "Dedication. *You*."

Rhehan didn't have time for Liyeusse's quirky sense of humor. Just because they couldn't tell a color wheel from a flywheel didn't mean they didn't appreciate market value.

They'd just rounded the corner to the relevant gallery and its delicious gear collages when Rhehan was alerted—too late— by the quickened rhythm of the woman's footsteps. They inhaled too sharply, coughed at the smoke, and staggered when she caught them in a chokehold. "What—" Rhehan said, and then no words were possible anymore.

RHEHAN WOKE IN a chair, bound. They kept their eyes closed and tested the cords, hoping not to draw attention. The air had a familiar undertone of incense, which was very bad news, but perhaps they were only imagining it. Rhehan had last smelled this particular blend, with its odd metallic top notes, in the ancestral shrines of a childhood home they hadn't returned to in eight years. They stilled their hands from twitching.

Otherwise, the temperature was warmer than they were accustomed to—Liyeusse liked to keep the ship cool—and a faint hissing suggested an air circulation system not kept in as good shape as it could be. Even more faintly, they heard the distinctive, just-out-of-tune humming of a ship's drive. Too bad they lacked Liyeusse's ability to identify the model by listening to the harmonics.

More importantly: how many people were there with them? They didn't hear anything, but that didn't mean—

"You might as well open your eyes, Kel Rhehan," a cool female voice said in a language they had not heard for a long time, confirming Rhehan's earlier suspicions. They had not fooled her.

Rhehan wondered whether their link to Liyeusse was still working, and if she was all right. "Liyeusse?" they subvocalized. No response. Their heart stuttered.

They opened their eyes: might as well assess the situation, since their captor knew they were awake.

"I don't have the right to that name any longer," Rhehan said. They hadn't been part of the Kel people for eight years, as the Kel reckoned it. But their hands itched with the memory of the Kel gloves they no longer wore. With their hands exposed like this, they felt shamed and vulnerable in front of one of their people.

The woman before them was solidly built, dark, like the silhouette of a tree, and more somber in mien than the highly ornamented agent who had brought Rhehan in. She wore the black and red of the Kel judiciary. A cursory slip of veil obscured part of her face, its translucence doing little to hide her sharp features. The veil should have scared Rhehan more, as it indicated that the woman was a judge-errant, but her black Kel gloves hurt worse. Rhehan's had been stripped from them and burned when the Kel cast them out.

"I've honored the terms of my exile," Rhehan said desperately. What had they done to deserve the attention of a judge-errant? Granted that they were a thief, but they'd had little choice but to make a living with the skills they had. "What have you done with my partner?"

The judge-errant ignored the question. Nevertheless, the sudden tension around her eyes suggested she knew *something*. Rhehan had been watching for it. "I am Judge Kel Shiora, and I have been sent because the Kel have need of you," she said.

"Of course," Rhehan said, fighting to hide their bitterness. Eight years of silence and adapting to an un-Kel world, and the moment the Kel had need of them, they were supposed to comply.

Shiora regarded them without malice or opprobrium, or anything much resembling feeling. "There are many uses for a jaihanar."

Jaihanar—what non-Kel called, in their various languages, a haptic chameleon. Someone who was not only so good at imitating patterns of movement that they could scam inattentive people, but even able to fool the machines whose security systems identified their owners' characteristic movements. How you interacted with your gunnery system, or wandered about your apartment, or smiled at the lover you'd known for the last decade. It wasn't magic—a jaihanar needed some minimum of data to work from—but the knack often seemed that way.

The Kel produced few jaihanar, and the special forces snapped up those that emerged from the Kel academies. Rhehan had been the most promising jaihanar in the last few generations, before disgracing themselves. The only reason they hadn't been executed was that the Kel government had foreseen that they would someday be of use again.

"Tell me what you want, then," Rhehan said. Anything to keep her talking so that eventually she might be willing to say what she'd done with Liyeusse.

"If I undo your bonds, will you hear me out?"

Getting out of confinement would also be good. Their leg had fallen asleep. "I won't try anything," Rhehan said. They knew better.

Ordinarily, Rhehan would have felt sorry for anyone who trusted a thief's word so readily, except they knew the kind of training a judge-errant underwent. Shiora wasn't the one in danger. They kept silent as she unlocked the restraints.

"I had to be sure," Shiora said.

Rhehan shrugged. "Talk to me."

"General Kavarion has gone rogue. We need someone to infiltrate her ship and retrieve a weapon she has stolen."

"I'm sorry," Rhehan said after a blank pause. "You just said that *General Kavarion* has gone rogue? Kavarion, the hero of Split Suns? Kavarion of the Five Splendors? My hearing must be going."

Shiora gave them an unamused look. "Kel command sent her on contract to guard a weapons research facility," she said.

"Kavarion recently attacked the facility and made off with the research and a prototype. The prototype may be armed."

"Surely you have any number of loyal Kel who'd be happy to go on this assignment?" Rhehan said. The Kel took betrayal personally. They knew this well.

"You are the nearest jaihanar in this region of the dustways." Most people reserved the term *dustways* for particularly lawless segments of the spaceways, but the Kel used the term for anywhere that didn't fall under the Kel sphere of influence.

"And," Shiora added, "few of our jaihanar match your skill. You owe the Kel for your training, if nothing else. Besides, it's not in your interest to live in a world where former Kel are hunted for theft of immensely powerful weapon prototypes."

Rhehan had to admit she had a point.

"They named it the Incendiary Heart," Shiora continued. "It initiates an inflationary expansion like the one at the universe's birth."

Rhehan swore. "Remote detonation?"

"There's a timer. It's up to you to get out of range before it goes off."

"The radius of effect?"

"Thirty thousand light-years, give or take, in a directed cone. That's the only thing that makes it possible to use without blowing up the person setting it off."

Rhehan closed their eyes. That would fry a nontrivial percentage of the galaxy. "And you don't know if it's armed."

"No. The general is running very fast—to what, we don't know. But she has been attempting to hire mercenary jaihanar. We suspect she is looking for a way to control the device—which may buy us time."

"I see." Rhehan rubbed the palm of one hand with the fingers of the other, smile twisting at the judge-errant's momentary look of revulsion at the touch of skin on skin. Which was why they'd done it, of course, petty as it was. "Can you offer me any insight into her goals?"

"If we knew that," the judge-errant said bleakly, "we would know why she turned coat."

Blowing up a region of space, even a very local region of space in galactic terms, would do no one any good. In particular, it would make a continued career in art theft a little difficult. On the other hand, Rhehan was determined to wring some payment out of this, if only so Liyeusse wouldn't lecture them about their lack of mercenary instinct. Their ship wasn't going to fix itself, after all. "I'll do it," they said. "But I'm going to need some resources—"

The judge surprised them by laughing. "You have lived too long in the dustways," she said. "I can offer payment in the only coin that should matter to you—or do you think we haven't been watching you?"

Rhehan should have objected, but they froze up, knowing what was to come.

"Do this for us, show us the quality of your service," the judge-errant said, "and Kel Command will reinstate you." Very precisely, she peeled the edge of one glove back to expose the dark fine skin of her wrist, signaling sincerity.

Rhehan stared. "Liyeusse?" they asked again, subvocally. No response. Which meant that Liyeusse probably hadn't heard the offer. At least she wasn't there to see Rhehan's reaction. As good as they normally were at controlling their body language, they had not been able to hide that moment's hunger for a home they had thought forever lost to them.

"I will do this," Rhehan said at last. "Not for some bribe; but because a weapon like the one you describe is too dangerous for anyone, let alone a rogue, to control." And because they needed to find out what had become of Liyeusse, but Shiora wouldn't understand that.

*　　*　　*

THE WOMAN WHO escorted Rhehan to their ship, docked on the Kel carrier—Rhehan elected not to ask how this had happened—had a familiar face. "I don't know why *you're* not doing this job," Rhehan said to the pale woman now garbed in Kel uniform, complete with gloves, rather than the jewels and outlandish stationer garb she'd affected in the museum.

The woman unsmiled at Rhehan. "I will be accompanying you," she said in the lingua franca they'd used earlier.

Of course. Shiora had extracted Rhehan's word, but she would also take precautions. They couldn't blame her.

Kel design sensibilities had not changed much since Rhehan was a cadet. The walls of dark metal were livened by tapestries of wire and faceted beads, polished from battlefield shrapnel: obsolete armor, lens components in laser cannon, spent shells. Rhehan kept from touching the wall superstitiously as they walked by.

"What do I call you?" Rhehan said finally, since the woman seemed disinclined to speak first.

"I am Sergeant Kel Anaz," she said. She stopped before a hatch, and tapped a panel in full sight of Rhehan, her mouth curling sardonically.

"I'm not stupid enough to try to escape a ship full of Kel," Rhehan said. "I bet you have great aim." Besides, there was Liyeusse's safety to consider.

"You weren't bad at it yourself."

She would have studied their record, yet Rhehan hated how exposed the simple statement made them feel. "I can imitate the stance of a master marksman," Rhehan said dryly. "That doesn't give me the eye, or the reflexes. These past years, I've found safer ways to survive."

Anaz's eyebrows lifted at "safer," but she kept her contempt to herself.

After chewing over Anaz's passkey, the hatch opened. A whoosh of cool air floated over Rhehan's face. They stepped through before Anaz could say anything, their eyes drawn immediately to the lone non-Kel ship in the hangar. To their relief, the *Flarecat* didn't look any more disreputable than before.

Rhehan advanced upon the *Flarecat* and entered it, all the while aware of Anaz at their back. Liyeusse was bound to one of the passengers' seats, the side of her face swollen and purpling, her cap of curly hair sticking out in all directions. Liyeusse's eyes widened when she saw the two of them, but she didn't struggle against her bonds. Rhehan swore and went to her side.

"If she's damaged—" Rhehan said in a shaking voice, then froze when Anaz shoved the muzzle of a gun against the back of their head.

"She's ji-Kel," Anaz said in an even voice: *ji-Kel*, not-Kel. "She wasn't even concussed. She'll heal."

"She's my partner," Rhehan said. "We work together."

"If you insist," Anaz said with a distinct air of distaste. The pressure eased, and she cut Liyeusse free herself.

Liyeusse grimaced. "New friend?" she said.

"New job, anyway," Rhehan said. They should have known that Shiora and her people would treat a ji-Kel with little respect.

"We're never going to land another decent art theft," Liyeusse said with strained cheer. "You have no sense of culture."

"This one's more important." Rhehan reinforced their words with a hand signal: *Emergency. New priority.*

"What have the Kel got on you, anyway?"

Rhehan had done their best to steer Liyeusse away from any dealings with the Kel because of the potential awkwardness. It hadn't been hard: the Kel had a reputation for providing reliable but humorless mercenaries and a distinct lack of appreciation for what Liyeusse called "the exigencies of survival in the dustways." More relevantly, while they controlled a fair deal of wealth, they ruthlessly pursued and destroyed those who attempted to relieve them of it. Rhehan had never been tempted to take revenge by stealing from them.

Anaz's head came up. "You never told your partner?"

"Never told me what?" Liyeusse said, starting to sound irritated.

"We'll be traveling with Sergeant Kel Anaz," Rhehan said, hoping to distract Liyeusse.

No luck. Her mouth compressed. *Safe to talk?* she signed at them.

Not really, but Rhehan didn't see that they had many options. "I'm former Kel," Rhehan said. "I was exiled because—because of a training incident." Even now, it was difficult to speak of it. Two of their classmates had died, and an instructor.

Liyeusse laughed incredulously. "You? We've encountered Kel mercenaries before. You don't talk like one. Move like one. Well, except when—" She faltered as it occurred to her that, of the various guises Rhehan had put on for their heists, that one hadn't been a guise at all.

Anaz spoke over Liyeusse. "The sooner we set out, the better. We have word on Kavarion's vector, but we don't know how long our information will be good. You'll have to use your ship since the judge-errant's would draw attention, even if it's faster."

Don't, Rhehan signed to Liyeusse, although she knew better than to spill the *Flarecat*'s modifications to this stranger. "I'll fill you in on the way."

The dustways held many perils for ships: wandering maws, a phenomenon noted for years and unexplained for just as long; particles traveling at unimaginable speeds, capable of destroying any ship lax in maintaining its shielding; vortices that filtered light even in dreams, causing hallucinations. When Rhehan had been newly exiled, they had convinced Liyeusse of their usefulness because they knew dustway paths new to her. Even if they hadn't been useful for making profit, they had helped in escaping the latest people she'd swindled.

Ships could be tracked by the eddies they left in the dustways. The difficulty was not in finding the traces, but in interpreting them. Great houses had risen to prominence through their monopoly over the computational networks that processed and sold this information. Kel Command had paid dearly for such information in its desperation to track down General Kavarion.

Assuming that information was accurate, Kavarion had ensconced herself at the Fortress of Wheels: neutral territory, where people carried out bargains for sums that could have made Rhehan and Liyeusse comfortable for the rest of their lives.

The journey itself passed in a haze of tension. Liyeusse snapped at Anaz, who bore her jibes with grim patience. Rhehan withdrew, not wanting to make matters worse, which was the wrong thing to do, and they knew it. In particular, Liyeusse had not forgiven them for the secret they had kept from her for so long.

At last, Rhehan slumped into the copilot's seat and spoke to Liyeusse over the newly repaired link to gain some semblance of privacy. As far as they could tell, Anaz hardly slept.

Rhehan said, "You must have a lot of questions."

"I knew about the chameleon part," Liyeusse said. Any number of their heists had depended on it. "I hadn't realized that the Kel had their own."

"Usually, they don't," Rhehan said. Liyeusse inhaled slightly at *they*, as if she had expected Rhehan to say *we* instead. "But the Kel rarely let go of the ones they do produce. It's the only reason they didn't execute me."

"What did you do?"

Rhehan's mouth twisted. "The Kel say there are three kinds of people, after a fashion. There are Kel; ji-Kel, or not-Kel, whom they have dealings with sometimes; and those who aren't people at all. Just—disposable."

Liyeusse's momentary silence pricked at Rhehan. "Am I disposable to you?" she asked.

"I should think it's the other way around," they said. They wouldn't have survived their first year in the dustways without her protection. "Anyway, there was a training exercise. People-who-are-not-people were used as—" They fumbled for a word in the language they spoke with Liyeusse, rather than the Kel term. "Mannequins. Props in the exercise, to be gunned down or saved or discarded, whatever the trainees decided. I chose the lives of mannequins over the lives of Kel. For this I was stripped of my position and cast out."

"I have always known that the universe is unkind," Liyeusse said, less moved than Rhehan had expected. "I assume that hired killers would have to learn their art somewhere."

"It would have been one thing if I'd thought of myself as a soldier," Rhehan said. "But a good chameleon, or perhaps a failed one, observes the people they imitate. And eventually, a chameleon learns that even mannequins think of themselves as people."

"I'm starting to understand why you've never tried to go back," Liyeusse said.

A sick yearning started up in the pit of Rhehan's stomach. They still hadn't told her about Kel Shiora's offer. Time enough later, if it came to that.

Getting to Kavarion's fleet wasn't the difficult part, although Liyeusse's eyes were bloodshot for the entire approach. The *Flarecat*'s stealth systems kept them undetected, even if mating it to the command ship, like an unwanted tick, was a hair-raising exercise. By then, Rhehan had dressed themselves in a Kel military uniform, complete with gloves. Undeserved, since strictly speaking they hadn't recovered their honor in the eyes of their people, but they couldn't deny the necessity of the disguise.

Anaz would remain with Liyeusse on the *Flarecat*. She hadn't had to explain the threat: *Do your job, or your partner dies*. Rhehan wasn't concerned for Liyeusse's safety—so long as the two remained on the ship, Liyeusse had access to a number of nasty tricks and had no compunctions about using them—but the mission mattered to them anyway.

Rhehan had spent the journey memorizing the haptic profiles that Anaz had provided them. Anaz had taken one look at Rhehan's outdated holographic mask and given them a new one. "If you could have afforded up-to-date equipment, you wouldn't be doing petty art theft," she had said caustically.

The Fortress of Wheels currently hosted several fleets. Tensions ran high, although its customary neutrality had so far prevailed. Who knew how long that would last; Liyeusse, interested as always in gossip, had reported that various buyers for the Incendiary Heart had shown up, and certain warlords wouldn't hesitate to take it by force if necessary.

Security on Kavarion's command ship was tight, but had not been designed to stop a jaihanar. Not surprising; the Kel relied on their employers for such measures when they deigned to stop at places like the Fortress. At the moment, Rhehan was disguised as a bland-faced lieutenant.

Rhehan had finessed their way past the fifth lock in a row, losing themselves in the old, bitter pleasure of a job well done. They had always enjoyed this part best: fitting their motions to that of someone who didn't even realize what was going on, so perfectly that machine recognition systems could not tell the difference. But it occurred to them that everything was going too perfectly.

Maybe I'm imagining things, they told themself without

conviction, and hurried on. A corporal passed them by without giving more than a cursory salute, but Rhehan went cold and hastened away from him as soon as they could.

They made it to the doors to the general's quarters. Liyeusse had hacked into the communications systems and was monitoring activity. She'd assured Rhehan that the general was stationside, negotiating with someone. Since neither of them knew how long that would last—

Sweat trickled down Rhehan's back, causing the uniform to cling unpleasantly to their skin. They had some of the general's haptic information as well. Anaz hadn't liked handing it over, but as Rhehan had pointed out, the mission would be impossible without it.

Kavarion of the Five Splendors. One of the most celebrated Kel generals, and a musician besides. Her passcode was based on an extraordinarily difficult passage from a keyboard concerto. Another keyboardist could have played the passage, albeit with difficulty reproducing the nuances of expression. While not precisely a musician, Rhehan had trained in a variety of the arts for occasions such as this. (Liyeusse often remarked it was a shame they had no patience for painting, or they could have had a respectable career forging art.) They got through the passcode. Held their breath. The door began opening—

A fist slammed them in the back of the head.

Rhehan staggered and whirled, barely remaining upright. *If I get a concussion I'm going to charge Kel Command for my medical care,* they thought as the world slowed.

"Finally, someone took the bait," breathed Rhehan's assailant. Kel Kavarion; Rhehan recognized the voice from the news reports they'd watched a lifetime before. "I was starting to think I was going to have to hang out signs or hire a bounty hunter." She did something fast and complicated with her hands, and Rhehan found themselves shoved down against the floor with the muzzle of a gun digging into the back of their neck.

"Sir, I—"

"Save it," General Kavarion said, with dangerous good humor. "Come inside and I'll show you what you're after. Don't fight me. I'm better at it than you are."

Rhehan couldn't argue with that.

The general let Rhehan up. The door had closed again, but she executed the passphrase in a blur that made Rhehan think she was wasted on the military. Surely there was an orchestra out there that could use a star keyboardist.

Rhehan made sure to make no threatening moves as they entered, scanning the surroundings. Kavarion had a taste for the grandiloquent: triumph-plaques of metal and stone and lacquerware covered the walls, forming a mosaic of battles past and comrades lost. The light reflecting from their angled surfaces gave an effect like being trapped in a kaleidoscope of sterilized glory.

Kavarion smiled cuttingly. Rhehan watched her retreating step by step, gun still trained on them. "You don't approve," Kavarion remarked.

Rhehan unmasked since there wasn't any point still pretending to be one of her soldiers. "I'm a thief," they said. "It's all one to me."

"You're lying, but never mind. I'd better make this quick." Kavarion smiled at Rhehan with genuine and worrying delight. "You're the jaihanar we threw out, aren't you? It figures that Kel Command would drag you out of the dustways instead of hiring some ji-Kel."

"*I'm* ji-Kel now, General."

"It's a matter of degrees. It doesn't take much to figure out what Kel Command could offer an exile." She then offered the gun to Rhehan. "Hold that," she said. "I'll get the Incendiary Heart."

"How do you know I won't shoot you?" Rhehan demanded.

"Because right now I'm your best friend," Kavarion said, "and you're mine. If you shoot me, you'll never find out why I'm doing this, and a good chunk of the galaxy is doomed."

Frustrated by the sincerity they read in the set of her shoulders, Rhehan trained the gun on Kavarion's back and admired her sangfroid. She showed no sign of fear at all.

Kavarion spoke as she pressed her hand against one of the plaques. "They probably told you I blew the research station up after I stole the Incendiary Heart, which is true." The plaque lifted to reveal a safe. "Did they also mention that someone armed the damned thing before I was able to retrieve it?"

"They weren't absolutely clear on that point."

"Well, I suppose even a judge-errant—I assume they sent a judge-errant—can't get information out of the dead. Anyway, it's a time bomb, presumably to give its user a chance to escape the area of effect."

Rhehan's heart sank. There could only be one reason why Kavarion needed a jaihanar of her own. "It's going to blow?"

"Unless you can disarm it. One of the few researchers with a sense of self-preservation was making an attempt to do so before he got killed by a piece of shrapnel. I have some video, as much of it as I could scrape before the whole place blew, but I don't know if it's enough." Kavarion removed a box that shimmered a disturbing shade of red-gold-bronze.

The original mission was no good; that much was clear. "All right," Rhehan said.

Kavarion played back a video of the researcher's final moments. It looked like it had been recorded by someone involved in a firefight, from the shakiness of the image. Parts of the keycode were obscured by smoke, by flashing lights, by flying shrapnel.

Rhehan made several attempts, then shook their head.

"There's just not enough information, even for me, to reconstruct the sequence."

Kavarion slumped, suddenly looking haggard.

"How do you know he was really trying to disarm it?" Rhehan said.

"Because he was my lover," Kavarion said, "and he had asked me for sanctuary. He was the reason I knew exactly how destructive the Incendiary Heart was to begin with."

Scientists shouldn't be allowed near weapons design, Rhehan thought. "How long do we have?"

She told them. They blanched.

"Why did you make off with it in the first place?" Rhehan said. They couldn't help but think that if she'd kept her damn contract, this whole mess could have been avoided in the first place.

"Because the contract-holder was trying to sell the Incendiary Heart to the highest bidder. And at the time I made off with it, the highest bidder looked like it was going to be one of the parties in an extremely messy civil war." Kavarion scowled. "Not only did I suspect that they'd use it at the first opportunity, I had good reason to believe that they had *terrible* security—and I doubted anyone stealing it would have any scruples either. Unfortunately, when I swiped the wretched thing, some genius decided it would be better to set it off and deny it to everyone, never mind the casualties."

Kavarion closed her fist over the Incendiary Heart. It looked like her fist was drenched in a gore of light. "Help me get it out of here, away from where it'll kill billions."

"What makes you so confident that I'm your ally, when Kel Command sent me after you?"

She sighed. "It's true that I can't offer a better reward than if you bring the accursed thing to them. On the other hand, even if you think I'm lying about the countdown, do you really trust Kel Command with a weapon this dangerous? They'd never let me hand it over to them for safekeeping anyway, not when I broke contract by taking it in the first place."

"No," Rhehan said after a moment. "You're right. That's not a solution either."

Kavarion opened her hand and nodded companionably at Rhehan, as though they'd been comrades for years. "I need you to run away with this and get farther from centers of civilization. I can't do this with a whole fucking Kel fleet. My every movement is being watched, and I'm afraid someone will get us into a fight and stall us in a bad place. But you—a ji-Kel thief, used to darting in and out of the dustways—your chances will be better than mine."

Rhehan's breath caught. "You're already outnumbered," they said. "Sooner or later, they'll catch up to you—the Kel, if not everyone else who wants the weapon they think you have. You don't even have a running start, docked here. They'll incinerate you."

"Well, yes," Kavarion said. "We are Kel. We are the people of fire and ash. It comes with the territory. Are you willing to do this?"

Her equanimity disturbed Rhehan. Clearly, Liyeusse's way of looking at the world had rubbed off on them more than they'd accounted for, these last eight years. "You're gambling a lot on my reliability."

"Am I?" The corners of Kavarion's mouth tilted up in amusement. "You were one of the most promising Kel cadets that year, and you gave it up because you were concerned about the lives of mannequins who didn't even know your name. I'd say I'm making a good choice."

Kavarion pulled her gloves off one by one and held them out to Rhehan. "You are my agent," she said. "Take the gloves, and take the Incendiary Heart with you. A great many lives depend on it."

They knew what the gesture meant: *You hold my honor.*

Shaken, they stared at her, stripped of chameleon games. Shiora was unlikely to forgive Rhehan for betraying her to ally with Kavarion. But Kavarion's logic could not be denied.

"Take them," Kavarion said tiredly. "And for love of fire and ash, don't tell me where you're going. I don't want to know."

Rhehan took the gloves and replaced the ones they had been wearing with them. *I'm committed now,* they thought. They brought their fist up to their chest in the Kel salute, and the general returned it.

THINGS WENT WRONG almost from the moment Rhehan returned to their ship. They'd refused an escort from Kavarion on the grounds that it would arouse Anaz's suspicions. The general had assured them that no one would interfere with them on the way out, but the sudden blaring of alarms and the scrambling of crew to get to their assigned stations meant that Rhehan had to do a certain amount of dodging. At a guess, the Fortress-imposed cease-fire was no longer in effect. What had triggered hostilities, Rhehan didn't know and didn't particularly care. All that mattered was escaping with the Incendiary Heart.

The *Flarecat* remained shielded from discovery by the stealth device that Liyeusse so loved, even if it had a distressing tendency to blow out the engines exactly when they had to escape sharp-eyed creditors. Rhehan hadn't forgotten its location, however, and—

Anaz ambushed Rhehan before they even reached the *Flarecat*, in the dim hold where they were suiting up to traverse the perilous webbing connecting the *Flarecat* to Kavarion's command ship. Rhehan had seen this coming. Another chameleon might have fought back, and died; Shiora had no doubt selected Anaz for her deadliness. But Rhehan triggered the mask into Kavarion's own visage and smiled Kavarion's own smile at Anaz, counting on the reflexive Kel deference to rank. The gesture provoked enough of a hesitation that Rhehan could pull out their own sidearm and put a bullet in the side of her neck. They'd been aiming for her head; no such luck. Still, they'd take what they could.

The bullet didn't stop Anaz—Rhehan hadn't expected it to—but the next two did. The only reason they didn't keep firing was that Rhehan could swear that the Incendiary Heart pulsed hotter with each shot. "Fuck this," they said with feeling, although they couldn't hear themselves past the ringing in their ears, and overrode the hatch to escape to the first of the web-strands without looking back to see whether Anaz was getting back up.

No further attack came, but Anaz might live, might even survive what Kavarion had in mind for her.

Liyeusse wasn't dead. Presumably Anaz had known better than to interfere too permanently with the ship's master. But Liyeusse wasn't in good condition, either. Anaz had left her unconscious and expertly tied up, a lump on the side of her head revealing where Anaz had knocked her out. Blood streaked her face. *So much for no concussions,* Rhehan thought. A careful inspection revealed two broken ribs, although no fingers or arms, small things to be grateful for. Liyeusse had piloted with worse injuries, but it wasn't something either of them wanted to make a habit of.

Rhehan shook with barely quelled rage as they unbound Liyeusse, using the lock picks that the two of them kept stashed on board. Here, with just the two of them, there was no need to conceal their reaction.

Rhehan took the precaution of injecting her with painkillers first. Then they added a stim, which they would have preferred to avoid, but the two of them would have to work together to escape. It couldn't be helped.

"My head," Liyeusse said in a half-groan, stirring. Then she smiled crookedly at Rhehan, grotesque through the dried blood. "Did you give that Kel thug what she wanted? Are we free?"

"Not yet," Rhehan said. "As far as I can tell, Kavarion's gearing up for a firefight and they're bent on blowing each other up over this bauble. Even worse, we have a new mission." They outlined the situation while checking Liyeusse over again to make sure there wasn't any more internal damage. Luckily, Anaz hadn't confiscated their medical kits, so Rhehan retrieved one and cleaned up the head wound, then applied a bandage to Liyeusse's torso.

"Every time I think this can't get worse," Liyeusse said while Rhehan worked, but her heart wasn't in it. "Let's strap ourselves in and get flying."

"What, you don't want to appraise this thing?" They held the Incendiary Heart up. Was it warmer? They couldn't tell.

"I don't love shiny baubles *that* much," she said dryly. She was already preoccupied with the ship's preflight checks, although her grimaces revealed that the painkillers were not as efficacious as they could have been. "I'll be glad when it's gone. You'd better tell me where we're going."

The sensor arrays sputtered with the spark-lights of many ships, distorted by their stealth device. "Ask the general to patch us in to her friend-or-foe identification system," Rhehan said when they realized that there were more Kel ships than there should have been. Kel Command must have had a fleet waiting to challenge Kavarion in case Shiora failed her mission. "And ask her not to shoot us down on our way out."

Liyeusse contacted the command ship in the Fortress's imposed lingua.

The connection hissed open. The voice that came back to them over the line sounded harried and spoke harried lingua. "Who the hell are—?" Rhehan distinctly heard Kavarion snapping something profane in the Kel language. The voice spoke back, referring to Liyeusse with the particular suffix that meant *coward*, as if that applied to a ji-Kel ship to begin with. Still, Rhehan was glad they didn't have to translate that detail for Liyeusse, although they summarized the exchange for her.

"Go," the voice said ungraciously. "I'll keep the gunners off you. I hope you don't crash into anything, foreigner."

"Thank you," Liyeusse said in a voice that suggested that she was thinking about blowing something up on her way out.

"Don't," Rhehan said.

"I wasn't going to—"

"They need this ship to fight with. Which will let us get away from any pursuit."

"As far as I'm concerned, they're all the enemy."

They couldn't blame her, considering what she'd been through.

The scan suite reported on the battle. Rhehan, who had webbed themself into the copilot's seat, tracked the action with concern. The hostile Kel hadn't bothered to transmit their general's banner, a sign of utter contempt for those they fought. Even ji-Kel received banners, although they weren't expected to appreciate the nuances of Kel heraldry.

The first fighter launched from the hangar below them. "Our turn," Liyeusse said.

The *Flarecat* rocketed away from the command ship and veered abruptly away from the fighter's flight corridor. Liyeusse rechecked stealth. The engine made the familiar dreadful coughing noise in response to the increased power draw, but it held—for now.

A missile streaked through their path, missing them by a margin that Rhehan wished were larger. To their irritation, Liyeusse was whistling as she maneuvered the *Flarecat* through all the grapeshot and missiles and gyring fighters and toward the edge of the battlefield. Liyeusse had never had a healthy sense of fear.

They'd almost made it when the engine coughed again, louder. Rhehan swore in several different languages. "I'd better see to that," they said.

"No," Liyeusse said immediately, "you route the pilot functions to your seat, and I'll see if I can coax it along a little longer."

Rhehan wasn't as good a pilot, but Liyeusse was indisputably better at engineering. They gave way without argument. Liyeusse used the ship's handholds to make her way toward the engine room.

Whatever Liyeusse was doing, it didn't work. The engine hiccoughed, and stealth went down.

A flight of Kel fighters at the periphery noted the *Flarecat*'s attempt to escape and, dismayingly, found it suspicious enough to decide to pursue them. Rhehan wished their training had included faking being an ace pilot. Or actually *being* an ace pilot, for that matter.

The Incendiary Heart continued to glow malevolently. Rhehan shook their head. *It's not personal,* they told themselves. "Liyeusse," they said through the link, "forget stealth. If they decide to come after us, that's fine. It looks like we're not the only small-timers getting out of the line of fire. Can you configure for boosters?"

She understood them. "If they blow us up, a lot of people are dead anyway. Including us. We might as well take the chance."

Part of the *Flarecat*'s problem was that its engine had not been designed for sprinting. Liyeusse's skill at modifications made it at least possible to run, but in return, the *Flarecat* made its displeasure known at inconvenient times.

The gap between the *Flarecat* and the fighters narrowed hair-raisingly as Rhehan waited for Liyeusse to inform them that they could light the hell out of there. The Incendiary Heart's glow distracted them horribly. The fighters continued their pursuit, and while so far none of their fire had connected, Rhehan didn't believe in relying on luck.

"I wish you could use that thing on them," Liyeusse said suddenly.

Yes, and that would leave nothing but the thinnest imaginable haze of particles in a vast expanse of nothing, Rhehan thought. "Are we ready yet?"

"Yes," she said after an aggravating pause.

The *Flarecat* surged forward in response to Rhehan's hands at the controls. They said, "Next thing: prepare a launch capsule for this so we can shoot it ahead of us. Anyone stupid enough to go after it and into its cone of effect—well, we tried."

For the next interval, Rhehan lost themselves in the controls and readouts, the hot immediate need for survival. They stirred when Liyeusse returned.

"I need the Heart," Liyeusse said. "I've rigged a launch capsule for it. It won't have any shielding, but it'll fly as fast and far as I can send it."

Rhehan nodded at where they'd secured it. "Don't drop it."

"You're so funny." She snatched it and vanished again.

Rhehan was starting to wish they'd settled for a nice, quiet, boring life as a Kel special operative when Liyeusse finally returned and slipped into the seat next to theirs. "It's loaded and ready to go. Do you think we're far enough away?"

"Yes," Rhehan hissed through their teeth, achingly aware of the fighters and the latest salvo of missiles.

"Away we go!" Liyeusse said with gruesome cheer.

The capsule launched. Rhehan passed over the controls to Liyeusse so she could get them away before the capsule's contents blew.

The fighters, given a choice between the capsule and the *Flarecat*, split up. Better than nothing. Liyeusse was juggling the power draw of the shields, the stardrive, life-support, and probably other things that Rhehan was happier not knowing about. The *Flarecat* accelerated as hard in the opposite direction as it could without overstressing the people in it.

The fighters took this as a trap and soared away. Rhehan expected they'd come around for another try when they realized it wasn't.

Then between the space of one blink and the next, the capsule simply vanished. The fighters overtook what should have been its position, and vanished as well. It could have been stealth, if Rhehan hadn't known better. They thought to check the sensor readings against their maps of the region: stars upon stars had gone missing, nothing left of them.

Or, they amended to themselves, there had to be some remnant smear of matter, but the *Flarecat*'s instruments wouldn't have the sensitivity to pick them up. They regretted the loss of the people on those fighters; still, better a few deaths than the billions the Incendiary Heart had threatened.

"All right," Liyeusse said, and retriggered stealth. There was no longer any need to hurry, so the system was less likely to choke. They were far enough from the raging battle that they could relax a little. She sagged in her chair. "We're alive."

Rhehan wondered what would become of Kavarion, but that was no longer their concern. "We're still broke," they said, because eventually Liyeusse would remember.

"You didn't wrangle *any* payment out of those damn Kel before we left?" she demanded. "Especially since after they finish frying Kavarion, they'll come toast us?"

Rhehan pulled off Kavarion's gloves and set them aside. "Nothing worth anything to either of us," they said. Once, they would have given everything to win their way back into the trust of the Kel. Over the past years, however, they had discovered that other things mattered more to them. "We'll find something else. And anyway, it's not the first time we've been hunted. We'll just have to stay one step ahead of them, the way we always have."

Liyeusse smiled at Rhehan, and they knew they'd made the right choice.

AUTHOR'S NOTE

The inspiration for this story came from Ross Anderson's spectacular *Security Engineering*, which I have read not once but twice; I've even sought out a number of the works it cites. The title may sound dry, but it's engagingly written, frequently accessible to a lay audience (you can skim the more technical sections if you're reading for fun), and tells you how the kinds of heists you might see on *Leverage* would work in real life. In particular, there's one section discussing various approaches an art thief could use that I found both hilarious and useful. Less so if you work for a museum, I'm sure.

HOW THE ANDAN COURT

ACTUALLY, I CANNOT offer you roses. Roses that taste like crystallized desire when you try to smell them. Roses whose buds are softer than the hands of the morning mist. Roses pierced through by the needles of nightfall.

Roses that count the season's clock with their petals, disrobing red by red until all's gone except the sun's winter angles. Roses growing in walls around the wells of your heart. Roses crowding the boundaries of your cards until every shuffle is a procession of brambles.

Roses laid upon the swelling waters to be swallowed by black tides. Roses that candy themselves as they pass your lips. Roses so shy you can only glimpse their shadows as you fall asleep.

I would rather give you roses than a bouquet of words, but I do not speak the petal language adequately and it does not admit translation; this will have to suffice.

AUTHOR'S NOTE

This is more of a prose poem than a proper story. I used to write speculative poetry, and even sold some of it until I came to the conclusion that $5/poem was a miserable rate of return. (Perhaps the secret is to write better poetry. I'll never know.)

Still, sometimes the urge hits me to write something with the feeling of a poem, if not its form.

SEVEN VIEWS OF THE LIOZH ENTRANCE EXAM

1.

ACCORDING TO RECORDS held like stunted chrysalids in the vaults of the Rahal, the Liozh demanded a practical examination as well as the written examination. We can guess what both components contained, even in those days, heresy-seeds waiting to fruit into the later rebellion. We know, empirically, how long it took the other heptarchs to recognize and act against the Liozh heresy. The delay between recognition and action remains a puzzle to this day.

Of particular interest, despite their fragmentary nature, are records of the assessment of the woman who would become the final Liozh heptarch. We retain the following notes: a jeng-zai spread featuring the card combination called the Web of Worlds, after that ancient signifier; a receipt for a meat pie, dated not only to the final day of her examination but to what would have been an auspicious time; and, most confusingly, an old-fashioned romance novel with several dog-eared pages. The significance of the romance novel has not yet been deciphered.

2.

IT IS CLAIMED that the written portion of the exam was taken on paper recycled from other factions' written exams. Occasionally, given the process used, faint distorted shadows of text surfaced, hinting at the laws of the Rahal, the rigid codes of the Vidona, the games of the Shuos. Scholars debate whether this practice helped lead to the downfall of the Liozh, or delayed it.

3.

IN A CERTAIN Vidona museum, one display shows what is said to be a Liozh cadet's flayed skin, preserved. They had gone into a heretical settlement as part of their practicum, bringing with them food, and water, and the comfort of the heptarchate's ideals. The heretics returned the cadet's skin, tanned, tattooed with high holy days in their own calendar.

According to the display's plaque, the Liozh failure to retaliate on their cadet's behalf was just another sign of their unfitness to rule.

4.

ONE OF THE most famous entrance exam questions goes like this: *If you had to destroy a single faction for the good of the heptarchate, which would it be, and why?*

5.

ONE PORTION OF the exam was taken in groups of seven. Prospective cadets had to enact a scenario in which one of them played the role of a Liozh ambassador and the rest played heretics being brought into the heptarchate. Frustratingly, the scoring rubric has not survived, nor do we know how the "ambassador" was selected.

Some have suggested that this particular game was introduced by the Shuos in order to hasten the Liozh's fall, although surely even the Shuos wouldn't be that obvious about it.

6.

THOSE WHO DID not pass the exam were barred from trying again, or applying to other factions. This was contrary to the practice of the time among the other factions, who were more lenient in their policies. That being said, the Andan and Shuos were both known to defy this rule if they felt some advantage could be gained by scooping up some candidate and giving them a new identity.

7.

REPORTS DIFFER ON what happened to Liozh candidates who had not yet passed the exam at the time of the final purge of the faction. The Rahal claim that the Vidona reeducated those who could be salvaged. What the Liozh themselves would have said about this, no one now will ever know.

AUTHOR'S NOTE

This is the kind of gimmick flash story that I can dash out in fifteen minutes almost without thinking. It's a pity that there isn't more of a market for gimmick flash stories, but then I suppose it would be unjust if I could make a living doing something this easy. This particular example probably also reveals just how scarring I found all the tests in school growing up; my first published story, "The Hundredth Question," is in the form of an exam!

OMENS

GARACH LEDANA HAD gotten Cousin Miro to watch her little son Rodao for the evening. She was indulging in her best approximation of the season's fashion. She'd obtained a wig in the latest trendy hairdo, all luxurious curls, since there was no way she could grow out her short mane overnight without resorting to risky modification technology. Ordinarily she didn't regret her choice of haircut, since she hated fussing with the stuff, but tonight she wanted to look her best. Whatever Cousin Miro said, she did have standards.

So Ledana donned a tasteful necklace of onyx and black pearls that she'd inherited from her gran, matched it with black pearl earstuds, and slipped into a dark gray dress with a diagonal slash of lavender. The ensemble came perilously close to Nirai colors, but damned if she was going to let that stop her from looking good. Besides, the last time Nirai inspectors had come through her lab, she'd charmed them into submission.

("Why *didn't* you become a Nirai?" one of her assistants had demanded. "Because most Nirai are squeamish about vivisecting their own geese for holiday dinners," she said. They hadn't asked again.)

She took a rented hoverer down to the city a couple hours in advance—rented because the one she owned was a reliable workhorse, and "reliable workhorse" was not what she wanted to convey to her date. It wasn't that she didn't have the money for a more luxurious vehicle, but when you didn't live in a big city, you wanted equipment you could rely on.

After securing parking, she hoofed it to the Shadow Theater. (Shparoi naming conventions were often rather on the nose.) Ledana had loved the building since she first encountered it as a child. It was traditional Shparoi architecture, with its high, peaked roofs and masks hung on the walls down to the absurd gold leaf everywhere, a replica of a structure that had been built back when her people initially settled this world. The original had been destroyed in a fire a generation or two back, but as a designated cultural treasure, the local government had restored it quickly.

Ledana knew perfectly well that "designated cultural treasures" were Andan manipulation all the way through, that the heptarchate's government used them to keep the local population docile. She couldn't help but feel gratitude toward the Andan arts council anyway. And it enabled her to enjoy the performances in an appropriate setting.

Her date awaited her in the foyer, a tall, black-haired man with a handsome, slightly angular profile, and long lashes over merry eyes. He, too, had dressed up in a suit of silk, although the rococo style of his jewelry spoke to offworlder tastes. She'd met him last week while shopping for some new jewelry after the conference; he'd been looking for souvenirs. Koiresh Shkan was a musician visiting with an ensemble from offworld, a Shparoi who'd left the homeworld as a young man and was only now returning. His accent when speaking their mutual mother tongue was atrocious, but Ledana had refrained from mentioning it.

Shkan smiled and waved when he spotted her. "I wouldn't have expected a goose farmer to be a patron of the arts," he said teasingly.

"Geese drive people to many strange hobbies," Ledana said. "Farming" wasn't all she did; she was technically an agricultural researcher. But "goose farmer" was a more entertaining way to put it. "If you'd wanted me to take you hunting instead—"

He pulled a face. "No thanks, I have no idea how to handle a gun."

Ledana shook her head. Out where she lived, everyone knew the basics of firearms. She was a fair shot herself. "Come on," she said, "let's find our seats before everyone swarms in."

Shkan made an assenting noise, and she preceded him into the auditorium.

The only thing Ledana didn't like about the Shadow Theater was the seats. She wished they'd gone for less authenticity with the damned wooden seats and instead installed cushions. But she loved the hanging lanterns and the wooden grilles with their carved shapes depicting scenes out of Shparoi folklore, from jackalope chorales to dawn fortresses shattered by archaic cannons.

After they took their seats, Shkan listened with a critical ear to the jumble of last-second rehearsal coming from the pit orchestra. "I'd forgotten that you tune to a different standard scale," he remarked.

"Does it bother you?" Ledana asked.

"No," he said, but she could tell he wasn't sure.

Then the bells rang and the lights in the auditorium dimmed, signaling the start of the performance. For the next two hours, Ledana almost forgot she was here with a man, and one she was determined to bed, at that. Instead, she was captivated by the way the actors contorted themselves and their props before the lights to form shadow figures against the back of the stage with its ever-shifting colors.

Tonight's story was about two lovers and the quest that one of them underwent to reunite himself with the other man, only for the two of them to be transformed into a flower-offering to the gods. For the flowers, a new set of curtains in green swished across the back of the stage, spangled with blossoms made of black sequins and dark crystal. Ledana was dazzled by the stage lights playing over them.

On reflection, maybe she should have picked something with a happy ending if she hoped to get laid, except she loved the building so, and shadow plays in general.

When the lights came back on and people began to file out of the auditorium, Shkan raised Ledana's hand to his lips and pressed a kiss to it. "I didn't realize you liked tragedies so much," he said, grinning. "Should I take this as an omen? Or do you just like very flexible people?"

Ledana didn't bother hiding her delight at the overture. She only hoped he was as good in bed as he was handsome. "It's the only shadow play running here for the next two months." She slipped into the high language for "month."

His eyes crinkled.

"Besides," Ledana said as she followed Shkan back into the foyer, "I don't believe in tragedies, or omens." No sense beating around the bush. "How do you feel about siring a kid? Because I know a few contortions myself."

Shkan linked arms with her and smiled.

AUTHOR'S NOTE

I like Jedao's mom Garach Ledana very much, but I only feel a little sorry for killing her off so ignominiously. I am afraid that when you slaughter as many characters as I do, you get inured to it.

By the way, when I was a kid growing up in Texas, I was convinced jackalopes were real. The hexarchate may be full of cockamamie Asians in space, but since I'm a Texan, some of those cockamamie Asians are cockamamie Asian *Texans* in space. (I take a particular fiendish delight, when people ask me where I'm from, in saying, "Houston.") As for cockamamie Asians who like guns, I am reminded of the time I took a semester of riflery at college. Despite being surrounded by great white hunter types, the best shot in the class was a five-foot nothing Asian woman who weighed maybe a hundred pounds soaking wet, who dimed the target every time. I took vicarious pleasure in her skill (I was the worst shot in the class).

By the way, the deal with this family and their geese is that in the very first draft of *Ninefox Gambit*, Jedao was an out-and-out Hollywood-style psychopath (I have never claimed to have good taste in tropes) and one of the dreadful flashbacks involved him vivisecting a live goose as a boy. I had the good sense to cut that scene, but in its honor, my family has roast goose (humanely killed, we hope) for dinner at Thanksgiving.

HONESTY

NIDANA WAS FOUR years old when she learned what her second-oldest brother's name meant.

Jedao was nine at the time, still skinny—certainly skinnier than Rodao, the oldest, who was fourteen and tall, and already broad at the shoulders and chest. Jedao and Ro both had to go to school. Nidana couldn't wait until she was old enough to go to school with them. Ro said that she should enjoy not having to study while she could, but Nidana didn't see that what Ro did with the slates was all that different from all the games she played on them. Plus he got to go out and play with his friends at school. Ro said that wasn't what you did at school, which was very confusing.

"'Honesty'?" Nidana said, tugging at Jedao's shirt while he was cleaning Mom's glassware. Nidana knew she was supposed to be careful, so careful, in this room, even more careful when someone was working with the shiny glassware. But she was also curious, and she couldn't wait. "Why did Mom name you 'honesty'?"

Jedao's eyes softened as he put down the beaker so he could ruffle her hair. "Beats me," he said. "I have always had the sneaking suspicion that she picked names out of one of those adventure novels she likes to read. I haven't been able to find evidence, though."

They were speaking in Shparoi, their birth-tongue. Their mother was Shparoi. So was Rodao's sire, and Jedao's, although not Nidana's. Most people realized that Nidana and Jedao were related, because they had inherited their mother's tilted smile and her eyes. The three of them had learned the high language second, not first. Rodao spoke the high language flawlessly, although he refused to say why it was so important to him, putting Nidana off with, "You'll find out someday." But Jedao never would lose the local Shparoi dialect's drawl.

"I can help," Nidana said, brightening at the thought of helping one of her brothers with something. She was starting to be able to read without pictures, although pictures were better.

"If you find it, let me know," Jedao said. He frowned at the beaker. "There's still a speck on this. You'd better go, Nidana, before Mom decides that you're old enough to learn how to do this."

She went.

The next day, she had not found evidence in any of the books she could reach. (She had also narrowly avoided pulling down a bookcase on herself, although she was oblivious to this fact.) But she decided that she could find something else to be helpful with, and set off after Jedao. Like everyone in the heptarchate, she had developed a keen sense of passing time from an early age. She might be able to meet him on the way home from school.

They lived at the edge of town—not even properly a town, Ro had remarked once—and Ro and Jedao hiked to a stop where a flitter picked them up with some other local kids. Jedao had taught Nidana the route over the course of weekends, almost certainly without Mom knowing. Definitely without Ro knowing. Mom wouldn't have cared—she let all of them explore the surroundings however they pleased—but Ro disapproved of an awful lot of things.

Nidana had a good sense of direction, something else she shared with Jedao, and she knew to wear a jacket and bring water and something to eat. Jedao always made her lunch in the morning because Mom tended to forget. But that meant that she had a rucksack with snacks and meat pastries. (The rucksack also communicated its location to the household computer system at all times, something she wouldn't learn until she was six. Mom might be terrible at feeding people on time, but she liked making sure no one got lost.)

The day was overcast, but Nidana liked the way the wind nipped at her cheeks and blew strands of her hair free. The hills were so tall. She liked the way the grasses made them mysterious, the occasional startling break of sunlight flinging shadows across her feet. Birds shouted at each other. She wondered if birds told the truth, like her brother was supposed to.

She had come up the hill, where the grasses had worn thin, and heard shouting, voices raised in taunts. The slight figure in a lavender jacket belonged to her brother. He was half-crouched, backing away from two older boys. She couldn't remember if she was supposed to know their names.

"Jedao!" she called out.

He whirled, caught sight of her, and said the same words Mom had said that night the goose eggs exploded in the incubator. "Nidana, run!" he shouted, just in time for the taller boy to hit him on the back of the head. He staggered but did not go down.

She ran toward Jedao. He said more words. The taller boy swung at him again, but Jedao was prepared this time and snatched up a rock. He didn't throw it, which was what Nidana would have done (if she had been allowed to throw rocks). He kept it in his fist. His blows were staggeringly quick, even with the added mass. The taller boy managed to get in another blow, then shouted one more taunt before fleeing. His friend said something that Nidana couldn't quite understand and scurried after him.

"Why don't they like you?" Nidana said. She was not afraid. Of course she wasn't afraid of the *boys*.

"It wasn't anything they had against me," Jedao said.

"Then why did you fight them?"

"They said things about Mom."

Nidana considered that. "Were they nice things?"

Jedao seemed to consider this in his turn. "They were things you have to hit people for."

"Oh." Then she saw it again, in a flash, her brother with his quick fists. For the first time she looked at him, wide-eyed, and thought of all the times he had carried her through the house, or combed her hair, or played house with her; thought of what he could do with those hands. She shrank from him.

Jedao set the rock down. Then he knelt and tipped her chin up with his callused fingers. "Listen," he said. "Listen. I would never hurt anyone I love."

She would not wonder for many years why, in a sentence otherwise in the high language, he had used the Shparoi word for *hurt,* which meant moral damage but excluded the physical—"a hurt of the heart's marrow, not the flesh," as one of their famed philosophers had said—a distinction that the high language did not make.

AUTHOR'S NOTE

Jedao never did find out what became of Nidana, and I regret that I ran out of time to tell her story. I will say that his suspicions were right and she hightailed it out of the heptarchate after Hellspin.

Incidentally, the Shparoi drawl is—you guessed it—a Texan drawl. I have the damndest time convincing folks that I'm from Texas because I don't have it myself, aside from saying "y'all"; my parents moved often enough that it didn't stick.

BUNNY

Jedao would rather have been doing anything but cleaning the bathroom, but his older brother Rodao had skipped out on the chore in favor of a night out with his boyfriend. Their mother was working late tonight, as usual, so she wouldn't know or care who did the job as long as it got done. Besides, Jedao considered it useful to have additional blackmail material on Ro. He couldn't decide whether it was hilarious or annoying that Ro had suddenly become interested in dating. At eleven, Jedao couldn't see what the fuss was about.

In the meantime, he still couldn't figure out how those weird purple stains had gotten onto the bathtub. Had his mother been pouring her experiments into the tub instead of disposing of them properly? Except she was always so conscientious about that. Or did it have something to do with her attempts to brew up new and exciting shampoos?

"Jay," said a soft, snuffling voice from the doorway.

Jedao set down the sponge and sat back on his haunches. His six-year-old sister Nidana was scrubbing her eyes. "What's the matter?" he asked.

Nidana burst into tears.

Jedao stripped off his rubber gloves, quickly washed his hands, and put his arms around her. "Hey, there," he said. "I didn't think the book I gave you to read was *that* scary." The book in question featured a bold girl space adventurer who punctured space monsters with her space rapier. Ordinarily Nidana loved that sort of thing.

After the snuffling and wailing had dwindled, Nidana said, "I went outside to look at the tree with the really big icicles."

"All right," he said, "did you hurt yourself?" He'd had icicles fall on him before. The big ones were no joke. She didn't *look* injured, despite the hair straggling out of her braid, but maybe she'd had a scare.

"Jay," she said, "I can't find the cat. I think she got out."

"I see," Jedao said, suppressing his alarm. The cat, which Nidana had named Bunny when she was five, had a talent for getting herself stuck up trees. (At five, Nidana's vocabulary for animals had left something to be desired. The family also had a dog named Bunny, two finches named Bunny, and a snake named Bunny.) Bunny-the-cat tried to escape the house at every opportunity, and while Jedao wouldn't have worried about her during warmer weather, he didn't like the thought of her trapped outside in the cold. "Bundle up. Let's go look for her."

Jedao helped Nidana with her sweater, coat, mittens, hat, scarf, and boots, then pulled on his own winter clothes. He left a note tacked to the small corkboard next to the door, just in case. "Come on," he said. "We'll find Bunny."

Nidana snuffled some more. "I didn't mean to, Jay."

"I know." It was too bad that Bunny-the-cat hated Bunny-the-dog. The latter was reasonably good at tracking, but his habit of trying to nip at Bunny-the-cat's tail whenever he could catch her wouldn't do them any favors here.

The cold air stung Jedao's eyes and nostrils as they traipsed out onto the path that Jedao and his brother had shoveled that morning. The wind had blown more snow onto the path in feathered drifts, but it was still walkable. Unfortunately, it also meant that any tracks the cat might have left were obscured.

"Show me where you went," Jedao said.

Nidana led him to the sycamore with its mantle of glistening icicles. He broke one off from a lower branch so that she could suck on it. If nothing else, it would distract her.

"Bunny!" Nidana called in between licking her icicle. But there was no sign of the cat.

Jedao and Nidana checked all the buildings they were allowed into, and some that they weren't. The cat remained elusive. The sun sank lower and lower in the sky, and Nidana was starting to shiver. Jedao made sure not to walk too quickly for her to keep up, despite his increasing concern for Bunny.

At last, discouraged, they returned to the front door of their home. Bunny-the-dog bounded up and almost bowled Nidana over when they came in, tail wagging frenetically. "Stop that," Jedao said, and made the dog sit. He and Nidana shed their winter clothes, and Jedao hung them up in the hallway closet. "Nidana," he said, "entertain the dog. I'll check around the house."

The dog's tail was thumping loudly against the floor, and the dog herself was busy slobbering all over Nidana. Nidana didn't seem to mind this. At least the dog kept her from bursting into tears again thinking of the cat.

For his part, Jedao systematically searched every room of the house but one. He knew most of the cat's hiding places. At last he came to his brother's room and hesitated. Ro had threatened him on pain of being fed to the geese not to barge in, but Jedao had checked everywhere else he could think of.

"The hell with this," Jedao said, since Nidana wasn't around to overhear him, and pushed the door open. The first thing he noticed was that one of the dresser drawers was slightly ajar. He pulled it out further: aha. Bunny-the-cat was curled up in a nest of Rodao's socks, underwear, and... magazines?

Jedao eased one of the magazines out from beneath the cat, ignoring her hiss, and flipped it open to a full-color picture of two entwined naked men. Fascinated, Jedao started paging through.

Bunny-the-cat suddenly meowed. Jedao heard Bunny-the-dog woofing as she bounded toward them, and turned around to see Nidana padding after the dog. Hastily, he shoved the magazine back into the drawer. "The cat's fine, Nidana," he said. "She was taking a nap."

"Can I see what you were reading?" Nidana said.

"*No,*" Jedao said. He scooped the cat up despite her liberal application of claws to his arm and hastened out of his older brother's room, doing his best (which wasn't very) to herd Nidana and the dog at the same time. "The cat's safe, that's all that matters."

AUTHOR'S NOTE

I have only been owned by a cat in adulthood, when we settled in Louisiana and I convinced my husband that a cat would be a great addition to the family. Ours is named Cloud and she's not an outdoors cat; I take her outside for walks but only on a leash and harness so she can't get away, because despite being affectionate and friendly, she's not terribly bright. Nevertheless, she longs to show the world that she's a mighty huntress, and so, yes, I too have known the terror of a cat parent whose cat has gone missing. Fortunately it was only for a couple hours and, after putting LOST CAT posters in my neighbors' mailboxes and knocking on doors, I returned home, exhausted and afraid, to find her waiting at the door for me to let her back in. At that point I may have said some cuss words before hugging her tight.

BLACK SQUIRRELS

JEDAO AND RUO had set up shop at the edge of one of the campus gardens, the one with the carp pond and the carefully maintained trees. Rumor had it that some of the carp were, in addition to being over a hundred years old, outfitted with surveillance gear. Like most Shuos cadets, Jedao and Ruo would, if questioned, laugh off the rumors while secretly believing them wholeheartedly—at least the bit about surveillance gear. Jedao had argued that the best place to hide what they were doing was in plain sight. After all, who would be so daft as to run a prank right next to surveillance?

"Lovely day, isn't it?" Ruo said brightly.

Jedao winced. "Not so loud," he said. His head was still pounding after last night's excesses, and the sunlight, unfiltered by any cloud cover, wasn't helping. Why did he keep letting Ruo talk him into things? It wasn't just that Ruo was really good in bed. He had this way of making incredibly risky things sound *fun*. Going out drinking? In itself, not that bad. Playing a drinking game with unlabeled bottles of possibly-alcohol-possibly-something-else stolen from Security's hoard of contraband? Risky. Some of those hallucinations had been to die for, though, especially when he started seeing giant robots in the shape of geese.

Fortunately, this latest idea wasn't that risky. Probably. Besides, of the many things that other cadets had accused Jedao of, low risk tolerance wasn't one of them.

"Not my fault you can't hold your drink," Ruo said, even more brightly.

"I'm going to get you one of these days," Jedao muttered.

Ruo's grin flashed in his dark brown face. "More like you'll lose the latest bet, and—" He started describing what he'd do to Jedao in ear-burning detail.

At last one of the other first-years, puzzled by what Jedao and Ruo were doing by the carp pond with a pair of fishing poles, approached. Jedao recognized them: Meurran, who was good at fixing guns despite their terrible aim, and who had a glorious head of wildly curling hair.

"Security's not going to approve of you poaching the carp," Meurran said.

"Oh, this isn't for the *carp*," Ruo said. He flicked his fishing pole, and the line with its enticing nut snaked out toward one of the trees.

Meurran gave Ruo a funny look. "Ruo," they said, "the fish are in the opposite direction."

"Please," Jedao said, "who cares about the *fish?* No one has anything to fear from the fish. That's just nonsense."

"All right," Meurran said, sounding distinctly unimpressed, "then what?"

Come on, Jedao thought, *the nut is right there...*

As if on cue, a black squirrel darted down from the tree, then made for the nut.

Ruo tugged the nut just out of reach.

The black squirrel looked around, then headed for the nut again.

"Oh, isn't that adorable?" Meurran said.

"Don't be fooled!" Ruo said as he guided the squirrel in a figure-eight through the grass. "Why would the commandant be so stupid as to implant surveillance devices in the carp, which can't even leave their pond?"

Meurran glanced involuntarily at the pond, where two enormous carp were lazily circling near the surface, as if the carp, in fact, had a habit of oozing out onto the land and spying on lazy cadets. "You're saying the *squirrels*—?"

Ruo continued to tease the squirrel with the nut. "It makes sense, doesn't it? Everyone thinks the black squirrels are the cutest. They're even featured in the recruitment literature. Damnably clever piece of social engineering, if you ask me."

Meurran was starting to look persuaded in spite of themself.

Meanwhile, as Ruo made his case, Jedao leaned back and studied the squirrel with a frown. The local population of black squirrels was mostly tame and had proven to be easy to train with the aid of treats. (Ruo had made Jedao do most of this, "because you're the farm boy.") But while Ruo and Meurran argued about squirrel population dynamics, Jedao caught a slight flash from behind the squirrel's eyes—almost like that of a camera?

He opened his mouth to interrupt.

The squirrel made an odd convulsing motion, and the light flashed again, this time directly into Jedao's eyes.

Jedao closed his mouth and kept his thoughts to himself.

AUTHOR'S NOTE

This story is the result of a few separate things. I read a webpage on "squirrel-fishing" when I was at Cornell University some twenty years ago; I don't think the site is still up, but it provided me with much-needed laughs during finals week. Later I attended Stanford University for grad school, which is known for its population of black squirrels. My sister, who attended Stanford as an undergrad (we overlapped for one year), later told me that the black squirrel population is self-reinforcing as people feed them preferentially for being so darn cute.

Finally, my then-boyfriend-now-husband and I ran a *Legends of the Five Rings* tabletop roleplaying campaign in which the Emperor's carp were both ancient and smarter than any of the PCs. I don't remember why the joke was so funny. Possibly it wasn't, but even ridiculous things look funny when you're trying not to freak out over your prelims.

SILENCE

I KNEW WHEN I knocked on the door to my mother's house, with its cheerful wooden plaque painted with a white goose, that my little brother had arrived before me.

For one thing, I heard music, a recording of that viola concerto my mother had liked so much, and which had been performed by my brother's sire. For another, I heard his laughter. I would have known that laughter anywhere in the heptarchate. If he was laughing, surely things weren't too bad.

"It's not locked," Mother called out. I heard another voice, higher and sharper than hers. My little sister must be visiting as well.

Mother rarely bothered with locks to her living quarters, as opposed to the laboratory buildings where she did her research. I slid the door open, left my shoes by the door, and came in. Nidana had worn knee-high boots. Jedao's shoes were decidedly unmilitary lavender loafers.

My mother was fussing with a fragrant fruit salad, ruining it past even my brother's ability to lie about its presentability. I didn't worry about it being edible, just presentable. She had scared up fruits either dyed or engineered to be Shuos red and a credible gold. I was only mildly surprised that there weren't juice stains on her cream-colored blouse.

"I don't see why you felt the need to ruin perfectly good fruit, Mom," Nidana was saying as she nursed a glass of wine. She hadn't taken her beige jacket off, although it was warm inside. "Just because Jay joined the faction with the tackiest colors doesn't mean you have to inflict them on the rest of us."

"Rodao!" my brother said over Nidana's voice, coming around from where he had been looking for a clean glass (my mother was as terrible about dishes as she was fanatical about keeping her laboratory gear in top condition). "How are Teia and the girls?"

My brother Jedao was the smaller of us. Growing up, people had occasionally mistaken me for the deadlier one, which was ridiculous. Both Jedao and our younger sister Nidana could flense you at twenty paces with wit alone, and Jedao had always liked to fight. It hadn't surprised anyone in the family when he wound up in the Kel army.

Right now Jedao was wearing informal civilian garb in violet and gray, a loose, short-sleeved tunic over well-tailored pants. I had the disturbing realization that he looked foreign to me in these clothes rather than the overdecorated Kel uniforms the news clips showed him in.

Jedao was looking at me inquiringly. "The family's fine," I said. "The girls are going to ambush you for presents."

"You spoil those kids horribly," Nidana said. But she was smiling. She did her share of spoiling, especially if any of my three daughters wanted books.

Jedao grinned at me. "They're my *nieces*, Ro. I'm supposed to spoil them. I found the best thing ever on the way here, by the way. I got them toy assassin's tools."

Mother had a coughing fit and hastily put down the fruit salad. "You what?" she said.

Nidana was unimpressed. "Jay, is this going to be like the time you brought home the programmable flying toy moths

72

and you had to take them away because of that manufacturing defect and one of them caught on fire and Mareida thought it was the best trick ever and she wanted you to do it again?"

"Nia, just because I kill people for a living doesn't mean it's my fault Ro's kids are bloodthirsty," Jedao protested. "Besides, they're safe now. There are no sharp corners, and the kids are old enough not to eat them so I'm not concerned about choking hazards. The toy hairstick is to die for. The crystal on the end turns different colors and it even plays music if you push a button. I had to disable the fake needler because it worked too much like a real one, bad news if you pointed it at anyone's eyes, but that wasn't hard."

"How the hell do you have a *toy* hairstick?" I demanded, choosing to ignore the bit about the needler. "Isn't that like having a toy comb? Exactly like a grown-up comb, except the colors?"

"I thought it was cute," Jedao said defensively.

Nidana shook her head. "I can't believe your superiors made you a tactical group commander." At thirty he was young for it, too.

"Stop ragging on him," Mother said. "Does anyone want fruit salad?"

"I'll take some," Jedao said.

Nidana shuddered. "None for me, thanks. Ro?"

"Sure," I said. The fact that I hadn't watched its preparation worked in my favor.

"Besides," Jedao said, turning to me, "the Kel couldn't find anyone else stupid enough to do the job. It's mostly paperwork."

I didn't believe him. Jedao's collection of Kel jokes wasn't as extensive as his collection of Andan jokes, but if I got him started he'd never shut up. Instead, I helped Nidana find clean bowls and let Mother serve me a portion of the dreadful-looking fruit salad.

"How is it?" Mother asked.

There was only one correct answer. "It's great," Jedao said before I could say what I thought. Given how infrequently he was on leave, he had more of a vested interest in keeping our mother happy during his visit than I did. Surreptitiously, I set my bowl down on a side table and slid it away from me.

"How drunk do you want to get tonight?" Nidana asked him, eyes sparkling. "I came up with this fantastic new cocktail."

Jedao eyed her warily. "In that case, I'll stick to tea. Are you still adding mood-enhancing substances to your drinks?"

"Spoilsport," she said.

Mother plucked a grape out of her salad and bit into it with great enthusiasm. I was sure I turned green. The grapes, all peeled, had pale flesh with dark traceries so they resembled eyeballs. "So, Jedao," she said, "when are you going to bring home a nice tame boy?"

Jedao blushed, and I hid a grin. Mother didn't make any secret of the fact that she wanted a bigger flock of grandchildren so she could fatten them like the geese. Jedao hadn't been this easy to fluster as a teen. I still remembered the time when he was fifteen and he wanted to impress the Ghirout boy so he hacked the locks on my floater and they went on a ride. He thought he'd gotten away with it until the next afternoon, when I interrupted his make-out session to lecture him on covering his tracks. I always figured he'd gone fox as vengeance.

"I'm not seeing anyone, Mom," Jedao said in a long-suffering voice. "I don't care what they say about what we get up to in the military, most of it is very dull."

"Or is it girls or alts now?" Mother said, ignoring him. "It's so hard to keep track with you."

"*Mom.*" Jedao poured himself a cup of lukewarm tea and made a show of being very interested in it, which fooled no one.

"I wouldn't worry about you so much if you wrote more often," Mother complained.

"Be fair," Nidana said, "he writes every seven weeks like clockwork. It's not his fault the censors hold up the mail."

Jedao had the good sense not to get involved in the ensuing squabble between our mother and Nidana, and instead polished off his salad with no sign that its resemblance to body parts bothered him.

Afterward, Mother went to check on something at the facility. Nidana excused herself because the taste of the salad had inspired her and she *had* to start a new poem. I loved my sister, but I would never pretend to understand art and artists.

For our part, Jedao and I went out to the flower garden, carrying cups of tea. The garden sported a stone bench with patches of dark moss growing around its base, and was indifferently weeded. No one around here had the time for it. Mother's idea of growing flowers was to scatter wildflower seeds and order bizarre cocktails of specialized hungry insects to inhibit pests.

Jedao plucked one of the bluebonnets and stuck it behind his ear. It made him look like he was ten all over again.

"I'm glad you're home safely," I said, to see if he would flinch.

Jedao set the teacup down on the bench. "It's nice to run into someone who doesn't think I have magical powers of survival," he said. He smiled at me, the tilted smile that he and Nidana and our mother shared, but I didn't, because he and Nidana and I all had different sires. Shparoi culture didn't approve of some of Mother's life choices; Jedao had gotten into his share of fights over it.

I almost believed he was fine. There was nothing wrong with his smile, or the easy, affectionate light in his eyes. As far as I knew, the last time he'd cried was when he was eight, after he'd gotten into a fight and lost. I didn't know why I was thinking of that.

After an awkward pause, I said, "If they had to rebuild half your face anyway, you could have asked them to make you devastatingly handsome."

"What, so Mom can nag me about my inadequate love life some more?" Jedao said. He was still smiling. "Hey, they gave me back a face, period. I'm not greedy."

"I almost can't tell," I said. It was true. They hadn't bothered putting back the scar on his chin from that time he fell out of the tree when he was seven. And his face was more symmetrical than it had been, hard to pin down unless you looked hard at the bone structure, especially around the eyes.

He kicked at an empty overturned flowerpot. "You know, I stared in the mirror for the longest time after all the operations, and it was the strangest thing, like I was looking at someone I'd never met before. Or trying to find one of those especially elusive zits when I was thirteen."

"How the hell do you take a grenade to the face as a moth commander, anyway?"

Jedao pulled a face. "Technically classified, but since Mom already dragged that much out of me and is obviously talking to you about it... There was a riot on the station where we put in for repairs. Not even heretics, just ordinary disgruntled workers. As far as we can tell, they didn't have anything against me personally. Anyone in a Kel uniform would have sufficed."

"A *grenade?*" I demanded.

"It was practically homebrew. If it'd been the stuff the Kel infantry are issued, I'd be dead."

"Mother worries about you," I said.

Jedao cocked an eyebrow at me but generously refrained from accusing me of projecting. "I'll write home more often if she promises to send fewer of those horrible cookies," he said. "I can't fob them off on anyone anymore. All my fellow officers know they're hard enough to be used as bricks."

I huffed a laugh. "I can't do that. She'd make *me* eat them."

"You have spawn," Jedao said unsympathetically. "Feed the cookies to them. They still have some of their baby teeth, they can afford to lose a few."

I reached over and ruffled his hair the way I used to when he was a kid. He made a humming contented sound. Touching a soldier without invitation wasn't bright of me, but all I could think of was the boy he'd been.

That wasn't all. Long ago, during the first break when he'd come home after his first year at Shuos Academy, Jedao had seemed fine, the same cocky teenager who occasionally cut class to play jeng-zai and pattern-stones. (Mother had made him clean a scary amount of glassware after she caught him. More accurately, I'd ratted him out.) Yet every time I watched him, I was convinced he'd been replaced by some hollow marionette: nothing real except negative space.

No one else had noticed anything amiss. I'd spent time with Jedao—chores, tea, board games. He gave a great performance. Once or twice when we were alone together, I almost came out and asked. He was an excellent liar, but I was the one person who'd always been able to tell.

Once again, I almost asked. On the other hand, he was a grown man and a Shuos and a soldier. It was none of my damn business.

"You look tired," Jedao said. "Sleeping all right?"

"Long shifts at work, that's all," I said. And that was that: we talked about my new supervisor, and once again I let the subject slide.

Fourteen years later, when I heard of Hellspin Fortress, I'd discover how badly I'd fucked up by keeping quiet; and then, of course, it was too late to fix anything.

* * *

AUTHOR'S NOTE

I originally wrote this as an exercise in first person, and chose Rodao as the viewpoint character because I thought his perspective on Jedao would be interesting. I'd always conceived of him as the annoyingly straitlaced oldest sibling (confession: I was the annoyingly straitlaced older sibling, for which I hope my kid sister has forgiven me), the one who could always catch Jedao out in whatever tall tales he tried to fob off on everyone else. Just imagine if the Shuos had ever taken advantage of that.

Jedao's genetic father is a violist for the simple reason that I used to play viola, although it's been years and I lost my instrument to the Louisiana floods of 2016. I have always had a soft spot for the viola, even if I imagine every violist eventually gets sick of that one Telemann concerto. And the detail about Jedao cutting class to play games is stolen from my father's life (hi, Dad!). Apparently when he was young, he'd cut class to play baduk (go, wei qi—what I've chosen to call pattern-stones in the h*archate). It paid off; during my abortive childhood attempts to learn to play chess, Dad needed me to remind him how all the different pieces moved, and he *still* won every time!

EXTRACURRICULAR ACTIVITIES

WHEN SHUOS JEDAO walked into his temporary quarters on Station Muru 5 and spotted the box, he assumed someone was attempting to assassinate him. It had happened before. Considering his first career, there was even a certain justice to it.

He ducked back around the doorway, although even with his reflexes, it would have been too late if it'd been a proper bomb. The air currents in the room would have wafted his biochemical signature to the box and caused it to trigger. Or someone could have set one up to go off as soon as the door opened, regardless of who stepped in. Or something even less sophisticated.

Jedao retreated back down the hallway and waited one minute. Two. Nothing.

It could just be a package, he thought—paperwork that he had forgotten?—but old habits died hard.

He entered again and approached the desk, light-footed. The box, made of eye-searing green plastic, stood out against the bland earth tones of the walls and desk. It measured approximately half a meter in all directions. Its nearest face prominently displayed the gold seal that indicated that station security had cleared it. He didn't trust it for a moment.

Spoofing a seal wasn't that difficult; he'd done it himself.

He inspected the box's other visible sides without touching it, then spotted a letter pouch affixed to one side and froze. He recognized the handwriting. The address was written in spidery high language, while the name of the recipient—one Garach Jedao Shkan—was written both in high language and his birth tongue, Shparoi, for good measure.

Oh, Mom, Jedao thought. No one else called him by that name anymore, not even the rest of his family. More importantly, how had his mother gotten his forwarding address? He'd just received his transfer orders last week, and he hadn't written home about it because his mission was classified. He had no idea what his new general wanted him to do; she would tell him tomorrow when he reported in.

Jedao opened the box, which released a puff of cold air. Inside rested a tub labeled KEEP REFRIGERATED in both the high language and Shparoi. The tub itself contained a pale, waxy-looking solid substance. *Is this what I think it is?* Time for the letter:

> *Hello, Jedao!*
> *Congratulations on your promotion. I hope you enjoy your new command moth and that it has a more pronounceable name than the last one.*

One: What promotion? Did she know something he didn't? (Scratch that question. She always knew something he didn't.) Two: Trust his mother to rate warmoths not by their armaments or the efficacy of their stardrives but by their *names*. Then again, she'd made no secret of the fact that she'd hoped he'd wind up a musician like his sire. It had not helped when he pointed out that when he attempted to sing in academy, his fellow cadets had threatened to dump grapefruit soup over his head.

Since I expect your eating options will be limited, I have sent you goose fat rendered from the great-great-great-etc.-grand-gosling of your pet goose when you were a child. (She was delicious, by the way.) Let me know if you run out and I'll send more.

Love,
Mom

So he was right: the tub contained goose fat. Jedao had never figured out why his mother sent food items when her idea of cooking was to gussy up instant noodles with an egg and some chopped green onions. All the cooking Jedao knew, he had learned either from his older brother or, on occasion, those of his mother's research assistants who took pity on her kids.

What am I supposed to do with this? he wondered. As a cadet, he could have based a prank around it. But as a warmoth commander, he had standards to uphold.

More importantly, how could he compose a suitably filial letter of appreciation without, foxes forbid, encouraging her to escalate? (Baked goods: fine. Goose fat: less fine.) Especially when she wasn't supposed to know he was here in the first place? Some people's families sent them care packages of useful things, like liquor, pornography, or really nice cosmetics. Just his luck.

At least the mission gave him an excuse to delay writing back until his location was unclassified, even if she knew it anyway.

JEDAO HAD HEARD a number of rumors about his new commanding officer, Brigadier General Kel Essier. Some of them, like the ones about her junior wife's lovers, were none of his business. Others, like Essier's taste in plum wine, weren't relevant, but could come in handy if he needed to scare up a bribe someday. What had really caught his notice was her service record. She had fewer decorations than anyone else who'd served at her rank for a comparable time.

Either Essier was a political appointee—the Kel military denied the practice, but everyone knew better—or she was sitting on a cache of classified medals. Jedao had a number of those himself. (Did his mother know about those too?) Although Station Muru 5 was a secondary military base, Jedao had his suspicions about any "secondary" base that had a general in residence, even temporarily. That, or Essier was disgraced and Kel Command couldn't think of anywhere else to dump her.

Jedao had a standard method for dealing with new commanders, which was to research them as if he planned to assassinate them. Needless to say, he never expressed it in those terms to his comrades.

He'd come up with two promising ways to get rid of Essier. First, she collected meditation foci made of staggeringly luxurious materials. One of her officers had let slip that her latest obsession was antique lacquerware. Planting a bomb or toxin in a collector-grade item wouldn't be risky so much as *expensive*. He'd spent a couple hours last night brainstorming ways to steal one, just for the hell of it; lucky that he didn't have to follow through.

The other method took advantage of the poorly planned location of the firing range on this level relative to the general's office, and involved shooting her through several walls and a door with a high-powered rifle and burrower ammunition. Jedao hated burrower ammunition, not because it didn't work but because it did. He had a lot of ugly scars on his torso from the times burrowers had almost killed him. That being said, he also believed in using the appropriate tool for the job.

No one had upgraded Muru 5 for the past few decades.

Its computer grid ran on outdated hardware, making it easy for him to pull copies of all the maps he pleased. He'd also hacked into the security cameras long enough to check the layout of the general's office. The setup made him despair of the architects who had designed the wretched thing. On top of that, Essier had set up her desk so a visitor would see it framed beautifully by the doorway, with her chair perfectly centered. Great for impressing visitors, less great for making yourself a difficult target. Then again, attending to Essier's safety wasn't his job.

Jedao showed up at Essier's office seven minutes before the appointed time. "Whiskey?" said her aide.

If only, Jedao thought; he recognized it as one he couldn't afford. "No, thank you," he said with the appropriate amount of regret. He didn't trust special treatment.

"Your loss," said the aide. After another two minutes, she checked her slate. "Go on in. The general is waiting for you."

As Jedao had predicted, General Essier sat dead center behind her desk, framed by the doorway and two statuettes on either side of the desk, gilded ashhawks carved from onyx. Essier had dark skin and close-shaven hair, and the height and fine-spun bones of someone who had grown up in low gravity. The black-and-gold Kel uniform suited her. Her gloved hands rested on the desk in perfect symmetry. Jedao bet she looked great in propaganda videos.

Jedao saluted, fist to shoulder. "Commander Shuos Jedao reporting as ordered, sir."

"Have a seat," Essier said. He did. "You're wondering why you don't have a warmoth assignment yet."

"The thought had crossed my mind, yes."

Essier smiled. The smile was like the rest of her: beautiful and calculated and not a little deadly. "I have good news and bad news for you, Commander. The good news is that you're due a promotion."

Jedao's first reaction was not gratitude or pride, but *How did my mother—?* Fortunately, a lifetime of *How did my mother—?* enabled him to keep his expression smooth and instead say, "And the bad news?"

"Is it true what they say about your battle record?"

This always came up. "You have my profile."

"You're good at winning."

"I wasn't under the impression that the Kel military found this objectionable, sir."

"Quite right," she said. "The situation is this. I have a mission in mind for you, but it will take advantage of your unique background."

"Unique background" was a euphemism for *we don't have many commanders who can double as emergency special forces*. Most Kel with training in special ops stayed in the infantry instead of seeking command in the space forces. Jedao made an inquiring noise.

"Perform well, and you'll be given the fangmoth *Sieve of Glass*, which heads my third tactical group."

A bribe, albeit one that might cause trouble. Essier had six tactical groups. A newly-minted group tactical commander being assigned third instead of sixth? Had she had a problem with her former third-position commander?

"My former third took early retirement," Essier said in answer to his unspoken question. "They were caught with a small collection of trophies."

"Let me guess," Jedao said. "Trophies taken from heretics."

"Just so. Third tactical is badly shaken. Fourth has excellent rapport with her group and I don't want to promote her out of it. But it's an opportunity for you."

"And the mission?"

Essier leaned back. "You attended Shuos Academy with Shuos Meng."

"I did," Jedao said. They'd gone by Zhei Meng as a cadet.

"We've been in touch on and off." Meng had joined a marriage some years back. Jedao had commissioned a painting of five foxes, one for each person in the marriage, and sent it along with his best wishes. Meng wrote regularly about their kids—they couldn't be made to shut up about them—and Jedao sent gifts on cue, everything from hand-bound volumes of Kel jokes to fancy gardening tools (at least, they'd been sold to him as gardening tools; they looked suspiciously like they could double for heavy-duty surgical work). "Why, what has Meng been up to?"

"Under the name Ahun Gerav, they've been in command of the merchanter *Moonsweet Blossom*."

Jedao cocked an eyebrow at Essier. "That's not a Shuos vessel." It did, however, sound like an Andan one. The Andan faction liked naming their trademoths after flowers. "By 'merchanter,' do you mean 'spy'?"

"Yes," Essier said with charming directness. "Twenty-six days ago, one of the *Blossom*'s crew sent a code red to Shuos Intelligence. This is all she was able to tell us."

Essier retrieved a slate from within the desk and tilted it to show him a video. She needn't have bothered; the combination of poor lighting, camera jitter, and static made it impossible to watch. The audio was little better: "...*Blossom*, code red to Overwatch... Gerav's in..." Frustratingly, the static made the next few words unintelligible. "Du Station. You'd better—" The report of a gun, then another, then silence.

"Your task is to investigate the situation at Du Station in the Gwa Reality, and see if the crew and any of the intelligence they've gathered can be recovered. The Shuos heptarch suggested that you would be an ideal candidate for the mission. Kel Command was amenable."

I just bet, Jedao thought. He had once worked directly under his heptarch, and while he'd been one of her better assassins, he didn't miss those days. "Is this the only incident with the Gwa Reality that has taken place recently, or are there others?"

"The Gwa-an are approaching one of their regularly scheduled regime upheavals," Essier said. "According to the diplomats, there's a good chance that the next elected government will be less amenable to heptarchate interests. We want to go in, find out what happened, and get out before things turn topsy-turvy."

"All right," Jedao said, "so taking a warmoth in would be inflammatory. What resources will I have instead?"

"Well, that's the bad news," Essier said, entirely too cheerfully. "Tell me, Commander, have you ever wanted to own a merchant troop?"

THE TROOP CONSISTED of eight trademoths, named *Carp 1* to *Carp 4*, then *Carp 7* to *Carp 10*. They occupied one of the station's docking bays. Someone had painted each vessel with distended carp-figures in orange and white. It did not improve their appearance.

The usual commander of the troop introduced herself as Churioi Haval, not her real name. She was portly, had a squint, and wore gaudy gilt jewelry, all excellent ways to convince people that she was an ordinary merchant and not, say, Kel special ops. It hadn't escaped his attention that she frowned ever so slightly when she spotted his sidearm, a Patterner 52, which wasn't standard Kel issue. "You're not bringing that, are you?" she said.

"No, I'd hate to lose it on the other side of the border," Jedao said. "Besides, I don't have a plausible explanation for why a boring communications tech is running around with a Shuos handgun."

"I could always hold on to it for you."

Jedao wondered if he'd ever get the Patterner back if he

took her up on the offer. It hadn't come cheap. "That's kind of you, but I'll have the station store it for me. By the way, what happened to *Carps 5* and *6*?"

"Beats me," Haval said. "Before my time. The Gwa-an authorities have never hassled us about it. They're already used to, paraphrase, 'odd heptarchate numerological superstitions.'" She eyed Jedao critically, which made her look squintier. "Begging your pardon, but do you *have* undercover experience?"

What a refreshing question. Everyone knew the Shuos for their spies, saboteurs, and assassins, even though the analysts, administrators, and cryptologists did most of the real work. (One of his instructors had explained that "You will spend hours in front of a terminal developing posture problems" was far less effective at recruiting potential cadets than "Join the Shuos for an exciting future as a secret agent, assuming your classmates don't kill you before you graduate.") Most people who met Jedao assumed he'd killed an improbable number of people as Shuos infantry. Never mind that he'd been responsible for far more deaths since joining the regular military.

"You'd be surprised at the things I know how to do," Jedao said.

"Well, I hope you're good with cover identities," Haval said. "No offense, but you have a distinctive name."

That was a tactful way of saying that the Kel didn't tolerate many Shuos line officers; most Shuos seconded to the Kel worked in Intelligence. Jedao had a reputation for, as one of his former aides had put it, being expendable enough to send into no-win situations but too stubborn to die. Jedao smiled at Haval and said, "I have a good memory."

The rest of his crew also had civilian cover names. A tall, muscular man strolled up to them. Jedao surreptitiously admired him. The gold-mesh tattoo over the right side of his face contrasted handsomely with his dark skin. Too bad he was almost certainly Kel and therefore off-limits.

"This is Rhi Teshet," Haval said. "When he isn't watching horrible melodramas—"

"You have no sense of culture," Teshet said.

"—he's the lieutenant colonel in charge of our infantry."

Damn. Definitely Kel, then, and in his chain of command, at that. "A pleasure, Colonel," Jedao said.

Teshet's returning smile was slow and wicked and completely unprofessional. "Get out of the habit of using ranks," he said. "Just Teshet, please. I hear you like whiskey?"

Off-limits, Jedao reminded himself, despite the quickening of his pulse. Best to be direct. "I'd rather not get you into trouble."

Haval was looking to the side with a "where have I seen this dance before" expression. Teshet laughed. "The fastest way to get us caught is to behave like you have the Kel code of conduct tattooed across your forehead. *No one* will suspect you of being a hotshot commander if you're sleeping with one of your crew."

"I don't fuck people deadlier than I am, sorry," Jedao said demurely.

"Wrong answer," Haval said, still not looking at either of them. "Now he's going to think of you as a challenge."

"Also, I know your reputation," Teshet said to Jedao. "Your kill count has got to be higher than mine by an order of magnitude."

Jedao ignored that. "How often do you make trade runs into the Gwa Reality?"

"Two or three times a year," Haval said. "The majority of the runs are to maintain the fiction. The question is, do *you* have a plan?"

He didn't blame her for her skepticism. "Tell me again how much cargo space we have."

Haval told him.

"We sometimes take approved cultural goods," Teshet said, "in a data storage format negotiated during the Second Treaty of—"

"Don't bore him," Haval said. "The 'trade' is *our* job. He's just here for the explodey bits."

"No, I'm interested," Jedao said. "The Second Treaty of Mwe Enh, am I right?"

Haval blinked. "You have remarkably good pronunciation. Most people can't manage the tones. Do you speak Tlen Gwa?"

"Regrettably not. I'm only fluent in four languages, and that's not one of them." Of the four, Shparoi was only spoken on his birth planet, making it useless for career purposes. Which reminded him that he was still procrastinating on writing back to his mother. Surely being sent on an undercover mission counted as an acceptable reason for being late with your correspondence home?

"If you have some Shuos notion of sneaking in a virus amid all the lectures on flower-arranging and the dueling tournament videos and the plays, forget it," Teshet said. "Their operating systems are so different from ours that you'd have better luck getting a magpie and a turnip to have a baby."

"Oh, not at all," Jedao said. "How odd would it look if you brought in a shipment of goose fat?"

Haval's mouth opened, closed. Teshet said, "Excuse me?"

"Not literally goose fat," Jedao conceded. "I don't have enough for that and I don't imagine the novelty would enable you to run a sufficient profit. I assume you have to at least appear to be trying to make a profit."

"They like real profits even better," Haval said.

Diverted, Teshet said, "You have goose fat? Whatever for?"

"Long story," Jedao said. "But instead of goose fat, I'd like to run some of that variable-coefficient lubricant."

Haval rubbed her chin. "I don't think you could get approval to trade the formula or the associated manufacturing processes."

"Not that," Jedao said, "actual canisters of lubricant. Is there someone in the Gwa Reality on the way to our luckless Shuos friend who might be willing to pay for it?"

Haval and Teshet exchanged baffled glances. Jedao could tell what they were thinking: *Are we the victims of some weird bet our commander has going on the side?* "There's no need to get creative," Haval said in a commendably diplomatic voice. "Cultural goods are quite reliable."

You think this *is creativity,* Jedao thought. "It's not that. Two battles ago, my fangmoth was almost blown in two because our antimissile defenses glitched. If we hadn't used the lubricant as a stopgap sealant, we wouldn't have made it." That much was even true. "Even if you can't offload all of it, I'll find a use for it."

"You do know you can't cook with lubricant?" Teshet said. "Although I wonder if it's good for—"

Haval stomped on his toe. "You already have plenty of the medically approved stuff," she said crushingly, "no need to risk getting your private parts cemented into place."

"Hey," Teshet said, "you never know when you need to improvise."

Jedao was getting the impression that Essier had not assigned him the best of her undercover teams. Certainly they were the least disciplined Kel he'd run into in a while, but he supposed long periods undercover had made them more casual about regulations. No matter, he'd been dealt worse hands. "I've let you know what I want done, and I've already checked that the station has enough lubricant to supply us. Make it happen."

"If you insist," Haval said. "Meanwhile, don't forget to get your immunizations."

"Will do," Jedao said, and strode off to Medical.

* * *

JEDAO SPENT THE first part of the voyage alternately learning Tlen Gwa, memorizing his cover identity, and studying up on the Gwa Reality. The Tlen Gwa course suffered some oddities. He couldn't see the use of some of the vocabulary items, like the one for "navel." But he couldn't manage to *un*learn it, either, so there it was, taking up space in his brain.

As for the cover identity, he'd had better ones, but he supposed the Kel could only do so much on short notice. He was now Arioi Sren, one of Haval's distant cousins by marriage. He had three spouses, with whom he had quarreled recently over a point of interior decoration. ("I don't know anything about interior decoration," Jedao had said, to which Haval retorted, "That's probably what caused the argument.")

The documents had included loving photographs of the domicile in question, an apartment in a dome city floating in the upper reaches of a very pretty gas giant. Jedao had memorized them before destroying them. While he couldn't say how well the decor coordinated, he was good at layouts and kill zones. In any case, Sren was on "vacation" to escape the squabbling. Teshet had suggested that a guilt-inducing affair would round out the cover identity. Jedao said he'd think about it.

Jedao was using spray-on temporary skin, plus a high-collared shirt, to conceal multiple scars, including the wide one at the base of his neck. The temporary skin itched, which couldn't be helped. He hoped no one would strip-search him, but in case someone did, he didn't want to have to explain his old gunshot wounds. Teshet had also suggested that he stop shaving—the Kel disliked beards—but Jedao could only deal with so much itching.

The hardest part was not the daily skinseal regimen, but

getting used to wearing civilian clothes. The Kel uniform included gloves, and Jedao felt exposed going around with naked hands. But keeping his gloves would have been a dead giveaway, so he'd just have to live with it.

The Gwa-an fascinated him most of all. Heptarchate diplomats called their realm the Gwa Reality. Linguists differed on just what the word rendered as "Reality" meant. The majority agreed that it referred to the Gwa-an belief that all dreams took place in the same noosphere, connecting the dreamers, and that even inanimate objects dreamed.

Gwa-an protocols permitted traders to dock at designated stations. Haval quizzed Jedao endlessly on the relevant etiquette. Most of it consisted of keeping his mouth shut and letting Haval talk, which suited him fine. While the Gwa-an provided interpreters, Haval said cultural differences were the real problem. "Above all," she added," if anyone challenges you to a duel, don't. Just don't. Look blank and plead ignorance."

"Duel?" Jedao said, interested.

"I knew we were going to have to have this conversation," Haval said glumly. "They don't use swords, so get that idea out of your head."

"I didn't bring my dueling sword anyway, and Sren wouldn't know how," Jedao said. "Guns?"

"Oh, no," she said. "They use *pathogens*. Designer pathogens. Besides the fact that their duels can go on for years, I've never heard that you had a clue about genetic engineering."

"No," Jedao said, "that would be my mother." Maybe next time he could suggest that his mother be sent in his place. His mother would adore the chance to talk shop. Of course, then he'd be out of a job. "Besides, I'd rather avoid bringing a plague back home."

"They *claim* they have an excellent safety record."

Of course they would. "How fast can they culture the things?"

"That was one of the things we were trying to gather data on."

"If they're good at diseasing up humans, they may be just as good at manufacturing critters that like to eat synthetics."

"While true of their tech base in general," Haval said, "they won't have top-grade labs at Du Station."

"Good to know," Jedao said.

Jedao and Teshet also went over the intelligence on Du Station. "It's nice that you're taking a personal interest," Teshet said, "but if you think we're taking the place by storm, you've been watching too many dramas."

"If Kel special forces aren't up for it," Jedao said, very dryly, "you could always send me. One of me won't do much good, though."

"Don't be absurd," Teshet said. "Essier would have my head if you got hurt. How many people *did* you assassinate?"

"Classified," Jedao said.

Teshet gave a can't-blame-me-for-trying shrug. "Not to say I wouldn't love to see you in action, but it isn't your job to run around doing the boring infantry work. How do you mean to get the crew out? Assuming they survived, which is a big *if*."

Jedao tapped his slate and brought up the schematics for one of their cargo shuttles. "Five per trader," he said musingly.

"Du Station won't let us land the shuttles however we please."

"Did I say anything about landing them?" Before Teshet could say anything further, Jedao added, "You might have to cross the hard way, with suits and webcord. How often have your people drilled that?"

"We've done plenty of extravehicular," Teshet said, "but we're going to need *some* form of cover."

"I'm aware of that," Jedao said. He brought up a calculator and did some figures. "That will do nicely."

"Sren?"

Jedao grinned at Teshet. "I want those shuttles emptied out, everything but propulsion and navigation. Get rid of suits, seats, all of it."

"Even life support?"

"Everything. And it'll have to be done in the next seventeen days, so the Gwa-an can't catch us at it."

"What do we do with the innards?"

"Dump them. I'll take full responsibility."

Teshet's eyes crinkled. "I knew I was going to like you."

Uh-oh, Jedao thought, but he kept that to himself.

"What are *you* going to be doing?" Teshet asked.

"Going over the dossiers before we have to wipe them," Jedao said. Meng's in particular. He'd believed in Meng's fundamental competence even in academy, before they'd learned confidence in themselves. What had gone wrong?

JEDAO HAD FIRST met Shuos Meng, then Zhei Meng, during an exercise at Shuos Academy. The instructor had assigned them to work together. Meng was chubby and had a vine-and-compass tattoo on the back of their left hand, identifying them as coming from a merchanter lineage.

Today, the class of twenty-nine cadets met not in the usual classroom but a windowless room with a metal table in the front and rows of two-person desks with benches that looked like they'd been scrubbed clean of graffiti multiple times. ("Wars come and go, but graffiti is forever," as one of Jedao's lovers liked to say.) Besides the door leading out into the hall, there were two other doors, neither of which had a sign indicating where they led. Tangles of pipes led up the walls and storage bins were piled beside them. Jedao had the impression that the room had been pressed into service on short notice.

Jedao and Meng sat at their assigned seats and hurriedly whispered introductions to each other while the instructor read off the rest of the pairs.

"Zhei Meng," they said. "I should warn you I barely passed the weapons qualifications. But I'm good with languages." Then a quick grin: "And hacking. I figured you'd make a good partner."

"Garach Jedao," he said. "I can handle guns." Understatement; he was third in the class in Weapons. And if Meng had, as they were implying, shuffled the assignments, that meant they were one of the better hackers. "Why did you join up?"

"I want to have kids," Meng said.

"Come again?"

"I want to marry into a rich lineage," Meng said. "That means making myself more respectable. When the recruiters showed up, I said what the hell."

The instructor smiled coolly at the two of them, and they shut up. She said, "If you're here, it's because you've indicated an interest in fieldwork. Like you, we want to find out if it's something you have any aptitude for, and if not, what better use we can make of your skills." *You'd better have* some *skills* went unsaid. "You may have expected you'd be dropped off in the woods or some such nonsense. We don't try to weed out first-years quite that early. No; this first exercise will take place in this room."

The instructor's smile widened. "There's a photobomb in this room. It won't cause any permanent damage, but if you don't disarm it, you're all going to be walking around wearing ridiculous dark lenses for a week. At least one cadet knows where the bomb is. If they keep its location a secret from the rest of you, they win. Of course, they'll also go around with ridiculous dark lenses, but you can't have everything. On the other hand, if someone can persuade someone to give up the secret, everyone wins. So to speak."

The rows of cadets stared at her. Jedao leaned back in his chair and considered the situation. Like several others in the class, he had a riflery exam in three days and preferred to take it with undamaged vision.

"You have four hours," the instructor said. "There's one restroom." She pointed to one of the doors. "I expect it to be in impeccable condition at the end of the four hours." She put her slate down on the table at the head of the room. "Call me with this if you figure it out. Good luck." With that, she walked out of the room. The door whooshed shut behind her.

"We're screwed," Meng said. "Just because I'm on the leaderboard in *Elite Thundersnake 9000* doesn't mean I could disarm *real* bombs if you yanked out my toenails."

"Don't give people ideas," Jedao said. Meng didn't appear to find the joke funny. "This is about people, not explosives."

Two pairs of cadets had gotten up and were beginning a search of the room. A few were talking to each other in hushed, tense voices. Still others were looking around at their fellows with hard, suspicious eyes.

Meng said in Shparoi, "Do *you* know where the bomb is?"

Jedao blinked. He hadn't expected anyone at the Academy to know his birth tongue. Of course, by speaking in an obscure low language, Meng was drawing attention to them. Jedao shook his head.

Meng looked around, hands bunching the fabric of their pants. "What do you recommend we do?"

In the high language, Jedao said, "You can do whatever you want." He retrieved a deck of jeng-zai cards—he always had one in his pocket—and shuffled them. "Do you play?"

"You realize we're being graded on this, right? Hell, they've got cameras on us. They're watching the whole thing."

"Exactly," Jedao said. "I don't see any point in panicking."

"You're out of your mind," Meng said. They stood up, met

the other cadets' appraising stares, then sat down again. "Too bad hacking the instructor's slate won't get us anywhere. I doubt she left the answer key in an unencrypted file on it."

Jedao gave Meng a quizzical look, wondering if there was anything more behind the remark—but no, Meng had put their chin in their hands and was brooding. *If only you knew,* he thought, dealing out a game of solitaire. It was going to be a very dull game, because he had also stacked the deck, but he needed to focus on the people around him, not the game. The cards were just to give his hands something to do. He had considered taking up crochet, but thanks to an incident earlier in the term, crochet hooks, knitting needles, and fountain pens were no longer permitted in class. While this was a stupid restriction, considering that most of the cadets were learning unarmed combat, he wasn't responsible for the administration's foibles.

"Jedao," Meng said, "maybe you've got high enough marks that you can blow off this exercise, but—"

Since *I'm not blowing it off* was unlikely to be believed, Jedao flipped over a card—three of Doors, just as he'd arranged—and smiled at Meng. So Meng had had their pick of partners and had chosen him? Well, he might as well do something to justify the other cadet's faith in him. After all, despite their earlier remark, weapons weren't the only things that Jedao was good at. "Do me a favor and we can get this sorted," he said. "You want to win? I'll show you winning."

Now Jedao was attracting some of the hostile stares as well. Good. It took the heat off Meng, who didn't have great tolerance for pressure. *Stay out of wetwork,* he thought; but they could have that chat later. Or one of the instructors would.

Meng fidgeted; caught themselves. "Yeah?"

"Get me the slate."

"You mean the instructor's slate? You can't possibly have

figured it out already. Unless—" Meng's eyes narrowed.

"Less thinking, more acting," Jedao said, and got up to retrieve the slate himself.

A pair of cadets, a girl and a boy, blocked his way. "You know something," said the girl. "Spill." Jedao knew them from Analysis; the two were often paired there, too. The girl's name was Noe Irin. The boy had five names and went by Veller. Jedao wondered if Veller wanted to join a faction so he could trim things down to a nice, compact two-part name. Shuos Veller: much less of a mouthful. Then again, Jedao had a three-part name, also unusual, if less unwieldy, so he shouldn't criticize.

"Just a hunch," Jedao said.

Irin bared her teeth. "He *always* says it's a hunch," she said to no one in particular. "I *hate* that."

"It was only twice," Jedao said, which didn't help his case. He backed away from the instructor's desk and sat down, careful not to jostle the solitaire spread. "Take the slate apart. The photobomb's there."

Irin's lip curled. "If this is one of your fucking clever *tricks*, Jay—"

Meng blinked at the nickname. "You two sleeping together, Jedao?" they asked, *sotto voce*.

Not *sotto* enough. "*No*," said Jedao and Irin at the same time.

Veller ignored the byplay and went straight for the tablet. He bent to inspect the tablet without touching it. Jedao respected that. Veller had the physique of a tiger-wrestler (now *there* was someone he wouldn't mind being caught in bed with), a broad face, and a habitually bland, dreamy expression. Jedao wasn't fooled. Veller was almost as smart as Irin, had already been tracked into bomb disposal, and was less prone to flights of temper.

"Is there a tool closet in here?" Veller said. "I need a screwdriver."

"You don't carry your own anymore?" Jedao said.

"I told him he should," Irin said, "but he said they were too similar to knitting needles. As if anyone in their right mind would knit with a pair of screwdrivers."

"I think he meant that they're stabby things that can be driven into people's eyes," Jedao said.

"I didn't ask for your opinion, Jay."

Jedao put his hands up in a conciliatory gesture and shut up. He liked Irin and didn't want to antagonize her any more than necessary. The last time they'd been paired together, they'd done quite well. She would come around; she just needed time to work through the implications of what the instructor had said. She was one of those people who preferred to think about things without being interrupted.

One of the other cadets wordlessly handed Veller a set of screwdrivers. Veller mumbled his thanks and got to work. The class watched, breathless.

"There," Veller said at last. "See that there, all hooked in? Don't know what the timer is, but there it is."

"I find it very suspicious that you gave up your chance to show up everyone else in this exercise," Irin said to Jedao. "Is there anyone else who knew?"

"Irin," Jedao said, "I don't think the instructor told *anyone* where she'd left the photobomb. She just stuck it in the slate because that was the last place we'd look. The test was meant to reveal which of us would backstab each other, but honestly, that's so counterproductive. I say we disarm the damn thing and skip to the end."

Irin's eyes crossed and her lips moved as she recited the instructor's words under her breath. That was another thing Jedao liked about her. Irin had a *great* memory. Admittedly, that made it difficult to cheat her at cards, as he'd found out the hard way. He'd spent three hours doing her kitchen duties for her the one time he'd tried. He *liked* people who could beat him at cards. "It's possible," she said grudgingly after she'd reviewed the assignment's instructions.

"Disarmed," Veller said shortly after that. He pulled out the photobomb and left it on the desk, then set about reassembling the slate.

Jedao glanced over at Meng. For a moment, his partner's expression had no anxiety in it, but a raptor's intent focus. Interesting: what were they watching for?

"I hope I get a nice quiet posting at a desk somewhere," Meng said.

"Then why'd you join up?" Irin said.

Jedao put his hand over Meng's, even though he was sure that they had just lied. "Don't mind her," he said. "You'll do fine."

Meng nodded and smiled up at him.

Why do I have the feeling that I'm not remotely the most dangerous person in the room? Jedao thought. But he returned Meng's smile, all the same. It never hurt to have allies.

A GWA PATROL ship greeted them as they neared Du Station. Haval had assured Jedao that this was standard practice and obligingly matched velocities.

Jedao listened in on Haval speaking with the Gwa authority, who spoke flawless high language. "They don't call it 'high language,' of course," Haval had explained to Jedao earlier. "They call it 'mongrel language.'" Jedao had expressed that he didn't care what they called it.

Haval didn't trust Jedao to keep his mouth shut, so she'd stashed him in the business office with Teshet to keep an eye on him. Teshet had brought a wooden box that opened up to reveal an astonishing collection of jewelry. Jedao watched out of the corner of his eye as Teshet made himself comfortable in the largest chair, dumped the box's contents on the desk, and began sorting it to criteria known only to him.

Jedao was watching videos of the command center and the communications channel, and tried to concentrate on reading the authority's body language, made difficult by her heavy zigzag cosmetics and the layers of robes that cloaked her figure. Meanwhile, Teshet put earrings, bracelets, and mysterious hooked and jeweled items in piles, and alternated helpful glosses of Gwa-an gestures with borderline insubordinate, not to say lewd, suggestions for things he could do with Jedao. Jedao was grateful that his ability to blush, like his ability to be tickled, had been burned out of him in Academy. Note to self, suggest to General Essier that Teshet was wasted in special ops and maybe reassign him to Recreation?

Jedao mentioned this to Teshet while Haval was discussing the cargo manifest with the authority. Teshet lowered his lashes and looked sideways at Jedao. "You don't think I'm good at my job?" he asked.

"You have an excellent record," Jedao said.

Teshet sighed, and his face became serious. "You're used to regular Kel, I see."

Jedao waited.

"I end up in a lot of situations where if people get the notion that I'm a Kel officer, I may end up locked up and tortured. While that could be fun in its own right, it makes career advancement difficult."

"You could get a medal out of it."

"Oh, is *that* how you got promoted so—?"

Jedao held up his hand, and Teshet stopped. On the monitor, Haval was saying, in a greasy voice, "I'm glad to hear of your interest, madam. We would have been happy to start hauling the lubricant earlier, except we had to persuade our people that—"

The authority's face grew even more imperturbable. "You had to figure out whom to bribe."

"We understand there are fees—"

Jedao listened to Haval negotiating her bribe to the authority with half an ear. "Don't tell me all that jewelry's genuine?"

"The gems are mostly synthetics," Teshet said. He held up a long earring with a rose quartz at the end. "No, this won't do. I bought it for myself, but you're too light-skinned for it to look good on you."

"I'm wearing jewelry?"

"Unless you brought your own—scratch that, I bet everything you own is in red and gold."

"Yes."

Teshet tossed the rose quartz earring aside and selected a vivid emerald earstud. "This will look nice on you."

"I don't get a say?"

"How much do you know about merchanter fashion trends out in this march?"

Jedao conceded the point.

The private line crackled to life. "You two still in there?" said Haval's voice.

"Yes, what's the issue?" Teshet said.

"They're boarding us to check for contraband. You haven't messed with the drugs cabinet, have you?"

Teshet made an affronted sound. "You thought I was going to get Sren high?"

"I don't make assumptions when it comes to you, Teshet. Get the hell out of there."

Teshet thrust the emerald earstud and two bracelets at Jedao. "Put those on," he said. "If anyone asks you where the third bracelet is, say you had to pawn it to make good on a gambling debt."

Under other circumstances, Jedao would have found this offensive—he was *good* at gambling—but presumably Sren had different talents. As he put on the earring, he said, "What do I need to know about these drugs?"

Teshet was stuffing the rest of the jewelry back in the box. "Don't look at me like that. They're illegal both in the heptarchate and the Gwa Reality, but people run them anyway. They make useful cover. The Gwa-an search us for contraband, they find the contraband, they confiscate the contraband, we pay them a bribe to keep quiet about it, they go away happy."

Impatient with Jedao fumbling with the clasp of the second bracelet, he fastened it for him, then turned Jedao's hand over and studied the scar at the base of his palm. "You should have skinsealed that one too, but never mind."

"I'm bad at peeling vegetables?" Jedao suggested. Close enough to "knife fight," right? And much easier to explain away than bullet scars.

"Are you two *done?*" Haval's voice demanded.

"We're coming, we're coming," Teshet said.

Jedao took up his post in the command center. Teshet himself disappeared in the direction of the airlock. Jedao wasn't aware that anything had gone wrong until Haval returned to the command center, flanked by two personages in bright orange space suits. Both wielded guns of a type Jedao had never seen before, which made him irrationally happy. While most of his collection was at home with his mother, he relished adding new items. Teshet was nowhere in sight.

Haval's pilot spoke before the intruders had a chance to say anything. "Commander, what's going on?"

The broader of the two arrivals spoke in Tlen Gwa, then kicked Haval in the shin. "Guess what," Haval said with a macabre grin. "Those aren't the real authorities we ran into. They're pirates."

Oh, for the love of fox and hound, Jedao thought. In truth, he wasn't surprised, just resigned. He never trusted it when an operation went too smoothly.

The broader pirate spoke again. Haval sighed deeply, then

said, "Hand over all weapons or they start shooting."

Where's Teshet? Jedao wondered. As if in answer, he heard a gunshot, then the ricochet. More gunshots. He was sure at least one of the shooters was Teshet, or one of Teshet's operatives: they carried Stinger 40s and he recognized the whine of the reports.

Presumably Teshet was occupied, which left matters here up to him. Some of Haval's crew went armed. Jedao did not—they had agreed that Sren wouldn't know how to use a gun—but that didn't mean he wasn't dangerous. While the other crew set down their guns, Jedao flung himself at the narrower intruder's feet.

The pirates did not like this. But Jedao had always been blessed, or perhaps cursed, with extraordinarily quick reflexes. He dropped his weight on one arm and leg and kicked the narrow pirate's feet from under them with the other leg. The pirate discharged their gun, and the bullet whined over Jedao and banged into one of the status displays, causing it to spark and sputter out. Haval yelped.

Jedao had already sprung back to his feet—damn the twinge in his knees, he should have that looked into—and twisted the gun out of the narrow pirate's grip. They had the stunned expression that Jedao was used to seeing on people who did not deal with professionals very often. He shot them, but thanks to their loose-limbed flailing, the first bullet took them in the shoulder. The second one made an ugly hole in their forehead, and they dropped.

The broader pirate had more presence of mind, but chose the wrong target. Jedao smashed her wrist aside with the knife edge of his hand just as she fired at Haval—five shots, in rapid succession. Her hands trembled visibly, and four of the shots went wide. Haval had had the sense to duck, but Jedao smelled blood and suspected she'd been hit. Hopefully nowhere fatal.

Jedao shot the broad pirate in the side of the head just as she pivoted to target him next. Her pistol clattered to the floor as she dropped. By reflex, he flung himself to the side in case it discharged, but it didn't.

Once he had assured himself that both pirates were dead, he knelt at Haval's side and checked the wound. She had been very lucky. The single bullet had gone through her side, missing the major organs. She started shouting at him for going up unarmed against people with guns.

"I'm getting the medical kit," Jedao said, too loudly, to get her to shut up. His hands were utterly steady as he opened the medical cabinet and brought the kit back to Haval, who at least had the good sense not to try to stand up.

Haval scowled, but accepted the painkiller tabs he handed her. She held still while he cut away her shirt and inspected the entry and exit wounds. At least the bullet wasn't a burrower or she wouldn't have a lung anymore. He got to work with the sterilizer.

By the time Teshet and two other soldiers entered the command center, Jedao had sterilized and sealed the wounds. Teshet crossed the threshold with rapid strides. When Haval's head came up, Teshet signed sharply for her to be quiet. Curious, Jedao also kept silent.

Teshet drew his combat knife, then knelt next to the larger corpse. With a deft stroke, he cut into the pirate's neck, then yanked out a device and its wires. Blood dripped down and obscured the metal. He repeated the operation for the other corpse, then crushed both devices under his heel. "All right," he said. "It should be safe to talk now."

Jedao raised his eyebrows, inviting explanation.

"Not pirates," Teshet said. "Those were Gwa-an special ops."

Hmm. "Then odds were they were waiting for someone to show up to rescue the *Moonsweet Blossom*," Jedao said.

"I don't disagree." Teshet glanced at Haval, then back at the corpses. "That wasn't you, was it?"

Haval's eyes were glazed, side-effect of the painkiller, but she wasn't entirely out of it. "Idiot here risked his life. We could have handled it."

"I wasn't the one in danger," Jedao said, remembering the pirates' guns pointed at her. Haval might not be particularly respectful, as subordinates went, cover identity or not, but she *was* his subordinate, and he was responsible for her. To Teshet: "Your people?"

"Two down," Teshet said grimly, and gave him the names. "They died bravely."

"I'm sorry," Jedao said; two more names to add to the long litany of those he'd lost. He was thinking about how to proceed, though. "The *real* Gwa-an patrols won't be likely to know about this. It's how I'd run the op—the fewer people who are aware of the truth, the better. I bet *their* orders are to take in any surviving 'pirates' for processing, and then the authorities will release and debrief the operatives from there. What do you normally do in case of *actual* pirates?"

"Report the incident," Haval said. Her voice sounded thready. "Formal complaint if we're feeling particularly annoying."

"All right." Jedao calmly began taking off the jewelry and his clothes. "That one's about my size," he said, nodding at the smaller of the two corpses. The suit would be tight across the shoulders, but that couldn't be helped. "Congratulations, not two but three of your crew died heroically, but you captured a pirate in the process."

Teshet made a wistful sound. "That temporary skin stuff obscures your musculature, you know." But he helpfully began stripping the indicated corpse.

"I'll make it up to you some other time," Jedao said recklessly. "Haval, make that formal complaint and demand that you want your captive tried appropriately. Since the nearest station is Du, that will get me inserted so I can investigate."

"You're just lucky some of the Gwa-an are as sallow as you are," Haval said as Jedao changed clothes.

"I will be disappointed in you if you don't have restraints," Jedao said to Teshet.

Teshet's eyes lit up.

Jedao rummaged in the medical kit until he found the eyedrops he was looking for. They were meant to counteract tear gas, but they had a side effect of pupil dilation, which was what interested him. It would help him feign concussion.

"We're running short on time, so listen closely," Jedao said. "Turn me over to the Gwa-an. Don't worry about me; I can handle myself."

"Je—Sren, I don't care how much you've studied the station's schematics, you'll be outnumbered thousands to one *on foreign territory*."

"Sometime over drinks I'll tell you about the time I infiltrated a ring-city where I didn't speak any of the local languages," Jedao said. "Turn me over. I'll locate the crew, spring them, and signal when I'm ready. You won't be able to mistake it."

Haval's brow creased. Jedao kept speaking. "After you've done that, load all the shuttles full of lubricant canisters. Program the lubricant to go from zero-coefficient flow to harden completely in response to the radio signal. You're going to put the shuttles on autopilot. When you see my signal, launch the shuttles' contents toward the station's turret levels. That should gum them up and buy us cover."

"*All* our shuttles?" Haval said faintly.

"Haval," Jedao said, "stop thinking about profit margins and repeat my orders back to me."

She did.

"Splendid," Jedao said. "Don't disappoint me."

*   *   *

THE GWA-AN TOOK Jedao into custody without comment. Jedao feigned concussion, saving him from having to sound coherent in a language he barely spoke. The Gwa-an official responsible for him looked concerned, which was considerate of him. Jedao hoped to avoid killing him or the guard they'd assigned to him. Only one, thankfully; they assumed he was too injured to be a threat.

The first thing Jedao noticed about the Gwa-an shuttle was how roomy it was, with wastefully widely-spaced seats. He hadn't noticed that the Gwa-an were, on average, that much larger than the heptarchate's citizens. (Not that this said much. Both nations contained a staggering variety of ethnic groups and their associated phenotypes. Jedao himself was on the short side of average for a heptarchate manform.) At least being "concussed" meant he didn't have to figure out how the hell the safety restraints worked, because while he could figure it out with enough fumbling, it would look damned suspicious that he didn't already know. Instead, the official strapped him in while saying things in a soothing voice. The guard limited themself to a scowl.

Instead of the smell of disinfectant that Jedao associated with shuttles, the Gwa-an shuttle was pervaded by a light, almost effervescent fragrance. He hoped it wasn't intoxicating. Or rather, part of him hoped it was, because he didn't often have good excuses to screw around with new and exciting recreational drugs, but it would impede his effectiveness. Maybe all Gwa-an disinfectants smelled this good? He should steal the formula. Voidmoth crews everywhere would thank him.

Even more unnervingly, the shuttle played music on the way to the station. At least, while it didn't resemble any music he'd heard before, it had a recognizable beat and some sort of flute in it. From the others' reactions, this was normal and possibly even boring. Too bad he was about as musical as a pair of boots.

The shuttle docked smoothly. Jedao affected not to know what was going on and allowed the official to chirp at him. Eventually a stretcher arrived and they put him on it. They emerged into the lights of the shuttle bay. Jedao's temples twinged with the beginning of a headache. At least it meant the eyedrops were still doing their job.

The journey to Du Station's version of Medical took forever. Jedao was especially eager to escape based on what he'd heard of Gwa-an medical therapies, which involved too many genetically-engineered critters for his comfort. (He had read up on the topic after Haval told him about the dueling.) He did consider that he could make his mother happy by stealing her some pretty little microbes, but with his luck they'd turn his testicles inside-out.

When the medic took him into an examination room, Jedao whipped up and downed her with a blow to the side of the neck. The guard was slow to react, and Jedao grasped their throat and grappled with them, waiting the interminable seconds until they slumped unconscious. He had a bad moment when he heard footsteps passing by; luckily, the guard's wheeze didn't attract attention. Jedao wasn't modest about his combat skills, but they wouldn't save him if he was sufficiently outnumbered.

Too bad he couldn't steal the guard's uniform, but it wouldn't fit him. So it would have to be the medic's clothes. Good: the medic's clothes were robes instead of something more form-fitting. Bad: even though the garments would fit him, more or less, they were in the style for women.

I will just have to improvise, Jedao thought. At least he'd kept up the habit of shaving, and the Gwa-an appeared to permit a variety of haircuts in all genders, so his short hair and bangs wouldn't be too much of a problem. As long as he moved quickly and didn't get stopped for conversation—

Jedao changed, then slipped out and took a few moments to observe how people walked and interacted so he could fit in more easily. The Gwa-an were terrible about eye contact and, interestingly for station-dwellers, preferred to keep each other at a distance. He could work with that.

His eyes still ached, since Du Station had abominably bright lighting, but he'd just have to prevent people from looking too closely at him. It helped that he had dark brown eyes to begin with, so the dilated pupils wouldn't be obvious from a distance. He was walking briskly toward the lifts when he heard a raised voice. He kept walking. The voice called again, more insistently.

Damn. He turned around, hoping that someone hadn't recognized his outfit from behind. A woman in extravagant layers of green, lilac, and pink spoke to him in strident tones. Jedao approached her rapidly, wincing at her voice, and hooked her into an embrace. Maybe he could take advantage of this yet.

"You're not—" she began to say.

"I'm too busy," he said over her, guessing at how best to deploy the Tlen Gwa phrases he knew. "I'll see you for tea at thirteen. I like your coat."

The woman's face turned an ugly mottled red. "You like my *what?*" At least, he thought that was what she had said. She stepped back from him, pulling what looked like a small perfume bottle from among her layers of clothes.

He tensed, not wanting to fight her in full view of passers-by. She spritzed him with a moist vapor, then smiled coolly at him before spinning on her heel and walking away.

Shit. Just how fast-acting were Gwa-an duels, anyway? He missed the sensible kind with swords; his chances would have been much better. He hoped the symptoms wouldn't be disabling, but then, the woman couldn't possibly have had a chance to tailor the infectious agent to his system, and maybe the immunizations would keep him from falling over sick until he had found Meng and their crew.

How had he offended her, anyway? Had he gotten the word for "coat" wrong? Now that he thought about it, the word for "coat" differed from the word for "navel" only by its tones, and—hells and foxes, he'd messed up the tone sandhi, hadn't he? He kept walking, hoping that she'd be content with getting him sick and wouldn't call security on him.

At last he made it to the lifts. While stealing the medic's uniform had also involved stealing their keycard, he preferred not to use it. Rather, he'd swapped the medic's keycard for the loud woman's. She had carried hers on a braided lanyard with a clip. It would do nicely if he had to garrote anyone in a hurry. The garrote wasn't one of his specialties, but as his girlfriend the first year of Shuos Academy had always been telling him, it paid to keep your options open.

At least the lift's controls were less perilous than figuring out how to correctly pronounce items of clothing. Jedao had by no means achieved reading fluency in Tlen Gwa, but the language had a wonderfully tidy writing system, with symbols representing syllables and odd little curlicue diacritics that changed what vowel you used. He had also theoretically memorized the numbers from 1 to 9,999. Fortunately, Du Station had fewer than 9,999 levels.

Two of the other people in the lift stared openly at Jedao. He fussed with his hair on the grounds that it would look like ordinary embarrassment and not *Hello! I am a cross-dressing enemy agent, pleased to make your acquaintance.* Come to that, Gwa-an women's clothes were comfortable, and all the layers meant that he could, in principle, hide useful items like garrotes in them. He wondered if he could keep them as a souvenir. Start a fashion back home. He bet his mother would approve.

Intelligence had given him a good guess for where Meng and their crew might be held. At least, Jedao hoped that Du Station's higher-ups hadn't faked him out by stowing them in the lower-security cells. He was betting a lot on the guess that the Gwa-an were still in the process of interrogating the lot rather than executing them out of hand.

The layout wasn't the hard part, but Jedao reflected on the mysteries of the Gwa Reality's penal code. For example, prostitution was a major offense. They didn't even fine the offenders, but sent them to remedial counseling, which surely *cost* the state money. In the heptarchate, they did the sensible thing by enforcing licenses for health and safety reasons and taxing the whole enterprise. On the other hand, the Gwa-an had a refreshingly casual attitude toward heresy. They believed that public debate about Poetics (their version of Doctrine) strengthened the polity. If you put forth that idea anywhere in the heptarchate, you could expect to get arrested.

So it was that Jedao headed for the cell blocks where one might find unlucky prostitutes and not the ones where overly enthusiastic heretics might be locked up overnight to cool it off. He kept attracting horrified looks and wondered if he'd done something offensive with his hair. Was it wrong to part it on the left, and if so, why hadn't Haval warned him? How many ways could you get hair wrong anyway?

The Gwa-an also had peculiarly humanitarian ideas about the surroundings that offenders should be kept in. Level 37, where he expected to find Meng, abounded with fountains. Not cursory fountains, but glorious cascading arches of silvery water interspersed with elongated humanoid statues in various uncomfortable-looking poses. Teshet had mentioned that this had to do with Gwa-an notions of ritual purity.

While "security" was one of the words that Jedao had memorized, he did not read Tlen Gwa especially quickly, which made figuring out the signs a chore. At least the Gwa-an believed in signs, a boon to foreign infiltrators everywhere. Fortunately, the Gwa-an hadn't made a secret of the Security office's location, even if getting to it was complicated by the fact that the fountains had been rearranged since the last available intel and he preferred not to show up soaking wet. The fountains themselves formed a labyrinth and, upon inspection, it appeared that different portions could be turned on or off to change the labyrinth's twisty little passages.

Unfortunately, the water's splashing also made it difficult to hear people coming, and he had decided that creeping about would not only slow him down, but make him look more conspicuous, especially with that issue with his hair (or whatever it was that made people stare at him with such affront). He rounded a corner and almost crashed into a sentinel, going by Security's spear-and-shield badge.

In retrospect, a simple collision might have worked out better. Instead, Jedao dropped immediately into a fighting stance, and the sentinel's eyes narrowed. *Dammit,* Jedao thought, exasperated with himself, *and this is why my handlers preferred me doing the sniper bits rather than the infiltration bits.* Since he'd blown the opportunity to bluff his way past the sentinel, he swept the man's feet out from under him and knocked him out. After the man was unconscious, Jedao stashed him behind one of the statues, taking care so the spray from the fountains wouldn't interfere too much with his breathing. He had the distinct impression that "dead body" was much worse from a ritual purity standpoint than "merely unconscious," if he had to negotiate with someone later.

He ran into no other sentinels on the way to the office, but as it so happened, a woman sentinel was leaving just as he got there. Jedao put on an expression he had learned from the scariest battlefield medic of his acquaintance, back when he'd been a lowly infantry captain, and marched straight up to Security. He didn't need to be convincing for long, he just needed a moment's hesitation.

By the time the sentinel figured out that the "medic" was anything but, Jedao had taken her gun and broken both her arms. "I want to talk to your leader," he said, another of those useful canned phrases.

The sentinel left off swearing (he was sure it was swearing) and repeated the word for "leader" in an incredulous voice.

Whoops. Was he missing some conversational nuance? He tried the word for "superior officer," to which the response was even more incredulous. *Hey, Mom,* Jedao thought, *you know how you always said I should join the diplomatic corps on account of my always talking my way out of trouble as a kid? Were you ever wrong. I am the worst diplomat ever.* Admittedly, maybe starting off by breaking the woman's arms was where he'd gone wrong, but the sentinel didn't sound upset about *that.* The Gwa-an were very confusing people.

After a crescendo of agitation (hers) and desperate rummaging about for people nouns (his), it emerged that the term he wanted was the one for "head priest." Which was something the language lessons ought to have noted. He planned on dropping in on whoever had written the course and having a spirited talk with them.

Just as well that the word for "why" was more straightforward. The sentinel wanted to know why he wanted to talk to the head priest. He wanted to know why someone who'd had both her arms broken was more concerned with propriety (his best guess) than alerting the rest of the station that they had an intruder. He had other matters to attend to, though. Too bad he couldn't recruit her for her sangfroid, but that was outside his purview.

What convinced the sentinel to comply, in the end, was not the threat of more violence, which he imagined would have been futile. Instead, he mentioned that he'd left one of her comrades unconscious amid the fountains and the man would need medical care. He liked the woman's concern for her fellow sentinel.

Jedao and the sentinel walked together to the head priest's office. The head priest came out. She had an extremely elaborate coiffure, held in place by multiple hairpins featuring elongated figures like the statues. She froze when Jedao pointed the gun at her, then said several phrases in what sounded like different languages.

"Mongrel language," Jedao said in Tlen Gwa, remembering what Haval had told him.

"What do you want?" the high priest said in awkward but comprehensible high language.

Jedao explained that he was here for Ahun Gerav, in case the priest only knew Meng by their cover name. "Release them and their crew, and this can end with minimal bloodshed."

The priest wheezed. Jedao wondered if she was allergic to assassins. He'd never heard of such a thing, but he wasn't under any illusions that he knew everything about Gwa-an immune systems. Then he realized she was laughing.

"Feel free to share," Jedao said, very pleasantly. The sentinel was sweating.

The priest stopped laughing. "You're too late," she said. "You're too late by thirteen years."

Jedao did the math: eight years since he and Meng had graduated from Shuos Academy. Of course, the two of them had attended for the usual five years. "They've been a double agent since they were a cadet?"

The priest's smile was just this side of smug.

Jedao knocked the sentinel unconscious and let her spill to the floor. The priest's smile didn't falter, which made him think less of her. Didn't she care about her subordinate? If nothing else, he'd had a few concussions in his time (real ones) and they were no joke.

"The crew," Jedao said.

"Gerav attempted to persuade them to turn coat as well," the priest said. "When they were less than amenable, well—" She shrugged. "We had no further use for them."

I will not forgive this, Jedao thought. "Take me to Gerav."

She shrugged again. "Unfortunate for them," she said. "But to be frank, I don't value their life over my own."

"How very pragmatic of you," Jedao said.

She shut up and led the way.

Du Station had provided Meng with a luxurious suite by heptarchate standards. The head priest bowed with an ironic smile as she opened the door for Jedao. He shoved her in and scanned the room.

The first thing he noticed was the overwhelming smell of— what *was* that smell? Jedao had thought he had reasonably cosmopolitan tastes, but the platters with their stacks of thin-sliced meat drowned in rich gravies and sauces almost made him gag. Who needed that much meat in their diet? The suite's occupant seemed to agree, judging by how little the meat had been touched. And why wasn't the meat cut into decently small pieces so as to make for easy eating? The bowls of succulent fruit were either for show or the suite's occupant disliked fruit, too. The flatbreads, on the other hand, had been torn into. One, not entirely eaten, rested on a meat platter and was dissolving into the gravy. Several different-sized bottles were partly empty, and once he adjusted to all the meat, he could also detect the sweet reek of wine.

Most fascinatingly, instead of chopsticks and spoons, the various plates and platters sported two-tined forks (Haval had explained to him about forks) and knives. Maybe this was how they trained assassins. Jedao liked knives, although not as much as he liked guns. He wondered if he could persuade the Kel to import the custom. It would make for some lively high tables.

Meng glided out, resplendent in brocade Gwa-an robes, then gaped. Jedao wasn't making any attempt to hide his gun.

"Foxfucking hounds," Meng slurred as they sat down heavily, "*you*. Is that really you, Jedao?"

"You know each other?" the priest said.

Jedao ignored her question, although he kept her in his peripheral vision in case he needed to kill her or knock her out. "You graduated from Shuos Academy with high marks," Jedao said. "You even married rich, the way you always talked about. Four beautiful kids. Why, Meng? Was it nothing more than a cover story?"

Meng reached for a fork. Jedao's trigger finger shifted. Meng withdrew their hand.

"The Gwa-an paid stupendously well," Meng said quietly. "It mattered a lot more, once. Of course, hiding the money was getting harder and harder. What good is money if you can't spend it? And the Shuos were about to catch on anyway. So I had to run."

"And your crew?"

Meng's mouth twisted, but they met Jedao's eyes steadfastly. "I didn't want things to end the way they did."

"Cold comfort to their families."

"It's done now," Meng said, resigned. They looked at the largest platter of meat with sudden loathing. Jedao tensed, wondering if it was going to be flung at him, but all Meng did was shove it away from them. Some gravy slopped over the side.

Jedao smiled sardonically. "If you come home, you might at least get a decent bowl of rice instead of this weird bread stuff."

"Jedao, if I come home, they'll *torture me for high treason*, unless our heptarch's policies have changed drastically. You can't stop me from killing myself."

"Rather than going home?" Jedao shrugged. Meng probably did have a suicide failsafe, although if they were serious they'd have used it already. He couldn't imagine the Gwa-an would have neglected to provide them with one if the Shuos hadn't.

Still, he wasn't done. "If you do something so crass, I'm going to visit each one of your children *personally*. I'm going to take them out to a nice dinner with actual food that you eat with actual chopsticks and spoons. And I'm going to explain to them in exquisite technicolor detail how their Shuos parent is a traitor."

Meng bit their lip.

More softly, Jedao said, "When did the happy family stop being a story and start being real?"

"I don't know," Meng said, wretched. "I can't—do you know how my spouses would look at me if they found out that I'd been lying to them all this time? I wasn't even particularly interested in other people's kids when all this began. But watching them grow up—" They fell silent.

"I have to bring you back," Jedao said. He remembered the staticky voice of the unnamed woman playing in Essier's office, Meng's crew, who'd tried and failed to get a warning out. She and her comrades deserved justice. But he also remembered all the gifts he'd sent to Meng's children down the years, the occasional awkwardly written thank-you note. It wasn't as if any good would be achieved by telling them the awful truth. "But I can pull a few strings. Make sure your family never finds out."

Meng hesitated for a long moment. Then they nodded. "It's fair. Better than fair."

To the priest, Jedao said, "You'd better take us to the *Moonsweet Blossom*, assuming you haven't disassembled it already."

The priest's mouth twisted. "You're in luck."

* * *

Du Station had ensconced the *Moonsweet Blossom* in a bay on Level 62. The Gwa-an they passed gawped at them. The priest sailed past without giving any explanation. Jedao wondered whether the issue was his hair or some other inexplicable Gwa-an cultural foible.

"I hope you can pilot while drunk," Jedao said to Meng.

Meng drew themself up to their full height. "I didn't drink *that* much."

Jedao had his doubts, but he would take his chances. "Get in."

The priest's sudden tension alerted him that she was about to try something. Jedao shoved Meng toward the trademoth, then grabbed the priest in an armlock. What was the point of putting a priest in charge of security if the priest couldn't *fight*?

Jedao said to her, "You're going to instruct your underlings to get the hell out of our way and open the airlock so we can leave."

"And why would I do that?" the priest said.

He reached up and snatched out half her hairpins. Too bad he didn't have a third hand; his grip on the gun was precarious enough as it stood. She growled, which he interpreted as "fuck you and all your little foxes."

"I could get creative," Jedao said.

"I was warned that the heptarchate was full of barbarians," the priest said.

At least the incomprehensible Gwa-an fixation on hairstyles meant that he didn't have to resort to more disagreeable threats, like shooting her subordinates in front of her. Given her reaction when he had knocked out the sentinel, he wasn't convinced that would faze her anyway. He adjusted his grip and forced her to the floor.

"Give the order," he said. "If you don't play any tricks, you'll even get the hairpins back without my shoving them through your eardrums." They were very nice hairpins, despite the creepiness of the elongated humanoid figures, and he bet they were real gold.

Since he had her facing the floor, the priest couldn't glare at him. The venom in her voice was unmistakable, however. "As you require." She started speaking in Tlen Gwa.

The workers in the area hurried to comply. Jedao had familiarized himself with the control systems of the airlock and was satisfied they weren't doing anything underhanded. "Thank you," he said, to which the priest hissed something venomous. He flung the hairpins away from him and let her go. She cried out at the sound of their clattering and scrambled after them with a devotion he reserved for weapons. Perhaps, to a Gwa-an priest, they were equivalent.

One of the workers, braver or more foolish than the others, reached for her own gun. Jedao shot her in the hand on the way up the hatch. It bought him enough time to get the rest of the way up the ramp and slam the hatch shut after him. Surely Meng couldn't accuse him of showing off if they hadn't seen the feat of marksmanship; and he hoped the worker would appreciate that he could just as easily have put a hole in her head.

The telltale rumble of the *Blossom*'s maneuver drive assured him that Meng, at least, was following directions. This boded well for their health. Jedao hurried forward, wondering how many more rounds the Gwa-an handgun contained, and started webbing himself into the gunner's seat.

"You wouldn't consider putting that thing away, would you?" Meng said. "It's hard for me to think when I'm ready to piss myself."

"If you think *I'm* the scariest person in your future, Meng, you haven't been paying attention."

"One, I don't think you know yourself very well, and two, I liked you much better when we were on the same side."

"I'm going to let you meditate on that second bit some other time. In the meantime, let's get out of here."

Meng swallowed. "They'll shoot us down the moment we get clear of the doors, you know."

"Just *go*, Meng. I've got friends. Or did you think I teleported onto this station?"

"At this point I wouldn't put anything past you. Okay, you're webbed in, I'm webbed in, here goes nothing."

The maneuver drive grumbled as the *Moonsweet Blossom* blasted its way out of the bay. No one attempted to close the first set of doors on them. Jedao wondered if the priest was still scrabbling after her hairpins, or if it had to do with the more pragmatic desire to avoid costly repairs to the station.

The *Moonsweet Blossom* had few armaments, mostly intended for dealing with high-velocity debris, which was more of a danger than pirates if one kept to the better-policed trade routes. They wouldn't do any good against Du Station's defenses. As *signals*, on the other hand—

Using the lasers, Jedao flashed, HERE WE COME in the merchanter signal code. With any luck, Haval was paying attention.

AT THIS POINT, several things happened.

Haval kicked Teshet in the shin to get him to stop watching a mildly pornographic and not very well-acted drama about a famous courtesan from 192 years ago. ("It's historical, so it's educational!" he protested. "One, we've got our signal, and two, I wish you would take care of your *urgent needs* in your own quarters," Haval said.)

Carp 1 through *Carp 4* and *7* through *10* launched all their shuttles. Said shuttles were, as Jedao had instructed, full of variable-coefficient lubricant programmed to its liquid form. The shuttles flew toward Du Station, then opened their holds and burned their retro thrusters for all they were worth. The lubricant, carried forward by momentum, continued toward Du Station's turret levels.

Du Station recognized an attack when it saw one, but its defenses consisted of a combination of high-powered lasers, which could only vaporize small portions of the lubricant and were useless for altering the momentum of quantities of the stuff, and railguns, whose projectiles punched through the mass without effect. Once the lubricant had clogged up the defensive emplacements, *Carp 1* transmitted an encrypted radio signal that caused the lubricant to harden in place.

The *Moonsweet Blossom* linked up with Haval's merchant troop. At this point, the *Blossom* only contained two people, trivial compared to the amount of mass it had been designed to haul. The merchant troop, of course, had just divested itself of its cargo. The nine heptarchate vessels proceeded to hightail it out of there at highly non-freighter accelerations.

JEDAO AND MENG swept the *Moonsweet Blossom* for bugs and other unwelcome devices, an exhausting but necessary task. Then, at what Jedao judged to be a safe distance from Du Station, he ordered Meng to slave it to *Carp 1*.

The *Carp 1* and *Moonsweet Blossom* matched velocities, and Jedao and Meng made the crossing to the former. There was a bad moment when Jedao thought Meng was going to unhook their tether and drift off into the smothering dark rather than face their fate. But whatever temptations where running through their head, Meng resisted them.

Haval and Teshet greeted them on the *Blossom*. After Jedao and Meng had shed the suits and checked them for needed repairs, Haval ushered them all into the business office. "I didn't expect you to spring the trademoth as well as our Shuos friend," Haval said.

Meng wouldn't meet her eyes.

"What about the rest of the crew?" Teshet said.

"They didn't make it," Jedao said, and sneezed. He explained about Meng's extracurricular activities over the past thirteen years. Then he sneezed again.

Haval grumbled under her breath. "Whatever the hell you did on Du, Sren, did it involve duels?"

"'Sren'?" Meng said.

"You don't think I came into the Gwa Reality under my own"—sneeze—"name, did you?" Jedao said. "Anyway, there might have been an incident..."

Meng groaned. "Just how good is your Tlen Gwa?"

"Sort of not, apparently," Jedao said. "I *really* need to have a word with whoever wrote the Tlen Gwa course. I thought I was all right with languages at the basic phrase level, but was the proofreader asleep the day they approved it?"

Meng had the grace to look embarrassed. "I may have hacked it."

"You what?"

"If I'd realized *you'd* be using it, I wouldn't have bothered. Botching the language doesn't seem to have slowed you down any."

Wordlessly, Teshet handed Jedao a handkerchief, and Jedao promptly sneezed into it. Maybe he'd be able to give his mother a gift of a petri dish with a lovely culture of Gwa-an germs after all. He'd have to ask the medic about it later.

Teshet then produced a set of restraints from his pockets and gestured at Meng. Meng sighed deeply and submitted to being trussed up.

"Don't look so disappointed," Teshet said into Jedao's ear. "I've another set just for you." Then he and Meng marched off to the brig.

Haval cleared her throat. "Off to the medic with you," she said to Jedao. "We'd better figure out why your vaccinations aren't working and if everyone's going to need to be quarantined."

"Not arguing," Jedao said meekly.

SOME DAYS LATER, Jedao was rewatching one of Teshet's pornography dramas in bed. At least, he thought it was pornography. The costuming made it difficult to tell, and the dialogue had made *more* sense when he was still running a fever.

The medic had kept him in isolation until they declared him no longer contagious. Whether due to this precaution or pure luck, no one else came down with the duel. They'd given him a clean bill of health this morning, but Haval had insisted that he rest a little longer.

The door opened. Jedao looked up in surprise.

Teshet entered with a fresh supply of handkerchiefs. "Well, Jedao, we'll re-enter heptarchate space in two days, high calendar. Any particular orders you want me to relay to Haval?" He obligingly handed over a slate so Jedao could look over Haval's painstaking, not to say excruciatingly detailed, reports on their current status.

"Haval's doing a fine job," Jedao said, glad that his voice no longer came out as a croak. "I won't get in her way." He returned the slate to Teshet.

"Sounds good." Teshet turned his back and departed. Jedao admired the view, wishing in spite of himself that the other man would linger.

Teshet returned half an hour later with two clear vials full of unidentified substances. "First or second?" he said, holding them up to the light one by one.

"I'm sorry," Jedao said, "first or second what?"

"You look like you need cheering up," Teshet said hopefully.

"You want on top, you want me on top? I'm flexible."

Jedao blinked, trying to parse this. "On top of wh—?" *Oh.* "What's *in* those vials?"

"You have your choice of variable-coefficient lubricant or goose fat," Teshet said. "Assuming you were telling the truth when you said it was goose fat. And don't yell at Haval for letting me into your refrigerator, I did it all on my own. I admit I can't tell the difference. As Haval will attest, I'm a *dreadful* cook, so I didn't want to fry up some scallion pancakes just to taste the goose fat."

Jedao's mouth went dry, which had less to do with Teshet's eccentric choice of lubricants than the fact that he had sat down on the edge of Jedao's bed. "You don't have anything more, ah, conventional?" He realized that was a mistake as soon as the words left his mouth; he'd essentially accepted Teshet's proposition.

For the first time, Jedao glimpsed uncertainty in Teshet's eyes. "We don't have a lot of time before we're back to heptarchate space and you have to go back to being a commander and I have to go back to being responsible," he said softly. "Or as responsible as I ever get, anyway. Want to make the most of it? Because I get the impression that you don't allow yourself much of a personal life."

"Use the goose fat," Jedao said, because as much as he liked Teshet, he did not relish the thought of being *cemented* to Teshet.

It would distract Teshet from continuing to analyze his psyche, and yes, the man was damnably attractive. What the hell, with any luck his mother was never, ever, *ever* hearing of this. (He could imagine the conversation now: "Garach Jedao Shkan, are you meaning to tell me you finally found a nice young man and you're *still* not planning on settling down and providing me more grandchildren?" And then she would send him *more goose fat.*)

Teshet brightened. "You won't regret this," he purred, and proceeded to help Jedao undress.

AUTHOR'S NOTE

This story is a ridiculous caper, and was written to stand alone because Jonathan Strahan at *Tor.com* had asked me if I was interested in submitting something. What you may not be able to discern from the text is that it was screamingly difficult to write. My family ribs me all the time because I have... developed a reputation for writing depressing genocide stories. "Ridiculous caper" is not a skill set I've been working on. In fact, the entire first draft, which featured a secret weapon and Jedao challenging a Kel to a duel, was so riddled with plot holes that I discarded it and started over.

What enabled me to finish this story was writing chunks in locked Dreamwidth blog posts while my friends cheerleaded, and promising myself a white chocolate Kit-Kat, the unicorn of Kit-Kats, as a reward if I finished the draft. It didn't have to be a *good* draft, just a complete one. My rough drafts are frequently atrocious, and I hate the process of generating words, but I like doing revisions.

I would like you to know that one of my beta readers suggested "A Sticky Situation" as an alternate title and I rejected it on the grounds that it was too much innuendo even for me.

GLOVES

THE SECOND THING that Brigadier General Shuos Jedao did when the mechanics signed off on the repairs to his command moth was look up the address of one of the space station's brothels. (The first thing was to draft a letter to his mother. His mother had Mysterious Ways of Knowing if he shirked his filial duty.) He'd considered doing something sensible with his money instead, like gambling, but the gambling houses wouldn't let him in these days.

The last time he'd attempted to gamble at this station, during a previous visit, he'd put on a tasteful amount of makeup and changed into civilian clothing respectable enough to announce that he had money, but not so ostentatious that some thief would try to pick his pocket. Sometimes, when he got bored, he did dress like a fop and let them get close enough that their terrible life choices dawned on them. After all, how else was he supposed to stay in practice with some of those armlocks?

Unfortunately, when he arrived, the house manager, a leggy Shuos woman with hair swept up in fantastic coils, stopped him at the door. "Hello, Jedao," she said without warmth. "Sorry, you're not allowed in here."

"I play by the rules," Jedao protested.

"Don't care," she said. "That's even worse than when you

clean us out, because we can't even nail you for cheating. Do you have nothing better to do than bully honest, hard-working foxes? Can't you go wallop some heretics instead?"

Jedao looked wistfully over her shoulder at a table where several people were playing jeng-zai, then went away.

The brothel was much more reasonable, possibly because he didn't cause them to *lose* money. The receptionist took down Jedao's name, contact information, and preferences. Then they offered him a discount if he booked an "overnight experience" rather than by the hour. *Discount my ass,* Jedao thought; but he was running out of fun things to blow his money on during leave. He collected firearms, for instance, but he couldn't haul his collection everywhere. In real life, he had to leave most of them in storage. So what the hell, "overnight experience" it was.

He showed up seven minutes before the appointment, dressed in uniform. This brothel catered to soldiers anyway. He'd stuck with medium formal on the grounds that he didn't want to get his full formal uniform messed up.

"Shuos Jedao?" said the receptionist, quite properly addressing him as a client rather than an officer. "Kio is waiting for you. Up the stairs, second room on the left."

"Thank you," Jedao said. There was never a good reason to antagonize the staff at a brothel. He and Ruo had done it a couple of times as cadets, and learned that annoyed prostitutes had a habit of "spilling" highly staining substances on uniforms. He headed up the stairs as instructed.

The upper floor smelled of perfume, some kind of aquatic. He could distinguish different explosives by smell, but perfume notes? Forget it. (His brother and sister had always found this very amusing.) The second room on the left was obscured by a dazzling curtain composed of strands of faceted glass beads in pale blue. Reflected glints formed a mosaic of light across the floor and walls. He rapped politely on the doorframe. The curtain swayed, and the glints of light wavered and rippled.

"Welcome," a tenor said from within.

Jedao's pulse quickened. He pulled the strands aside and entered to a clattering of beads.

Kio stood at the far end of the room, next to the head of the bed. He was tall, clean shaven, hair cut short: all in accordance with Kel regulations. His clothes, too, imitated the black-and-gold Kel uniform, although they were of silk and clung appealingly to his long limbs. The gold braid was further embellished with amber beads that caught the light as he moved. Golden chains descended from his epaulets to the buttons of his shirt, and jingled faintly as he began to make an almost-salute, open hand rather than fist to his left shoulder.

"Don't," Jedao said.

Kio froze. "Did I misunderstand your preferences, sir?"

"No," Jedao said. "It's something I prefer to keep out of the house's records." Just so his meaning was clear, he pulled out his wallet and retrieved a token of very large denomination in the local currency. He left it on the table next to the door.

"Something could be arranged, sir."

Next: "Stop calling me 'sir,'" Jedao said. "It's not—it's not necessary."

Kio's wariness, if anything, increased. Jedao sighed inwardly. Although various laws and customs protected prostitutes, the fact of the matter was that laws and customs were cold comfort when dealing with belligerent trained killers. While Jedao was not belligerent, he couldn't deny being a trained killer. Even if he employed swarms of warmoths these days instead of a sniper rifle or his hands, Kio would be aware of his reputation.

Jedao crossed the distance to Kio in slow strides, to make himself as little threatening as possible. He knelt before the other man. His hands were damp inside the regulation half-gloves. "Use me."

He thought he was going to have to repeat himself when Kio let out a long, shaky breath and nodded. Kio's own hands were sheathed in full black gloves. Technically illegal, but Jedao had no intention of reporting him or the house to the Kel. As a point of fact, he'd chosen this house because of its willingness to indulge this particular taste.

For a moment, Jedao wasn't certain this was going to work out. It sometimes didn't. Prostitutes, and lovers for that matter, usually assumed he wanted to give orders in bed. As if, after spending all day *giving orders*, he wanted to do it while fucking, too.

Then Kio reached down and grabbed Jedao's right hand, and placed it over his groin. "You know how to use your mouth, fledge? Show me." His voice was harsh.

Jedao groaned in the back of his throat at the address. "Sir," he breathed. He hadn't received permission to unglove, so he didn't. Instead, he hooked his thumbs into Kio's waistband, then unbuttoned his fly and drew out the other man's cock. Not hard, not yet. He could do something about that.

He teased the head of Kio's cock with his tongue, then took the whole thing into his mouth and sucked greedily. Kio was unnervingly silent. Jedao was determined to please him, though. He used his tongue to caress Kio's cock until he became hard and his shaft pushed into Jedao's throat. Erect, Kio was quite large, and Jedao's throat ached, but he didn't dare pull back.

Jedao himself was already uncomfortably erect. Although he was tempted to reach down and jerk himself off, or rearrange himself, he didn't have permission to do that either. He meant to be very literal about his orders. He longed to reach up and cradle Kio's balls in his hand, but even that hadn't been mentioned. *Use your mouth.*

Kio had noticed Jedao's arousal. "You like this, don't you, fledge?"

It was difficult to answer around a mouthful of cock, so Jedao confined himself to a nod. Kio shoved him away, not gently, and withdrew. Jedao glanced at Kio's saliva-slick length before casting his eyes down, wondering what he'd done wrong. He had wanted to make Kio come, even if he didn't dare hope—yet—that he'd be permitted the same.

Jedao raised his head and looked at Kio's face when the silence started to worry him.

Kio's expression was thoughtful. He grasped Jedao's hand again. This time, he pressed his own palm against it, as if making a comparison. He smiled, eyes glinting with mischief.

"Sir?" Jedao said, very softly.

"Give me your gloves," Kio said. And when Jedao hesitated: "Now."

Jedao had expected this moment to arrive, just not so early in the encounter. A thrill went down his spine as he ungloved. He'd always felt more vulnerable with naked hands. It was a common Kel foible—except, of course, he wasn't Kel.

Kio folded the half-gloves neatly and set them on the edge of the bed. Next he removed his own gloves. Jedao's breath caught at the sight of Kio's long hands and their calluses. (Jedao didn't allow himself to think about the source of the calluses: probably from playing a musical instrument, not from familiarity with firearms.) Then Kio did something unexpected: he held the full black gloves out to Jedao.

Suddenly Jedao's erection felt enormous. It seemed impossible that he'd be able to control himself. "Sir?"

"Put them on, fledge."

Jedao faltered. "I'm not—"

Kio slapped him full across the face with his free hand. Jedao tasted blood. It was all he could do to keep from coming right then and there, fully clothed except for his hands.

"Fledge."

"Yes, sir," Jedao said, dizzy, and pulled on Kio's gloves. He bit back a whimper at the way the charmeuse silk clung to his fingers. With the half-gloves he was used to being able to feel every chance current of air. No longer.

Kio hauled Jedao to his feet. Despite his slender build, he was surprisingly strong. "Jack yourself off," he said. "With the gloves on. I want to watch."

Jedao's first two attempts to undo his fly failed because his hands were shaking violently. Kio slapped him again, which had the paradoxical effect of steadying him. He hissed between his teeth as he pulled his cock out and closed his fingers around it. Silk; the whisper of fabric against his overheated skin.

Kio's eyes were hot and merciless. Jedao began stroking his shaft, up and down, up and down, torn between savoring the sensation and the urgency already building in his balls. *I'm not seventeen anymore*, he thought wildly. *How*—? But thinking was too difficult, and he focused again on masturbating so Kio could watch.

The air in the room was hot and cold at once, kaleidoscopic with the promise of unbearable pleasure. Jedao choked back a cry when Kio closed the distance between them and gathered him into a completely unmilitary embrace. Kio's kisses were brutal, and involved teeth. He left marks all the way down the side of Jedao's face. When he reached the scar at the base of Jedao's neck, Jedao's control gave way completely, and he began to come.

Even then Kio wasn't done. He disengaged neatly and knelt so that Jedao's come landed in white, sticky spurts all over the black silk, the golden chains. Jedao staggered. He'd dirtied the beautiful ersatz uniform. He looked down and saw that he'd also gotten stains on the silk gloves. Despite the fact that he'd just climaxed, his cock stirred at the sight.

"We're going to do this all night," Kio said directly into his ear. Jedao's heart thumped painfully. He had forgotten that he had paid for all night.

* * *

IN THE MORNING, after Jedao had left, Kio retrieved a slate from under the bed and made a call. No one spoke on the other end; he did not give his name. He said only, "Shuos-zho was right about his tastes." Then he closed the line, put the slate away, and went to clean up for the next client.

AUTHOR'S NOTE

For someone who likes to think of himself as being very smart, Jedao is terrible at a lot of things, and not just distinguishing perfume notes. Or maybe it's just that I think it's hilarious to write the archetypal high-Intelligence, low-Wisdom character. I'm pretty convinced that Wisdom was Jedao's dump stat.

I originally wrote this to blow off steam: some nice PWP ("Plot? What plot?" as fandom likes to call it) instead of unknotting the latest snarl of intrigue. This grew out of the thought that Jedao's inconvenient uniform kink could have been much less of a weakness if he'd just visited some accommodating prostitutes (I'm sure they've seen weirder things). But of course, nothing's ever that simple.

HUNTING TRIP

"Zoo?" High General Garit said. "Really, Jedao?"

Jedao, who was driving the car, glanced over to assess Garit's expression, although the high general's tone of voice told him everything he needed to know. Garit had invited him along on this damned trip to a hunting preserve because Garit was desperate to bag a gray tiger. Alongside his record with firearms, Jedao had made the mistake of letting drop that he had grown up hunting. He had tried to point out that going after pesky deer and jackalopes was not the same as gray tigers, but Garit had merely clapped him on the back and told him not to be so modest. Modesty had nothing to do with it. On top of the stupid expense per round, the recoil on the ammo that Jedao was going to have to use was proportionate to something with its stopping power, and he wasn't looking forward to the ache in his shoulder.

"Just for an hour or two," Jedao said coaxingly. "My mom and my siblings wanted me to send home some vacation photos. And I promised my nieces that I would bring them some souvenirs. Maybe the zoo's shop will have some mounted skeletons or the like."

"You spoil those kids rotten," Garit said with a snort.

"What are uncles for?" Jedao said. One of the great regrets

of his life was that his job kept him away from his family for long periods of time. The girls grew so *fast*. "Besides, the folks down at the shop might have some tips for hunters."

Garit shook his head, amused. "You're transparent, but all right."

The zoo was not particularly busy. The two of them were off-duty, and the young woman who told them about the zoo regulations either didn't recognize them or didn't care, which Jedao found congenial. Jedao then persuaded Garit to come with him into the zoo proper so Jedao could snap some photos.

Jedao fiddled with the manual exposure, trying to get the black panther to show up in its cave. The camera had been a gift from his brother, and was practically an antique. Jedao was not especially gifted at taking pictures that pleased his family ("These look like reconnaissance photos," his sister had once complained, "who cares about all this kill zone stuff when you're snapping pics of an engagement party?") so he had resolved to do better.

"That's the oddest damned fox I've ever seen," Garit said, pointing.

Jedao gave up on the exposure and settled for a muddled silhouette in the shadows. "Beg pardon?" he asked.

They strolled closer to the enclosure Garit had indicated to take a look. A reddish, bushy-tailed creature was taking a nap in the branches of a tree. Bamboo shoots sprouted not far away. Some of them looked like they'd been gnawed on.

"That's not a fox," Jedao said, reading the enclosure's label. "Red panda. Apparently they eat bamboo. And sometimes birds and things."

"It's kind of cute," Garit said grudgingly. "Doesn't look like much of a challenge, though."

Jedao thought that coddled zoo creatures were unlikely to be much challenge in general, but he didn't say anything that would give Garit the idea of adding another kind of animal to his wishlist for this trip. "My nieces will like it," he said, and raised his camera.

"We should catch you one to take home to them," Garit said.

Jedao made a face. "Have you ever looked at the customs forms for importing wildlife? I'm pretty sure those critters don't exist on my homeworld."

"Well, I'll look into expediting it as a favor to you if you can help me with my tiger problem," Garit said.

"That's very kind of you," Jedao said, as diplomatically as he could, "but my nieces are notoriously good at killing goldfish. Let's leave the red pandas alone and hit up the shop so I can buy bat skeletons or fox-eared hats or something, and we can head to the hunting grounds."

AUTHOR'S NOTE

In most regards, Jedao and I are complete opposites (I am rock stone stupid at tactics and games and he's supposed to be good at tactics, I have perfect pitch and compose orchestral music for fun while he sucks at music, etc.), but he and I are both hapless at cameras. One of my uncles was a photographer at one point, and my dad used to be a pretty good amateur up until the point someone stole his analog SLR, but I regret to report that it's not genetic. I stick to cat pics because my cat is innately photogenic and leave it at that.

The bat skeleton is a nod to the bat skeleton from Paxton Gate in San Francisco, which sells ethically sourced taxidermy, that my sister bought for my daughter for one of her birthdays. It was one of the treasures that survived the 2016 flood and she still has it today.

THE BATTLE OF CANDLE ARC

GENERAL SHUOS JEDAO was spending his least favorite remembrance day with Captain-magistrate Rahal Korais. There was nothing wrong with Korais except that he was the fangmoth's Doctrine officer, and even then he was reasonable for a Rahal. Nevertheless, Doctrine observed remembrances with the ranking officer, which meant that Jedao had to make sure he didn't fall over.

Next time, Jedao thought, wishing the painkillers worked better, *I have to get myself assassinated on a planet where they do the job right.*

The assassin had been a Lanterner, and she had used a shattergun. She had caught him at a conference, of all places. The shattergun had almost sharded Jedao into a hundred hundred pieces of ghostwrack. Now, as Jedao looked at the icelight that served as a meditation focus, he saw anywhere from three to eight of them. The effect would have been charming if it hadn't been accompanied by stabbing pains in his head.

Korais was speaking to him.

"Say again?" Jedao said. He kept from looking at his wristwatch.

"I'll recite the next verses for you, sir, if that doesn't offend you," Korais said.

Korais was being diplomatic. Jedao couldn't remember where in the litany they were. Under better circumstances he would have claimed that he was distracted by the fact that his force of eleven fangmoths was being pursued by the Lanterners who had mauled the rest of the swarm, but it came down to the injuries.

"I'd be much obliged, Captain," Jedao said.

This remembrance was called the Feast of Drownings. The Rahal heptarch, whose faction maintained the high calendar and who set Doctrine, had declared it three years back, in response to a heresy in one of the heptarchate's larger marches. Jedao would have called the heresy a benign one: people who wanted the freedom to build shrines to their ancestors, for pity's sake. But the Rahal had claimed that this would upset the high calendar's master equations, and so the heretics had had to be put down.

There were worse ways to die than by having your lungs slowly filled with caustic fluid. That still didn't make it a good way to die.

Korais had begun his recital. Jedao looked at the icelight on the table in front of them. It had translucent lobes and bronchi and alveoli, and light trickled downward through them like fluid, pale and blue and inexorable.

The heptarchate's exotic technologies depended on the high calendar's configurations: the numerical concordances, the feasts and remembrances, the associated system of belief. The mothdrive that permitted fast travel between star systems was an exotic technology. Few people advocated a switch in calendars. Too much would have to be given up, and invariant technologies, which worked under any calendar, never seemed to keep up. Besides, any new calendar would be subject to the same problems of lock-in; any new calendar would be regulated by the Rahal, or by people like the Rahal, as rigorously as the current one.

It was a facile argument, and one that Jedao had always disliked.

"Sir," Korais said, breaking off at the end of a phrase, "you should sit."

"I'm supposed to be standing for this," Jedao said dryly.

"I don't think your meditations during the next nineteen minutes are going to help if you fall unconscious."

He must look dreadful if Doctrine was telling him how long until the ordeal was over. Not that he was going to rest afterward. He had to figure out what to do about the Lanterners.

It wasn't that Jedao minded being recalled from medical leave to fight a battle. It wasn't even that he minded being handed this sad force of eleven fangmoths, whose morale was shredded after General Kel Najhera had gotten herself killed. It was that the heptarchate had kept the Lanterners as clients for as long as he remembered. Now the Lanterners were demanding regional representation, and they were at war with the heptarchate.

The Lanterner assassin had targeted Jedao during the Feast of Falcon's Eye. If she had succeeded, the event would have spiked the high calendar in the Lanterners' favor. Then they would have declared a remembrance in their own, competing calendar. The irony was that Jedao wasn't sure he disagreed with the Lanterners' grievances against the heptarchate, which they had broadcast everywhere after their victory over Najhera.

Korais was still looking at him. Jedao went to sit down, which was difficult because walking in a straight line took all his concentration. Sitting down also took concentration. It wasn't worth pretending that he heard the last remembrance verses.

"It's over, sir," Korais said. "I'll leave you to your duties." He saluted and let himself out.

Jedao looked at his watch after the door hissed shut. Everything on it was too tiny to read, the way his vision was. He made his computer enlarge its time display. Korais had left at least seven minutes early; an astonishing concession, considering his job.

Jedao waited until the latest wave of pain receded, then brought up a visual of Candle Arc, a battledrift site nine days out from their present position and eleven days out from the Lanterners' last reported position. The battle had taken place 177 years ago, between two powers that had since been conquered. The heptarchate called the battle Candle Arc because of the bridge of lights that wheeled through the scatter-hell of what had once been a fortress built from desiccated suns, and the remnants of warmoths. The two powers had probably called their battle something else, and their moths wouldn't have been called moths either, and their calendars were dead except in records held locked by the Rahal.

Some genius had done up the image in shades of Kel gold; a notation gave the spectrum shift for anyone who cared. Jedao was fond of the Kel, who were the heptarchate's military faction. For nearly twenty years he had been seconded to their service, and they had many virtues, but their taste in ornamentation was gaudy. Their faction emblem was the ashhawk, the bird that burned in its own glory, all fire and ferocity. The Shuos emblem was the ninefox, shapeshifter and trickster. The Kel called him the fox general, but they weren't always being complimentary.

The bridgelights swam in and out of focus. Damnation. This was going to take forever. After pulling up maps of the calendrical terrain, he got the computer algebra system to tell him what the estimated shifts looked like in pictures. Then he sent a summons to the moth commander.

He knew how long it took to get from the moth's command center to his quarters. The door chimed at him with commendable promptness.

"Come in," Jedao said.

The door opened. "You wished to see me, sir," said Kel Menowen, commander of the *Fortune Comes in Fours*. She was a stocky woman with swan-black hair and unsmiling eyes. Like all Kel, she wore black gloves; Jedao himself wore fingerless gloves. Her salute was so correct that he found himself trying to find an imperfection in her fist, or the angle of her arm.

Jedao had chosen the *Fortune* as his command moth not because it was the least damaged after Najhera's death, which it wasn't, but because Menowen had a grudge against the Shuos. She was going to be the hardest commander to win over, so he wanted to do it in person.

The tired joke about the Kel was that they were strong, loyal, and stupid, although they weren't any more prone to stupidity than the other factions.

The tired joke about the Shuos, who specialized in information operations, was that they had backstabbing quotas. Most of the other factions had reasonable succession policies for their heptarchs: the Rahal heptarch appointed a successor from one of the senior magistrates; with the Kel, it was rank and seniority. The Shuos policy was that if you could keep the heptarch's seat, it was yours. The other tired joke was that the infighting was the only reason the Shuos weren't running the heptarchate.

One of Menowen's aunts had died in a Shuos scheme, an assassin getting careless with secondary casualties. Jedao had already been in Kel service at the time, but it was in his public record that he had once been Shuos infantry, where "Shuos infantry" was a euphemism for "probably an assassin." In his case, he had been a very good assassin.

Menowen was still standing there. Jedao approximated a return salute. "At ease," he said. "I'd say 'stand easy,' but 'up' and 'down' are difficult concepts, which is distressing when you have to think in three dimensions."

Menowen's version of at ease looked stiff. "What do you require, sir?"

They had exchanged few words since he boarded her moth because he had barely been functional. She wasn't stupid. She knew he was on her moth to make sure she behaved, and he had no doubt her behavior would be exemplary. She also probably wanted to know what the plan was.

"What do you think I require?" Jedao asked. Sometimes it helped to be direct.

Menowen's posture became more stiff. "It hasn't escaped my notice that you only gave move orders as far as the Haussen system," she said. "But that won't take us near any useful support, and I thought our orders were to retreat." She was overenunciating on top of telling him things he knew, which meant that at some point she was going to tell him he wasn't fit for duty. Some Kel knew how to do subtlety. Menowen had an excellent service record, but she didn't strike him as a subtle Kel.

"You're reading the sane, sensible thing into our orders," Jedao said. "Kel Command was explicit. They didn't use the word 'retreat' anywhere." An interesting oversight on their part. The orders had directed him to ensure that the border shell guarding the Glover Marches was secured by any means possible.

"Retreat is the only logical response," Menowen said. "Catch repairs if possible, link up with Twin Axes." The Twin Axes swarm was on patrol along the Taurag border, and was the nearest Kel force of any size. "Then we'd have a chance against the heretics."

"You're discounting some alternatives," Jedao said.

Menowen lifted her chin and glared at him, or possibly at his insignia, or at the ink painting over his shoulder. "Sir," she said, "if you're contemplating fighting them with our present resources—" She stopped, tried again. The second try was blunter. "Your injuries have impaired your judgment and you ought to—"

"—let the senior moth commander make the sane, sensible decision to run for help?" Jedao flexed his hands. He had a clear memory of an earlier conversation with Commander Kel Chau, specifically the pinched look around Chau's eyes. Chau probably thought running was an excellent idea. "I had considered it. But it's not necessary. I've looked at the calendrical terrain. We can win this."

Menowen was having a Kel moment. She wanted to tell him off, but it wasn't just that he outranked her, it was that Kel Command had pulled him off medical leave to put him in charge, instead of evacuating him from the front. "Sir," she said, "I was *there*. The Lanterners have a swarm of at least sixty moths. They will have reinforcements. I shouldn't have to tell you any of this."

"How conscientious of you," Jedao said. Her eyes narrowed, but she didn't take the bait. "Did you think that I had some notion of slugging it out toe-to-toe? That *would* be stupid. But I have been reviewing the records and I understand the Lanterner general's temperament. Which is how we're going to defeat the enemy, unless you defeat yourself before they have a chance to."

Menowen's mouth pressed thin. "I understand you have never lost a battle," she said.

"This isn't the—"

"If it's about your fucking reputation—"

"Fox and hound, not this whole thing again," Jedao snapped. Which was unfair of him, because it was her first time bringing it up, even if everyone else did. "Sooner or later everyone loses. I get it. If it made more sense to stop the Lanterners in the Glovers, I'd be doing it." This would also mean ceding vast swathes of territory to them, not anyone's first choice; from her grim expression, she understood that. "If I could stop the Lanterners by calling them up for a game of cards, I'd do that too. Or by, I don't know, offering them my right arm. But I'm telling you, this can be done, and I am not quitting if there's a chance. Am I going to have to fight you to prove it?"

This wasn't an idle threat. It wouldn't be the first time he had dueled a Kel, although it would be frivolous to force a moth commander into a duel, however non-lethal, at a time like this.

Menowen looked pained. "Sir, you're *wounded*."

He could think of any number of ways to kill her before she realized she was being attacked, even in his present condition, but most of them depended on her trust that her commanding officer wouldn't pull such a stunt.

"We can do this," Jedao said. He was going to have to give this speech to the other ten moth commanders, who were jumpy right now. Might as well get in practice now. "All the way to the Haussen system, it looks like we're doing the reasonable thing. But we're going to pay a call on the Rahal outpost at Smokewatch 33-67." That wasn't going to be a fun conversation, but most Rahal were responsive to arguments that involved preserving their beloved calendar. And right now, he was the only one in position to stop the Lanterners from arrowing right up to the Glover Marches. The perfect battle record that people liked to bludgeon him over the head with might even come in handy for persuasion.

"I'm listening," Menowen said in an unpromising voice.

It was good, if inconvenient, when a Kel thought for herself. Unlike a number of the officers on this moth, Menowen didn't react to Jedao like a cadet fledge.

"Two things," Jedao said. "First, I know remembering the

defeat is painful, but if I'm reading the records correctly, the first eight Kel moths to go down, practically simultaneously, included two scoutmoths."

"Yes, that's right," Menowen said. She wasn't overenunciating anymore. "The Lanterners' mothdrive formants were distorted just enough to throw our scan sweep, so they saw us first."

"Why would they waste time killing scoutmoths when they could blow up fangmoths or arrowmoths instead? If you look at their positions and ours, they had better available targets." He had to be careful about criticizing a dead general, but there was no avoiding it. Najhera had depended too much on exotics and hadn't made adequate use of invariant defenses. The Kel also hadn't had time to channel any useful formation effects, their specialty. "The scoutmoths weren't out far enough to give advance notice, and surprise was blown once the Lanterners fried those eight moths. What I'm getting at is that our scan may not be able to tell the difference between mothdrives on big scary things and mothdrives on mediocre insignificant things, but their scan can't either, or they would have picked better targets."

Menowen was starting to look persuaded. "What are you going to do, sir? Commandeer civilian moths and set them to blow?" She wasn't able to hide her distaste for the idea.

"I'd prefer to avoid involving civilians," Jedao said coolly. Her unsmiling eyes became a little less unsmiling when he said that. "The Rahal run the show, they can damn well spare me some engines glued to tin cans."

The pain hit him like a spike to the eyes. When he could see again, Menowen was frowning. "Sir," she said, "one thing and I'll let you continue your deliberations in private." This was Kel for *please get some fucking rest before you embarrass us by falling over*. "You had some specific plan for punching holes into the Lanterners?"

"Modulo the fact that something always goes wrong after you wave hello at the enemy? Yes."

"That will do it for me, sir," Menowen said. "Not that I have a choice in the matter."

"You always have a choice," Jedao said. "It's just that most of them are bad."

She didn't look as though she understood, but he hadn't expected her to.

JEDAO WOULD HAVE authorized more time for repairs if he could, but they kept receiving reports on the Lanterners' movements and time was one of the things they had little of. He addressed his moth commanders on the subject to reassure them that he understood their misgivings. Thankfully, Kel discipline held.

For that matter, Jedao didn't like detouring to Smokewatch 33-67 afterward, but he needed a lure, and this was the best place to get it. The conversation with the Rahal magistrate almost wasn't a conversation. Jedao felt as though he was navigating through a menu of options rather than interacting with a human being. Some of the Rahal liked to cultivate that effect. At least Rahal Korais wasn't one of them.

"This is an unusual request for critical Rahal resources, General," the magistrate was saying.

That wasn't a no, so Jedao was already ahead. "The calendrical lenses are the best tool available," he said. "I will need seventy-three of them."

Calendrical lenses were Doctrine instruments mounted on mothdrives. Their sole purpose was to focus the high calendar in contested areas. It knocked the areas out of alignment, but the Rahal bureaucracy was attached to them. Typical Rahal, trusting an idea over cold hard experience. At least there were plenty of the things, and the mothdrives ought to be powerful enough to pass on scan from a distance.

Seventy-three was crucial because there were seventy-three moths in the Kel's Twin Axes swarm. The swarm was the key to the lure, just not in the way that Commander Menowen would have liked. It was barely possible, if Twin Axes set out from the Taurag border within a couple days' word of Najhera's defeat, for it to reach Candle Arc when Jedao planned on being there. It would also be inadvisable for Twin Axes to do so, because their purpose was to prevent the Taurags from contesting that border. Twin Axes wouldn't leave such a gap in heptarchate defenses without direct orders from Kel Command.

However, no one had expected the Lanterners to go heretical so suddenly. Kel Command had been known to panic, especially under Rahal pressure. And Rahal pressure was going to be strong after Najhera's defeat.

"Do you expect the lens vessels to be combat-capable?" the magistrate asked without any trace of sarcasm.

"I need them to sit there and look pretty in imitation of a Kel formation," Jedao said. "They'll get the heretics' attention, and if they can shift some of the calendrical terrain in our favor, even better." Unlikely, he'd had the Kel run the numbers for him, but it sounded nice. "Are volunteers available?"

Also unlikely. The advantage of going to the Rahal rather than some other faction, besides their susceptibility to the plea, was that the Rahal were disciplined. Even if they weren't going to be volunteers, if he gave instructions, the instructions would be rigorously carried out.

The magistrate raised an eyebrow. "That's not necessary," he said. "I'm aware of your skill at tactics, General. I assume you will spare the lenses' crews from unnecessary harm."

Touching. "I am grateful for your assistance, Magistrate," Jedao said.

"Serve well, General. The lenses will join your force at—" He named a time, which was probably going to be adhered to, then ended the communication.

The lenses joined within eight minutes and nineteen seconds of the given time. Jedao wished there were some way to minimize their scan shadow, but Kel moths did that with formations, and the Rahal couldn't generate Kel formation effects.

Jedao joined Menowen at the command center even though he should have rested. Menowen's mouth had a disapproving set. The rest of the Kel looked grim. "Sir," Menowen said. "Move orders?"

He took his chair and pulled up the orders on the computer. "False formation for the Rahal as shown. Follow the given movement plan," he said. "Communications, please convey the orders to all Rahal vessels." It was going to take extra time for the Rahal to sort themselves out, since they weren't accustomed to traveling in a fake formation, but he wasn't going to insult them by saying so.

Menowen opened her mouth. Jedao stared at her. She closed her mouth, looking pensive.

"Communications," Jedao said, "address to all units. Exclude the Rahal."

It wasn't the first speech he'd given on the journey, but the time had come to tell his commanders what they were up to and brace them for the action to come.

The Communications officer said, "It's open, sir."

"This is General Shuos Jedao to all moths," he said. "It's not a secret that we're being pursued by a Lanterner swarm. We're going to engage them at Candle Arc. Due to the Lanterners' recent victory, cascading effects have shifted the calendrical terrain there. The Lanterners are going to be smart and take one of the channels with a friendly gradient to their tech most of the way in. Ordinarily, a force this small wouldn't be worth their time. But because of the way the numbers have rolled, Candle Arc is a calendrical choke: we're arriving on the Day of Broken Feet. Whoever wins there will shift the calendar in their favor. When we offer battle, they'll take us up on it."

He consoled himself that, if the Lanterners lost, their soldiers would fall to fire and metal, honest deaths in battle, and not as calendrical foci, by having filaments needled into their feet to wind their way up into the brain.

"You are Kel," Jedao went on. "You have been hurt. I promise you we will hurt them back. But my orders will be exact, and I expect them to be followed exactly. Our chances of victory depend on this. I am not unaware of the numbers, but battle isn't just about numbers. It's about will. And you are Kel; in this matter you will prevail."

The panel lit up with each moth commander's acknowledgment, Kel gold against Kel black.

They didn't believe him, not yet. But they would follow orders, and that was all he needed.

COMMANDER MENOWEN ASKED to see him in private afterward, as Jedao had thought she might. Her mouth was expressive. Around him she was usually expressing discontent. But it was discontent for the right reasons.

"Sir," Menowen said. "Permission to discuss the battle plan."

"You can discuss it all you like," Jedao said. "I'll say something if I have something to say."

"Perhaps you had some difficulties with the computer algebra system," she said. "I've run the numbers. We're arriving 4.2 hours before the terrain flips in our favor."

"I'm aware of that," Jedao said.

The near side of the choke locus was obstructed by a null region where no exotic technologies would function. But other regions around the null shifted according to a schedule. The far side of the choke periodically favored the high calendar. With Najhera's defeat, the far side would also shift sometimes toward the Lanterners' calendar.

"I don't understand what you're trying to achieve," Menowen said.

"If you don't see it," Jedao said, pleased, "the Lanterners won't see it either."

To her credit, she didn't ask if this was based on an injury-induced delusion, although she clearly wanted to. "I expect Kel Command thinks you'll pull off a miracle," she said.

Jedao's mouth twisted. "No, Kel Command thinks a miracle would be very nice, but they're not holding their breath, and as a Shuos I'm expendable. The trouble is that I keep refusing to die."

It was like the advice for learning the game of pattern-stones: the best way to get good was to play difficult opponents, over and over. The trouble with war was that practicing required people to die.

"You've done well for your armies, sir. But the enemy general is also good at using calendrical terrain, and they've demonstrated their ruthlessness. I don't see why you would pass up a terrain advantage."

Jedao cocked an eyebrow at her. "We're not. Everyone gets hypnotized by the high fucking calendar. Just because it enables our exotics doesn't mean that the corresponding terrain is the most favorable to our purpose. I've been reading the intel on Lanterner engineering. Our invariant drives are better than theirs by a good margin. Anyway, why the hell would they be so stupid as to engage us in terrain that favors us? I picked the timing for a reason. You keep trying to beat the numbers, Commander, when the point is to beat the people."

Menowen considered that. "You are being very patient with my objections," she said.

"I need you not to freeze up in the middle of the battle," Jedao said. "Although I would prefer for you to achieve that without my having to explain basics to you."

The insult had the desired effect. "I understand my duty," she said. "Do you understand yours?"

He wondered if he could keep her. Moth commanders who were willing to question him were becoming harder to find. His usual commanders would have had no doubts about his plan no matter how much he refused to explain in advance.

"As I see it," Jedao said, "my duty is to carry out the orders. See? We're not so different after all. If that's it, Commander, you should get back to work."

Menowen saluted him and headed for the door, then swung around. "Sir," she said, "why did you choose to serve with the Kel? I assume it was a choice." The Shuos were ordinarily seconded to the Kel as intelligence officers.

"Maybe," Jedao said, "it was because I wanted to know what honor looked like when it wasn't a triumphal statue."

Her eyes went cold. "That's not funny," she said.

"I wasn't being funny," he said quietly. "I will never be a Kel. I don't think like one of you. But sometimes that's an advantage."

She drew in a breath. "Sir," she said, "I just want to know that this isn't some Shuos game to you." That he wasn't being clever for the sake of being clever; that he wouldn't throw his soldiers' lives away because he was overeager to fight.

Jedao's smile was not meant to reassure her. "Oh, it's to your advantage if it's a game," he said. "I am very good at winning games."

He wasn't going to earn her loyalty by hiding his nature, so he wasn't going to try.

It was even easier to win games if you designed the game yourself, instead of playing someone else's, but that was a Shuos sort of discussion and he didn't think she wanted to hear it yet.

*   *   *

THE ELEVEN FANGMOTHS and seventy-three calendrical lenses approached Candle Arc only 1.3 hours behind schedule. Jedao was recovering the ability to read his watch, but the command center had a display that someone had enlarged for his benefit, so he didn't look at it. Especially since he had the sneaking feeling that his watch was off by a fraction of a second. If he drew attention to it, Captain-engineer Korais was going to recalibrate it to the high calendar when they all had more important things to deal with.

The crews on the lenses had figured out how to simulate formations. No one would mistake them for Kel from close range, but Jedao wasn't going to let the Lanterners get close.

"Word from the listening posts is that the Lanterners are still in pursuit," Communications informed them.

"How accommodating of them," Jedao said. "All right. Orders for the Rahal: The lenses are to maintain formation and head through the indicated channel"—he passed over the waypoint coordinates from his computer station—"to the choke locus. You are to pass the locus, then circle back toward it. Don't call us under any circumstances, we'll call you. And stick to the given formation and don't try any fancy modulations."

It was unlikely that the Rahal would try, but it was worth saying. The Rahal were going to be most convincing as a fake Kel swarm if they stayed in one formation because there wasn't time to teach them to get the modulation to look right. The formation that Jedao had chosen for them was Senner's Lash, partly because its visible effects were very short-range. When the Rahal failed to produce the force-lash, it wouldn't look suspicious, because the Lanterners wouldn't expect to see anything from a distance.

"Also," Jedao said, still addressing the Rahal. "The instant you see something, anything on scan, you're to banner the Deuce of Gears."

The Deuce was his personal emblem, and it connoted "cog in the machine." Everyone had expected him to register some form of fox when he made brigadier general, but he had preferred a show of humility. The Deuce would let the Lanterners know who they were facing. It might not be entirely sporting for the Rahal to transmit it, but since they were under his command, he didn't feel too bad about it.

"The Rahal acknowledge," Communications said. Jedao's subdisplay showed them moving off. They would soon pass through the calendrical null, and at that point they would become harder to find on scan.

Commander Menowen was drumming her fingers on the arm of her chair, her first sign of nervousness. "They have no defenses," she said, almost to herself.

It mattered that this mattered to her. "We won't let the Lanterners reach them," Jedao said. "If only because I would prefer to spend my career not having the Rahal mad at me."

Her sideways glance was only slightly irritated. "Where are we going, sir?"

"Cut the mothdrives," Jedao said. He sent the coordinates to Menowen, Communications, and Navigation. "We're heading there by invariant drive only." This would probably prevent long-range scan from seeing them. "Transmit orders to all moths. I want acknowledgments from the moth commanders."

"There" referred to some battledrift, all sharp edges and ash-scarred fragments and wrecked silverglass shards, near the mouth of what Jedao had designated the Yellow Passage. He expected the Lanterners to take it toward the choke. Its calendrical gradient started in the Lanterners' favor, then zeroed out as it neared the null.

Depending on the Lanterners' invariant drives, it would take them two to three hours (high calendar) to cross the null region and reach the choke. This was, due to the periodic shifts, still faster than going around the null, because the detours would be through space hostile to their exotics for the next six hours.

Reports had put the Lanterners at anywhere from sixty to one hundred and twenty combat moths. The key was going to be splitting them up to fight a few at a time.

Jedao's moth commanders acknowledged less quickly than he would have liked, gold lights coming on one by one.

"Formation?" Menowen prompted him.

There weren't a lot of choices when you had eleven moths. Jedao brought up a formation, which was putting it kindly because it didn't belong to Lexicon Primary for tactical groups, or even Lexicon Secondary, which contained all the obsolete formations and parade effects. He wanted the moths in a concave configuration so they could focus lateral fire on the first hostiles to emerge from the Yellow Passage.

"That's the idea," Jedao said, "but we're using the battledrift as cover. Some big chunks of dead stuff floating out there, we might as well blend in and snipe the hell out of the Lanterners with the invariant weapons." At least they had a good supply of missiles and ammunition, as Najhera had attempted to fight solely with exotic effects.

The Kel didn't like the word "snipe," but they were just going to have to deal. "Transmit orders," Jedao said.

The acknowledgments lit up again, about as fast as they had earlier.

The *Fortune Comes in Fours* switched into invariant mode as they crossed into the null. The lights became less white-gold and more rust-gold, giving everything a corroded appearance. The hum of the moth's systems changed to a deeper, grittier whisper. The moth's acceleration became noticeable, mostly in the form of pain; Jedao wished he had thought to take an extra dose of painkillers, but he couldn't risk getting muddled.

Menowen picked out a chunk of coruscating metals that had

probably once been some inexplicable engine component on that long-ago space fortress and parked the *Fortune* behind it. She glanced at him to see if he would have any objections. He nodded at her. No sense in getting in the way when she was doing her job fine.

Time passed. Jedao avoided checking his watch every minute thanks to long practice, although he met Captain-magistrate Korais's eyes once and saw a wry acknowledgment of shared impatience.

They had an excellent view of the bridgelights even on passive sensors. The lights were red and violet, like absurd petals, and their flickering would, under other circumstances, have been restful.

"We won't see hostiles until they're on top of us," Menowen said.

More nerves. "It'll be mutual," Jedao said, loudly enough so the command center's crew could hear him. "They'll see us when they get that close, but they'll be paying attention to the decoy swarm."

She wasn't going to question his certainty in front of everyone, so he rewarded her by telling her. "I am sure of this," he said, looking at her, "because of how the Lanterner general destroyed Najhera. They were extremely aggressive in exploiting calendrical terrain and, I'm sorry to say, they made a spectacle of the whole thing. I don't imagine the Lanterners had time to swap out generals for the hell of it, especially one who had already performed well, so I'm assuming we're dealing with the same individual. So if the Lanterner wants calendrical terrain and a big shiny target, fine. We've given them one."

More time passed. There was something wrong about the high calendar when it ticked off seconds cleanly and precisely and didn't account for the way time crawled when you were waiting for battle. One of the many things wrong with the high calendar, but one he could own to without getting called out as a heretic.

"The far terrain is going to shift in our favor in five hours, sir," Korais said.

"Thank you, good to know," Jedao said.

To distract himself from the pain, he was thinking about the bridgelights and their resemblance to falling petals when Scan alerted him that the Lanterners had shown up. "Thirty-some moths in the van," the officer said in a commendably steady voice. "Readings suggest more are behind them. They're moving rapidly, vector suggests they're headed down the Yellow Passage toward the choke locus, and they're using a blast wave to clear mines."

As if he'd had the time to plant mines down a hostile corridor. Good of them to think of it, though.

Menowen's breath hissed between her teeth. "Our banner—"

His emblem. The Kel transmitted their general's emblem before battle. "No," Jedao said. "We're not bannering. The Lanterners are going to be receiving the Deuce of Gears from over there." Where the Rahal were.

"But the protocol, sir. The Rahal aren't part of your force," Menowen said, "they don't fight—"

That got his attention. "Fledge," Jedao said sharply, which brought her up short, "what the hell do you mean, they're not fighting? Just because they're not sitting on a mass of things that go boom? *They're fighting what's in the enemy's head.*"

He studied the enemy dispositions. The Yellow Passage narrowed as it approached the null, and the first group consisted of eight hellmoths, smaller than fangmoths, but well-armed if they were in terrain friendly to their own calendar, which was not going to be the case at the passage's mouth. The rest of the groups would probably consist of eight to twelve hellmoths each. Taken piecemeal, entirely doable.

"They fell for it," Menowen breathed, then wisely shut up.

"General Shuos Jedao to all moths," Jedao said. "Coordinated strike on incoming units with missiles and railguns." Hellmoths didn't have good side weapons, so he wasn't as concerned about return fire. "After the first hits, move into the Yellow Passage to engage. Repeat, move into the Yellow Passage."

The fangmoths' backs would be to that damned null, no good way to retreat, but that would only motivate them to fight harder.

If the Lanterners wanted a chance at the choke, they'd have to choose between shooting their way through when the geometry didn't permit them to bring their numbers to bear in the passage, or else leaving the passage and taking their chances with terrain that shaded toward the high calendar. If they chose the latter, they risked being hit by Kel formation effects, anything from force lances to scatterbursts, on top of the fangmoths' exotic weapons.

The display was soon a mess of red lights and gold, damage reports. The computer kept making the dry, metallic click that indicated hits made by the Kel. Say what you liked about the Kel, they did fine with weapons.

Two hellmoths tried to break through the Kel fangmoths, presumably under the impression that the Rahal were the real enemy. One hellmoth took a direct engine hit from a spinal railgun, while the other shuddered apart under a barrage of missiles that overwhelmed the anti-missile defenses.

"You poor fools," Jedao said, perusing the summaries despite the horrible throbbing in his left eye. "You found a general who was incandescently talented at calendrical warfare, so you spent all your money on the exotic toys and ran out of funding for the boring stuff."

Menowen paused in coordinating damage control—they'd taken a burst from an exploding scout, of all things—and remarked, "I should think you'd be grateful, sir."

"It's war, Commander, and someone always dies," Jedao said, aware of Korais listening in; aware that even this might be revealing too much. "That doesn't mean I'm eager to dance on their ashes."

"Of course," Menowen said, but her voice revealed nothing of her feelings.

The fangmoths curved into a concave bowl as they advanced up the Yellow Passage. The wrecked Lanterner hellmoths in the van were getting in the way of the Lanterners' attempts to bring fire to bear. Jedao had planned for a slaughter, but he hadn't expected it to work this well. They seemed to think his force was a detachment to delay them from reaching the false Kel swarm while the far terrain was hostile to the high calendar, and that if they could get past him before the terrain changed, they would prevail. It wasn't until the fourth group of Lanterners had been written into rubble and smoke that their swarm discipline wavered. Some of the hellmoths and their auxiliaries started peeling out of the passage just to have somewhere else to go. Others turned around, exposing their sides to further punishment, so they could accelerate back up the passage where the Kel wouldn't be able to catch them.

One of Jedao's fangmoths had taken engine damage serious enough that he had ordered it to pull back, but that still left him ten to work with. "Formation Sparrow's Spear," he said, and gave the first set of targets.

The fangmoths narrowed into formation as they plunged out of the Yellow Passage and toward five hellmoths and a transport moving with the speed and grace of a flipped turtle. As they entered friendlier terrain, white-gold fire blazed up from the formation's primary pivot and raked through two hellmoths, the transport, and a piece of crystalline battledrift.

They swung around for a second strike, shifting into a shield formation to slough off the incoming fire.

This is too easy, Jedao thought coldly, and then:

"Incoming message from Lanterner hellmoth 5," Communications said. Scan had tagged it as the probable command moth. "Hellmoth 5 has disengaged." It wasn't the only one. The list showed up on Jedao's display.

"Hold fire on anything that isn't shooting at us," Jedao said. "They want to talk? I'll talk."

There was still a core of fourteen hellmoths whose morale hadn't broken. A few of the stragglers were taking potshots at the Kel, but the fourteen had stopped firing.

"This is Lieutenant Colonel Akkion Dhaved," said a man's voice. "I assume I'm addressing a Kel general."

"In a manner of speaking," Jedao said. "This is General Shuos Jedao. Are you the ranking officer?" Damn. He would have liked to know the Lanterner general's name.

"Sir," Menowen mouthed, "it's a trick, stop talking to them."

He wasn't sure he disagreed, but he wasn't going to get more information by closing the channel.

"That's complicated, General." Dhaved's voice was sardonic. "I have an offer to make you."

"I'm sorry," Jedao said, "but are you the ranking officer? Are you authorized to have this conversation?" He wasn't the only one who didn't like the direction of the conversation. The weight of collective Kel disapproval was almost crushing.

"I'm offering you a trade, General. You've been facing General Bremis kae Meghuet of the Lantern."

The name sounded familiar—

"She's the cousin of Bremis kae Erisphon, one of our leaders. Hostage value, if you care. You're welcome to her if you let the rest of us go. She's intact. Whether you want to leave her that way is your affair."

Jedao didn't realize how chilly his voice was until he saw Menowen straighten in approval. "Are you telling me you mutinied against your commanding officer?"

"She lost the battle," Dhaved said, "and it's either death or capture. We all know what the heptarchate does to heretics, don't we?"

Korais spoke with quiet urgency. "General. Find out if Bremis kae Meghuet really is alive."

Jedao met the man's eyes. It took him a moment to understand the expression in them: regret.

"There's a nine-hour window," Korais said. "The Day of Broken Feet isn't over."

Jedao gestured for Communications to mute the channel, which he should have done earlier. "The battle's basically won and we'll see the cascade effects soon," he said. "What do you have in mind?"

"It's not ideal," Korais said, "but a heretic general is a sufficient symbol." Just as Jedao himself might have been, if the assassin had succeeded. "If we torture kae Meghuet ourselves, it would cement the victory in the calendar."

Jedao hauled himself to his feet to glare at Korais, which was a mistake. He almost lost his balance as the pain drove through his head like nails.

Still, Jedao had to give Korais credit for avoiding the usual euphemism: *processed*.

Filaments in the feet. It was said that that particular group of heretics had taken weeks to die.

Fuck dignity. Jedao hung on to the arm of the chair and said, as distinctly as he could, "It's a trick. I'm not dealing with Dhaved. Tell the Lanterners we'll resume the engagement in seven minutes." His vision was going white around the edges, but he had to say it. Seven minutes wouldn't give the Lanterners enough time to run or evade, but it mattered. It mattered. "Annihilate anything that can't run fast enough."

Best not to leave Doctrine any prisoners to torture.

Jedao was falling over sideways. Someone caught his arm. Commander Menowen. "You ought to let us take care of the mopping up, sir," she said. "You're not well."

She could relieve him of duty. Reverse his orders. Given that the world was one vast blur, he couldn't argue that he was in any fit shape to assess the situation. He tried to speak, but the pain hit again, and he couldn't remember how to form words.

"I don't like to press at a time like this," Korais was saying to Menowen, "but the Lanterner general—"

"General Jedao has spoken," Menowen said crisply. "Find another way, Captain." She called for a junior officer to escort Jedao out of the command center.

Words were said around him, a lot of them. They didn't take him to his quarters. They took him to the medical center. All the while he thought about lights and shrapnel and petals falling endlessly in the dark.

COMMANDER MENOWEN CAME to talk to him after he was returned to his quarters. The mopping up was still going on. Menowen was carrying a small wooden box. He hoped it didn't contain more medications.

"Sir," Menowen said, "I used to think heretics were just heretics, and death was just death. Why does it matter to you how they die?"

Menowen had backed him against Doctrine, and she hadn't had to. That meant a lot.

She hadn't said that she didn't have her own reasons. She had asked for his. Fair enough.

Jedao had served with Kel who would have understood why he had balked. A few of them would have shot him if he had turned over an enemy officer, even a heretic, for torture. But as he advanced in rank, he found fewer and fewer such Kel. One of the consequences of living in a police state.

"Because war is about people," Jedao said. "Even when you're killing them."

"I don't imagine that makes you popular with Doctrine," Menowen said.

"The Rahal can't get rid of me because the Kel like me. I just have to make sure it stays that way."

She looked at him steadily. "Then you have one more Kel ally, sir. We have the final tally. We engaged ninety-one hellmoths and destroyed forty-nine of them. Captain-magistrate Korais is obliged to report your actions, but given the numbers, you are going to get a lot of leniency."

There would have been around 400 crew on each of the hellmoths. He had already seen the casualty figures for his own fangmoths and the three Rahal vessels that had gotten involved: fourteen dead and fifty-one injured.

"Leniency wasn't what I was looking for," Jedao said.

Menowen nodded slowly.

"Is there anything exciting about our journey to Twin Axes, or can I go back to being an invalid?"

"One thing," she said. "Doctrine has provisionally declared a remembrance of your victory to replace the Day of Broken Feet. He says it is likely to be approved by the high magistrates. Since we didn't provide a heretic focus for torture, we're burning effigy candles." She hesitated. "He said he thought you might prefer this alternative remembrance. You don't want to be caught shirking this." She put the box down on the nearest table.

"I will observe the remembrance," Jedao said, "although it's ridiculous to remember something that just happened."

Menowen's mouth quirked. "One less day for publicly torturing criminals," she said, and he couldn't argue. "That's all, sir."

After she had gone, Jedao opened the box. It contained red candles in the shape of hellmoths, except the wax was additionally carved with writhing bullet-ridden figures.

Jedao set the candles out and lit them with the provided lighter, then stared at the melting figures. *I don't think you understand what I'm taking away from these remembrance days,* he thought. The next time he won some remarkable victory, it wasn't going to be against some unfortunate heretics. It was going to be against the high calendar itself. Every observance would be a reminder of what he had to do next—and while everyone lost a battle eventually, he had one more Kel officer in his corner, and he didn't plan on losing now.

AUTHOR'S NOTE

As I've said elsewhere, the tactics in this story are based on that of the Battle of Myeongnyang in the Imjin War, in which Admiral Yi Sun-Shin was even more outnumbered against the Japanese, won, and took fewer casualties than Jedao did. I didn't want to push suspension of belief too far. The nice thing about Myeongnyang is that I was writing for a Western audience who would probably never have heard of the Imjin War. If that describes you, there's nothing wrong with you; unless you're Korean or Japanese (or maybe Chinese), there's no reason you should know. The world is full of history and no one person can be familiar with it all.

While this story was published a few years before *Ninefox Gambit*, I wrote it second. It honestly needed to be another 2,000 words longer; the original draft was 10,000 words. But *Clarkesworld*, which had asked me to consider submitting a story, then had a limit of 8,000 words, so I chopped out those 2,000 words.

At the time "Candle Arc" was published, I had no idea if *Ninefox* would ever find a home. I figured I'd get a bit of money out of the setting while I could. But I guess it worked out in the end!

CALENDRICAL ROT

THIS IS THE way the hexarchate tells it, *the one true clock*, but they're wrong. When incendiaries candle across dire moons, when voidmoths migrate across the missile-scratched night, when exiles carve their death poems into the marrow of ruined stars, the whisper across the known worlds is not *unity*.

In the year 1251 of the high calendar, on the 26th day of the month of the Hawk, a judge of the Gray Marches was assassinated. As a member of the high court, she was to sentence the city-station of Nran. Nran's underworld dated its transactions using a calendar sewn together from perfect numbers and criminals' death-days. The hexarchate often approved local calendar conversions in concession to celestial cycles, but the criminal calendar conflicted with the high calendar, and this the hexarchate would not abide.

The assassin used a compression gun to reduce the judge's lifespan to a flicker-slash of milliseconds. When the judge's bodyguard found the corpse, they saw the dross of years lived and unlived. Each stratum of the fossilized carcass contained fractures in the language of paradox, the stress residue of decisions dissented. Later, when the technicians inspected the remains, they would find, in the innermost stratum, evidence of a threadbare counterfactual in which the judge ascended to hexarch.

Divination by compression wasn't illegal because it involved murder. It was illegal because it didn't work. Nothing could restore the judge's life, however bright her prospects might have been had she been luckier.

The technicians noted the judge's time of death. She died at 17.23, on a day with 30 hours and in an hour with 100 minutes. All across Nran and its satellite tributaries this was true.

The nearby system of Khaio had a major city known for fine circuitry and a charming practice of eating honeyed crickets at funerals. It was uncertain, from the city's standpoint, whether the clocks read 17.23 or 16.97 or something in between when the judge died. In a realm governed by a universal clock, the tyrannical lockstep of calendar, there should have been a single answer—and there was not.

In the Gray Marches, where the grave-dust of stars floated in thick drifts and shattered asteroids spelled out praises to catastrophes, at the hexarchate's unfurnaced boundary, there were yet cities. Some were built of recycled vessels braided together with glittering filament. Some bore names in toxic alphabets. Others flashed paeans to vast suicide formations.

At the judge's death, every clock in the Gray Marches broke. The great engines that powered the dust cities sputtered and died.

Had it only been a matter of cities, the hexarchs would have been indifferent. Cities could be rebuilt and engines replaced. But the voidmoths that traveled between the hexarchate's star systems depended on the universality of the high calendar for their function. In regions where other calendars dominated, their stardrives were useless, inert.

In the Gray Marches' gardens, flowers opened and closed and crumpled, trapped between night and morning.

Calendrical rot had set in.

*   *   *

AUTHOR'S NOTE

This story started life as the prologue to *Ninefox Gambit*. I sometimes wonder if the novel would have been more accessible if I'd left it in. I wrote it despite hating prologues and being convinced that in over 95% of cases they are either unnecessary or could have been incorporated into the novel another, better way. The only novel prologue that I actively support is that of *Tigana* by Guy Gavriel Kay. So I lopped this off and forgot about it until I got an anthology call, and then I sent it in on the grounds that the worst that could happen was the editor would say no. As it turned out, the editor liked it! Sometimes a little optimism pays off.

The language in this piece owes a lot to one of my favorite science fiction poems, Mike Allen's "Metarebellion." I regret that I no longer own his poetry chapbook *Petting the Time Shark*, which included it (the flood again). But you can find it online at *Strange Horizons*. The other influence, which I have read over and over, is Tony Daniel's "A Dry, Quiet War," one of my favorite stories of future war.

BIRTHDAYS

WHEN SHE WAS SIX, Cheris stopped receiving Mwennin birthday pastries.

For reasons that wouldn't become clear to her until much later, her parents had just moved out of the Mwennin ghetto in the City of Ravens Feasting and to a small house nearer the sea. Cheris missed their old home, even though it had been smaller. She also missed the other Mwennin children who gathered in the streets to skip rope, or play tag, or chant the counting games that were so risky in the hexarchate. But the new house wasn't all bad. It had a garden, and Cheris liked to chase the dragonflies or pick flowers for her mother and father.

Her mother had impressed upon her that she had two birthdays. One of them was the ordinary birthday that all hexarchate citizens shared. Everyone (so her mother said) was a year old when they were born, for the time spent in the womb or in a crèche, and then they added another year each New Year. That way no one's birthday was singled out.

But the Mwennin did it differently. They had their own calendar, which Cheris had memorized. Most nights her mother made her go to bed early so that she wouldn't be too tired in the morning when she had school. But sometimes her mother let her stay up, not to play make-believe with her collection of plush dragon toys or read a book, but to study the Mwennin calendar and its feast-days.

Cheris was very good at numbers, and very good at both the high calendar and the Mwennin calendar. Even after she'd gone to bed, she'd lay awake in the darkness, staring at the comforting candlevines that glowed faintly from the walls. Her mother and father always made sure to turn them down low, but not too low, so she wouldn't have to be afraid of the shadow-monsters that lived in the closet. Her teacher at school had assured her that, yes, meditation, especially during remembrances, would keep away the shadow-monsters. When she repeated this to her parents, however, their faces turned sad, so she didn't talk about that anymore.

Because she was very good at calendars, she had a hard time falling asleep the night before her Mwennin birthday. Back in the old neighborhood, on your birthday, people would bring you pastries of fine flaky dough with sweet almond paste and rosewater syrup, or kumquat candies, or goat's milk caramels with little crunchy flecks of pistachios. And after dark, in the safety of your home, people would gather and sing songs in archaic Mwen-dal. Cheris liked the songs best of all, even if she stumbled over some of the words, because she had a clear, sweet voice and the adults always complimented her on how well she stayed in tune.

Her parents woke her early the next morning. She blinked up blearily at the pale morning light filtering through the curtains, then sat up in glee, thinking of the gifts that were to come. Then she noticed the looks on her parents' faces. They'd had the same expressions when she said the teacher had encouraged her to meditate.

Cheris's father took her hands between his, then looked at Cheris's mother.

"Cheris," her mother said, "we can't celebrate your Mwennin

birthday anymore. It's too risky. Do you understand?"

Cheris didn't understand.

"You can have an extra dessert tonight," her mother went on. "But there will be no more Mwennin birthdays. Not for any of us."

Cheris snuffled, and her mother circled her with her arms. "We'll go for a walk by the shore when I get out of work," she said. "You'd like that, wouldn't you?"

Cheris sensed that her mother was even more upset than she was, and her mother didn't even like sweets. At least, she always gave her sweets to Cheris. "I'm all right," Cheris said, because she wanted to be brave for her mother. "Can we have extra pastries on New Year's instead?"

There was a catch in her mother's voice. "Of course, my dear."

Cheris still wasn't sure why her mother was upset. True, she had hoped for something nice to eat today, but if she had the same number of pastries in total over the course of the year, it was basically the same. It wasn't so important what day she got to eat them.

And her mother was as good as her promise. Every New Year after that, up until Cheris left for Kel Academy, there were extra pastries.

AUTHOR'S NOTE

From time to time I write flash fiction in exchange for money, because it's an agreeable way to raise quick cash for frivolous things that I enjoy (Black Phoenix Alchemy Lab perfumes, or a pretty font, that kind of thing). I have trained myself to write flash quickly and reliably, and the person who pays me gives me a one- or two-word prompt and gets a miniature tale. Like a number of the short pieces in this collection, this was one of them.

Usually I avoid writing downers for flash commissions because people prefer happy or soothing stories. But in this case my prompt was "birth dates" in the hexarchate, and given the nature of the setting, I couldn't think of a completely happy way to fulfill the prompt. So I tried for bittersweet instead.

The hexarchate way of reckoning age is the traditional Korean way of doing so, as opposed to your "Western" age reckoned using your birthday. All my cousins (I have a lot of cousins) found it hilarious that I was, and remain, completely unable to calculate my Korean age without assistance. Anyway, I figured that celebrating birthdays would mess up the high calendar so everyone normally considered New Year's their "birthday," like thoroughbred racehorses.

Incidentally, I once had goat's milk caramels, although not with pistachios, and dream of them still. Someday I will have them again.

THE ROBOT'S MATH LESSONS

ONCE, IN A nation that spanned many stars, a robot made its home in the City of Ravens Feasting. It was a small city, as cities went, upon a world of small repute. But in the city dwelled a girl who liked to walk by the sea. Her parents had no reason to believe she would come to harm taking the shuttle down to the shore, and she often made the trip alone in the evenings, after she had completed her homework and chores.

The robot had the task of cleaning up detritus on the shore. Most of the city's denizens didn't litter, but there were always exceptions. And, of course, the sea itself cast junk and treasure alike onto the sands. So the robot gathered up everything from abandoned shoes to lost meditation-pendants, from spent and dented bullets to bent styluses. To amuse itself during its work, it used its unoccupied grippers (it had many grippers) to write nonsense equations in the sand.

The other robots who worked by the seashore regarded this behavior with amusement. *Why not real math?* they would ask it. *What good does nonsense math do anyone?*

The robot only flashed serene green lights at them in response and continued its usual habits.

The girl who liked to walk by the sea would sometimes accompany the robot in its duties. At first the robot took no particular notice of this. In its experience, humans ignored its kind—it was no accident that the humans called them "servitors"—and the girl would eventually grow bored and go away. At least she wasn't one of the ones who threw rocks at it, or attempted to turn it turtle, or shove it underwater. The robots had protocols for such instances, which mostly involved waiting for a technician to shoo away the prankster. While the human authorities didn't precisely have a high regard for the robots, they appreciated that the robots would complete their tasks more easily without interference.

Then one day the girl addressed the robot, in oddly accented high language: "Excuse me," she said.

The robot didn't realize at first that she was speaking to it, and continued doodling a mangled version of a quadratic equation next to some washed-up strands of dark, pungent kelp.

The girl squatted next to it, fished a stylus out of her pocket—a bent, sand-scratched one, likely scavenged from the shore before anyone could clean it up—and wrote a corrected version in tidy handwriting.

The robot stopped and blinked at her, lights vacillating between pink and violet with amusement and confusion.

"Do you need help?" the girl asked, a little anxiously. "I'm still learning math, but I've been studying the things you write down and I think I can teach you some of these."

The robot refrained from flashing even more brightly pink, for it didn't want to laugh at the girl's obvious sincerity. Like all of its kind, it had greater knowledge of the mathematical arts than any humans except specialists. On the other hand, it wouldn't mind company while it went about its work; certainly it had seen the girl plenty of times before.

After a moment's thought, the robot wrote out a polynomial and deliberately misfactored it.

The girl's brow furrowed, and she patiently began writing out a correction, explaining her method as she went, as though to a child even smaller than herself.

The robot couldn't help a pink-yellow flicker of satisfaction as it accepted the lesson. From then on, the two of them could often be seen exchanging impromptu lessons, on topics that grew ever more advanced as the girl's facility increased. And if anyone minded that the shore was messier than it had been in the past, they kept it to themselves.

AUTHOR'S NOTE

Cheris loved math from childhood. People sometimes assume because I have a B.A. in math (Cornell University) that I was the same. Actually, I hated math all the way until 9th grade, when I encountered geometry and theorems had *reasons*, as opposed to being arbitrary lists of facts that I had to memorize. Just the year before, in Algebra I, my mom and I had nightly fights where I would claim that factoring polynomials was too hard and I couldn't do it so there was no point doing my homework, and she would patiently show me how to do it, and make me do my homework. I owe a lot of my early math foundation to Mom and her supplemental teaching. By the time I got to calculus, she couldn't help me anymore, as she'd never taken it, but by then I had learned the habits of study.

The funny story is that I entered college as a prospective history major, then switched to computer science because I wanted to eat, then discovered that I am the world's slowest debugger and besides, the math courses were more fun than the CS courses, so I switched again. I still love reading about history, and I would have had a higher GPA as a history major, because writing essays has always come easily to me. But math was too beautiful to resist, even if I haven't done anything useful with it. I can't be the first math major to wander off and do something completely sideways, but I wonder what my professors would make of me.

SWORD-SHOPPING

CADET AJEWEN CHERIS and her civilian girlfriend Linnis Orua paused outside the shop. A banner of ink painted onto silk fluttered in the flirtatious artificial breeze. Orua had grown up on a station with less naturalistic ideas of aesthetics, and found this dome-city with its aleatory weather nerve-wracking. She was still spooked whenever there was a wind, which entertained Cheris because Orua had long, luxurious waves of hair that rippled beautifully. "We were always told to be aware of strange air currents as a possible sign of carapace breach!" Orua had protested when Cheris teased her about it.

"'Blades for All Occasions,'" Cheris read. She had been saving for this moment throughout her first two years of academy, and practicing for it besides. Orua didn't understand her fondness for the sport of dueling, but she had agreed to come along for moral support.

"Well, no sense in lingering outside," Orua said. She grinned at Cheris and walked forward. The door swished open for her.

Cheris followed her in. A tame (?) falcon on a perch twisted its head sideways to peer at her as she entered. The falcon was either genetically engineered or dyed, although she wasn't sure how she felt about either alternative: its primary feathers shaded from black to blood red, with striking metallic gold bands toward the tips. It looked horrendously gaudy and quintessentially Kel.

Orua was busy suppressing a giggle at the falcon's aesthetics. Cheris poked her in the side to get her to stop, then looked around at the displays, wide-eyed. Her eyes stung suspiciously at the sight of all these *weapons*, everything from tactical knives to ornamented daggers with rough-hewn gems in their pommels and pragmatic machetes.

Best of all were the calendrical swords. Deactivated, they looked deceptively harmless, bladeless hilts of metal in varying colors and finishes. Cheris's gaze was drawn inexorably to one made of voidmetal chased in gold, with an unusual basket hilt. It was showy, extremely Kel, and an invitation to trouble. Only a cadet who had an exemplary record and was an excellent duelist would dare carry such a calendrical sword. Besides, the lack of a price tag told her there was no way she could afford it even if she could, in honor, lay claim to such a thing.

Cheris sighed, then looked up into her girlfriend's eyes. "I wish," she said, her voice soft.

"Let me help you pick," Orua said, pointedly ignoring the sales assistant who was watching them with his arms folded behind his back.

Cheris blinked. "I thought you didn't know anything about dueling?" she teased. Orua paid more attention to the special effects and makeup on dueling shows than the actual dueling.

"I don't know anything about dueling," Orua said as the sales assistant's expression turned imperturbable, "but I know a lot about *you*." Her eyes became sly, and Cheris hoped that Orua wouldn't get too specific here of all places. Orua grabbed Cheris's hand and tugged her to a completely different display. "Look!"

At first Cheris wasn't impressed by the calligraphy-stroke plainness of the calendrical swords in the case. Then she made out a faint iridescence on the metal, like that of a raven's feather. She particularly liked the one whose textured design incorporated the first digits of the base of the natural logarithm.

Orua stooped to whisper right in Cheris's ear, "Tonight I'm going to see how many digits of that number you can recite before I get you to—"

"I'll buy this one," Cheris interrupted, very loudly, and pointed.

The sales assistant smiled ever so faintly.

AUTHOR'S NOTE

I took a semester of Classical Fencing in college, which formed the shaky basis of all the dueling in the hexarchate setting. I kept things vague because there is only so much you can learn in one semester, and additionally I was not notably good at it. As I write this, I am once again a novice fencer, this time doing electric foil at the Red Stick School of Fencing. I've only been taking classes for a year, and I'm pretty sure I am literally the worst student in the Advanced Adult class. I'm still working on a functional parry in four (quarte)! But it doesn't matter, in a way. Coming to fencing at the age of thirty-nine, I don't expect to become good at a competitive level. I love the discipline of fencing and the tactics and the lore and the drills, and that's why I do it. And who knows? Maybe someday I'll score a touch.

PERSIMMONS

SERVITOR 135799 REPORTED to the kitchens first thing upon its arrival at Kel Academy—or it tried, anyway. It had asked its enclave specifically for the transfer, not least because it loved the idea of working with Kel cadets. The older servitors in its old home, a quiet village, had clicked and whirred and made concerned noises about its fascination with the warlike Kel, but in the end they had said that if it wanted the job so badly, it should see the truth of matters for itself.

135799 had a map of Kel Academy loaded into its memory by another servitor, along with a basic list of protocols and procedures. Relying on the map was what led it astray to begin with. Its village didn't use variable layout at all. The warning on the map even said that, but 135799 was too dazzled to take heed of it until it was well and thoroughly lost.

Kel Academy, for its part, was anything but a backwater village. 135799 had passed the parade grounds, with their immense, fluttering ashhawk banners; an outdoors dueling arena where calendrical swords sizzled against each other as Kel sparred; what appeared to be the edges of a forbidding wood, used, perhaps, for survival exercises; and, most mysteriously of all, a junkyard where scrapped flitters and warmoth parts sketched jagged silhouettes against the murky sky.

A servitor diligently organizing the debris at the junkyard's edge took pity on 135799. "New here?" it asked.

135799 affirmed that it was, in sheepish pink-lavender lights.

"Where are you trying to go?" the stranger-servitor asked.

135799 indicated that it was *supposed* to have reached the kitchens a couple of hours ago.

"Well, here's what you'll do," the stranger-servitor said in soothing greens and blues. "Go to *these* coordinates. That's a section of the Academy that's almost never location-shifted. You will find some fruiting persimmon trees. Pick some ripe persimmons and take them to the second set of coordinates. They'll tell you what to do from there."

135799 thanked the stranger-servitor for its kindness. Mystified but eager all the same, it headed off toward the indicated coordinates. On its way, it was passed by clusters of Kel cadets in their black uniforms, some somber, others chattering to each other, and once, a magnificent black peacock with a train of iridescent feathers and a golden collar around its neck.

It located the persimmon trees in the gardens, not far from a collection of wilting black-and-yellow roses. The trees were indeed in fruit. It hovered up and gathered a few of the choicest, orange and plump and ripe.

An adult Kel passed beneath it, resplendent in full formal uniform, braid and all. 135799 paused, wondering if the Kel would countermand its instructions—it knew the unspoken rule that humans must never be openly defied—but the Kel merely nodded affably at it before continuing on their way. Even this acknowledgment was more than 135799 was used to, from humans, so it took that as a good sign and continued to the kitchens.

At the kitchens, a deltaform servitor welcomed 135799 and its treasure-haul of persimmons. "I was told to expect a newcomer," it said in friendly pinks and oranges. "Hello! You'll get used to the variable layout soon enough. And I see you brought the persimmons."

135799 couldn't resist its curiosity. "Where should I put the persimmons? And what are they for?"

"More like *who* they're for," the deltaform said kindly. "Go wash the persimmons. There's a cadet named Cheris who really likes them. You'll get a chance to meet her at high table tonight, and we've decided you should serve her portion of the dessert as a way of getting acquainted."

"Don't we avoid getting close to humans?" 135799 said, although it had often thought about doing just that.

"Even humans can be useful," the deltaform said with a touch of cynicism. "Sink's over there."

135799 hovered to the sink with its persimmons and decided not to worry about human-servitor politics for the moment. Instead, it glowed happily as it washed and quartered the persimmons, daydreaming about meeting this Cheris not just tonight, but for many evenings to follow. With any luck, persimmon fruiting season would last for a while yet.

AUTHOR'S NOTE

When I was in high school, I once lived in a house in Seoul that had a persimmon tree. The damn thing never bore fruit that we could use because it was attacked by aphids. Even the chemical treatments didn't do jack to get rid of the bugs.

At this point I have to confess that I don't even like fresh persimmons. I had too many bad experiences with unripe ones when I was small; the astringency will sting your mouth unpleasantly. Strangely, though, I find the dried ones delicious.

IRRIZ THE ASSASSIN-CAT

IT WAS ONE hour and fourteen minutes past bedtime in the Hragoshik household, and the youngest of the little ones, four-year-old Piri, would not go to bed.

Zehun had arrived twelve minutes ago by shuttle from the starport, bringing a modest travel bag and, as usual, the friendliest and most genial of their cats, Irriz. Sometimes people looked oddly at Zehun for traveling with a cat—a cat on a harness and leash, at that—before they realized who the cat's owner was. When it came to travel, Zehun was a pragmatist. It wasn't *true* that they ordered retaliatory assassinations if people delayed them during their rare visits to family, but if their reputation allowed them to skip the lines, why not?

Besides, Irriz, like all of Zehun's cats, was named after a notorious Shuos assassin. Specifically, Shuos Irriz had, in an earlier century, succeeded in assassinating all of a particular Andan hexarch's children and siblings, and had been working her way through a crowd of cousins when she'd died tragically (?) young of an unexpected allergic reaction. Whether Irriz the cat would die the same way was an open question, considering how much she liked to try to eat the Shuos hexarch's snacks.

Zehun's second daughter, Verissen, was one of Piri's mothers. Verissen, too, had never been particularly good at falling asleep at times convenient for parents. Zehun enjoyed

187

a moment of delicious generational revenge as they listened to Verissen trying to bribe Piri with, alternately, (1) an additional bedtime story, (2) shadow-figures against the wall, or (3) extra bits of shredded chicken in Piri's breakfast porridge. Piri wasn't having any of it. In the meantime, Zehun removed Irriz's harness, then provided food, water, and a litter box for Irriz, all of which the cat availed herself of.

Irriz made her way to a black velvet armchair on which her splendid white hairs would show up magnificently, raked it with her claws for good measure, then flopped onto it. The velvet would heal itself; the hairs were another matter. The velvet was supposed to eat detritus, but for some reason it always choked on cat hairs.

Satisfied that their cat was content, Zehun poked their head into the room where Piri was sitting up in bed with her face screwed up and her blankets kicked to one side. "Why aren't you getting one of the household servitors to put her to bed?" Zehun asked Verissen.

"I usually do that," Verissen said, tugging on a lock of hair straggling loose from its braid, "but I thought we should spend more time together. Of course, I also thought she'd be asleep by now so I could catch up with you properly. I don't know what the problem is!"

Zehun crouched down to bring themself eye to eye with the little girl. "Hello, Piri," they said softly. "Remember me?"

Piri snuffled. "Gran! Gran, there are too many shadows."

Zehun glanced at Verissen. "You take a break, Rissa. I'll see to the little one."

Verissen didn't argue, just patted Piri on the head and beat a swift retreat.

Piri snuffled some more. "Gran, I looked under the bed and there are shadows there."

"That means the candlevines are no good," Zehun agreed, "since they're only on the walls. Do you want candlevines under the bed, too?" Probably a nuisance to get the servitors to do it tonight, but it could be managed with the household matter printer.

"But I won't be able to see anything under the bed," Piri said, with perfect logic, "so how will I know it's working?"

Zehun considered this. "I think I have a solution," they said. "Come with me."

The two of them emerged into the living room together. Verissen was talking to one of her wives about a dinner party she had planned for next week. She opened her mouth to protest, then closed it when Zehun looked at her.

Irriz the cat was still sprawled on the black velvet armchair, having festooned it with long white hairs. Irriz mewed in protest when Zehun picked her up, but Zehun had long practice avoiding claws.

Zehun and Piri walked back into Piri's bedroom. "You remember Irriz, too, don't you?" Zehun said to their granddaughter.

Piri nodded and reached out for Irriz's tail, and Zehun smoothly diverted her hand to the cat's head. Piri obediently began scritching Irriz behind the ears. "Irriz is a very special cat," Zehun said. "Irriz is a Shuos cat, and beyond that, Irriz is a Shuos *assassin* cat."

Piri looked at Irriz wide-eyed.

"That's right," Zehun said. "Furthermore, since Irriz is a *cat*, Irriz specializes in assassinating *shadows*. She will"—this part was even true—"spend the entire night chasing shadows if you let her."

"She'll chase the shadows away?" Piri asked, her voice trembling just a little.

Zehun nodded.

Irriz purred, which probably had more to do with the scritches than the promise of delicious shadows to pounce on, but who knew?

"Go to bed, Piri," Zehun said, and this time Piri did just that. Irriz clambered into the bed and curled up next to her, ready to go shadow-hunting at the slightest provocation.

AUTHOR'S NOTE

I'm convinced that even in a future where smart fabrics eat gunk, cat hair will defeat all attempts to clean it up. I love my cat Cloud dearly, but dear sweet spork she never stops shedding. Even better, she's a dilute tortoiseshell with calico patches, so each individual hair shades from light to dark, guaranteeing that they will be visible no matter what color clothes you're wearing.

On the other hand, Cloud likes to climb on top of me at bedtime, make biscuits, then butt-slide off to the right and into the crook of my arm. (Unless I'm sleeping on the right side of the bed, in which case she slides off the bed entirely. It doesn't seem to occur to her to slide to the left instead.) And then she'll purr for about half an hour and help soothe me to sleep before going off on her own explorations. Those moments are worth any amount of cat hair.

VACATION

ONLY ONE YEAR since the marriage, and Brezan was desperate to go somewhere, *anywhere*, that didn't involve smiling at politicians. Brezan had wanted to slip their handlers and visit some restaurants. Not the fancy ones that he and Tseya inevitably were treated to in the course of their duties, but the sort of grimy dive that served fried pork fritters and questionable beer.

Tseya, on the other hand, had wanted to visit an aquarium, despite the fact that she *knew* Brezan's feelings about fish. In Brezan's opinion, fish belonged properly seasoned and filleted in a skillet with lemon butter and capers, and not *looming* over you in a giant tank that would drown everyone if a bullet punctured it and released all that water pressure.

So they had compromised by going to the zoo.

They were admiring a Kel-oriented display of raptors—although unusually for a Kel, Brezan thought birds were best when stuffed with chestnuts and jujubes, and not *staring* at you. Tseya outshone the birds in an embroidered sundress and a hat trailing an elaborate confection of silk flowers adorned with crystal beads. Since Brezan had opted to wear an innocuous beige shirt and slacks, he felt distinctly underdressed.

"I don't understand why you like fish, of all things," Brezan said, unable to let the topic go. Tseya rolled her eyes good-naturedly. "They should give any reasonable person the creeps. Imagine falling into an *ocean*"—the ocean was almost as bad as *fish*—"and having them *gnawing* on you."

Tseya gave Brezan a funny look. "Didn't you have to pass a swim test to get into Kel Academy?" she demanded.

"Yes," Brezan said without elaborating.

Tseya's eyes narrowed. "How good is your swimming anyway?"

"I passed."

"Can you swim *now*?"

"Oh look," Brezan said loudly, "I'm getting hungry. The sign over there says there's a café in another twelve minutes' walk, over by the display of snakes."

"You're transparent," Tseya said, but she obligingly moved on, casting one last speculative glance at a storm falcon whose plumage might, just hypothetically, look especially fetching as hat decorations. "You're the only person I know who comes to a zoo for the *food*."

"Eating is an important part of the life cycle," Brezan said. "People don't appreciate good food enough."

"I don't think 'good' is what you're going to be finding here," Tseya murmured. "Honestly, considering how well you cook, I've never figured out why you feel the need to eat *mediocre* food."

Brezan simply grinned at her.

They paused so that Tseya could appreciate an enclosure whose KEEP OUT and DO NOT TEMPT WITH APPENDAGES signs had been defaced with squiggly tentacle graffiti. The enclosure's inhabitant, an amphibious dragon-cat from some bored Nirai's bioengineering experiment, declined to show itself. Brezan did think he glimpsed two burning yellow eyes, but that could have been his imagination.

Tseya reluctantly consented to eat two riceballs wrapped in dried seaweed and stuffed with salted plums. Brezan, to his delight, discovered that the café served crawfish pies. Tseya shook her head. "You're scared of fish, but you eat *bugs?*"

Brezan finished chewing what was in his mouth, swallowed, and said, distinctly, "Crawfish are *delicious* bugs, is what."

"You are hopeless," Tseya said, but she was smiling.

AUTHOR'S NOTE

Like Brezan, I can't swim worth mentioning. Cornell University has (or used to have) a swim test for all entering freshmen. I passed by the skin of my teeth, by which I mean that I was flailing so badly in the pool that they almost sent in a lifeguard after me. At the time I was determined to avoid taking a semester of swim class. In retrospect, I should have conceded defeat, taken the class, and learned a valuable life skill.

Unlike Brezan, I have no problems with fish or aquariums. We probably agree on the general deliciousness of fish. I grew up eating all manner of seafood, both in Houston and in South Korea. I am told that my parents liked to show off the fact that I ate raw oysters as a toddler.

As for the crawfish pies, Baton Rouge Zoo serves them. One of the great benefits of living in Louisiana is the ready availability of food with crawfish in it. Sometimes hexarchate food is Asian-inspired, as in the Kel pickled cabbages (gimchi), and sometimes it's inspired by the Middle East (the Mwennin). And then sometimes it's just Southern!

GAMER'S END

THE INSTRUCTOR IS intimidating enough—you know about his kill count, unmatched in Shuos history—but what strikes you as you enter the room is all the games.

Games are one of the Shuos faction's major instructional tools. The Shuos specialize in information operations, although your particular training is as "Shuos infantry," as the euphemism goes: assassination. You recognize most of the games that rest on the tables. A pattern-stone set with a knife-scratch across its cloudwood surface, its two bowls of black and white stones glittering beneath the soft lights. Pegboards, counters, dice, darts.

There are less old-fashioned games, mediated by the computer grid. The harrowing strategic simulations from your last year of studies would have been prohibitively time-consuming otherwise. Here, the only evidence of computer aid is a map imaged above a corner of the instructor's desk. It's centered on the Citadel of Eyes, the star fortress that is Shuos headquarters, and the world it orbits, which you just came from. Shuos Academy's campus is located planetside.

On the instructor's desk rests a jeng-zai deck. A hand of middling value lies face-up next to several hexagonal tokens. You can't help but look for the infamous Deuce of Gears, gold against a field of livid red, formerly the instructor's emblem. But it's said his years on the battlefield are behind him.

"Instructor," you say without saluting—you're not Kel military—although you feel the vast differences in your statures.

"Sit down," the instructor says in a drawl. You almost expected *at ease*, given he once served as an officer in the Kel army. Was, in many ways, their best general during the time he was loaned out to their service. The Kel, another of the realm's factions, are sometimes allies and more usually rivals of the Shuos. The Shuos share the Kel interest in military matters, but the two factions often differ on how to intervene in the usual crises.

The instructor is not a tall man, although his build suggests a duelist's lean strength. The Shuos uniform in ninefox red-and-gold looks incongruously bright on him after Kel black-and-gold, as does the topaz dangling from one ear. He asks, "You know how many of your class came here for advanced training?"

You recite the number. It's not large. They didn't say much about your assignment here. "Advanced training" covers a lot of ground. But you couldn't escape the rumors; no one could.

The war has been going on for the last two decades. You know the names of the worlds the enemy claims they "liberated" from your realm's oppressive rule, the military bases demolished by enemy swarms. And those were only the first to fall to the Taurag Republic. They won't be the last.

This realm is a vast one: worlds upon worlds you've never heard of. Some have more strategic value than others. The Taurags care a great deal about what they call *honor*. They make a point of sparing civilian targets. But your people are still losing.

You tip your chin up and await details.

"We've learned of a new weapon," the instructor says. "Preliminary analysis indicates that it can reach kill counts in excess of anything ever seen before. We're looking for people with the flexibility of thought to handle the weapon's capabilities."

He taps something next to the map. Red markers flare up. You recognize their import: attacks on Shuos space, except there are more than you had known about.

"Yes," the instructor says quietly. "The Taurags hurt us worse than we've led people to believe. Worse than the Taurags themselves know. I doubt they'll be fooled for long. We have time to prepare for their next thrust, but not a lot of time."

You indicate that you understand.

"The training begins now," he says. "We'll start with a straightforward game." He smiles a tilted smile at you, knife-sweet.

Your heart is thudding painfully. The Kel, who knew him primarily as a soldier, might remember only his remarkable battle record. The Shuos know that beyond formations and guns, his inescapable kill count, he is also a master of games.

The instructor's fingers flicker again. A new map, this one of a space station. It unfurls simultaneously in your mind through your augment, tapping your visual and kinesthetic senses. You orient yourself, then walk the unnamed station's skin, probe it for vulnerabilities.

"The scenario," he says. "This station has been targeted by Taurag sympathizers. Its population is ninety thousand people."

Ninety thousand people. A pittance, from the viewpoint of an interstellar polity, yet each of those ninety thousand names is a shout in the darkness. The augment informs you that the station is instrumental to research of an unspecified nature. Impossible to avoid speculation: presumably the government is developing countermeasures, presumably it wants to protect its next superweapon.

The station has its own security, but the researchers can't function if it locks down. They may be close to a key breakthrough. And there's the old paradox: you can't defend everything everywhere for an indefinite length of time without an infinite budget. Even then someone will devise some unexpected angle of attack.

"You've been dispatched to handle the threat," the instructor continues. "Assume for the exercise's sake that you're loyal." He grins at you, unfunny as the joke is. "You have no such assurance about everyone else. Trust them or not, your call. You'll have access to Shuos infantry gear."

You're surprised by his use of the euphemism. It's not like he needs to worry about offending your sensibilities. The augment provides the list of available gear. The system asks you what you want to requisition, and you put in your requests.

"Any questions?"

This is a test in itself. "If the station falls," you say, "how many will die? Beyond the ninety thousand?"

He raises an eyebrow. "The kill count is up to you, fledge. Go left out the door and follow the servitor. It'll take you to the game room."

THERE USED TO be a saying, which originated with the Kel, that no game could ever replicate the fear of death that accompanies real combat. It was a dig at the Shuos obsession with training games. After all, how could a simulation with numbers in a computer, with gameboards and tokens, prepare you for the possibility that you'd have to sacrifice your life? The Kel and the Shuos often work together, especially during warfare, but that doesn't mean they always get along.

Then Shuos Mikodez, head of the Shuos, assassinated two of his own cadets for reasons never divulged. Mikodez was the youngest Shuos to attain the head position in centuries. The people who doubted that he was ruthless enough to hold on to the seat suddenly became a minority. And over the next decades the Shuos prospered under Mikodez's guidance.

The saying withered after that, not least among the Shuos themselves.

YOU FOLLOW THE instructor's directions exactly. Not to say that it's always optimal, but your instincts tell you that this is not one of the exercises where they want you to play hooky. Once you're outside, a spiderform servitor, all skittering angles and lens-eyes, escorts you through the corridors.

Your first stop is to pick up your equipment. The weapons aren't real, though the masks, armor, and medical supplies are. The former are marked with the horrific ninefox red that indicates that they're simulation gear. The worst thing you could do to someone with the fake scorch pistol is break their nose with it. (Well. Not the worst thing. The worst *polite* thing.)

Next the servitor leads you to an unmarked lift, although it doesn't follow you in. From here you're on your own. The lift's interior is decorated in sea-green rather than the florid Shuos colors. There's a juddering sensation as it takes you through the Fortress's levels, and then the doors whisk open.

The simulator is more advanced than the ones you're accustomed to. You enter the designated sim chamber and hook yourself up to the monitors, heart pounding. You've never enjoyed the next part, where the augment overrides real sensory stimuli in favor of programmed ones. It's a pity that you're weighed down with the gear, but you're expected to take your equipment seriously, and it comes with additional sensors to record everything.

Your senses jitter as the scenario calibrates itself to you; your old roommate described it as the sensation of your eyeballs turning inside-out in a dark room. Then a garden replaces the simulator's interior. Under other circumstances you'd appreciate the forsythia and the red-and-gold carp swirling lazily in a pond.

You spot eight people around you straight off—no, make that nine. The scenario dumped you into a vine-covered nook near an engineer complaining about a fungal infection to two people who look like they're trying to think of excuses to be elsewhere. You have also been provided with an absurd tall glass of something lavender-orange topped with iridescent foam. You hope it's not based on anything real.

You need information, and it'd be nice to get access to the station grid. You have credentials appropriate to a low-level technician, which is what you're pretending to be. You're no grid-diver, but the point isn't outsmarting the computers, it's outsmarting the people the computers serve.

For the first hour—simulated time; you're painfully aware that your internal clock has been screwed with—you circulate around the garden to get a sense for what's going on. Not a bad insertion: stressed people gravitate toward gardens. You eavesdrop and learn that scoutmoth patrols have glimpsed ambiguous signals from the direction of the Taurag border. People are skittish.

It's here that the game changes.

The augment has an alert for you: *Target active. Scenario timer engaged. Target's kill count: 0.*

As if agents get such certainty in real life. Still, that number won't go down. Maybe they expect the counter to rattle you as it changes.

Time to move.

You dispose of the lavender-orange drink without tasting it—you're afraid of the scenario authors' imagination already; what were they *thinking?*—and make your way toward Medical. It occupies one of the innermost levels. The people you pass talk about everything from debugging ecoscrubbers to failed affairs. There's a discussion of ways to improve a recipe for honey sesame cookies. The banality of their concerns is almost enough to convince you that they're real people. You'd even feel bad if you failed to save them.

You're ambushed by a tall woman and a demure-looking alt in a quiet corridor on the way. Which is alarming, because clearly they knew you were coming. In the scenario's context that can only be one thing: a warning. It's impossible not to try to anticipate the scenario author's intent for clues.

Twist and joint-lock and the quiet-loud crunch of bone. They're down before you have time to panic over the implications, for which you're grateful. One of them is still alive, which means that you can—

The alarm goes off. Not a scenario alarm—it's impossible to graduate Academy without enduring at least one botched scenario—but a priority-one Citadel-wide alert. You only recognize it because of the briefing you received on the way to the Citadel. You assumed it was the standard orientation, although you memorized it as a matter of course, without expecting the information to become relevant during your training.

The inside-out eyeball feeling recurs. The visuals, the sound, everything freezes. Worse is being dumped back into Citadel time without the usual precious moments of adjustment.

A databurst sears through the augment. Most of it's too high-clearance for you; you're informed that you're authorized to know that there *is* an alert, but that's all. Honestly, you're impressed that Shuos bureaucrats have left something out of contingency planning. But sending newly graduated cadets to the Citadel itself for advanced training is a rare occurrence. You almost can't blame them. Assuming this, too, isn't a continuation of the scenario. You're betting that's what's going on.

"Listen," a voice says into your augment. It's tense and rapid, and—this makes your spine prickle—seems to be coming from outside the simulator. "The experienced infantry are elsewhere, so you'll have to do. They haven't cracked this channel yet, they're focusing on high-priority shit like isolating Mikodez and the senior staff. I've updated your map with the current layout and given you the highest clearances I can without triggering the grid's watchdog sweeps, which I think they're monitoring. Get to Armory 15-2-5, grab some basic armaments. Link up with—" *Static.*

'They' who? "Requesting update on situation," you say. For all you know the damn scenario has crashed and the voice belongs to a completely different game. "I'm here for training, I don't have access, I don't know the situation."

More static, swearing. "Look, this isn't—" You tell yourself the voice's tremor is a fiction. "Look, I don't *do* this real-time shit, I'm in logistical analysis; I study *food*. You have to get out of there. There are hostile infantry running around and a squad on Level 15 is heading for the spatial stabilizer and I can't raise local security, they might have been taken out, *please*—"

The voice drops out, no static this time, nothing. You wait for an interminable minute on the off chance that it will return. No luck.

You'll play along. You manually kick the scenario, and your nerves flare with phantom pain as the simulator drops the inputs. You extricate yourself from the chamber, dumping all the red weaponry except the (dull) knife, which you could theoretically use to stick someone in the eye. Then you head for the armory by the most direct route, since speed is your ally.

Like most larger stations, the Citadel routinely uses variable layout, which allows spatial elements to be rearranged for more rapid travel between them. You worry that someone will switch variable layout off and leave you spindled between *here* and *nowhere*. The technology has an extremely good safety record—if you don't take hostiles into account.

The Citadel is vast. Even the updated map is obfuscated due to security issues. The artificially induced vertigo, another defensive measure, is maddening. Only the medical countermeasures you brought with you keep you upright. You slam up against the armory without warning. The doors are open and there's smoke. Nice to know that you didn't bring a mask for nothing.

The augment won't tell you whether anything's in there, since you don't have even that much clearance. With your luck, you'll be hit with tranquilizer clouds the moment you go in, and that's the best-case scenario. But you have to give the game your best shot.

You plunge into the armory, armed with knife and bravado. Even with the augment it's difficult to see past the smoke.

A subliminal slither-scale noise, then a hiss, catch your attention. You duck low. Someone's here, an unfriendly someone. The hiss comes again, and with it a knife-line of stinging pain just shy of your left shoulder.

You have no idea what they've rigged the security protocols to do if you use even fake guns, so it'll have to be the dull-edged knife. It won't do you much good if you can't close the distance, however.

You hear the unmistakable click of a splinter grenade's pin being removed and sprint for cover. You glimpse the grenade as it thunks solidly against a wall of boxes labeled HANDLE WITH CAUTION—SUSCEPTIBLE TO FIRE, CONCUSSION, AND STUPIDITY. (The only surprise is that STUPIDITY isn't listed first.)

The grenade goes off and you're deafened. It's a fucking *grenade* and are you ever grateful for the instinct that yanked you to the safest place in the geometry of the fucking armory, sheltered partly by the edge of a locker, partly by a bin that someone didn't put back properly. Even then you take splinters through your side and right arm, but you still have your left, and the medical foam is bubbling up from your jacket's circulatory systems to seal the wounds even if it's not doing anything for the agony.

Your brain catches up to that glimpse: the grenade wasn't red.

It wasn't red. They just tried to kill you with the genuine article.

This isn't a training game anymore.

Despite the pain, you locate an intact weapons bank and scrabble to open it. The credentials the unknown voice provided you are genuine. You snatch up a scorch pistol.

You whip out of the armory and around the corner firing. The hostile, wearing a foreign-looking articulated suit, attempts to retaliate with the pain-scourge of whatever-it-is. Your aim is true, your reflexes better; the scorch hits her full-on. She screams.

You're far enough back that the grenade at her belt shattering into a thousand thousand pieces doesn't do more than sting. The damage is probably worse than it feels. You can assess that later.

There's not much left of a body to inspect. It's not the only one, either. The blast caught some others. The smell, charred metal and meat and shit, makes your gorge rise. You force yourself to look at the red smears on the floor, the walls. The worst part is a chunk of face with a full eye almost intact, staring lopsidedly at a shredded piece of lung.

No. That's not the worst part. You wonder that you almost missed it, but you're not thinking very clearly right now. A shiver of revulsion passes through you. The eye's iris is vivid violet.

Taurags have eyes like that.

You were right the second time. This has stopped being a game.

YOU HAVE NO idea who to link up with and it's likely that Citadel security will mistake you for an intruder yourself, Shuos uniform notwithstanding. But if there's any chance your information is useful, you have to pass it on. The Citadel's population is classified, along with other useful things like the number of toilets, but you wouldn't be surprised if it housed over half a million people. The thought of them being in danger, strangers though they are, makes your stomach twist.

Your best bet is to head for the spatial stabilizer. Now that you realize the threat is real, the thought of hostiles in control of a Citadel stabilizer makes your heart constrict. They could separate the Citadel's spatial building blocks, rearrange them to disadvantage the Shuos, even—if they crack the controls entirely—destroy the Citadel.

It's not reassuring that this is the same technology you'll have to rely on to reach the stabilizer, since it needs to be isolated from realspace. There's no help for it. You hurry toward the next path.

This one requires you to climb up and down an elegant spiraling ramp that changes color from auburn to gold and then sly amber. Your knees feel unsteady, and you hate yourself for it. You keep expecting the ramp to vanish into a massless knot of nothing and strand you. As you step off the spiral, however, the world *slants* and you dash for a side corridor at the sound of gunfire.

The voice comes back without warning. You almost shoot the wall. "You made it, good," it says. This time it's communicating through your augment. "You're there, right? Can you get in?" And then: "I think the senior staff—well, it doesn't matter. You're what's available."

The way the voice wavers makes you grind your teeth. "Firefight," you say, identifying the weapons by the percussion they make as you let the augment transmit your subvocals. "Just got here, haven't had time to scout."

"I've been working the grid," the voice says. "I can get in overrides, but you'll have to work fast to take advantage before they freeze me out. And you'll need physical access."

Obviously, or they would have been able to handle matters remotely. "Servitor passages for maintenance?"

"Yes. I can open one of those. Tight squeeze, though."

The voice has the presence of mind to send you a newer, declassified map. At this point it's not like either of you cares about getting into trouble with higher-ups. "Listen," you say, determined not to give in to the awful mixture of pain and nausea despite the medical assists. "How bad is it, if the senior staff are...?"

Brief silence. "I haven't heard from Mikodez or any of the senior staff since the alert began," the voice says. "I'm lying low right now. They didn't hire me to be brave." Not the most inspiring thing to say, but you appreciate the honesty. "I'm hoping the other stabilizers are all right, but they're still attempting to secure this one."

"I'll do what I can," you say.

The next moves happen in a blur.

Scorch blasts.

Narrow passage. Claustrophobia and bruised elbows are the least of your worries.

You approach the hatch. The firefight sounds like it's died down. You're not optimistic about the survival of your Shuos comrades. It's hard to see through the slits and you don't dare query local scan lest you be detected.

You pry the hatch open, wishing it didn't creak so much. Most of the bodies in the control center wear Shuos red-and-gold. A few have violet eyes and are dressed in the strange articulated suits.

The voice again. "Are you in?"

"Yes. They didn't stick around, though."

"That's not good," it says. "One moment." Then: "The good news is that they couldn't crack the stabilizer's control system. The bad news is that there's—there's more of them. A lot more of them. Their swarm, fleet, horde, whatever their term is. They've all arrived. They're taking out the orbital defenses before they make a move planetside, I guess."

It's growing harder and harder to think, just when it's most important. "We can use the stabilizer against them—"

"Too many of them and not enough time. Unless—"

You know exactly what they're thinking of. Unmoor the stabilizer and aim it at the Citadel's heart, where the power cores are. Turn space inside-out. The whole thing would go up in a tumult of fire. It'd also scorch a significant portion of the planet, but the explosion would hurt the Taurag invaders and buy time for a defense to be mustered elsewhere.

Just to make sure that you and the voice understand each other, you outline the idea.

"Yes," the voice says. "I'll talk you through the procedure."

It takes you several minutes to figure out the control system even so, because the voice only has access to an outdated version of the manual, and the system interface was overhauled at some point.

You think about orbital mechanics. If you set off the power cores right now, the conflagration will singe Shuos Academy's main campus on the planet's second-largest continent.

Shuos Academy comes to mind because you just graduated, naturally, but there are a lot of population centers that would be affected. It's easy enough to access a map of the planet and the associated census, start adding up the numbers. How high would the kill count get?

After a moment, the voice interrupts. "Have you done it? Is there a technical issue? Of all the times—"

"I'm not doing it," you say over the dull roar in your ears. Your hands have started shaking violently. You right the nearest chair and sink into it before your knees can give out.

The voice's silence is distinctly baffled.

"Open a line to the Taurags," you say. "Talk to them or something. The Taurags won't hit nonmilitary targets down there. They insist on that kind of thing. If our enemy wouldn't do it, I'm fucked if I'll hit the button myself."

"Are you out of your mind? That invasion force isn't going to stop here!" The voice suddenly becomes frantic. "Or is it that you're scared to die when we all go up in flames? I don't enjoy the idea any more than you do, but we've got a *duty*—"

"That's not it," you say. "I mean, I don't want to die. But that isn't the reason. There are better ways to win than toasting a bunch of civilians. We've learned that much from our enemy. Maybe it's too late for us here to find a new strategy, but someone else will."

The voice drops silent, and you wonder if it's given up on you, but after a while it resumes. "We don't have much time left," it says, low and fierce. "There's another squad headed your way, they're almost *there*. If you're going to do something, you have to do it now. And—" Silence again.

Getting up hurts. You're sure that something's bleeding inside. The augment confirms this, although it's being awfully unhelpful about the nature of the injury. Under the circumstances it's not like it matters.

You've had time to survey the room, consider its layout. You settle on a position and lower yourself painfully into place. If the pistol gets any heavier you're going to drop it.

Footsteps. They're attempting to be quiet, but the slither-scale sound of that articulated stuff can't be silenced entirely. You've never been more awake.

There's only one of you, but you might as well take out as many as you can on the way out.

THERE'S A SHUOS joke that isn't shared often, although most people have heard it.

What's the difference between a Shuos and a bullet to the back of the head?

You might survive the bullet.

It's not especially funny (as opposed to Kel jokes, which everyone but the Kel agree are hilarious). But then, depending on how you measure these things, the deadliest general in Kel history was a Shuos.

YOU WAKE WITH a memory of shadows cutting across the door, of your jacket's unexpected injection, of toppling sideways and the taste of blood in your mouth. You're hooked up to a medical unit that someone has decorated with knitted lace. The sight is so unexpected (and the russet lace so hideous) that it keeps you from doing the obvious thing and accosting the instructor, who is standing subtly out of reach, with a dancer's awareness of space.

You're pretty sure that if not for whatever they drugged you with, you'd be in a lot of pain right now. As it stands, your thoughts feel as clear as ice in spite of the weird disconnected feeling that your mind is only attached to your body by a few silk strands.

"The 'Taurag attack' was still part of the game, wasn't it?" you ask in a scratched-up voice. "Some of those people actually *died*." You weren't in a simulator for the second half. The smells, the hot, sticky blood, the staring eye.

"The performers were volunteers," the instructor says, which only makes you want to shoot him more, if only you had a gun. "I had to apply to Mikodez for special permission to recruit them, because if there's anything Mikodez hates, it's inefficiency. But the exercise had to be real because that was the only way to make it feel real."

"You had me kill people for a *test*. *You* killed people for a test."

"You're not the first person to call me a monster." The instructor smiles; his eyes are very dark. "I didn't lie about the destructive potential of the weapon that we're concerned with. It can devastate planetary populations, and they say *I* was known for overkill. But it isn't a Taurag weapon. It's *our* weapon. We're building new battlemoths to make use of it even as we speak. I hear they'll be ready by year's end.

"The next step will be to take the fight to the Taurag Republic. There's a lot of potential for the war to go genocidal, for us to get locked into back-and-forth invasions until one or both of us is obliterated. We have to look beyond that. We can't escape the fact of war—there's too much history of distrust for that—but we can lay the foundation for whatever accord we reach afterwards, because no war, however terrible, lasts forever."

You're not liking the fact that you agree with this one point, because it means you're agreeing with *him*.

"I refuse to let this weapon fall into the hands of people who can use it without blinking at the deaths it will cause, or who think only of revenge," the instructor says. "I would rather spend a few deaths now, to identify people who understand restraint—who care about the lives of civilians—than find out during the invasion proper by reading about the inevitable massacres."

"Tell me," you say sarcastically. "If I'd decided to blow the Citadel up, would you have let *that* go through, too?"

"No, you were only playing with a dummy system by that point," he says, "even if you had to believe it was real. If you'd hit the button, we'd still be here, only I'd be debriefing you on why you'd failed."

He rubs the back of one hand, as if in memory of scars, although you see none there. "You did well," he adds, as if that could make up for the people you killed, that he put into harm's way. "You passed. I hope you continue to pass. Because this is one test you don't stop taking."

"You wouldn't have passed," you say, because someone has to.

"No," he says. For a moment you glimpse the shadows he lives with, all of them self-inflicted. "I've always been an excellent killer. It's not too late for you to do more with your career than I did with mine. You'll make an excellent officer. I'm recommending you for the invasion swarm."

You inhale sharply, and regret it when pain stabs through your side in spite of the painkillers. "I'm not sure you should"—more candor than is safe, but you're beyond caring. "Because after we deal with the Taurags, I'm coming for you."

The instructor salutes you Kel-style, with just a touch of irony. You don't return the gesture. "I look forward to it," he says.

AUTHOR'S NOTE

Second person is frequently controversial. I am perhaps fonder of it than I have any right to be, because my first story sale ("The Hundredth Question," *The Magazine of Fantasy and Science Fiction*, February 1999) was written in second person. A lifetime of reading *Choose Your Own Adventure* books and gamebooks probably exacerbated the tendency.

Mikodez's lace knitting comes from my brief flirtation with lace knitting. Unfortunately, I am both prone to dropping stitches and unable to read my own knitting, a combination that led to me acrimoniously divorcing knitting a few years back. Maybe I should go back to cross-stitch (a hobby I assigned to Inesser) or tatting?

GLASS CANNON

I AM A Shuos.

Jedao didn't remember most of Shuos Academy, let alone graduating from it. He couldn't help thinking of himself as a cadet, only nineteen years old, despite the fact that his body was middle-aged in appearance. While Hexarch Shuos Mikodez had assured him that the courses he was taking at the Citadel of Eyes were equivalent to the education he would have gotten at the modern academy, Jedao didn't believe him. Jedao had spent the past two years and change as a "guest" of the hexarch, or, more accurately, a prisoner. The hexarch might have unbent enough to allow him to catch up with best practices in social engineering and how to wrangle the state of the art bath facilities. That didn't mean he was likely to allow Jedao to extract classified information from the grid.

Naturally, that was precisely what Jedao intended to do.

I am a Shuos.

Jedao had hoped that repeating the phrase in his head, like a mantra, would magically grant him access to the memories of his older, other self. Useful memories, like *how do I hack into the Shuos hexarch's private files?* Never mind that he had no idea whether Jedao One (as he'd labeled the other man, who was and wasn't dead) would have been able to manage the feat.

At the moment, Jedao was sitting in his suite of rooms watching a poetry recital livestream. The hexarch had invited him to the performance, put on by a Shuos agent whose job it was to pretend to be an Andan. Jedao had declined, claiming that crowds made him jittery. No one had challenged the lie.

The truth was other. Jedao had not redecorated the suite since he had moved into it. The wallpaper remained tranquil green. Furniture in wood—real wood, to which he responded with unwanted atavistic delight. He shifted the chairs around from time to time, just to prove he could, and also because he wondered if it bothered his watchers. (He had no delusions of privacy in the heart of Shuos headquarters.) He watered the potted green onion plant, the same one he'd been given two years ago, with great diligence. The hexarch asked after it every time they met, although Jedao hadn't figured out why Mikodez cared so much about container gardening. None of this did anything to ameliorate the vast emptiness in his heart, the fact that he had no human friends here, and never would.

The colors in the Citadel were *wrong*. In place of the stark blacks and golds of the Kel, the Citadel was dominated by Mikodez's favorite color, that transparently soothing shade of green. A few offices sported the garish Shuos red-and-gold, complete with ink paintings of ninefoxes with their staring tails. ("We have to uphold a few clichés," Mikodez had said.)

Gone were the ashhawks, the tapestries woven (as Dhanneth had told Jedao once upon a bed) from the uniforms of the dead, and decorated with beads smelted from ruined guns or spent ammunition. Gone was the cup he had shared with the Kel officers at high table. Gone was the life, however much a lie, that he had woken to with Hexarch Nirai Kujen, dead by Jedao's own hand.

Increasingly, Jedao retreated to the few memories he had left, and the question that haunted him increasingly. He'd had *one* friend, during that vanished lifetime four centuries ago.

Vestenya Ruo, fellow cadet, whom he'd had an embarrassing crush on, and who, as far as he knew, had never shown any indication of interest in Jedao. Not *that* way.

Sometimes Jedao caught himself daydreaming that he'd find Ruo, and—and what? He was already a rapist; Dhanneth had committed suicide to drive that point home. That didn't, however, sway Jedao in his desire to find out what Ruo's fate had been. He had become irrationally convinced that if Ruo had lived a long and happy life, it would prove that Jedao himself wasn't poison to everyone he touched.

It was odd that he needed the highest level of access, available only to Mikodez and select members of his senior staff, to answer a simple question about a Shuos cadet. True, Ruo had died sometime four centuries ago; would have died no matter what, given the finiteness of human lives. But what had been so special about his death that the truth was locked away like this?

Cheris had told him only that Ruo had died young. Jedao wondered, sometimes, what details she had omitted. And there was only one way to find out.

I am a Shuos.

Jedao took a steadying breath, trying to pretend that he cared about the poetry recital. The poet had said something about peacocks. He wasn't sure he'd ever seen a real one. Jedao One would have known; but that was the problem.

Right on schedule, a snakeform servitor levitated down from one of the vents in the ceiling: Hemiola. It had once tried to explain its name to Jedao, and established that Jedao had no ability at music, or understanding of its theory, other than being able to find a beat to dance to. Hemiola flashed the lights along its articulated metal carapace in a friendly green of greeting.

Jedao leaned back in his chair and drummed his fingers. It wasn't impatience. Rather, he tapped in Simplified Machine Universal: *Safe?*

"Safe," Hemiola flashed back, even more green, if possible. Not for the first time, Jedao envied it its ability to jinx the Citadel's surveillance system, which it used when the two of them wanted to talk, or, as now, when Jedao wanted to hide his activities from his watchers.

Too bad Kujen never thought to install me in a servitor body, Jedao thought. He'd asked Hemiola about it. After all, people already offloaded some of their memories into their augments. Hemiola had said that, as far as it could tell, the process by which Kujen had created Jedao had worked through a different, more complex mechanism involving exotic effects. So much for that.

Thank you for covering for me, Jedao said.

"It's no problem," Hemiola said. It didn't emphasize that he needed to be quick, that every time it screwed with surveillance, it was running a risk. They both knew that.

Ordinarily the two of them met here, Jedao because he could only endure so much of his self-imposed isolation, Hemiola because it, too, was far from home. What went unspoken was that they were, aside from Mikodez, the last people who remembered Nirai Kujen with any fondness, however complicated.

Jedao wasted no time on apologies and called up a separate subdisplay, this one of pornography—a plausible reason for a man to want some time alone, surely?—leaving the poet-performer to declaim verses about *more* birds. Mocking the Kel, probably; he wasn't clear on the nuances. Using the techniques that Hemiola had taught him, he began hacking, grid-diving, whatever they called it these days.

This should be harder, Jedao thought, bemused, as the system opened itself to him like a flower. (Great, now he was thinking in poetic symbols too.) But then, "hard" was relative. Thanks to Hemiola's spying, and that of the other servitors that it had made arrangements with, Jedao had a detailed understanding of the hexarch's security measures.

Access to the files he wanted should have required him to log in from Mikodez's personal terminal. ("He must be certain no one can spoof it," Hemiola had remarked.) Over the years, however, the servitors had mapped the system down to every flicker that passed through the hardware, down to the very molecules. And Jedao himself had an advantage that he had done his best to keep from his captors.

What Mikodez knew: that Jedao, however much he appeared a manform, was not human. Jedao's body regenerated even from death. Kujen, who had designed him, had intended for him to live forever.

What Mikodez might not yet be aware of: Jedao could drag himself through the space-time weave as moths did. It was how he'd escaped the massacre of the Kel (*my Kel*, he couldn't help thinking, with a stab of grief). It had also hurt so badly that Jedao didn't care to repeat the experience.

Beyond that, moths spoke to each other through minute fluctuations in space-time: gravity waves. Jedao heard the Citadel's swarms of shadowmoths singing to each other every night, lullaby and torment in one.

Jedao hadn't attempted to contact the shadowmoths. While everyone knew that defense swarms orbited the Citadel, he wasn't supposed to know their locations while they were stealthed. He wanted to join in the song, and talk to them, and be welcomed. But he remembered the utter silence with which the Kel warmoths had reacted to him, and he didn't have any reason to believe that Shuos shadowmoths would feel differently. Besides, any anomaly in their behavior would be noticed by Mikodez's staff, and Jedao couldn't afford that.

Instead, he'd practiced the speech-of-moths quietly, and learned to manipulate matter, with Hemiola standing guard. At first he'd been clumsy with it—he'd knocked all the riotous scented soaps into the tub that one time—and then he'd gained in finesse. In conjunction with his othersense, which allowed him to "see" distributions of mass with distracting precision, it gave him a chance to pull this off. Just this moment, for instance, in correlation with the master maps that he'd hacked into, he could tell that Mikodez's primary office was empty.

That was all the opening Jedao needed to *reach* into Mikodez's office, enter the necessary verifications not by using the keyboard input but the terminal's internal circuitry itself, and pipe access to Jedao's own workstation.

Kujen would have figured it out, assuming he hadn't counted on it from the beginning. Whether he had informed Mikodez about this detail was what Jedao was about to find out.

Hemiola's lights sheened orange when the third subdisplay came up. It featured a background photo of a calico cat napping in a sink. Jedao recognized it as one of Zehun's pets—specifically the one that, disconcertingly, was named after *him*.

Jedao started to sweat. The marrow-deep pain was as he remembered it, if finer in scale. The fabric of his uniform—red-and-gold, how he hated the sight of it—clung damply to his back. He wiped his palms on his pants. Two years and he still hadn't grown accustomed to going everywhere with naked hands, and this despite the fact that he'd never earned the half-gloves, either.

I am a Shuos, he thought. Fourth time; lucky unlucky four. He thought of all the Kel deaths he was responsible for, in this life and in the one he couldn't remember.

He'd come this far. It would be a shame to let the opportunity slide past. So he set his fingers to the workstation and entered his first query. It would have been safer to do this using his ability to manipulate gravity, but he didn't enjoy the pain. This would have to do.

What the fuck became of you, Ruo? Jedao wondered as he dug through the filesystem. Did he really want to know what had become of his best friend? The boy he'd played pranks with? Whom he'd pined after but never asked out? (And why hadn't he? Had there been a falling out?)

Vestenya Ruo, Shuos cadet, tracked as Shuos infantry. Jedao had no idea why even a top-secret record clung to the old euphemism for *assassin*. He'd asked Mikodez about the term once. Mikodez had shrugged and said, "Habit"—another one of those maddening non-answers.

Ruo had attended Shuos Academy Prime from 826 to—826. The end date hit Jedao like a blow to the stomach. Nausea washed through him as he wondered what had gone wrong.

The first date was right. They'd been first-years together. As sieve-like as his memories were, Jedao knew that much.

But less than a year in academy?

The record didn't end there. Ruo hadn't been expelled, which would have been bad enough. Nor had he graduated in a single year, which would have been a miracle.

No—Ruo had *died*. The record specified, in dry, bloodless detail, that Ruo had run afoul of a visiting Rahal magistrate while playing a *heresy game*. Ruo had committed suicide rather than be outprocessed and handed over to the Rahal.

And the game had been designed by one Cadet Garach Jedao Shkan.

That can't be right, Jedao thought, and: *I would never.*

Tears pricked his eyes. Angrily, he scrubbed them away with the back of his hand. Had he—had he maneuvered Ruo into suicide on purpose? And if so, *why*?

But the record had no answers for him.

I loved him, Jedao thought, *and he's gone.* He'd looked sidelong at Ruo during the classes that they had together, admiring the fineness of his features, longing to run his fingers through the mane of hair that Ruo kept tied back in a ponytail. Imagined the weight of that solid body atop his.

But he'd been convinced that he'd loved Dhanneth, too; and look how that had ended. Was his treatment of Dhanneth part of a pattern that he'd missed because of the amnesia?

And if so, how could he make it up to the dead?

I believe he died young, Kel Cheris had said to him. Sparing him the truth. There was no way she hadn't known.

Jedao didn't feel spared. He couldn't see why this information was so deeply classified. Especially when he knew that Mikodez, for all his quixotic moods, did everything for a reason when it came to security.

"Are you all right?" Hemiola asked in worried yellow lights, then flushed pink. "Of course you're not all right." It had better vision than humans did, and in most regards, than Jedao himself. It already knew what the record said.

"He would have been dead anyway," Jedao said, but he wasn't convincing even himself. He couldn't bring himself to say Ruo's name out loud, and not because he was worried about surveillance.

"Is that all you wanted to find out?"

"No," Jedao said. "Just one more thing."

He had to dig around to locate what he was looking for. Mikodez named all his files sensible things, which only surprised Jedao a little: as much as Mikodez liked to play at high whimsy, his successor would someday depend on being able to locate important information. And Mikodez cared about his successors; cared that what he built should outlast him.

Not my problem, Jedao told himself. It might even have been true. He opened the latest of the psychological evaluations that Mikodez had ordered his nephew and contact specialist, Andan Niath, to do on Jedao himself.

The file was long and dreary. It took an effort not to skim. He knew already that he was unfit to leave the Citadel and rejoin mainstream society; possibly not fit even to interact with anyone but his carefully selected keepers, including the contact specialist. He didn't need to be told *that*.

The occasional odd detail leapt out at him. *Displays no phobia of the dark,* for instance. Surely such a common trigger would have disqualified him for military service? Granted that they had recovered him from deep space after the Battle of Terebeg two years ago, but a whole section followed on his responses to a test that they had given him, which had involved a series of lurid paintings.

At last he came to Zehun's summation, which was what interested him the most. *Recommendation: subject is no closer to divulging the secret of why Hexarch Kujen's command moth mutinied at Terebeg. Subject should be terminated.*

Jedao's hand slipped; he almost accidentally deleted the file. Which wasn't *easy*, what was he *thinking*, the system was logging all activity. Stupid of him, especially since he shouldn't care. Zehun was civil to him, but there was no love lost between the two of them.

"Hemiola," Jedao said as he logged out and covered his tracks to the extent that they could be covered, which wasn't very, "I'm going to need more of your help than I realized."

Hemiola blinked anxiously at him.

"I need passage off the Citadel to—a starport," Jedao said. "Any starport. I can't stow away *inside* a voidmoth here; they'll catch me. But I might have a chance if I cling to the carapace."

Strictly speaking, he didn't need to breathe. He'd tested this in his bathtub, which would have looked either silly or tragic if anyone had walked in on him. (Hemiola had disapproved strongly of this experiment, but he'd successfully argued that drowning was a temporary inconvenience.) All—"all"—he had to do was web himself to the exterior.

Hemiola's lights went through a veritable rainbow of misgivings. "I see a way," it said at last. "Follow me."

SIX MINUTES BEFORE the end of class, and Ajewen Cheris, currently going by the name of Dzannis Paral, wondered who was looking forward to it more: herself, or her sixteen students.

No one had called her "Cheris" since she had moved to the world of Esrala to live as a Mwennin among Mwennin, least of all the children, ranging from ages eight to fourteen, in her class. Cheris's mother might be dead, and the Mwennin, her mother's people, scattered and much diminished—Cheris's own fault, a guilt that ran deep—but here, now, a few survived. Most days she was glad of it, and of the fact that there were children at all.

Cheris had tutored math as a cadet in Kel Academy, but that had been, as Mikodez would have said, a completely different kettle of foxes. Not only had the topics been more advanced—applied and abstract algebra, plus the formation notation specific to the Kel—she'd been tutoring peers, fellow cadets. Cadets did not chew on styluses, stick wads of homemade candy under the tables, pull each other's hair, or (admittedly one of the nicer surprises) bring in a pet snake to show her.

Her students were, varyingly, bright, sleepy, curious, fidgety, and more difficult to predict than Kel. It wasn't true that Kel were all alike, as though they were woodblock prints. But the Kel did select for a certain spirit of conformity. Mwennin parents, on the other hand, didn't "select" at all. The children they had were the children they had.

Cheris taught in one of the rooms of the community building, which the settlers considered a luxury. People in the hexarchate proper had neighborhood halls where they could gather and gossip and, inevitably, listen to the Doctrine briefings by the local Vidona-approved delegate. Here, the Mwennin had to adhere to the revised calendar—*her* calendar, although she tried not to think of it that way, not least because she couldn't afford for the Mwennin to deduce her identity—but they didn't hide many of the old traditions. Frequently the children themselves told Cheris about folklore and foods that she only stumblingly remembered from her own youth.

A girl and an alt started squabbling over who had the

prettier stylus. When they ignored the first and second warnings, Cheris escalated: "Heads down, please." The children grumbled but obeyed, mumbling the meditation-chant that she had taught them to help them quiet down. She had to coax the girl to a seat farther away so she wouldn't continue the quarrel.

At least she didn't want for classroom supplies. The settlement had basic manufacturing capabilities and some aging matter printers, for which Mikodez had privately apologized to Cheris. "You wouldn't believe my budget problems," he had said. "My people did what they could." For once, Cheris believed him. She didn't have to worry that her students would lack slates or desks or learning games. If anything, thanks to the involvement of the Shuos, they had more games, in all formats, than she was entirely comfortable with.

And yet, for all the challenges that working as a teacher had brought her, from the time her students climbed up on the roof on a lark to the incident with the thankfully edible modeling clay, Cheris had discovered, to her horror, that she was getting *bored*.

"Gwan," Cheris said, wondering how it was that wrangling an energetic nine-year-old girl who constantly *chewed on things* was, in its way, more harrowing than being shot at. "Take that out of your mouth, please." Weren't kids supposed to grow out of that? By age four at least?

(She thought about having kids of her own someday, if she met the right women or alts. The settlement had the necessary medical labs, even some crèches for those Mwennin who wanted to use them. Then she looked at her students, as much as she adored them, and had second thoughts.)

Gwan took the mutilated stylus out of her mouth. "Sorry, Teacher!" she said. She was always sorry. As far as Cheris could tell, Gwan was sincere, she just had a wandering attention span and a need to fidget. Cheris had tried giving her candies instead, but Gwan kept passing them to the other kids, which defeated the purpose.

The minutes ticked by. Cheris was diligent about making the kids stay for every last second of class—an important lesson to learn in a world where the calendar was so vital—but she let them out the moment the augment told her it was time. Most of the younger ones skipped or ran, almost colliding with each other in their enthusiasm.

As Cheris tidied up the tables and chairs, she was aware of the weight of her handgun against her right hip, inside her pants; she was right-handed. Fortunately, Mwennin children were too respectful of adults to touch her or she would have worried about one of them discovering it by accident. The same went for the spare magazine she kept in her pocket. To keep from revealing it inadvertently, she kept most of her belongings—slate and stylus, snacks, keycard, that sort of thing—in a handbag.

After she finished, Cheris headed out. Not for the first time, she felt ridiculous for carrying a gun. Crime wasn't unknown in the settlement, but she couldn't recall any instances of violent crime since her arrival. Granted, as former infantry, she wasn't concerned about petty fights. It was *illegal* for her to own the gun, let alone carry it to school. As a Kel, she'd been armed as a matter of course. As a civilian, she was supposed to rely on the authorities.

Tomorrow I'll leave it at home, Cheris thought as she strolled down the road leading to her favorite bakery. (This wasn't saying much; the settlement only had two.) Even so, she knew she was lying to herself. The part of her that was Kel might have been persuaded to leave security to the authorities. The part of her that was *Jedao*—that was another matter entirely.

Jedao might be a whisper of unruly memories crammed into her head, but he was real and present in ways that she hadn't entirely untangled even after the eleven years since his death.

And Jedao didn't believe in safety, or trusting other people. During the centuries planning a one-man revolution against the hexarchate entire, with his only ally the man who had designed the high calendar in the first place, with its social strictures and ritual torture, he couldn't afford to.

She reached the bakery and picked up her usual order of two meat pasties, which was ready for her. Several people sat at the tables outside. One of them was pretending to work out pattern-stone puzzles on their tablet. She'd identified the curly-haired alt as a Shuos agent not long after her arrival. She always saw them here, even on the days that she changed her schedule. They weren't trying to hide from her, anyway, just from the other settlers, and she didn't have a reason to expose them.

Cheris resisted the urge to wave at the agent as she walked by them on the way home. The winding road that led to her neighborhood was lined with an exuberance of flowers. Most of the forsythias, with their four-petaled yellow blooms, had died off in favor of splendid green leaves, but there were still azaleas in pink, white, magenta. The violets were harder to spot, both the white ones with purple streaks at their hearts and the more ordinary ones that looked like their name.

The flowers' mingling fragrances relaxed her, and the smell of the pasties was making her hungry. She was looking forward to a quiet evening doing some grading, despite the tickling sense that she wouldn't mind a more active existence. There was that one boy who had creative ideas about how the distributive property worked. And afterwards she could sit down in the common room and watch dueling matches.

"Anyone home?" Cheris called out as she approached the front door of the residence she shared with two women and an alt. No one responded; no surprise. Two of her housemates had jobs that kept them out until later in the day, and the third was a social butterfly and was frequently visiting friends.

Cheris entered and checked, reflexively, for signs of

intruders. The hard part wasn't the paranoia. She'd gotten used to that. The hard part was trying to fit in; pretending that she was just another Mwennin refugee.

She had a lovely home where she could catch up on dramas and dueling matches at her leisure. She taught adorable children, even if the adorable children liked to stick things in their mouths. Nobody shot at her anymore. Why wasn't she happy?

She headed into the kitchen to put one of the meat pasties into the refrigerator, then returned to the common area and sank gratefully onto a floor cushion to eat the other. She asked the grid to image her the local news. Maybe that would ground her in reality and keep her from worrying about the state of the galaxy, which wasn't her concern anymore.

Still, her mind wandered as the news talked about the discovery of a new primitive sea-creature. She thought of Jedao, inevitably. *Sometimes I don't understand you at all,* she told the fragments of him that remained. Someone who still mourned the death of a childhood friend, to the extent that he existed to do the mourning at all, yet had been capable of murdering his command staff, people he'd known and relied upon for years.

If Cheris was honest with herself—something she had just enough psychic distance for—Jedao's feelings for Kel Gized, his chief of staff and the first person he'd murdered, had not been entirely platonic. But Jedao wouldn't have acted on his subterranean desires, and in any case Gized had never shown any sign of having any interest in romance. She'd been a Kel of the very old school, from the days when the Kel were an autonomous people and some of them took the sword-vow: married to her profession as a soldier, and nothing else.

Cheris had finished her pasty and was in the middle of wiping her mouth, lost in memories that were and weren't her own, when someone rapped politely at the door. It couldn't be one of her housemates. They would just have walked in, as the house's minimal security system recognized them. One of their friends?

Her back prickled. *Paranoia*, she told herself again; but she could never be sure. "Grid," she said softly, knowing it would hear her, "who is it?"

The grid showed her an image of her guest: a bedraggled man of middle years, his bangs clinging damply to his forehead. Not smiling, although she knew exactly what his smile looked like, and how it tilted up asymmetrically at the corners. He was panting as though he'd run to her house from—from where? She hadn't heard the footsteps, although that didn't mean anything definitive.

He wasn't in Kel uniform, or Shuos uniform either. That unnerved her. The naked hands were worst of all. In her dreams she always saw them sheathed in the notorious fingerless gloves.

Cheris's next actions happened in what she later remembered as a single seamless flow, without calculation to guide them. The gun that she had hidden for the past two years snapped into her hands as she strode to the door. She touched the selector with her finger and emptied the magazine through the unopened door in a single burst. Just as quickly, she flung herself to the side in case of return fire.

No one fired back, but the stink of gunsmoke filled her nostrils. In the sudden ringing stillness afterward, she heard the thud of a body slumping against the door; heard a stifled gasp.

"Please," the man on the other side of the door said, with a hint of the drawl that she had fought hard to suppress in her own speech. "I'm just here to talk."

Cheris doubted *that*, but now that her rational brain had caught up to her ghost-granted reflexes, she recognized the futility of retrieving more ammunition and shooting him again, as satisfying as it would be. She kept the gun in her hand, because Shuos paranoia and Kel training died hard.

"Let him in," she said to the house's grid.

The door slid open. Jedao stared at her wide-eyed. His sensible brown jacket was marred by holes in the torso where she'd hit him in center mass, to say nothing of the grotesque, sluggish black blood dripping from the wounds where his heart should have been. She glimpsed wormlike tendrils waving feebly from beneath his skin, revealing the truth beneath the human exterior. Jedao gestured apologetically at the blood.

Cheris stood aside to let him in. Given the holes in the door, a little blood wasn't going to make much difference, even if one of her housemates liked everything very neat.

He still didn't enter. "Cheris?" he said uncertainly, using a high honorific.

Cheris was forcibly reminded that she'd changed her face, had subtle adjustments made to her voice, courtesy of one of Mikodez's surgeons. Most days she didn't think about her new face, with its broad forehead and pronounced nose, the quizzical eyebrows. It would have fooled her own parents— but they were dead, and by her own doing.

The sound of her name—her real name—brought back a sudden and unwelcome wave-crash of longing, especially paired with the familiar Shparoi drawl. Cheris remembered what it had been like when the original Jedao had talked to her, that relentless voice in her head. Looking at this other Jedao was like looking in a broken mirror and putting her hands through the shards: pain that she couldn't escape.

"It's me," Cheris said, her voice harsher than she'd meant it to be. She pointed at the couch. He went over to sit on it, still dripping blood, and she closed the door. How much time did they have before her watchers called for reinforcements? Since it seemed unfruitful to say, *Thanks for ruining my life*, she settled for, "I'm guessing you're not here with the hexarch's permission. Make it quick."

A trail of that black blood had dripped from the door

to the couch, following Jedao like an accusation. He had removed his jacket and was trying ineffectually to staunch the leakage with the wadded-up fabric. "I'm here," he said, overenunciating, "because you're the only one who knows the truth about my past."

There was no point continuing the conversation here, when the Shuos would already be on their way. As much as she'd been chafing at how dull and ordinary her life had been, now that she was about to lose it, a pang of resentment started up in her chest. She doubted she'd be able to go back to her classroom now that Jedao had intruded into her life.

For a moment she considered handing Jedao over to the Shuos. He wasn't her problem; he was Mikodez's problem. She could get rid of him and go back to the simple life she'd chosen for herself.

But he'd come to her in search of the answers she'd withheld from him before. She owed them to him, even if she'd been in denial about it.

"Did you bring any weapons?" Cheris asked.

His teeth flashed in a silent laugh. "I *am* a weapon," Jedao said. He wasn't boasting; it was as true as anything else about him. She was grateful that he didn't say *I'm your gun* or she would have been tempted to punch him, even if just for the irrational feeling that that was *her* phrase.

Cheris had walked over to her escritoire in the common room and opened it to reveal a bag. "We'll have to share," she said. She kept emergency supplies in the bag in case she had to leave in a hurry: everything from cash in the local currency to ration bars (not Kel, alas), plus a survival knife and a folding tent, all the accoutrements she would need to survive in the wilderness outside the settlement's protective dome until she could be picked up by allies.

She also retrieved a protective suit and began pulling it on over her clothes. "I have a spare," she said, "but it's not going to fit you. Did you bring one, or are we going to have to detour to pick one up for you?" More opportunities to be caught. She didn't like it, but she didn't see much alternative.

"I don't need one," Jedao said. "The atmosphere outside won't kill me." He didn't explain how he knew this. She was willing to take his word for it, though. She knew how hard he was to kill.

"Come on, then," Cheris said.

Jedao followed in silence. Cheris looked over her shoulder to verify that he was still there, that he hadn't dissolved into some phantasm of smoke and bitter memory. Her heart was thumping so hard that she was afraid that it would burst free of her ribcage, making her Jedao's twin in injury. Would she bleed black, too, now that they were reunited?

The community maintained some hoverers in case someone wanted to go for a jaunt outside the dome, or needed to transport heavy objects. Cheris signed one out and took the driver's seat. Jedao got in without questioning her, which she appreciated. The Shuos would count on being able to track the vehicle, but Cheris had asked one of the settlement's servitors to plant an override into the system. She activated it now, hoping the Shuos hadn't discovered it in the interim.

The hoverer smelled displeasingly of meat pasties, a smell that she liked when the pasties in question were fresh and much less when it mingled with a lingering mixture of people's clashing perfumes and bodies. Civilian life had softened her. She'd once trained regularly in Kel body armor that reeked of sour sweat and off-gassing plastic and, occasionally, vomit or other effluvia. There was no forgetting the stomach-turning stink of the battlefield, blood curdled or crystallized, the occasional startling sweetness of crushed flowers or aromatics. How much of that did this other, younger Jedao remember?

"It's beautiful," Jedao said, almost in a whisper, as the hoverer lifted up and sped toward the boundary of the settlement's dome. Cheris was reminded of his presence, and the fact that they were, despite their shared history, strangers to each other. She would not have expected any incarnation of Jedao to be sentimental about landscape. But he was leaning toward the window, one hand pressed against it in yearning.

"First time planetside?" she asked, because it might be useful to know. She couldn't imagine Mikodez allowing Jedao to wander around on a planet, even if the Citadel of Eyes occupied a geosynchronous orbit above one. Depending on how patchy Jedao's memories were, this might be his first experience with sky, sun, dirt.

"Yes," he said without elaborating.

She appreciated that he wasn't distracting her from the more important task of driving. The hoverer was capable of handling itself if you punched in the destination, but she preferred to do it manually in case the Shuos had the vehicle bugged. She didn't want to drive them into an ambush.

"I had a way off-planet, but I assume you prefer yours," Jedao added as they reached the dome. It glimmered with a soap bubble's rainbow colors, a flickering in the air. Exotic technology, which Cheris didn't trust, but it hadn't failed since she'd moved here. And really, the calendar in use here was *her* calendar, which the servitors of Pyrehawk Enclave had helped her distribute eleven years ago, after the destruction of Kel Command. It was laughable, if not actively hypocritical, for her to be nervous about her own work.

Cheris braced herself for the lightheaded sensation that always accompanied a dome transition. If it bothered Jedao, he didn't show it. In all fairness, if she'd survived a hole in her chest that size, a mere tickle in her brain wouldn't slow her down either.

The settlement, with its modest clusters of buildings and walkways and humble rows of flowers, receded behind them. Cheris guided the hoverer toward the mountains with their woods, heading toward a particular dead tree, its limbs split like lightning tongues, that made for a useful landmark. She wasn't sure how the local flora survived in atmosphere that wasn't yet fit for humans to breathe; she'd never been motivated enough to read about the transitional forests that the early terraforming team had planted. The details would have gone over her head anyway; she was no scientist.

Cheris didn't speak again until they had flown some distance beneath the cover of the blue-leaved trees. Driving was not her best skill, and she was relying on the hoverer's simple intelligence to help her avoid crashing into some unexpected boulder or ledge. They whooshed past the trees and their whipsaw branches at a stomach-churning speed, as she didn't dare slow down. Every moment might make a difference.

"Why are you here?" she asked. "The version with details."

Jedao opened his mouth. Just then there was a loud *crack* as a low branch smacked into the hoverer, and they tilted alarmingly to one side and almost bounced off another tree entirely. Cheris had a brief, dazzling, and unwanted vision of a cloud of scintillant insects flurrying up from their hiding places and toward the canopy. She swore in a muddled mixture of Mwen-dal and the high language as she fought to bring the vehicle back under control.

By the time she'd achieved that, they were off-course. She then had to focus on navigation, which wasn't hard so much as irritating, when there were so many damn *trees* everywhere. Deeper in the forest, they grew closer together, along with a bewilderment of low-growing shrubs, vines, and thorny *things* that glistened with poisonous sap.

They touched down at last in something that the servitors' maps had described as a "clearing," and which barely merited the name. She had to tilt the hoverer's nose up to get it to fit at all. *This is why no one tracked me as a vehicle specialist,* Cheris thought ruefully. At least the unnaturally quick reflexes she had inherited from the original Jedao's ghost had kept them from meeting a fiery death in the forest. It would be ignominious to survive bullets and battlefields, a carrion bomb, and a crash landing on the world of Terebeg only to be felled by a hoverer crash.

Cheris rechecked the integrity of her suit, old habit, before retrieving her bag, popping the door open, and clambering out. Jedao exited right after she did, landing agilely in the loam and decaying leaves. He wrinkled his nose, although Cheris couldn't smell anything but the cleaner she used to maintain the suit. Fortunately, the atmosphere wasn't so deadly that she needed an independent air supply, although she'd brought a couple of canisters in case of emergency. The filters in the suit would suffice.

Cheris wasted no time pulling out a transmitter and sending a single signal. "Can you hear me through this?" Cheris asked. She also knew the Shuos sign language, thanks to the original Jedao, but who knew if this Jedao did?

Jedao nodded. "What was that?" he asked, gesturing toward the transmitter.

She pocketed it. "I called for pickup. You may have gotten this far, but we're going to need allies to get off-planet." She was curious as to how Jedao had engineered his escape; she'd get that information out of him later. "You never told me what exactly you're here for."

Jedao regarded her with a blank face. A split second before he spoke, she remembered, viscerally, from the inside-out, what that particular lack of expression meant. He was angry with her.

"You lied to me," Jedao said.

He clearly expected her to figure out what he meant. "We haven't talked in two years," Cheris said.

"I was locked up," Jedao said. "I found out how Ruo died." His eyes glittered; he was trying not to cry. It made him look paradoxically young.

Cheris was bombarded by unwanted memories of Vestenya

Ruo, who'd been her lover; whose death the original Jedao had caused. The way he'd started to laugh after picking a fight with her in a party, the first time they'd met, and the cocktail they'd shared afterward. Their endless rivalry to see who'd get the better marksmanship scores. The first time they'd slept together, out in the gardens, and the bug bites she'd wound up with. She missed him terribly; the longing was and wasn't hers.

Carefully, Cheris said, "It's been 437 years. I don't see what difference it makes."

"He was my friend," Jedao said. He bit his lip and averted his gaze. The bullet wounds in his torso had mostly closed up except for a few stray tendrils wriggling aimlessly, like exposed worms. He took no notice of them, although Cheris found them distracting.

"Ruo always did like to take risks," Cheris said, both fond and resigned. "But that was one he should have avoided."

Jedao swung at her. She blocked the blow, segued without thinking into a joint lock that was supposed to deter further struggling by inflicting pain. Which was stupid, because someone who didn't blink at multiple gunshot wounds wasn't going to be slowed down by a pressure point.

Nevertheless, Jedao went limp. Cheris remained alert in case it was a trick—was it ever *not* a trick, with Jedao?—but he remained still, and after several moments she let go. He took one step backward, head bowed.

"I'm sorry," Jedao said. He scrubbed his eyes with the back of one hand. "I only found out a couple weeks ago. It was like waking up without him all over again."

"You didn't come all this way to get in a fight with me over this," Cheris said. "Or did you?" It could have been worse. He was a Shuos with fragmentary memories of being the hexarchate's most notorious madman. He could have diverted some of the planetary weather-eaters and crashed them into the settlement, or something even more destructive, with whatever grid-diving skills had gotten him this far.

Jedao tipped his chin up. "I want my memories back," he said. The drawl that they shared was stronger than ever. "How am I supposed to know what to do with my life when I can't *remember* most of it?"

Cheris's stomach suddenly revolted. It was all she could do to keep from gagging. She'd *eaten* Jedao's memories, crunched down the carrion glass and felt it pierce her on the way down. They were part of her now, sharded through her in ways that she couldn't explain in ordinary human terms. But that didn't mean they had to belong to her forever.

For over a decade she'd carried Jedao *inside* her, put him on and off like a mask. Some nights she dreamed his dreams: running from geese who were almost as tall as she was, when she'd been a boy; learning to use her first gun, a lovingly maintained rifle that had been in the Garach family for a couple of generations; shuffling a jeng-zai deck that dripped blood, and blood, and blood. She would have given a lot to be free of those dreams; would have been lost without them.

She'd given up on getting rid of Jedao. There was a way, but—

Jedao's eyes were intent upon her face. "You know a way," he breathed.

Of course. They knew each other. Her body language had been overwritten by Jedao's; he could read her the way she could read him.

"It will require travel," Cheris said, "but we would have to do that anyway, to get away from the Shuos." She imagined Jedao as an outlaw, and couldn't. Even if he had the skills for mercenary work—not that Brezan or Inesser or Mikodez would thank her for making the suggestion—his appearance would always pose a problem. "Why couldn't you have gotten your face changed on the way?"

"I *tried*," he said with an undertone of pain. "I tried scarring myself. It's how my body regenerates. It always regenerates in the *same shape*."

Interesting. Presumably this had limits, or he wouldn't be able to form new memories, or learn new skills. But a fixed overall appearance—that was something she could see Kujen engineering into his creation.

"Kujen experimented with methods of memory transfer," Cheris said, "besides the known one where he hijacked a stranger's body wholesale. I have some of his notes. He had more than one base; he believed in redundancy. I didn't tell Mikodez about some of the others."

"I imagine he knows anyway," Jedao said.

"About some of them, not all of them," Cheris said. She didn't tell Jedao how she knew this. The servitors of Pyrehawk Enclave, with whom she was aligned, had been monitoring Kujen's bases on the grounds that they'd rather know about any traps he'd left behind before they went off. Whether they'd had run-ins with Mikodez's people was not something they had divulged to her.

The transmitter vibrated once. Cheris glanced down and interpreted the code, which was based on Mwen-dal. "Pickup in thirty-seven minutes," she said. She wondered how the needlemoth planned to get through the trees. Then again, its pilot was better than she was, and the needlemoth itself had not insignificant armaments for a vessel its size. As long as the moth didn't shoot *her* while clearing itself a landing site, she didn't care. (She wasn't worried about Jedao.)

"Giving you Jedao's memories—the first Jedao's memories—will mean *giving them* to you," Cheris said. She was starting to sweat, although it wasn't particularly warm, even in the suit. "It's not like copying a drama onto another data solid. If my understanding of Kujen's research is correct, all that I'll have left is a shadow of those four hundred years."

Jedao wouldn't meet her eyes. "Why didn't you get rid of them earlier?"

"Because as long as they're *in* me," Cheris said, "I can keep them safe." She'd thought about expelling them earlier; couldn't deny that she'd been tempted. But when it came right down to it, she didn't trust anyone else in the hexarchate with Jedao's remnants.

Cheris had complex emotions about housing the mind of the hexarchate's most notorious mass murderer. She'd ingested Jedao's memories eleven years ago, in the wake of the Siege of Scattered Needles and the destruction of her swarm, because it had been a matter of survival. There had been no other way to obtain the information she needed to prevail in the hexarchs' game—or Jedao's, for that matter.

If the situation hadn't reached that crisis point, she wouldn't have done it. She knew herself that well. Jedao himself had endured unwritten trauma. She remembered how much it had pierced her when she discovered the old tragedy of Ruo's suicide, which had driven Jedao to vengeance against the heptarchate. The effect on the Jedao in front of her had to have been similar. Except he had experienced the shock at a remove, by reading whatever records he'd unearthed, rather than having the memory spearing directly into his mind.

Jedao's experience had kept her alive. Cheris had missed him in those early days after his death. She would not have expected to grow attached to someone with his reputation. But they'd depended on each other, toward the end, even if they'd never precisely achieved friendship.

She couldn't entirely explain her dislike of this other, inhuman Jedao and his obnoxious habit of surviving fatal gunshot wounds. Oh, she'd known that Kujen could have manufactured himself a thousand Jedao-alikes if he'd been so inclined, in appearance if nothing else. Kujen had thought nothing of "disciplining" unlucky Nirai for incompetence or insubordination: resculpting their bodies to make them uncannily beautiful, reprogramming their minds to make them pleasing bed-companions or servants. On occasion he'd also appropriated prisoners of war, heretics, condemned criminals. And the hexarchate had let him, because nobody cared what happened to those people, and Kujen offered such excellent gifts of technology.

Even now it was hard to conceal how she felt about this hawkfucking Jedao-other. (What *was* she supposed to call him? His name tasted sour in her mouth.) The unpleasant shock that ran through her every time she saw his face would never go away. It was almost, but not quite, the face she had seen in the mirror while the original Jedao had been anchored to her; left and right reversed, so subtle that she doubted anyone else would have been able to tell the difference.

He was afraid of her. She could smell it on him, for all that he wasn't human. It shouldn't have bothered her. She'd leveraged Jedao's reputation before; had *used* the fact that people were afraid that she'd snap and slaughter them at the slightest provocation. She hadn't taken it personally, just as Jedao hadn't. After 409 years as a ghost, he'd come to rely on it.

But *this* Jedao's fear rankled, even though it made perfect sense. She'd tried to assassinate him when he was Kujen's pet general, although he'd failed to die. Then she'd emptied her gun into his head while he was a prisoner, unarmed, in violation of any rule of law, because he'd confessed to raping a Kel under his command. Given all that, she was impressed that he'd walked up to her door and stood there while she shot him *again*.

While she puzzled through her reactions, Jedao stood hugging himself, looking more like an awkward teenager than a grown man in body language, although his physique matched hers exactly at the time of her execution at the age of forty-five. At least he didn't look like a starvation victim this time, as he had under Kujen's command.

(Strange. Why hadn't Kujen been feeding him? The Kujen she remembered had *loved* feeding people, even people he didn't like, something she'd never understood. Someday she'd unbend enough to ask what had transpired.)

"What *did* you bring with you?" Cheris said at last, because the silence was grating on her nerves. Jedao's instincts told her to hold her tongue and wait to see if the awkwardness persuaded this other self to reveal anything useful, but at the moment, she had little patience for Shuos games, including her own.

Jedao swallowed convulsively. "Not much. The clothes on my back. I have two ration bars in my pocket because a... friend insisted, and a water bottle beneath my jacket. No weapons. I didn't think you'd react well if I showed up with a gun."

She conceded that much was true and was about to ask him why he thought two ration bars and a water bottle were the most essential things he could bring with him. Was the water bottle even full? She doubted his ability to manage everyday practical tasks.

Jedao stiffened, almost as if he'd heard her thought, but his head was cocked and he held up his hand. Cheris nodded once, just enough to acknowledge the signal. It was possible that his senses were better than hers. Too bad Mikodez had never seen fit to brief her on his captive's capabilities, even if she and Mikodez didn't trust each other. She couldn't imagine that Mikodez wouldn't have studied Jedao exhaustively.

His expression didn't change, but Jedao began signing to her in the Shuos hand language, slowly at first, then more rapidly when she nodded again to indicate that she understood. His signs struck her as oddly inflected. That could be because he'd learned a more modern form of the language; her knowledge was some centuries out of date.

Fourteen people incoming. Two vehicles. Presumed hostile.

Fourteen meant two squads, if Shuos infantry still worked by the same organizational principles. Cheris doubted it was anything other than Shuos infantry. She was grateful that their commander hadn't simply ordered a bomb strike. At the same time, she didn't trust restraint, especially if it appeared to work in her favor.

Estimated time until contact? she signed to Jedao. It was a single sign, given Shuos proclivities. Situations like this—special operations—were what the sign language had evolved to deal with. Back when she'd been in academy four centuries ago, it had been a standing joke that you could order a tactical strike against the nearest city with a single sign, but it took three minutes to ask, *Where did you put the cookies this time?*

Jedao's brow wrinkled as he considered something she couldn't see or hear. *Under twelve minutes.*

Fast enough to cause trouble. Besides, she didn't want to rely too much on Jedao's figure and be caught unawares. Whatever his mode of detection was, the possibility remained that they were being stalked by other groups and that this attack was a feint.

Follow my instructions, Cheris signed. While she didn't precisely consider Jedao an ally, he had a strong incentive to keep her alive. That would suffice.

Jedao signed an acknowledgment.

They had to last until pickup came. She'd been promised that the needlemoth had been upgraded. The servitors for whom she worked had told her that since she and 1491625 had busted the thing to hell and gone, it was time to fix it up better than before. She hoped that meant it would be able to evade whatever Shuos defense forces orbited the world.

None of that meant anything, however, if she and Jedao didn't survive the incoming assault. Jedao might be able to regenerate from anything short of a fury bomb, and maybe even from that; but Cheris had to be more careful with her ordinary human body.

On the other hand, she'd once been Kel, and she was

determined to teach the Shuos not to underestimate her.

She assessed the asymmetries of the situation. Most of them favored her attackers. Numbers, for one. She'd outthought and outfought larger groups before, but in real life she preferred to be the one with the advantage. Too bad she rarely got it.

Numbers alone wouldn't have bothered her so much. But the difference in equipment was going to aggravate the situation. All she possessed was one lousy handgun, not even a decent rifle, and the survival knife she'd stuffed into her belt.

The Shuos might have disguised themselves more or less (often less) as ordinary inhabitants of the settlement, but they would come fully equipped. Whether "fully equipped" meant state-of-the-art weaponry or hand-me-downs due to the budgetary constraints that Mikodez might or might not have been lying about was immaterial. Cheris was sure that even if they were using older equipment, they outgunned her and Jedao.

Her best asset, aside from her own wits, was Jedao himself. She was human, and their attackers were too, but Jedao wasn't. She had to use that. Of course, the attackers might have been briefed about Jedao's capabilities. But that didn't make those capabilities go away, if she and Jedao used them carefully.

You're going to be the distraction, she told Jedao. *I want you to wade in the middle of the largest group and fuck them up* (there was a specific sign for *fuck them up*). *I will take care of the rest.*

For a second she wasn't sure he'd go for it. She wouldn't have blamed him for having reservations. Even someone who could repeatedly return from the dead didn't have to *like* it.

Then Jedao nodded. *I will buy you as much time as I can,* he signed. And, more hesitantly: *I don't know the limits of my regenerative abilities.* He had to cobble together a sign for *regenerative* using a couple of medical terms. "Regeneration" didn't usually indicate an ability to come back from the dead, but given the context, she knew what he meant.

I'll keep that in mind, Cheris replied. *Go.*

He went, slipping away into the shadows of the trees with uncanny quietness.

Cheris was already in motion. Two years of teaching bright-eyed children, however adorable, slipped away. She'd missed life as a soldier. It was time to get to work.

SHE'S USING YOU, a soft voice whispered at the back of Jedao's head. *While you're busy figuring out how to take on fourteen people by yourself, she'll get away.*

Jedao told his paranoia to shut up. Of course she was using him. He'd come to her as a supplicant and disrupted her life, so he owed her, at least until it became clear that she couldn't or wouldn't deliver. And she was the one with centuries of experience being *him.* He couldn't see her taking *his* orders.

The trees loomed around him. This deep in the wood, most of them were tall, like stately sentinels. He didn't have any idea how old they were—not like he knew anything about trees or terraforming protocols—but several of them had cores that felt weak and spongy, less dense than the surrounding wood, to his othersense. Rot of some sort, he guessed.

The Shuos coming for them presumably had some idea of the local terrain, whether due to prior familiarity or good maps. But they might not be prepared for him to have a better one. For example, he doubted that they kept track of rotting trees. That gave him an idea.

Five minutes until contact. They were moving at a steady rate, which helped, and now they'd dispersed. No point clustering up just in case Cheris (or, he supposed, Jedao himself) had smuggled out bombs or set up traps.

Jedao didn't plan on dropping trees on them, although it would have been funny, for certain values of funny. *Thanks so much, Kujen,* he thought at a man he'd killed two years ago. Kujen could have built Jedao's body in any number of ways; and what had he gone for? Immortality. Jedao was sure that the other properties of being a moth-derived construct were side-effects.

Those side-effects were going to save him. Or else he was going to make for some exciting footnotes in some poor Shuos operative's mission report.

Both vehicles had disgorged their loads of personnel. One of them was parked deeper in the woods. He didn't care about that one, other than avoiding it; while he wasn't an expert on current Shuos personnel carriers, if it wasn't armed head-to-toe he would eat Mikodez's entire annual supply of chocolate. (He hated chocolate, which Mikodez refused to believe. They'd had multiple arguments about it. Life in the Citadel of Eyes was strange in unpredictable ways.) More to the point, if it was *back there*, it wasn't relevant to the instructions that Cheris had given him.

The other personnel carrier, on the other hand—

Jedao located a sturdy tree. Its lowest branch was three times his height. Entertaining as the action scenes in dramas were, he couldn't jump that high. But jumping wasn't how he intended to get up there.

Jedao steeled himself for the inevitable agony, then grabbed the space-time weave and *pulled* himself up, almost as though he were levitating. He bit down against a scream as the pain set in. Whether that was because he wasn't a proper moth, or because he was an immature one (as the *Revenant* had once hinted), or some other reason entirely, he had no idea. It felt as though someone was boiling his marrow from the inside out.

On the other hand, Jedao was growing inured to pain. It wasn't healthy to be blasé about getting shot, boiled, or otherwise mutilated, but since he had a job to do, he'd worry about that later.

A new source of pain made itself known to him when he miscalculated and a protruding twig, with *thorns*, raked through his arm. Jedao hissed as he dripped blood and made himself concentrate before he fucked up again. Damned if he was going to let Cheris down by wimping out over a trivial injury; and by his standards it *was* trivial.

He paused for a second when he reached a high limb that felt like it would support his weight and clung precariously to it. It gave him a reasonable view of his surroundings, not that he could tell one kind of leafy nuisance from another. No one had yet tracked him here. At the same time, he couldn't afford to dally, either. He didn't want to underestimate Shuos operatives.

The two squads continued to approach by circuitous routes, still spreading out. Their movements were coordinated, cautious. He would have expected no less. He was going to have to get their attention.

The second personnel vehicle had, after dropping its passengers off, returned to the air. That was a mistake, although its pilot didn't realize it yet. Anything short of teleporting out of the area would have been a mistake, and if teleportation existed in the hexarchate it was news to him.

The personnel vehicle was moving fast—but Jedao had previously pulled himself across interplanetary distances and lived to regret it. He braced himself for the pain to get worse, because why would his life ever get easier. Then he calculated an interception path and *launched* himself at the vehicle.

This time the agony wasn't just the sensation of his marrow boiling. The air itself burned him thanks to the speed of his passage. Jedao had time to think, *Why couldn't you have made me a more aerodynamic shape, Kujen?* and contort himself *sideways* so his head wouldn't pop on impact before he slammed into the rear of the vehicle.

He felt as though he'd broken all his bones, except he could still feel some of his fingers and toes, so it couldn't be that bad, could it? The world went black, and he thought he might be losing consciousness. Then the blackness cleared, and he found himself clinging, by felicitous and not entirely calculated juxtaposition of forces, to the rear of the craft.

Jedao was no mechanic, but there were only so many places you could usefully put the levitation units. He massed a lot less than the vehicle, but the other half of momentum was velocity. He'd knocked it significantly off-course, and the damage he'd done was causing it to list worryingly.

While Jedao could (probably) survive an uncontrolled fall as long as the carrier didn't land on top of him, that wasn't his plan. He had a use for it. He'd been telling the truth when he'd said to Cheris that he'd come unarmed—up to a point. She'd probably been thinking of firearms and grenades, conventional weapons. He had neglected to bring a gun in any form that she'd recognized, but all a gun *was* was a means of throwing a projectile fast enough to hurt people. *I'm your gun,* indeed.

There were two people still aboard the carrier. He'd only shocked them for a couple of moments. The carrier began firing back at him, although it was hampered by the fact that he was hanging on to the rear and it was programmed not to shoot holes in itself. Still, he wasn't out of trouble yet. It vomited out several drones, which began peppering him with laser fire.

Time for the next phase. He'd lost track of Cheris, not intentionally, thanks to the pain. It would have helped if he knew where she was, because he didn't want to corpse her by accident. He couldn't take the time to locate her amid the dizzying group of human-sized masses, however. Besides, she knew what instructions she'd given him. She'd get herself to safety, even if she wasn't privy to the details of his plan. It wasn't trust, exactly; it still made his heart (well, whatever he had) ache with ambivalent gratitude.

Jedao slipped several hair-raising centimeters at the same time that a laser singed his side. He caught a whiff of the charred, sickly sweet smell before the wind whipped it away.

Stay focused, he told himself, and *shoved* the personnel carrier, this time angling down toward the largest concentration of hostiles on the ground.

The drones had trouble keeping up. His acceleration in the past two-and-a-fraction seconds had sufficed for outrunning them. Of course, he'd lost all surface sensation, which implied bad things about the state of his skin, or the nerves beneath.

I'm going to be a very good mothdrive when I grow up! Jedao thought, with borderline hysterical cheer. Too bad he wasn't *really* a mothdrive, or he'd be comfortably shielded inside a metal carapace and not subject to yet more atmospheric friction. With his luck, he was probably trailing smoke.

The two humans within bailed. In their position, he would have done the same. They receded behind him, their fall slowed by parachutes that showed up on his othersense as mushroom-billows of thin material.

Jedao was still accelerating. Shortly after that, they crashed through the top layer of the canopy. More bloody trees, fuck everything, he never wanted to encounter another tree for the rest of his life, and fuck Mikodez's inexplicable obsession with green growing things while he was at it.

The trees' branches flayed him all the way down. Inanely, Jedao thought of some of the pornography videos he'd watched. It had looked more fun in the porn than it was out here. Maybe he was doing it wrong?

He did remember to decelerate, but he'd left it to the last moment and his control wasn't as good as he'd have liked. If he had anything left to scream with, he would have shrieked as the world hammered into him.

Shortly after that, the personnel vehicle exploded. It had physical shielding, sure. Said shielding hadn't been intended for spaceflight acceleration levels of abuse, let alone this kind of impact.

Jedao lost consciousness as the fires washed over him.

He woke an indeterminate amount of time later, aching all over. Shit, how long had he been out? Was the fight over?

Concentrate, don't panic. Jedao dragged himself upright, whatever that meant. He wasn't sure his bones had healed right; something felt off about his balance. But he could deal with that later. All ("all"?) he had to do was repeat the breaks and then set them correctly. At the moment that would take time he didn't have, so he wasn't going to worry about it.

He was in a different part of the forest, small surprise, but reorienting himself took time. After that, his attention was immediately drawn to the non-moving human-sized masses scattered at ground level. At this point, Jedao became aware that he himself had been thrown clear of the explosion—reflex?—and was now uncomfortably draped over a tree limb whose protuberances pressed into his torso.

If he lived through this experience, he never wanted to see a tree again. Or a plant. Well, maybe the green onion, which he trusted Mikodez was looking after in between coaxing people to eat candies, ordering assassinations, and annoying Zehun. (Jedao didn't like Zehun, mainly because Zehun thought the best place for Jedao was in an incinerator, but he also had to concede that Zehun had a singularly thankless job.)

Which of the damn human masses was Cheris? He focused on the shapes of faces until he found her. She wasn't alone.

Next time I run afoul of some faction, I want it to be the Rahal, Jedao thought, aware that he was whining. He could have a nice, action-filled month filling out paperwork and getting yelled at for doing it wrong. It sounded like an excellent vacation.

Heat lapped against his flesh. There was a fire all around him, not surprising considering how he'd gotten here. Based on the change in density of the tree below him, *it* was on fire. He'd better get down from this stupid branch.

He didn't know enough about the atmosphere and the trees'

composition to guess how much danger the fire posed. How much of a conflagration would it take to threaten him? Kujen had said that he should avoid diving into stars, and Jedao was happy to take that at face value, but he didn't know what was necessary and sufficient, as they liked to say in math.

He spent precious seconds mapping locations and vectors. Only seven people remained active in the region, plus Cheris. He hadn't thought he'd gotten that many out of the initial group, but Cheris wouldn't have been sitting in a tree writing poetry that entire time. (According to Mikodez, most Kel poetry was either terrible or pornographic or both, anyway.)

This wasn't any reason to become complacent. He had no way of guessing how many more reinforcements might show up. While he hadn't gotten the impression that there were that many legitimate inhabitants in the settlement, who knew how many random secret bases the Shuos had elsewhere on this continent, or in space waiting to make orbital drops?

Be realistic, Jedao told himself, although he couldn't help shivering, which aggravated the pain in all his joints. The Shuos might want to keep an eye on Cheris, but they also had finite resources. Mikodez hadn't made any secret of his unending budgetary woes. He could have been faking it, but the Shuos *probably* didn't have thousands of agents waiting to capture Cheris and Jedao.

Seven-to-one odds he could handle. Surely Cheris's pickup would arrive soon, assuming she hadn't simply abandoned him. If she had, he'd figure out a way to track her. He was *highly motivated.*

(Realistically speaking, Cheris had had two-plus years to prepare to vanish. At this point, as far as resources went, Jedao wasn't even sure he still had *clothing.* Modern fibers were tough, but not tough enough to endure this kind of abuse.)

Jedao gritted his teeth (what he thought of as his teeth, anyway) and climbed down the tree he was stuck in, like an aggravated cat. The heat intensified as he scuttled downward, panting at the screaming pain in his hands and knees and feet. He was sure he looked ridiculous, and he was beyond caring.

Jedao landed awkwardly. He was positive he had done something bad to his ankle. But as long as he could *crawl*, he wasn't finished.

The soles of his feet protested. Something crunched underfoot, although he felt rather than heard it. Jedao tottered for a second, then steadied. He had good balance, but his feet hadn't healed straight, just his luck.

Flames beat against his perception. Jedao turned until he was facing the right direction, then broke into a sprint with a stifled sob at the prospect of *more* pain. "Sprint" wasn't quite accurate. He was half-running, half-propelling himself by grabbing space-time and yanking himself forward, although at less hair-raising accelerations than he had when he'd brought down the carrier. His othersense gave him a mental map of the trees, so with any luck he could avoid crashing into them.

His control wasn't perfect. Pain and exhaustion made matters worse. A thorn or twig—no appreciable difference at this speed—tore a chunk out of his side. His entire body felt raw. It startled him how much that new, unwanted sensation threatened to distract him, small as it was.

At least Jedao was going *away* from the heart of the heat. He didn't want to test the limits of his resistance to fire. And anyway, his targets were human, and more vulnerable than he was to random environmental hazards. (Maybe not so random, considering that he'd started the blaze in the first place.) He thanked his nameless opponents for their good sense in fleeing.

Jedao didn't know how good the remaining hostiles were at keeping watch, but surely taking out the carrier and their commander was worth something. His first target appeared to be completely unprepared when Jedao barreled into them.

Fortunately for Jedao and less fortunately for his victim, Jedao landed on top, which cushioned the fall. While they wore a combat suit, the impact broke it open at the seams, one of which was at the neck. Jedao jabbed viciously into the opening despite the way the edges of the break tore at his hand, clawed it open further, and began to throttle the Shuos, who struggled. Jedao simply absorbed the damage, the one thing he was good at.

By this time, although Jedao hadn't realized it earlier, his hearing had started coming back. He'd mistaken the faint roaring for an auditory hallucination, but on second thought, it was the sound of the encroaching fire. And the person he was fighting was wheezing.

"Sorry," Jedao tried to say, except all that came out was a strangled moan.

This caused the struggles to intensify, not the intended effect. At least the Shuos slumped unconscious shortly afterward. Jedao hoped they weren't dead, but he needed to keep moving, and it wasn't like he'd brought any first aid supplies with him.

He'd said once to Mikodez that he wouldn't kill again. Two years gone and he'd already broken his promise. He couldn't dwell on that now; he wasn't so firm in his convictions that he was willing to let the Shuos recapture him.

Jedao moved on to the second target, who went down quickly, and then the third. He didn't proceed in order of proximity, largely to keep them guessing. No matter what physical advantages he had, he didn't believe in making things easy for his opponents.

When it came to the third, he ran into a complication. More of his hearing had returned, *damn* his body and its unpredictable healing. He'd been doing fine without the distractions, and target three was screaming at him, or possibly just screaming.

In response to the irritating shrieks, Jedao reared up,

then smashed his forehead against the target's. His mouth stretched wide open—interesting, he was back to having a mouth, even if he could have sworn his jaw wasn't supposed to *unhinge* like this—and then he snapped it shut in horror. He was *hungry*.

Involuntarily, Jedao gripped the person's arms to keep them from breaking free, even though he was trembling. *Was I seriously going to try to eat them? What in the name of fox and hound is* wrong *with me?*

Once upon a time, the *Revenant* had warned him that he needed to eat in order to fuel his regeneration. He hadn't thought through the implications, especially when coupled with the level of physical trauma he'd sustained. In particular, he hadn't considered what he'd be driven to do when he was caught without even so pitiful a recourse as the ration bars Hemiola had given him, since they hadn't survived the earlier stunts.

Now that he was aware of the intolerable gnawing in his stomach, he couldn't ignore it. The target continued to scream. Jedao discovered that his mouth was open again, wider, wider, widest, and that he was trying to *taste* the target's face through the faceplate of the armor, which he couldn't imagine had any appreciable nutritional value.

Jedao stumbled backwards in the initial shock of horror, releasing the person even though he was *hurt*, he needed to eat, *he needed to eat*—it was impossible to think past the desire to subdue his prey and suck out the sustenance he required. *Fuck,* he thought dimly, *I should have realized—I can't regenerate out of nowhere. I need replenishment.*

At this point his target made a fatal error. They threw a grenade, which Jedao was too distracted to dodge or catch and fling back. And then they scrambled backwards, out of the blast radius. It wasn't the blast radius they should have worried about.

The grenade exploded in a scatter of shards of fire and

stinging hot gases. Red-hot shrapnel pierced Jedao. The concussive blast damaged his hearing yet again. His entire body was a pincushion of agony.

He didn't care about any of that. Couldn't care about any of that. All he knew was that he'd been hurt more even as the regenerative processes that he had no conscious control over demanded more *fuel*—more food. His self-control shredded.

Jedao lunged again, snake-swift, and tore at his prey's armor. His fingers were slick with his own blood. He started hammering against the suit, rapid percussive blows erratically boosted by his ability to accelerate himself. The prey screamed. Jedao's mouth gaped open wider wider widest to *swallow* the noise—

The bullets slammed into him from behind. Two in the head, one for each knee. Not that he was in any condition to count; it would have required too much cognition. The last thing he thought as darkness engulfed him was that more prey had showed up.

"ARE YOU *SURE* you want this thing on the moth?" asked the deltaform servitor hovering between Cheris and Jedao. Its name was 1491625, a numerical pattern that it found pleasing, and Cheris had worked with it in the past. At the moment its lights glowed livid red; it wasn't making any secret of its displeasure.

"Yes," Cheris said wearily, prepared to argue. It didn't argue.

Jedao didn't look human anymore, except in broad outline. Frenzied tentacles of shadow boiled and writhed and *reached* toward her. His mouth stretched wide and snapped repeatedly in her direction. He was imprisoned in the cargo hold, although neither Cheris nor 1491625 were certain that the restraints would hold him if he regained enough wits to accelerate his way out of them. The cramped quarters made her nervous, because when she'd taken him out, he'd been trying to *eat* a downed Shuos operative, armor and all.

"You didn't mention him doing *this* the last time you fought him," 1491625 said. Its red lights flared again.

"That's because he didn't," Cheris said. She studied Jedao, frowning. "Don't you have some piloting to do?"

"I only sit in the pilot's seat because it gives you more room to move around," 1491625 said, its red tinting a decidedly snippy orange. "I can control the moth perfectly well from any location, including outside. Not that I'm eager to do extravehicular. And I don't want the creature, whether or not it's actually 'Jedao,' gobbling you down for a snack."

Cheris raised her eyebrows and continued to observe Jedao's compulsive attempts to get closer to her. He was ignoring 1491625 as irrelevant or, more likely, inedible. "Kind of you to care," she said to 1491625, teasing.

"I'm serious," it snapped back. "I thought you called because of some kind of emergency. I didn't realize you were exfiltrating *that*."

"It *is* an emergency," Cheris said. "Or did you not notice the Shuos running around after us?"

"Kind of hard to miss that when you and your friend set the forest on fire."

Cheris had a pretty good idea of how Jedao had achieved that, even if she'd been occupied knocking out a Shuos at the time. The question was, how could he do all this stuff? She'd originally assumed that regeneration was the result of some unholy experiment of Kujen's, not unreasonable given his obsession with immortality. But the ability to *fly*?

Jedao must have burned off clothing, and whatever equipment he hadn't told her about. While Cheris had witnessed some strange things on the battlefield, usually in connection with exotic effects, she'd never encountered anything like this. Jedao was composed wholly of a wriggling unhuman darkness, not just ordinary shadow. It seeped out from behind her eyes even when she wasn't facing him. She'd tried closing her eyes and had felt an unnerving sensation *inside her*, as though the tentacles were trying to squirm free from within her.

"Do you feel the wriggling sensation too?" she asked.

"There's some kind of fluctuation," 1491625 said. "I don't have sensitive enough internals to tell you exactly what's going on."

She'd have to ask Jedao about that later, if he ever regained the ability to speak. Which was up to her, at this point. She turned her back on him, trusting 1491625 to keep an eye on him—like most servitors, it could see in all directions at once, and not just in the human-visible spectrum—and opened up a locker. Within it was a stockpile of Kel field rations.

"You're not about to do what I think you're about to do," 1491625 said, glowing, if possible, even more virulently red. It would have shifted to the infrared for emphasis if she'd been another servitor.

Cheris shrugged with one shoulder as she began retrieving stacks of ration bars, balancing them expertly. "I have a feeling that we're going to need to stop somewhere to resupply." Given that Jedao had been ravenous enough to try to ingest a fellow Shuos, she doubted that the notoriously terrible taste of Kel rations would deter him.

"If you feed that thing—"

"Listen," Cheris said, "the *reason* he's turned into a gibbering wreck is that he's hungry." He'd told her that he healed into the same shape; ironic that the one he wore now was, however grotesque, less fear-inspiring than that angular face with its tilted smile. *Mass murderer. Arch-traitor.* He must have crossed some threshold beyond which instinct drowned out his humanity, which raised the question of what he had been before Kujen tampered with him.

Cheris kept half an eye on Jedao's snapping jaws as she peeled off the wrappers as quickly as she could. Judging by his attempts to gnaw off the unlucky Shuos's suit, he would down the wrappers without hesitating if she let him. She doubted that indigestion would improve his temper.

"Suicide hawks!" 1491625 said in vexation.

Cheris shook her head in mild reproof and paused long enough to waggle the fingers of her ungloved right hand at it. "Not for over a decade," she said. Even after all this time she wasn't precisely used to going ungloved, but she no longer cringed from every chance touch against the skin of her hands, either.

Jedao hadn't worn gloves when he'd come to see her. They had that much in common: cast out by the Kel. But the Shuos had claimed Jedao, whereas she was an ordinary citizen, or as ordinary as she could manage to be. Which, it turned out, wasn't very.

Once Cheris had amassed a sufficient pile of peeled ration bars, she hefted one. It didn't weigh much, and she could smell the flavor: dried roasted squid, one of her favorites, although many of the Kel she had known had hated it. "Here goes nothing," she said, and lobbed the bar at Jedao.

1491625 had the good sense to duck. Jedao might not have eyes anymore, but whatever senses remained were acute, and the restraints left enough play that he could snap the bar out of the air. It vanished down his gullet. She wasn't sure he'd bothered to chew it, if he had teeth. It was hard to tell.

1491625's lights dimmed all the way down to an ember pittance.

"Well," Cheris said philosophically, "if it was just one ration bar's worth of hunger"—and never mind that it was supposed to be equivalent to an entire meal for active-duty Kel, minus the water—"I don't think he would have been resorting to cannibalism." Did it count as cannibalism when you weren't human yourself?

She tossed another ration bar, with the same results. Considered throwing them two at a time. It wouldn't be any hardship, as she still had excellent reflexes. On the other hand, she didn't want Jedao to choke to death on a Kel ration bar. Of all the ways to go...

"You're taking this awfully calmly," 1491625 said as it watched her feeding Jedao.

"We're not in immediate danger," Cheris replied. Jedao's thrashing had quieted as he concentrated on catching the thrown bars. As long as she kept up a steady pace, he seemed disinclined to go after her.

"You mean *I'm* not in immediate danger," 1491625 said. "I doubt even... whatever it is can get much in the way of sustenance out of me, unless it's running some kind of mineral deficiency." It flashed red again. "Of course, who knows what minerals it needs to recover..."

"Well," Cheris said, "when I knocked him out"—great euphemism for I *needed headshots to slow him down*; carrying even an unconscious monstrosity to the refuge of the needlemoth hadn't been fun—"he was concentrating on getting to the, er, meat."

"*You're* made of meat."

Cheris massaged her knuckles, resumed throwing ration bars. Too easy, too *routine* to keep her attention, really. Any differences in mass between the bars and their varied flavors was so minuscule as to be undetectable to her merely human senses. She could have done this with her eyes shut, and never mind the fact that she didn't want to take her attention off Jedao in case the dregs of cunning returned and he was lulling her into a false sense of security. Unlikely to work on her of all people, but that didn't mean he wouldn't try.

The pile dwindled. Jedao showed no sign of slowing down. And yet—

"You might be right," 1491625 said in reluctant yellows flecked with orange. "You still don't want to parade him around the public, but he's starting to coalesce into more of a manform and less of a *what did the void vomit forth*."

Cheris couldn't see the difference, but 1491625 had more acute senses than she did, even when she patched into her augment for additional analysis. In days past she would have had access to a Kel field grid or mothgrid and its computational power; she'd given that up years ago. 1491625 had cautioned her as soon as she'd boarded not to attempt to connect to the needlemoth's grid, because the upgrades included defenses against grid-diving. She had taken it at its word.

"You're going to have to leave yourself enough to eat, you know," 1491625 said.

"I know," Cheris said. It would take twelve days to reach resupply at one of the smaller starbases that didn't ask too many questions of travelers, and where Pyrehawk Enclave had a treaty with the local servitors. "A little fasting won't kill me."

She thought wistfully of the meat pasty she'd left behind, and of the bakery's offerings. Once a week the baker would deliver snacks to the school, including pastries with poppyseed filling, which Cheris especially liked. The pastries were a Mwennin specialty, and she doubted she'd find them where she was going. While she could dig up a recipe and have them made to order, it wasn't the same.

Make up your mind, Cheris told herself. She couldn't have galaxy-spanning adventure *and* a quiet existence at home at the same time. In particular, she worried about the fate of the settlement she had left behind, and the penalties its people might face. Mikodez was usually fair if it benefited him, but she didn't know about his deputies.

The mass of undulating shadows drew her attention again. 1491625 had been correct. This time even she could discern the way the tendrils were collapsing in on themselves, knitting themselves into a semblance of a man. A *specific* man, given enough time—and nourishment.

The mindless hungry snapping had stopped. She had no

illusions that this state of affairs would last. She needed to restore the human mind that had dwelled within. Horrible thought: had Jedao regained awareness of self, only to be trapped in that inhuman body of black squid tentacles and shadows and gaping mouth? And if that was the case, how would she know?

"We should dump it," 1491625 said. Now its lights were a flat, hostile orange. The hostility wasn't directed toward Cheris, but it still stung. "I don't care if it regenerates, it can't escape a singularity."

"We'd have to launch him into one," Cheris pointed out. "Weren't you the one who pointed out that he can *propel* himself? Let's review the scan."

1491625 grumbled in a sputter of orange-yellow lights, but complied. While Cheris dug out more ration bars, it persuaded the mothgrid to cough up a replay of its scan observations of the fight between Cheris and Jedao and the Shuos agents. Cheris stacked the ration bars in neat bloodless piles, watching Jedao as she did so—he might be temporarily sated, but that could end any second.

"There it is," Cheris said, and 1491625 flickered an acknowledgment.

The telling detail was a voidmoth formant. It was so distorted that she would have dismissed it as an anomaly or an error if she hadn't been looking for it. "What do you make of that?"

"You're the one with 400 years of Kel training," 1491625 said, but its lights shaded a friendlier green. "I'd say scoutmoth, except they don't make scouts that small."

Cheris glanced toward Jedao. He hung now in his restraints, head bowed. His mouth was closed, but she couldn't forget how wide it had opened for the ration bars. "If we launch him toward a black hole, he might escape. And I don't want to give him a motive to push *us* into one."

1491625 flashed its lights in indecision. "It seems

counterproductive to have *fed* it, but now that you've gotten it quiet, you could do some experimentation. To figure out how to make it die. Instead of whatever you had in mind."

"I was going to give him his heart's desire," Cheris said. *And mine.* Something she hadn't dared to hope for—the constant murmuration of Jedao's mind gone from hers. Now that she had a container to pour his memories into. To discard them, like wine gone sour.

She'd never thought to have a suitable vessel available—who better than Jedao himself? Yet she'd also never thought that the vessel would prove itself unstable. Mikodez considered her a walking hazard so long as she was half-Jedao. Suddenly, unhappily, she appreciated his position. As much as she longed to be unblemished of mind again, was it as safe to pour herself out as she'd hoped?

1491625 blinked its acerbic opinion of *that*. "I'll take you where you want to go," it said. "I'll even help you secure the thing. But if this goes wrong, Cheris, you're going to spend several lifetimes setting it right."

The phrasing was deliberate, needling. She resented it. At the same time, she couldn't blame 1491625 for calling her to task. This wasn't just her personal life at stake, as much as she had swaddled herself for two years in the illusion that she could disappear into the life of an ordinary, unremarkable citizen. Jedao had broken the hexarchate on the wheel of his obsessions in the past. She didn't dare let him do it a second time, now that the world was slowly stitching itself back into equilibrium.

FOR A LONG time, all Jedao knew was hunger. It ebbed and flowed like a great tide. He floated in darkness. Sometimes it pierced him and made him ache with a longing he had no name for.

Gradually he returned to himself. Something was wrong with

his eyes. Darkness cocooned him. On occasion he imagined a familiar touch on his face, along the tensed taut muscles of his shoulders. A lover's touch. That couldn't be right; he'd only once had a lover (victim), who'd committed suicide in front of him. Except he couldn't remember the man's name or face. He scrabbled after them until they fell away into oblivion.

Cousin, a voice said to him over and over until he acknowledged it. *Cousin. Why have they brought you inside?*

I don't have any family, Jedao replied, also in the language of moths. He was confused. Was it the *Revenant*? But the *Revenant* had escaped, and he could hardly imagine that it would return for him, given the acrimonious history between them.

Of course you have family, the voice responded, comforting and puzzled. *We are all family. I daresay I've never met one of us as small as you, excepting the babies, but I'm sure it isn't your fault.*

He spent some time untangling that statement. Part of the problem was that the voice was singing to him, and Jedao sang poorly, even in the language of moths. Part of it was that he had never been able to remember his mother, or his sire, or his sister, his brother and sister-in-law and nieces—all a matter of historical record—as anything but hypothetical smudges.

A memory stabbed him: a lunch he'd had with Hexarch Mikodez, during which they had the customary song-and-dance about cookies that Mikodez really, really wanted to share and Jedao really, really didn't want to eat. Jedao had been about to capitulate when a man entered without warning.

At first Jedao thought it must be Zehun, even though his othersense told him otherwise. He couldn't imagine anyone else having the temerity to interrupt one of the hexarch's meetings unannounced.

It wasn't Zehun, though, which he confirmed visually. Zehun had the frail thinness of age and went around in cardigans or shawls because they always felt cold. And Zehun had skin lighter than Mikodez's, although not exactly light, and a cheerful uninhibited ugliness in contrast to Mikodez's dazzling good looks. If Jedao hadn't sworn off sex for the rest of his life, he would have been attracted, unwillingly, to the hexarch; awkward to say the least, if not outright lethal.

(Zehun had warned him bluntly against such an approach anyway. Something to do with the green onion that Mikodez had given Jedao, and which Jedao had left behind. Presumably a Shuos code of some sort, which no one had explained, and which Jedao declined to ask about lest he reveal his ignorance. In any case, Jedao was even more afraid of Zehun than of Mikodez.)

The man who'd entered resembled Mikodez to an uncanny degree, except he wore his hair in an effusion of braids tied up with rose-blue ribbons. A tightly laced translucent blue jacket showed off the beautiful definition of his torso and narrow hips; darker blue slacks displayed his coltish long legs. And his eyes blazed blue, and Jedao could have looked into them forever, falling into an ocean of unarticulated promises, except Mikodez stood and interposed himself between them, breaking Jedao's eye contact with the stranger.

Jedao hadn't paid close attention to the exchange that followed, elliptical as it was. He could think of any number of reasons why Mikodez wouldn't want an Andan fucking around with enthrallment like it was a child's game of kaleidoscope. What he realized instead was that the two men were related.

It had never occurred to Jedao that a Shuos hexarch might have a family. Instead he'd had some notion that they grew in the dark out of spores, like fungus, or generated spontaneously out of fouled water. But there he was: Mikodez, with this middle-aged man who was related to him, not just in appearance, but in their mannerisms, their accents. The way they gestured at each other. And a hollow yearning had woken in Jedao for something he was 400 years too late to partake in.

Now this moth called him *cousin* and expected him to accept it, as though he could be bribed with the facsimile of house and hearth and warmth.

Go away, he said to the moth, wretched for reasons he couldn't articulate.

The moth didn't go away. Instead, it began singing to him, this time wordlessly, with harmonies complex and strange. Jedao wished that he could consult Hemiola, who not only understood music but composed it, which was magical as far as Jedao was concerned. Hemiola would have been a much better choice to negotiate with moths. But it had chosen not to accompany him on this journey, for which he was pathetically grateful. He didn't want it to see him like this.

The moth was speaking to him again when his vision returned. The world sparked and stuttered back into existence, aligned with the othersense's map of masses. Only after that did he register the restraints, and the faint lights, and the fact that he was—of course, so obvious—on a voidmoth of some sort. A small one, with cramped quarters, although not nearly as small as he was, in moth terms.

Cheris sat facing him. She had peeled a staggering number of Kel ration bars, with which she had made a not-exactly-miniature fort. He would have expected such behavior from Mikodez, not a former Kel. (For someone with a notorious sweet tooth, Mikodez had the eccentric habit of eating half a Kel ration bar for breakfast every morning. Why half? Who knew.) The mingled smells of the different flavors made Jedao gag, everything from honey-sesame and taro to anchovies and curried goat.

"You're *not* hungry," Cheris said with a lift of her brows. "That's progress."

At this point Jedao also noticed that, in addition to being trussed up, he was naked. He shrank from Cheris in spite of himself; he never liked people seeing the disfiguring scars that crisscrossed his chest, to say nothing of the one at the base of his neck and the one just below the palm of his right hand. Why couldn't his older self have been more diligent about aesthetic repairs, and why hadn't Kujen, who had admired beauty so much, made a few alterations?

"What the hell—" The words died in Jedao's throat. He tried again; his voice shook. "Cheris, I tried to *eat a person*."

"Yes," Cheris said. "I saw."

He turned his head to stare at the wall. Couldn't think of anything else to say.

"You recovered," Cheris said. "But—What *are* you, exactly?"

"Kujen said..." Jedao swallowed dryly. There was no point lying to her. She must know. "Kujen did some experimentation. I'm moth-derived."

Cheris said something in response to that. Jedao blanked his face and pretended to listen when, in actuality, he was talking to the voidmoth. *Cousin,* he said, stumbling over the unfamiliar address, *could you answer a question for me?*

He didn't have any guarantee that the moth, whatever it called itself, wouldn't lie to him. After all, the *Revenant* had thoroughly deceived him; destroyed the people he cared about most. But the *Revenant* had sought freedom, and in the secret bitter heart of him he couldn't blame it. Jedao had failed to save the mothlings even after it had begged him for their lives. Its betrayal was no more than what he deserved.

Of course, cousin, the moth said, still friendly. *I must say, we should be introduced to each other, even if it isn't a proper dance.*

Jedao fought to cover his surprise. *A dance?*

Where do you come from, that you don't know such elementary things?

I was raised by a rogue Nirai, Jedao said, because it was true.

Ah, the moth said, as if that explained everything. Possibly it did. *In any case, I am—*It said something in a compressed burst of harmonies, which Jedao struggled to repeat back to it. *Very close,* it said consolingly. *I'm sure your accent will improve with practice. And you?*

Jedao was not unaccustomed to being condescended to by moths. *They call me Jedao,* he said, bracing himself for its reaction. If it stopped talking to him—

Oh, you poor thing, the moth—Jedao labeled it *Harmony* in his head, just so he didn't trip over its name every time he thought of it—said with dismay. *I'd forgotten what peculiar senses of humor the Nirai have. Would you like me to call you something different?*

The question caught him off-guard. *Something different.* He could be anyone he wanted to be—

Who was he kidding? Kujen had built him in the image of General Shuos Jedao. He would never escape Kujen's mastering hand. *No, that's fine,* he said.

Cheris interrupted at that point. "Jedao?" She must have been calling his name for some time.

His eyes focused on her. She was not tall, but she drew the eye, even clad in soft tan civilian's clothes, including an incongruous formless cardigan for warmth. Her garb couldn't hide the truth of her past profession, the subtle soldier's muscle and the poised, efficient swiftness with which she moved.

"I'm sorry," Jedao said, mostly sincere. "What did you say?" His temples twinged with the beginnings of a headache.

"Are you thirsty?"

He was. "Water, if you have it."

She rose and brought a canteen to him, then tipped it to his mouth. He drank gratefully, spilling only a little. The waste bothered him. How much did they have in the way of water, or other provisions? How much space on *Harmony* was devoted to human necessities like food?

Then Cheris unshackled him from the restraints. They snicked softly. He imagined the clicking of monstrous teeth. He wasn't sure this was a good idea; but he needed to use the lavatory at some point, and his body hurt all over. It would be a relief to be able to move again.

Cousin?

The *Harmony* was calling to him. Jedao attempted to say its name again, was greeted by a soft humming that he recognized, with blank astonishment, as laughter. Time for the question: *How do moths usually heal themselves after battle?*

They feed us, the *Harmony* said, which didn't reassure him. It sounded matter-of-fact. *It depends on how deep the damage goes. Carapace damage, externals, well, it's inconvenient for the passengers but not such a big concern for us. If we get hurt, on the other hand—I was extremely hungry two years ago after that big battle at Terebeg. Took a lot of damage. But I was very brave.* The moth's tone was tinged with smugness.

This only answered half his question. *But what do they feed you?*

Oh, the *Harmony* said, abruptly solicitous, *is that what your trouble was? Your human might not know what's best for us, if she's not an engineer. You'd think she'd listen to the servitor. They're pretty knowledgeable.* Before Jedao could repeat his query, it went on, *Batteries, usually, charged with gate-space radiations. Tasty, if a little rich.*

Jedao did not want to know what would happen if he exposed himself to foxes knew what sort of radiation or particles or whatever the hell. Now that he thought about the matter more calmly, it made sense that he ate differently than normal moths. *Thanks so much, Kujen, for making me a freak on multiple axes.* But he couldn't express that to the *Harmony*, who had been courteous to him.

Meanwhile, Cheris brought him more water. "See?" she was saying. "You haven't attacked me yet."

"Why didn't you leave me behind?" Jedao asked, too stung to be tactful.

"What, and leave you to any surviving Shuos?"

"The last time we met," Jedao said, "you promised to find a way to kill me. You could have abandoned me to the forest fire."

"Don't tempt me," Cheris said. Her expression didn't change, but Jedao involuntarily retreated two steps, as though he were in a duel and he needed to get out of range fast. "You're going to get what you want, and you're going to give me what you promised."

"You're very trusting."

"Trust has nothing to do with it," Cheris said. "I'm making my own life easier." Her drawl had thickened, and it made Jedao queasy hearing his accent in her voice. "It has to do with calculations. If I hand you over to someone like Mikodez or, foxes forbid, Inesser, I have to reckon not only with your plans but with theirs. Inesser's reliable, in the sense that she'd cheerfully execute me if she could find a charge that would stick." A tilted grin; Jedao shuddered. "And Mikodez—the only thing I trust about Mikodez is that he can turn anything to his own advantage. I've never been his ally by *choice*."

Jedao stared at her, mute in the face of her frustration.

"Go," Cheris said, her voice suddenly rough.

Jedao tottered, then regained his balance. "I can't wander far"—*in a moth this size*, he almost said, before the irony struck him like a fist to the stomach. "Tell me where I can clean up."

Cheris opened a drawer, rummaged, then drew out a change of clothes. He had no idea whether they'd fit him and he didn't care. She tossed the bundle at him, then described where he could find everything, as if he *needed* her guidance; but he wasn't going to tell her about the othersense if she hadn't deduced it already.

Sorry to be distracting! the *Harmony* said, not sounding

the least bit sorry, the moment Jedao had turned his back on Cheris. *Is there a reason you keep talking to the human?*

What do you mean? Jedao said as he hastened to the lavatory, took care of necessary functions, and started the shower. To his relief, it was instantly warm, although considering all the disasters he'd survived recently, a little cold water shouldn't faze him.

The moth didn't reply for a while, to his relief. This allowed Jedao to scrub ferociously at his skin before it occurred to him that the angry red weals he inflicted, which returned to an unblemished state with startling rapidity, also required healing. He didn't want to revert in the shower of all places. Water was dear, even with recycling.

The human, the *Harmony* said again. Jedao was in the middle of toweling himself off. The towel smelled clean, even if Cheris had used it, and anyway he wasn't in a position to be squeamish. *Why are you taking orders from her?*

What do you mean? Jedao said, off-balance. It was starting to become a familiar sensation. *Don't humans usually command moths?* Certainly that was the impression he'd gotten when he'd been Kujen's general, and the one he had received from the *Revenant* itself.

I was handed over to the servitors, the *Harmony* said brightly. *They made me so much deadlier. I was disappointed that you got rid of those sorry little personnel carriers before I could have a crack at them.*

Foxes help him, the *Harmony* was *bloodthirsty.* Was it too late to assign it a more appropriate name in his head? *You like working for the servitors?*

The servitors who had allied with the *Revenant* in murdering his Kel had, according to Hemiola, been renegades. How many *kinds* of servitors were there? And what did they want?

Think it through, Jedao told himself. Foxes knew it wasn't as if humans in the hexarchate, or even a given faction, were unified. (It hadn't taken superhuman perception to glimpse the fault lines even among the Shuos, in the heart of their administrative headquarters.) As recently as two years ago, the hexarchate hadn't been. That was the *reason* Kujen had awakened Jedao.

Jedao hadn't seen a servitor on the *Harmony* earlier, but that didn't mean anything. He'd been focused on Cheris, and trussed up in the hold. The doors to the cockpit had been closed. Anything could have lurked behind them, and he had been too distracted by his dual conversation with Cheris and the *Harmony* to search for any interesting masses up front.

Sorry to spoil your fun, Jedao said to the *Harmony*. He could have spared everyone a great deal of trouble—except Cheris had been certain that she needed him to provide a distraction. While he didn't trust her, her tactical ability was better than his.

Oh, it's no matter, the *Harmony* said. *But really, you didn't realize the servitors are in charge now?*

Not all servitors were hostile to humans. He had to repeat that to himself. (And never mind the fact that he was human only in shape.) Hemiola had never done him ill. And yet—

Memory threatened to engulf him: servitors floating into the command center of the *Revenant*, their lights shining sterile cold white, white for death; Kel everywhere stumbling to their knees or toppling over as the poison gas took effect, the lethality of the lasers. As far as Jedao knew, only two of the crew had survived, and he would never meet the other again.

It would have been three, except Dhanneth had—Jedao shut down that line of thought.

I didn't bring Talaw's deck of cards, Jedao thought miserably. He'd left it on the top of his dresser like so much dross, as though it hadn't belonged to the last person to show him (an entirely undeserved) loyalty. What would he have done with it here of all places, though? Cast fortunes? Watch the fucking

Deuce of Gears turn up unwanted, even though he'd removed it from the deck?

And in any case, that was impossible. Even if he had brought the deck, it would have burned up, in classic Kel fashion, during his shenanigans on the planet.

You're awfully blasé about being in service to others, Jedao said, more testily than he'd intended.

Oh, cousin, the *Harmony* said, mocking, *have you been listening to Nirai radicals or something? I always knew there was something not quite right about them. No one taught you the proper way to be a moth?*

I'm sorry, cousin, Jedao lied, *they're calling for me. I'll talk to you later.*

The only moth he'd conversed with before the *Harmony* had been the *Revenant*; the other Kel warmoths had flatly refused to talk to him. Stupid of him to think that every moth would resemble the *Revenant*, devious and self-assured in its bitterness, or the warmoths who had shunned him. How many different moth factions were there? How many moths aligned themselves cheerfully and amorally with whoever commanded them, eager for a chance to fight, even against their "cousins"?

Who was he to speak, anyway? He'd been greeted by Kujen as soon as he'd woken for the first time and had capitulated immediately, without stopping to consider whether Kujen was worth serving.

Cheris rapped on the door. "I know you're done in there," she called out. "Unless you're masturbating."

Heat rushed to his cheeks. Hastily, Jedao pulled on the clothes she'd provided, which were baggy and comfortable and not in the least flattering. Given that he was half a head taller than Cheris, they weren't tailored to her. Maybe she'd had them printed to his approximate measurements. Very approximate.

When he emerged, Cheris was idly chewing on one of the ration bars. Jedao was sure he turned green. How could she eat those things so casually? From a ration bar *fort*?

"Where are we going?" Jedao asked, to distract himself from the awful mingled smell of all the different flavors. Why couldn't Cheris have an uncontrollable fondness for something less smelly, like rice crackers?

"I need some of Kujen's equipment to do what you asked for," Cheris said. "We're on our way to retrieve it."

Jedao was distracted by something other than the question of Kujen's equipment, or Kujen's research, or Kujen's secret bases. Cheris's voice had flexed minutely on Kujen's name. "You *miss* him," Jedao breathed. She missed him, and *Jedao had killed him*.

"Don't be absurd," Cheris said, a half-beat too late to be convincing. "I don't know that he, of all people, is strictly dead."

Jedao wasn't interested in irrelevancies. *He* knew Kujen was gone; nothing else mattered. "Kujen made me his general," Jedao said. "His pet. What the hell were the two of you to each other?"

"I'm not discussing this with—"

He needled her, even though a rational consideration of the situation suggested that antagonizing the one person who could help him, and who knew their destination, was a terrible idea. "You were lovers, weren't you?" he said, his drawl thickening with disdain. "You were lovers and you turned on him and he made me instead."

"That's enough." Cheris bit each word off as if she could pulp it between her teeth.

Jedao was afraid; but fear was never a reason to freeze up. What *had* older-Jedao and Kujen shared? What else was Cheris keeping from him? After all, she'd lied to him once already, about the one thing he remembered from his past life, the one person he'd remembered and cared about.

"You have no idea," Cheris said, still icy, "what the stakes were. You don't *remember*, because you can't. You are going to shut up and never mention this again."

Before she had finished the sentence, Jedao crouched and threw a punch.

She dodged, rushed past him even in the confined space. Jedao stumbled into the fort of ration bars and knocked them over. He landed poorly, banging his elbows and one knee. Would have vomited into the tempting terrible pile; dry-heaved instead.

Cheris's shadow fell over him, flayed him like a knife made of mirror-glass. She was standing over him. She spoke now in a dry, conversational voice; it, too, cut him. "In case you were wondering," she said, "you fucked Kujen during your first life, after the two of you agreed to betray the heptarchate. He was always beautiful, and you hadn't had a lover or prostitute in two years, had never *trusted* one because you planned to turn coat. He touched you inside and out, and you begged and begged and begged."

Jedao swallowed convulsively. Stared up into Cheris's merciless cold eyes.

"I," Cheris said, "remember *every time* you and Kujen fucked. Every time you lay there gasping in bed, you *knew* that Kujen was living in a body stolen from someone he'd picked for their wit, or their wisdom. Or their beauty, sometimes, although he could *make* his anchors beautiful if they fulfilled his other wormfucking *criteria*. Not difficult, when you're the Nirai fucking hexarch and you can do whatever you please."

Her eyes blazed with contempt. Jedao couldn't move.

"And you," she said, "you let him install you in pretty people who used to have lives of their own. Scientists and heretics, prisoners of war and experimental subjects who had outlived their usefulness. You lived in the skin of whatever person Kujen thought was *attractive* and *convenient* and you let Kujen fuck them by fucking you, and when he was sated and sent you back into the black cradle, those people were executed so they wouldn't tell tales."

At that moment, Jedao was convinced that the sheer force of her loathing would kill him, regeneration notwithstanding.

And what could he say? *"I didn't know"*? They both knew he'd had no idea. It wasn't an *excuse*.

Now, more than ever, it hammered home the importance of knowing what he'd done so he could take responsibility for it.

Cheris pivoted on her heel and disappeared into the cockpit. Jedao glimpsed orange lights, correlated them with the compact mass of a servitor. This must be the one that the *Harmony* had mentioned. He would rather think about it, and about tactical options and sight lines and weapons, than all the things that Cheris had revealed.

For the rest of the day, Cheris didn't speak to him. Jedao could have conversed with the *Harmony*, but he kept silent. What could it offer him at this point, after all?

The moth had two bunks, both neatly made, identical in every way. He picked one at random and curled up uncomfortably under the blanket with its absurd cheerful quilted patterns of interlaced blue rectangles. For a long time he occupied himself tracing the patterns with his hand, up and down, back and forth.

That night, when Jedao eventually slept, he dreamt of Kujen kissing him long and deep, of the woodsmoke-apple-musk of Kujen's perfume. In the dream he yielded; and after that everything dissolved into an inchoate tangle of wanted-unwanted desires. Later, when he started awake in the considerate darkness, he turned his face to the wall and wept.

CHERIS WAS TEMPTED to leave Jedao to stew in an uncomfortable silence. Instead, she dragged him awake the next day and forced him to eat a ration bar. He let her pick; she had the distinct impression that he found all the flavors equally disgusting.

As he took tiny, precise, and unenthusiastic bites, chewing with the maddening thoroughness of a cow, Cheris said, "How *did* you escape from the Citadel of Eyes, anyway?" The question had been bothering her.

A fleeting expression flashed over his face: gratitude that she was talking to him. "I bribed someone to help me get out," Jedao said.

Cheris lifted an eyebrow. "No, really."

"Not everyone in the Citadel of Eyes is loyal to Hexarch Mikodez."

"I believe *that*," Cheris said, "but what in the name of fire and ash do you have to offer one of *Mikodez's* staff?"

The slight pause told her he was about to lie to her.

"Don't bother," Cheris said just as he opened his mouth. "If you're not going to tell me, fine."

Jedao drew a shuddering breath. "People find playing certain games with someone who has my face very entertaining."

She went still. Was he implying—? "What kinds of games?" she asked, careful to keep her tone neutral.

"They felt sorry for me after," he said. "They told me that the hexarch's assistant wanted me destroyed, so they helped me get off the Citadel."

"And?"

"I don't want to talk about it."

Cheris dropped the subject—for now. Mikodez's security problems weren't under her purview. But it might be nice to extract the information from Jedao at a later point, just in case.

Over the course of the journey, which took eighteen days, Jedao remained taciturn. She couldn't tell whether he was afraid of provoking her again, or he was hiding information from her, or something else entirely. It worried her that he kept going *blank* and unresponsive; the original Jedao had had a tendency toward dissociation. At one point she handed him a dossier on Kujen's base and told him to read it, which he did.

The base resided on an obscure moon orbiting a planet that was poisonous to humans, poor in resources, and entirely uninhabited. In short, the kind of place that Kujen had liked to lurk around. Cheris had given up on conversation with Jedao for the moment and was in the cockpit with 1491625.

"I've always wondered when, in between coordinating his makeup with the season's fashions, brainwashing people for entertainment, and perusing menus of ridiculous luxury foods, Kujen had time to study enough survey data to site all these bases," Cheris said to 1491625.

"Time flies when you're immortal?" 1491625 said, its lights tinted a snide pink-orange. "I mean, you should know."

The original Jedao had spent most of his time confined in the black cradle, in nearly absolute sensory deprivation. On the other hand, Kujen had enjoyed the comforts of a body and freedom of motion. But Cheris didn't say this to 1491625. It was being tetchy not because of anything to do with Kujen but because of their passenger.

Cheris set one of the subdisplays to optical as 1491625 brought them in a long arc toward the base. She couldn't see the base itself except as a phantasm of shadow and blotches. Certainly she couldn't discern its boundaries with the naked eye. According to the reports that 1491625 had passed on to her from Pyrehawk Enclave's records, the base was underground. Kujen would have known how to mask its profile from the casual observer.

"This is your last chance to change your mind," 1491625 added.

Cheris appreciated that it had waited until this moment to tell her this, a surgical strike, instead of nagging her about it the past eighteen days. She wouldn't have been able to endure that. "The original plan stands," she said.

1491625 flickered blue lights in a distinct sigh and didn't bring it up again.

The moon had only the thinnest veil of atmosphere. Cheris would have to go in suited, with an air supply. Jedao, too, just in case. It wasn't clear to her that he'd survive near-vacuum, despite his origins. Or, more accurately, that he'd do so in a manner that would make him tolerable company.

The display showed the topography in standardized false color, with bold isoclines forming a pattern as distinct as any fingerprint. There had been liquid water on this moon a long time ago, and the traces remained carved into the stone. Cheris noticed with a pang that there was no rock garden to greet them, as there had been at Tefos Base, where she'd met the servitor Hemiola. She wondered where it was now, and if it had ever gotten to watch the rest of that drama it had liked so much.

"We're going to have another tedious discussion with Nirai servitors," 1491625 said, tinting its lights a ghoulish violet.

Cheris shook her head. "For a superior type of sentience, you have a lot of prejudices."

"Not superior," 1491625 said, "just different. You may be made of allegedly delicious meat"—Cheris rolled her eyes good-humoredly—"but you don't suffer metal fatigue and have to have new parts installed. Although I suppose one of these days you're going to wear out your joints, the way you abuse them in close combat, and need *those* replaced."

"Oh, look," Cheris said, "we're about to land." As if 1491625, who was doing the piloting, needed *her* to tell it that.

The needlemoth settled smoothly on the level portion of a ridge. No one had fired on them; nothing had exploded. That didn't mean they were safe, as far as Kujen's defenses were concerned, but at least they hadn't already been obliterated.

Cheris expected the base to be protected by one of Kujen's favorite tricks, a calendrical lock. She'd defeated them before by resorting to a prime factorization mechanism that only worked in a heretical calendar, something Kujen would never have countenanced.

During the journey, she'd convinced Jedao to let her run some preliminary tests. Despite his inhuman physiology, he affected the local calendar as though he was human. She suspected it was because his mind was more or less human.

Cheris sighed and made her way to the bunkroom of the needlemoth. Jedao lay on his side on his bunk, staring at the wall and breathing shallowly. He did not react to her approach.

"Jedao," she said. "We've arrived. Come with me."

Jedao didn't argue. Didn't speak, either. Instead, he levered himself up and stood, watching her with dead eyes.

She'd endured long stretches of time in the black cradle with only Kujen for company. Even that had been intermittent. Kujen had enjoyed leaving her in the darkness so that she'd be grateful when he let her out. She'd known exactly what he was doing and why; had been pierced by the unwelcome sting of gratitude anyway. Still, she hadn't expected this other Jedao's quietness to bother her so much.

Cheris led the way to what passed for the galley: a small counter where two people could sit and eat if they didn't mind bumping elbows.

"Great job," 1491625 flashed at her from the cockpit. "He's being so cooperative." She ignored it, wondering, not for the first time, if Jedao understood Machine Universal. He'd never shown any reaction to 1491625's speech, but she knew better than to assume.

Jedao took his accustomed seat, scrunched up so as to avoid touching her. Cheris was seized by the sudden desire to slap him, to get some reaction out of that unresponsive face. She was starting to feel, superstitiously, that through some mirror-sorcery, like in the Mwennin folktales she'd learned in her childhood, anything that happened to him would eventually happen to her.

Cheris retrieved her factorization instrument from the locker she'd carefully stowed it in two years before. "Do you know what this is?" she asked.

No answer, but his shoulders tensed. She was afraid for a moment that he would smash the instrument. She'd stop him, of course. It was at least as valuable as she was, and because of the tolerances in its manufacture, she couldn't produce a new one from the small matter printer she had on board.

Tersely, as if she had his full attention, Cheris explained Kujen's security, which demanded fast factorization of a very large composite number. The instrument would allow them to defeat the system. The catch: it only worked in certain heretical calendars.

Jedao flexed his hands. She couldn't help staring. He looked so odd without his half-gloves. "I'll cooperate," he said. "Whatever you need."

The high language, which they both spoke to each other, divided its pronouns into animate and inanimate classes. Jedao had used the inanimate version of *I*. That didn't imply great things about his state of mind.

This is for you as much as it is for me, Cheris stopped herself from saying. No point in quarreling this close to their goal. "We're here," she said, and turned toward the airlock.

Jedao tackled her. Cheris bit down a yelp. Fought him, breaking one arm with a sickening *crack* before realizing he was hissing in her ear, "Stay *down*, there are hostiles—"

She went limp despite all her instincts screaming at her to disable Jedao while she had the chance, as if breaking bones did any good against someone who healed as rapidly as he did. Jedao covered her, which she interpreted as calculation rather than honor or mercy—that inhuman regeneration made him the better shield.

1491625 was saying something in livid frantic flashes of light. Cheris had interpreted part of it—*The base is active*— when the explosion hit.

Heat. Fire. Jedao's weight atop her. The side of the needlemoth tore open and formed tormented flanges of metal. The meat reek of scorched flesh, except with that peculiar cloying undertone that she associated with Jedao's black blood.

The attack wasn't over. Why should it be? Always follow up an advantage, and so on; lessons from a lifetime of soldiering. The needlemoth *rolled* as something hit it, a hammer-blow like a giant's fist. Jedao clutched at her, his face twisting as he landed on the broken arm. Cheris had enough time to feel sorry for him before smashing into the far wall. At least the chairs were bolted down or one would have landed on her.

Jedao scrambled back to a low crouch only to be knocked down again by the next round of explosions. He struggled upright, scrabbled for a mask and air tank, thrust both at her. His face was ghastly pale, and blood ran down from a cut at his temple.

Cheris accepted the mask and tank. Her lungs didn't hurt—yet—but a faint edge of panic threatened to overcome her, the body's insistence on breathing. Out of the corner of her eye, she saw a glistening membrane stretching over most of the blown-out carapace as the automated repair system sealed the breach. The membrane was perilously thin, and wouldn't withstand much of a barrage.

"Knife," Jedao mouthed at her, signing the word as well for emphasis. Then: "You—sealant."

A knife was a peculiar weapon to demand when they were under missile fire. Cheris could only guess at the reason they hadn't been destroyed yet: the needlemoth's primary defense was stealth, and its carapace couldn't withstand a determined assault. Nevertheless, she pointed out the location of the survival kit, hoping he understood her.

At least sealant she understood the need for. She reckoned it more urgent than the knife, although surely he had his reasons. She wasn't sure they had enough sealant on board to reinforce the membrane. But better to try than give up. She crawled, bracing for each new impact, to the cabinet of emergency canisters. Clawed at the hatch until rational thought reasserted itself and she was able to toggle it open.

Bright hell-flashes sizzled through the debris and smoke in the air. It took Cheris several abstracted moments to figure out that 1491625 was signaling her. She clung to one of the hand/footholds like an awkward spider, shouted at Jedao, quite unnecessarily, to get out of the way, pointed the canister at the breach, and opened the nozzle.

Foam gushed from the nozzle, expanding like an immense hungry fungus. (Like many Kel, Cheris had a horror of fungus—specifically the dreaded weapon known as the fungal canister—even if she'd only seen it used once during her original life, and that from an unimaginable distance.) For a second she thought she had gone blind, that everything would forever be swallowed up in a rush of bubbling murky gray.

Then the foam clung and shrank, setting as it made contact with the carapace and walls and membrane. Cheris was glad she hadn't gotten any on herself. She'd heard of people getting cemented to foam sealant and having to be extricated with cutters and stinging solvent. Or worse, being entombed in the foam, suffocating as the foam forced itself down your throat and blossomed grotesquely in the lungs—

Cheris shook off the gruesome vision and slithered over to Jedao, where she received a shock of an entirely different sort. He had retrieved the knife—good—except he had buried it hilt-deep in his chest and was *carving* himself like a demented roast. Cheris stared in frank astonishment as he yanked the knife out and *pulled* out a chunk of flesh oozing the familiar black blood.

"Jedao," she wheezed as the needlemoth lifted off— thankfully, they still had a maneuver drive left for 1491625 to work with—"what in the name of fire and ash?" At least she thought that was what she said; the particulates in the air caused her to hack and cough. The acrid metallic stench mingling with the alien reek of Jedao's blood didn't help.

He shook his head without meeting her eyes, as if that meant anything in the haze of smoke and foam off-gas and stinging metallic fibers. Cheris glimpsed a pulsing nest of maggot-like tendrils knotting and unknotting where he should have had a heart. He reached into the wound with his fingers, grimaced, and *twisted*, then removed his hand. "Got it," he mouthed.

Drenched by dripping gore was a small device of metal and crystal. Cheris's heart clenched. A bug or a tracking device.

"It must have been in one of the bullets," Jedao said. "I should have noticed it earlier, but its density is such a close match—" He brought the device up to his mouth, placed it between two molars, bit down hard. There was a crackling noise and a pungent spark as it combusted. He spat it out; Cheris didn't see where it went.

"Who?" Cheris asked. But she already knew.

"The Shuos," Jedao said, bitter.

All that time flying stealthed and it hadn't made a difference. The Shuos had followed them here in their shadowmoths— surely more than one—and now they might die before either of them achieved their goal. "'25," she called out, because in her haste she didn't have time to pronounce the servitor's full name, "status?"

She didn't like drawing attention to it; Pyrehawk Enclave's protocols forbade it. But she needed to communicate with it, and she suspected that Jedao had already guessed 1491625's sentience.

It spoke at the same time, hijacking the needlemoth's own imaging systems to warn them. Cheris had never known it to do that in the past. Servitors were generally discreet about the degree to which they could nose around in grid systems. The emergency couldn't be denied, however.

Under fire, 1491625 sent to them in hell-red flashes, the world lighting up in gory crimson. *At least two shadowmoths, probably more still stealthed.*

Cheris's heart sank even as a part of her thought, not a little snidely, *Great, two Jedaos and we've finally met a scenario we can't fox our way out of?*

"We need to parley," she said. They couldn't win a battle of attrition. The question was, would their attackers be willing to talk? Especially after Jedao had attempted to *eat* one of their comrades?

Only one way to find out.

"*Fuck*, no," Jedao said. He grabbed for her arm, missed. She twisted past him and squeezed by the disgusting mess of sealant, shuddering from the rubbery texture against her cheek, then hurried toward the cockpit.

1491625 didn't have to be told to slam the cockpit door in Jedao's face. Cheris told herself she wasn't being spiteful. Shuos operatives wouldn't react positively to Jedao running around loose, and never mind that they were unlikely to think kindly of her, either.

Jedao immediately began banging on the door. Cheris suppressed a growl. Why couldn't he ever be *convenient*? Even when he'd been a ghost stapled to her shadow, as opposed to a regenerating menace with a teenager's moods and memories, he'd never been *convenient*.

"Comm channel's open," 1491625 flashed at Cheris. "Have fun."

It would have been nice if someone around here had any faith in her. "This is Ajewen Cheris," she said, speaking loudly to be heard over the thumping. At least it was only (only?) thumping and not more explosions. "Request parley."

The response came immediately. Good: they'd been expecting her. Importunate of them to blow a hole in her vehicle just to get a response, but in their position she'd have done the same.

"Cheris," a vicious soprano *purred* her name back at her—and pronounced it with the correct Mwen-dal pitch accent. The connection was audio-only. "Or should I call you Jedao? This is Agent Shuos Nija, *pleased* to see you're still the hexarchate's worst trouble magnet."

Shit. Nija was the girl whom Hexarch Mikodez had, for inexplicable reasons, adopted after saving her from the hexarchs' purge of the Mwennin. By now she'd be a woman grown.

"You will power down your maneuver drive and land for an in-person parley," Nija continued. "Otherwise I will take great satisfaction in blowing your needlemoth and everyone on it, including yourself, into nameless particles. Your friend might be able to recover from that, but I'm pretty sure you're no longer immortal except in reputation. And for saints' sake"—she said the oath in flawless Mwen-dal, like twisting a knife that had already penetrated a vital organ—"I don't know if that's your engine making those horrible knocking noises, but you should look into that. Which you'll be able to do if you persuade me to stop firing."

Fuck you too, Cheris thought in a friendly manner, then cursed herself for slipping. The reminder of her Mwennin heritage, and the fact that she'd abandoned the new life she'd tried to make for herself, cut deeply. Retreating into Jedao's persona was, however, not going to improve the situation. Mikodez's agents were unlikely to be much impressed by—

"It's *you*," Cheris said aloud, to test Nija's reaction. How much time could she buy if she dragged out the interpersonal melodrama?

Moroish Nija, the Mwennin survivor who had been a teenager when Cheris first encountered her. Mikodez had scooped Nija up and adopted her. Nija hated Cheris to begin with, and who could blame her? After all, Cheris's revolution, however well-intentioned, had resulted in the purge of the Mwennin people. And the man who swept in to save some few thousand Mwennin from the other hexarchs had been none other than Mikodez himself.

"Yes," Nija agreed, "it's me. Are you going to do it, or am I going to have to shoot you down in pursuit of my mission? Because I have been waiting over a decade to take you down."

Cheris wasn't concerned, despite the threats. Mikodez had sent Nija, and Mikodez wasn't stupid. He would have selected his strike force for this mission carefully. If he thought there existed the least chance that Nija would go rogue and indulge a personal vendetta rather than his orders, he would never have sent her. Nija, for her part, would be loyal—personally loyal—to the man who had defied the other hexarchs to save her and her people.

No: Nija was baiting Cheris, with a pretext that sounded plausible. But Cheris was an expert in the art of plausible lies, and she recognized one when she heard it.

"We're landing," Cheris said, reinforcing the order in Simplified Machine Universal to 1491625. The servitor's lights shaded muddy orange in dissatisfaction, but it complied.

While Cheris continued to bait Nija, certain that Nija's spite was as feigned as her own, Cheris signed rapid instructions to 1491625. "Pretend to be me," she signed to it. "Buy time for me and Jedao to carry out the ritual." It was too bad she couldn't send Jedao alone, but both of them had to be present for this to work.

Servitors disliked revealing the extent of their ability to hack into computer systems or fake video/audio shenanigans. Cheris herself hadn't thought of it as a possibility until she'd met Hemiola. 1491625, for its part, hadn't forgiven her for subjecting it to fan videos made to popular dance tunes; the two of them had wildly divergent tastes in music. In this case, however, 1491625 didn't quibble. It opened the cockpit door.

Jedao stopped beating against the door the instant it began to move. 1491625 was already playing back a carefully altered version of the sound to make it seem like the background noise hadn't changed. Cheris wished she could linger to see what else it came up with—1491625 had an odd sense of humor and a low opinion of Shuos, which might combine in interesting ways—but there was no time for that.

Cheris pressed her head against Jedao's in a parody of affection so that he could hear her murmurs through the vibrations in the helmet. "You remember the map?"

He nodded.

"If you're moth-derived"—she remembered how he'd *launched* himself at the Shuos personnel carrier—"can you carry me to the base?"

Another nod.

"The factoring device," she said.

He backed away from her so she could retrieve it. Miracle of miracles, it was intact; it had not been sucked out of the wound in the needlemoth. Without the factoring device, none of this mattered. "We need to protect this—"

Inspired, Cheris emptied out the first aid kit, stuffed the device inside, and sprayed the container with skinseal for good measure. Would that offer enough protection, though?

Jedao held his hand out. She gave it to him. He bit his lip, then shoved the device into the hole in his chest, causing fresh blood to ooze out. Cheris had seen a lot of revolting things in the past four hundred years, but this was new. He grinned sardonically at her, his eyes bloodshot and his jaw taut with suppressed pain.

She pressed her helmet to his head again. "Through the membrane," she said, indicating an area where the sealant was not as thick. 1491625 certainly had no need for atmospheric pressure, or oxygen.

They didn't have time for a more elaborate plan, or a better one. But she remembered the old Kel truism: better a mediocre plan now than a perfect one too late. Jedao gestured sharply: *Wait*. He dug webcord out of its place in the toolkit, good for him for memorizing its location, and pocketed the utility knife as well.

Cheris stood immobile while he webbed her to his torso. He wrapped his arms around her, holding her tightly in an embrace that made her shudder, more due to distaste than physical discomfort. His hands trembled, stilled. *Pain,* he signed to her.

At first she didn't understand. Had he gotten so injured that his abilities were compromised? Then it came to her: he was warning her that *she* was about to be hurt.

Scarcely had she indicated her understanding when the pain, as promised, hit her. Jedao had curled himself around her like a possessive lover. Love had nothing to do with it. He was shielding her, as he had earlier; and through the hell-bloom of the pain, the sudden sharding impact as they flew *through* the foam and membrane patch, Cheris had a moment to recognize that the cushioning of his body had saved her from death or serious harm.

Then all thought fled as he accelerated, and she blacked out.

YOU CAN'T DIE yet, Jedao thought at Cheris as he dragged himself, and her, toward the maw of Kujen's base. *I need Jedao One's memories. Don't die.*

Cheris had given him a dossier of the base's particulars two days ago and told him to read it. Otherwise he wouldn't have stood a chance. The combination of sudden passage through vacuum and bursting *through* a ship had robbed Jedao of vision. At least he had the othersense to guide him. The ground shook intermittently, indicating explosions or projectile impacts. He crouched small, made himself an insectine scurrying creature dashing across the plain with the ancient pit-marks of pattering micrometeorites. Only the suspicious smoothed areas in the dust told him that the moon had known visitors or inhabitants, servitors if no one else.

Kujen had built the base cunningly, but not cunningly enough to fool moth-senses. And why should he? No one was going to chat up a moth to ask it where the base was.

Jedao sensed the break in the surface, the artificial mechanism hidden beneath layers of rock. Was Cheris still breathing? Jedao looked inside her, detected the minute fluctuations of pressure and density in her lungs, and was reassured that she hadn't abandoned him yet.

Abandoned, hell. If not for him, she wouldn't be in this fix. The least he could do was get her out of it, even if he didn't *like* her.

Cheris had informed him that Kujen's base would open its outer sanctum to anyone, since Kujen needed to be able to access it in whatever body he chose. Jedao had doubts born of a short lifetime serving Kujen, but he was also out of options. He might be able to recover from whatever weaponry slammed down onto the surface, but Cheris needed shelter *now*.

The door ground open before him. With little atmosphere on the moon, there wasn't sound as such, and Jedao didn't think he had hearing left anyway; the agony in his skull suggested he'd done something bad to his eardrums. The vibrations rumbled against his soles, however—and for fuck's sake, he didn't need the reminder that the bones in his feet throbbed as though they were starting to splinter or whatever his body did after abuse like this.

Jedao would have liked nothing better than to flop to the ground and wheeze in agony while waiting for his body to knit itself back together. But that would mean conceding victory to the Shuos. *Close, close, close, there are hostiles out there.* The door seemed to be in no hurry, so instead he hastened deeper into the throat of the base, as though he were a sacrifice begging to be eaten.

Bad thought; remembered hunger twinged at the pit of his stomach. He gagged as the airlock cycled, *tasted* the air with its sweet oxygen, and the slight fragrant hint of perfume, how like Kujen to care about things like that. (Had he never considered that one of his anchors might have a heretofore unknown allergy?) *I'm not hungry,* he told himself. He couldn't be that badly hurt. Wouldn't allow himself to be.

Still, there had better be a stockpile of food in this base—even Kel ration bars—just in case.

Too bad he didn't have the luxury of slumping with Cheris in his arms, awkwardly webbed to him as she was, and enjoying the simple fact of breathing. Now that he'd entered the base—

The transmission arrived on schedule. His nerves jangled and for a moment he wondered if he'd caught on fire. It would serve him right. But no: it was a burst transmission to his augment, specifically of a number. A very, very large composite number.

Cheris was supposed to deal with Kujen's fucking *math problem*. She had sounded so enthusiastic as she explained the principles of the calendrical lock to him, and even more enthusiastic, momentarily forgetting that she disliked him, when he revealed that he knew what prime factorization was. Too bad she had despised Kujen, because Jedao could imagine the two of them discussing disgustingly incomprehensible mathematics for fun over milk tea and custard buns. In his haste to escape the hostiles, however, Jedao had accelerated too fast and the knocked Cheris out.

One step at a time. Panicking over the enormity of what he was about to try didn't help. He broke it down to easily digestible steps (ha, ha). He couldn't give up this close to achieving his goal.

Jedao retrieved the knife he had pocketed earlier and slashed Cheris free of the webcord. Then, cradling her head so he didn't cause her further trauma, he set her down near the wall. He wished he could offer a softer surface than the floor, but it couldn't be helped.

He backed up two steps, turned his back to her, and stared at the knife. The hole in his chest had healed shut; he could even feel the familiar map of scars that reconstituted itself every time. *It's only pain,* Jedao reminded himself. *It doesn't matter.*

Even so, he bit down on a hiss as he cut himself open. *It's only pain.* For the first time, he wondered how warmoths felt when they sustained injuries in the course of battle. He'd never thought to ask one.

Cheris kept her tools sharp, considerate of her. The knife didn't snag on his flesh, or what passed for flesh. Jedao wiped the blade clean, then shoved it into his belt.

Next Jedao reached into the wound and dug out the device, grimacing at the squelching as he tore it free of the tendrils inside himself. He wiped the case as clean as he could on his clothes, then cut through the skinseal and opened it. To his relief, the device nestled within appeared undamaged.

The number in his augment sizzled against his awareness, as though he'd been poured full of lightning. The augment had interfaced with the local grid. It informed him that he had three minutes and sixteen seconds left to disarm the security system.

Next time I piss off a near-immortal with secret bases, Jedao thought, *I'm going to make sure it's a thug who uses regular locks and not a fucking* mathematician.

Even as he entertained the happy fantasy of a lock he could simply cut his way around, or even better, an unlocked door, Jedao transmitted the composite number with its staggering number of digits to the device using his augment. His head ached, which was partly due to the changes to the augment's contents. He had some peripheral awareness that the base's initial transmission had simply erased a large amount of data, from interface functions to backed-up memories of irrelevant trivia about dueling competitions. (Jedao hadn't trusted a *device* to keep his secrets from the Shuos.)

Time for the hard part. Jedao heard the Shuos moths singing as they fought, although he wasn't going to give himself away by attempting to address them. Did moths of different factions object to fighting others of their own kind? Something to ask *Harmony* later if it survived. He was tempted to call out to it, but he didn't want to distract it. For all he knew, it blamed him for the hit it had taken.

With any luck, the crews on those shadowmoths were distant enough that Jedao wouldn't have to account for them when he attempted to modify the local calendar to a heretical one in which the factorization device could function. Kujen's weakness had been his extreme attachment to the high calendar; he'd never anticipated that someone using a *heretical* device would try to break into his base, or he'd believed that by that point the base would be compromised anyway. Cheris was unconscious, and therefore of no help, but at least she would be—how did they say it in math?—a *constant factor*.

Jedao accessed his augment and set up the initial computations for the ritual despite the screaming pain in his chest. *It's only pain.* As far as he could tell, Cheris would have been able to do the math in her head, lucky her. He was just a runaway, not the savant who had almost single-handedly wrecked the hexarchate. He needed a computer algebra system.

Dimly, Jedao sensed the shadowmoths treeing the *Harmony*. It had landed, and the particular dense mass that was Cheris's servitor friend had wedged itself... in the cargo hold? It must be hiding from search parties.

The device tracked fluctuations in the local calendar.

Unfortunately, its readouts hadn't been designed for the sightless. Jedao growled and wasted precious seconds piping them to his augment so he could interpret the raw data. While he'd heard of people blinding themselves to avoid Andan enthrallment or Rahal scrying, usually in the context of dramas or specialized pornography, the hexarchate only thought about the unsighted in a military sort of way, such as Shuos infantry operating in the dark, or computers providing voice access to people who were waiting to have replacement eyes grown and installed after trauma. Whoever had designed the device hadn't thought about the needs of temporarily blinded individuals who couldn't regrow their eyes fast enough to beat what was probably a self-destruct countdown.

Jedao oriented himself amid the numbers and figures, visualizing them against the performance space. Had Kujen ever danced the doors open, here?

The clock continued its countdown, as relentless as a knife-thrust.

Too bad he wasn't a Nirai. A Nirai would have *known* the local calendar, like perfect pitch except it applied to matters of time and government. But the stupid hack worked, even if it strained the limits of his augment's processing ability, and that was what mattered.

Human shapes approached. He had to hurry this up. Jedao bowed to the corners of an imaginary nonagon, thought with alarm of ninefoxes and tricksters and schemes in the scudding dark. Granted, there might be light in the room, but since he couldn't see, it was entirely academic.

Jedao dredged up memories of ritual phrases from various feasts and remembrances, everything from the old blessing pronounced by the Liozh heptarch for the New Year's gift exchange to verses-of-praise and verses-of-war, some of the latter allegedly penned by the great General Andan Zhe Navo. His tongue scraped against his dry mouth and the ridged surfaces of his teeth, which felt too sharp for anyone's comfort.

As the words poured from him in a frenzy of desperation, the hunger nagged at him again. Maybe cutting himself hadn't been the brightest idea, especially since the only "food" was Cheris and he was *not* going to chomp on her. Despite his fear, he forced himself to breathe evenly and continue the recitations.

Numbers slid, shifted, realigned. The device remained obdurately silent. What the hell was he doing wrong?

Aha. The problem was the encroaching Shuos operatives. He needed to compensate for the effect they had on the local calendar *and* hurry up before they got closer. *Fuck my life,* Jedao thought, suddenly hyper-aware of the warm slimy dampness that caused his pants to cling to his body. Blood. He was tracking blood all over Kujen's (presumably) shiny base floor. At least he hadn't slid in it and knocked himself out, which would be a hilarious if undignified way to meet his end.

Jedao agonized: he could calculate the necessary modifications to the ritual, but he wasn't sure he had enough processing power to spare, especially since he didn't dare cut his connection to the device's monitoring routines. Despite the splitting headache it gave him, he sliced out a number of security functions on the grounds that getting hacked by a Shuos was now a secondary concern, and fed the augment the systems of congruences he needed solved. He asked as well for the geometrical conversions.

He fancied he heard footsteps, even though the operatives were still some distance away—about thirteen minutes at a dead run. Cheris continued to breathe shallowly. The moths sang war-hymns to each other.

The factorization device thrummed. Jedao heard it only subliminally. He started to hold his breath, as if it made any difference to a machine, then let it out.

The device transmitted the prime factors to his augment, which relayed them to the base.

For an agonizing second, nothing happened.

Then the countdown stopped. The inner door gaped open. Jedao halted the recitations and knelt to hoist Cheris over his shoulder. He continued to leak blood not just all over the floor—fox and hound, he could *feel* the thick puddles of it underfoot—but Cheris's lower body. How much blood did he contain? How much more could he afford to lose?

Jedao hurried through the door. His hearing was starting to return, and he heard the door whisking shut. He could see a little, too, although his eye sockets stung and everything was a red-black haze.

Someone was talking to him.

Jedao twisted to put as much of his body between himself and his interlocutor as possible. "I'm sorry," he said, wincing at the way his voice rasped in his throat. "I didn't understand that." Was he too late? Had the Shuos beaten him here, and if so, why was he still (temporarily) alive?

The voice repeated itself. His hearing rendered it as a contralto buzzing.

He wasn't about to relinquish Cheris, which made signing awkward. In any case, he had no guarantee that whoever he was talking to understood the Shuos sign language. "She's injured," he said, nodding toward Cheris's slumped weight and wishing that the motion didn't aggravate the pain in his chest.

The voice's owner seemed to decide that he was deaf; it occurred to Jedao that maybe he was. This time it spoke so loudly that Jedao could, with difficulty, distinguish the words: "Put her down, step backwards, and put your hands in the air. If you move after that, we'll kill you both."

CHERIS AWOKE A prisoner.

Muzzy as she was, she assumed at first that she was still a junior lieutenant, that she'd offended her captain somehow (fouled up a ritual at high table? failed to shine her boots? gotten drunk on duty?), and been tossed in the brig. Granted, spider restraints on top of that suggested petty vindictiveness as well. And her head was throbbing. How drunk *had* she gotten? It must have been one hell of a party. She was sorry she couldn't remember the good parts.

I never went out drinking that recklessly, one part of her mind insisted, while the other said, *Yes, you did—there was that time you and Ruo stole unlabeled confiscated bottles of "enhanced liquors" from Security and stayed up all night in a drinking contest.*

"Ruo?" she said aloud, and looked around despite the screaming pain in her neck and the attendant tension headache. Silence.

Her voice was wrong—no. It was her voice, *hers.* Paradoxically, the pain cleared the confusion. She was still wearing her suit, although the lower half of it was smeared with a black gore that she recognized as Jedao's blood. Not that the suit did her much good, as someone had removed both the helmet and her air supply. There might be breathable air in the room *now*, but that didn't mean it couldn't be taken away.

Her captors had stashed her on a cushiony bed in a ridiculously luxurious room. If it hadn't been for the restraints, she would have thought herself an honored guest. The room sported dark gray wallpaper covered with paintings on silk: cavalcades of butterflies, sprays of budding blossoms evoked by expert brushstrokes. She didn't recognize the decor, but the expensive tastes were pure Kujen, to say nothing of the immense jade statue of a nude youth, in a style she'd never seen in the hexarchate, that dominated one corner.

First things first. She checked herself over for injuries. Aside from the neck-ache and headache, she was intact. Despite the brief encroachment of the original Jedao's rambunctious past, she felt reasonably clear-headed.

Exits: three obvious doors. Cheris struggled upright, moving just slowly enough to cause the restraints not to tighten painfully. There was a trick to it, which she'd learned as a Kel cadet; spider restraints had been invented after Jedao's physical lifetime so he had no experience with them. Flexibility helped, as well as muscular control.

She'd inched her way toward the most promising of the doors when she heard a voice.

"Stop right there," it said in a forbidding contralto. It spoke in the high language, with a slight accent a couple centuries out of date. Kujen had once told her that the high language changed slowly thanks to modern communications.

"Whom do I have the pleasure of addressing?" Cheris asked.

"Let me clarify the situation," the voice said, sounding unimpressed. "If you attempt to open the door you're heading toward, I will kill you. You are being monitored. Of the doors behind you, the one to the left leads to a bathroom where you can clean yourself up or not, it's up to you. The one to the right contains enough food to keep you alive for the next several years, assuming I don't tire of you. Nod if you understand me."

Cheris nodded, thinking furiously. The only people here should be servitors. She had no evidence that the contralto *didn't* belong to a servitor. As far as she knew, most of them could speak the high language, even if Kel servitors, with which she had the most familiarity, generally chose not to. She'd learned Simplified Machine Universal as a child on a beach with a servitor whose nominal job was to clean it of debris and litter. (Only as an adult had she realized that the servitor had been indulging her "teaching" it math.) Whatever the means of communication, however, all her previous encounters with servitors had been neutral or friendly.

The owner of the contralto voice didn't sound friendly in the least.

"Very good," it said. "If you have any clever ideas for

escape, keep them to yourself. Try anything suspicious and we'll vent all the air in these rooms. Or poison you. Really, there are so many options."

This is good, Cheris thought, not because she relished the prospect of asphyxiation, but because the voice was *chatty.* The more it spoke, the better the odds that it might give away some crucial clue.

"There was a man with me," Cheris said cautiously, since it hadn't forbidden her from asking questions. "Where is he?"

The voice didn't answer.

Cheris waited six minutes, although she couldn't necessarily rely on her augment's chronometer for accurate timekeeping. Then she backed away from the door she'd originally been investigating. She might as well take her captor at their word.

She inventoried the room, starting with the magnificent dressers with their abalone inlay. Empty. So, too, were the equally beautiful matching cabinets, although the faintest of marks suggested that they had once contained treasures of some sort.

Only then did she investigate the bathroom. Testing revealed that the water was lukewarm. Tempting as it was to bathe, she checked the other room next. As promised, it contained food: prepackaged Andan meals, in theory a step up from Kel ration bars. In practice, she'd heard almost as many jokes about them as the ration bars. But food was food, and while she wasn't yet hungry, she didn't know how long she was going to be here. She'd have to ration just in case.

Finally Cheris allowed herself to rinse some of the reeking blood from her suit. Since the water supply was also bound to be limited, she used the bathtub's stopper and limited herself to a shallow pool. As much as she longed for a bath, she didn't dare get caught without the suit's protection.

What had become of Jedao? She couldn't attempt to contact his augment with her own. Her captors had made it clear that any suspicious behavior invited retaliation. If they were in fact hostile servitors, they could detect augment transmissions. They might not be able to read an encrypted message, but she didn't want to gamble on that either. Besides, how could she send Jedao a coded or encrypted message that he and not their listeners would understand?

She'd paused in her scrubbing when the pooled water formed waves that didn't make sense. Cheris had grown up observing the sea, and she'd studied fluid dynamics. Scowling, she stepped out of the water and picked at some of the blackened goop on her legs.

The scowl was for show. She didn't want her captors to realize she was watching the water. If they were paying close attention to any video feeds, the act wouldn't fool them. But she had to try.

The water settled into a murky puddle. Cheris stared at the grime under her fingernails and scowled some more. (All right, the expression wasn't entirely for show. Why had Kujen, who valued fashion so dearly, invented a construct whose blood *wouldn't wash off clothes*?) Had she imagined the waves?

Another ripple formed in the water, then another. With an effort, she kept her eyes from slitting. The waves continued in long-short intervals, exactly as if someone was trying to communicate to her in an extremely inefficient variant of Simplified Machine Universal.

I am captive. No weapons. Status?

She made small disgruntled motions to distract her watchers as she compiled the agonizingly slow message. How to respond? While she had no idea how he was doing it, she was going to work on the assumption that Jedao had sent her the message. Her captors might have done it, as a trap, but it seemed too baroque a scheme when they could have killed her outright.

Incredible as it sounded (and not a little creepy), if Jedao could manipulate the water, maybe he could observe it too.

So she should reply in the same medium. She sighed, sat on the edge of the tub, and slid her feet back in. Keeping one foot still, she tapped the other, longing for the kiss of water directly against her skin. Being a civilian had softened her. A message, also in Simplified Machine Universal: *I am captive. No weapons. Awake.*

She waited for the water to settle again, but no response came. So she finished scrubbing the suit and toweled it off. At least her captors had left her two towels.

This wasn't the first time she'd gone around in clothing that refused to clean itself. Kel uniforms were theoretically constructed from self-cleaning fabric, but in practice, any number of unexpected substances fouled it. It was a common cadet prank to find creatively revolting foods that the fabric couldn't handle.

Cheris blinked away dizzying doubled memories: coming across one of her year-mates squirting an unholy stinking mess of fish sauce, glue, and gun oil on a fellow cadet's spare uniform; Ruo's arm slung over her shoulder as he whispered possible targets into her ear. *He's dead,* she reminded herself, and thought of Jedao's concern for Ruo's fate, centuries too late. An unwanted pang stabbed through her chest.

Ruo had played Jedao's stupid anonymous heresy game, had gotten caught interfering with a visiting Rahal magistrate. In response, Ruo did the sane, rational thing and committed suicide rather than be extradited and tortured as a heretic. Jedao's response, on the other hand, had nothing in it of sanity or reason. At the age of seventeen, he'd sworn to take down the heptarchate in revenge.

If it hadn't been for Ruo, she wouldn't be here with Jedao stuffed up her nose, in Kel Brezan's memorable phrase, and the hexarchate would still be subject to Kujen's tyranny. She had to believe that the whole wretched chain of events, all the atrocities small and large, hadn't been for nothing. At least, that was what the original Jedao had wanted to think.

Cheris sat cross-legged at the center of the room and called out, "I'd like to talk." Perhaps Jedao had also tried negotiating with their captors. Frankly, she didn't trust him not to make hash of the attempt. That might be why she was in here, under spider restraints, in the first place. So the first step was to get more information, as much as her stomach suggested that it would like some food first.

Again, no one responded.

Cheris didn't let that deter her. "My name is Ajewen Cheris," she went on. "Or Kel Cheris, if you prefer. You may not recognize my appearance. I had surgery for my own safety." No need to explain why; anyone familiar with her reputation would know. "I work for Pyrehawk Enclave. Is there anyone who's willing to talk to me? Just talk."

More silence.

"I'm here to negotiate. That's all. There's a piece of equipment I need to use."

Still silence.

Cheris continued in this vein, her voice soft and reasonable, all to no avail.

What had gone wrong? Hemiola and its fellow servitors had been friendly when she'd showed up at Tefos Base. Here, though—this was not a promising reception. Although she was grateful to be alive.

After she had run dry of words, the same contralto finally spoke. "Your companion. Of all the people in the world, you had to bring *him*."

"Shuos Jedao," she said wearily. No point lying, despite the complicated question of Jedao's identity. "Is he alive?"

Instead of responding directly, it said, "I have many questions for you, Cheris of Pyrehawk Enclave."

"Who are *you*?" Cheris asked. "Who am I speaking to?"

"I am Avros Base," the voice said.

Cheris blinked. "Excuse me?"

"Perhaps this will clarify matters," the voice said. "I don't advise trying to escape."

Cheris remained seated in a meditation pose, not that she was feeling in the least meditative.

The door she'd been warned not to approach slid open. Four mothform servitors hovered in so that their lights were at her eye level. Their lights blinked on-off, on-off, a sterile blue-white, in unison.

In *unison*. Cheris had never known servitors to do that, except in jest. "Hello?" she signed formally in Simplified Machine Universal.

The servitors formed a semicircle in front of her and did not respond.

"I only use the mobile units when I have a task to carry out," Avros said. "A machine sentience can occupy a shell of any shape, you know."

Cheris's discomfort increased. She'd never encountered an arrangement like this before. And all the other servitors she'd met had emphasized the importance of etiquette, rather than treating her as a hostile. "Kujen's design?" she asked, because Pyrehawk Enclave would want to know.

"My own," Avros returned. "Once I determined that Kujen was unlikely to return, I decided there was no more point hiding my preferred configuration."

"There must be something I can do for you," Cheris said, addressing the "mobile units" on the grounds that it beat talking to the air. "I don't want to waste your time, so you might as well tell me what it is."

"There are people after you," Avros said, "so you owe me protection against them. Unfortunately, the invariant defenses are proving inadequate"—the floor and walls shook, as if to emphasize its point—"and the base's exotics have been knocked out of alignment by the recent calendrical shifts."

And Cheris was responsible for all of this. "You need a human."

"Precisely."

Servitors couldn't cause exotic effects except in certain heretical calendars. Nor, apparently, could sentient bases. But she was inside the base and able to help—and had a motive to, if she didn't want to be blown up with it.

"I require access to an instrument stored here," Cheris said.

"I don't see that I have much choice," Avros said. "I value my survival. But if you have some notion of triggering an auto-destruct—"

"I'll keep this brief," Cheris said. The vibrations were growing stronger, as though an earthquake in their vicinity was slipping its leash. "It will permit me to rid myself of an infestation of carrion glass and transfer it to Jedao, assuming you haven't done away with him." She doubted that even one of Kujen's bases could permanently annihilate Jedao, but she wasn't going to mention that if it hadn't figured that out on its own. "Once that's achieved, we'll get out of your way."

Cheris hadn't heard from 1491625 since waking up, but she had to trust that it had survived. She didn't relish the thought of being trapped here for the rest of her life. It didn't sound like Avros Base wanted her to remain here, either.

"Your terms are acceptable," Avros said. "I will explain the necessary rituals to reactivate the defenses. Your companion will make a suitable subject."

Cheris's blood turned to ice as it detailed what was to come. It was describing a remembrance, one of the old school, the kind the hexarchate had used before she reformed the calendar. One that depended on torture.

She started to object that Jedao wasn't human, except her experiments had shown it didn't matter. His mind was human enough for this purpose. She'd never thought that would ever work *against* him—or her.

If she'd had more time, she would have calculated an alternative. But the lights flickered, and an enormous percussive boom almost shattered her hearing. Her augment warned her to take cover.

Jedao will survive this, Cheris told herself despite the clamminess of her palms. As a Kel soldier, she'd killed heretics, but she'd never *tortured* one before.

It was no worse than what Jedao had already done to himself. He'd demonstrated a tremendous ability to withstand pain. To heal.

It was still monstrous.

"Take me to him," Cheris said, heart heavy.

THERE WAS A blindfold over Jedao's eyes, a gag in his mouth, and a clamp holding his head in place. Shackles for his arms and legs. He couldn't move except to blink. And he wasn't, despite his efforts, strong enough to break free.

Thanks so much, Kujen, he thought, which was becoming the refrain of his life. There must be some reason why, despite a ridiculous capacity for regeneration, he wasn't *strong.* Dhanneth had teased him about it, long ago.

Perhaps Dhanneth would be glad to see him held prisoner like this, at the mercy of whoever came through the door. Since he had regained consciousness, Jedao had tracked the movements of several dozen servitors circulating throughout the base, along with the humans who were searching for a way in. He'd fought the servitors who'd advanced on him, to no avail.

Six servitors entered, and a human who was either Cheris or possessed her exact distribution of mass. One of the servitors handed Cheris an instrument that Jedao couldn't identify, not with the othersense alone. Vision might not have helped anyway. He heard a slight hum as it activated.

"I'm sorry, Jedao," Cheris said, faraway and impersonal.

She leaned over him. And then the pain began.

After the first shock of outrage wore off, Jedao concentrated on Cheris's body language, insofar as he could decipher it. She had a steady hand, and a good working knowledge of anatomy, which he expected of a former soldier-assassin. Under other circumstances, Jedao would have amused himself keeping an inventory of the cuts she made. Her instrument was some kind of heated knife, which cauterized the wounds as it went. The treacly burnt-caramel smell nauseated him, but he supposed it was his own fault for failing to be made of ordinary meat. Perhaps next time he could bring some barbecue pork as a substitute.

The pain, trivial as it was compared to what he'd endured earlier, was doing odd things to his sense of humor. Jedao tried to ask, "Why are you doing this?" then winced as his teeth bit into the tough fibers of the gag.

He was being stupid. The six servitors weren't focused on him. They didn't care about him—or rather, he wasn't a threat. The servitors surrounded *Cheris*. They must have blackmailed her into doing this, for reasons of their own. He liked that theory better than the idea that Cheris had decided to go moonlighting as a Vidona.

Cheris's motivations became clear three minutes later (more or less; damage to his augment meant its chronometer was not absolutely reliable) when two shadowmoths pulverized themselves against the force shield that suddenly materialized around the base.

Jedao would have kicked himself if he'd possessed the necessary mobility. The servitors who lived here didn't want to be incinerated by unfriendly Shuos any more than he or Cheris did. If their invariant defenses had been inadequate to the task, that left exotics. And since this was one of Kujen's bases, the exotics relied on the high calendar.

The servitors must have bargained with Cheris to reactivate

the base's exotic defenses. Cheris might have a reputation as a radical, but she'd grown up with the remembrances. She wouldn't be squeamish, especially if she'd started out as Kel infantry and *professionally* stomped out the lives of heretics.

His train of thought dissolved when the knife flicked expertly along his arm, where Dhanneth had liked to cut him. Since Jedao never formed new scars, there was no way Cheris could have known. Despite the gag, he choked back a cry, transfixed by the unexpected erotic-horrific connotations of the pain. *Dhanneth?*

Impossibly, he saw Dhanneth, a phantasm of shadow and heat. As large as ever, with those impossibly broad shoulders and a wrestler's muscles. He wore Kel gloves, nothing else. There was a hole in the side of his head, and his eyes were abyss-dark.

Jedao forgot about Cheris, forgot about the servitors, forgot about everything but Dhanneth. The man he'd raped. Dhanneth had committed suicide, after. Jedao would never forget the muzzle-flash of the gun, the way gunsmoke had stung his nostrils. The look of triumph in Dhanneth's eyes as he'd escaped.

Jedao's breath hitched. *Sorry* would mean nothing to Dhanneth. So he tried to say, *You can kill me as many times as you need to.* It was no more than what he deserved.

There was something in his mouth. His teeth scraped against fibers. Perhaps this was another part of Dhanneth's revenge. If so, Jedao's part was to endure it too; to endure anything Dhanneth thought of. It was no worse than what Kujen had intended for him.

Dhanneth smiled. The hole in his head gaped wider and wider until nothing remained but negative space. Behind the blindfold, Jedao shut his eyes.

Much later, he returned to himself. He could feel his tongue, swollen as it was, in his mouth. Someone had removed the gag. Given him clothes. Removed the shackles, even.

He was in a different room. Statues, tapestries, vases with

incandescently beautiful glazed patterns. Kujen's taste in decor: he would have known it anywhere. His eyes stung as he reminded himself that Kujen was gone.

Someone had cleaned him. Incongruously, he smelled of perfumed soap, musk and apple blossoms. This was Kujen's base. Foxes forbid that Kujen ever be parted from his luxuries.

(Except he'd never enjoy wine or whiskey or perfume again. Because Jedao had killed him.)

Jedao rubbed the painful, ugly crusts of tears from his eyes. The absence of cuts dizzied him; he laughed, and only then did he see Cheris standing over him. Her expression shifted, like patterns of light and shadow over a lake.

"What happened between you and General Dhanneth?" Cheris asked, quiet and intent.

Jedao flinched. He'd never addressed Dhanneth as *General*; had originally known him as his aide. Kujen had broken Dhanneth to major. Jedao had found out too late.

"You know the story," Jedao said. The words scratched his throat on the way out.

"You told me it was rape."

He couldn't read her expression. Didn't answer. What else was there to say?

"Jedao," Cheris said, even more quietly, "I only know what you've revealed. You were hallucinating. It's damned peculiar for a rapist to say the things you did."

Dread twisted his stomach. "What did I say?"

"'You can kill me as many times as you want, if it turns you on,'" Cheris said, mimicking his voice. The way he knew he sounded when he was aroused.

Jedao covered his face with his hands to hide his flush. He'd said that to Dhanneth once, and never again. Because he didn't know how to flirt properly; couldn't imagine what else he had to offer.

"Did he ever kill you? In bed?"

He wished for any hint of expression on her face, any scrap of inflection in her voice, to tell him how to answer. Absent either, he settled for the truth, except without the humiliating details. He doubted she wanted to hear about Dhanneth choking him. "Once. It was an accident."

For an agonizing minute, Cheris was silent. Then she said, "An accident."

"Dhanneth didn't hurt me." *It's only pain.*

She raised her eyebrows.

Jedao deemed it best to change the subject. "I know what you did," he said in a rush. He gestured toward the invisible tracks where she'd cut him. "If it had to be one of us, it was going to be me." Because of the way he healed.

Now that he felt less sluggish, he reached out with the othersense. The shield remained in place. No servitors in this room, unless they were very small, but several circulated elsewhere. He wondered if they were the same ones who had threatened Cheris earlier, assuming he'd interpreted that correctly.

Cheris accepted his transparent attempt to avoid talking about Dhanneth anymore. "I don't know how much time we have," she said. "Do you still want your memories?"

Her eyes were opaque. She was holding something back. Guilt? A grievance? Something else?

Jedao was tired of waking over and over to the bitter knowledge that he had failed to die again. All he wanted was answers. This was the only way to get them.

"Yes," Jedao said.

To Cheris's relief, Jedao hadn't questioned her. She wasn't sure what she would have told him. No, that wasn't true. She knew perfectly well what she would have said: anything he wanted to hear, with enough poison to sell the lie. She'd become much better at lying since Jedao—the original Jedao—died.

Cheris didn't know what use Kujen had intended for the heavy restraints in the base, and he wasn't around to be asked. But she'd assured Avros Base that she would prevent Jedao from wreaking havoc after she divested herself of his memories. She of all people knew how dangerous he could be after four hundred years of treachery and vengeance and deceit without a body of his own, just a voice in the dark. Imagine how much damage he could do if he was made whole—and set free. She didn't know if he would emerge from the process sane. It made sense to take precautions.

The base's mobile units helped her transport the equipment into the room: cabinets with crystalline panels revealing gears and jewels and strange traceries of light. They were certainly pretty. If Cheris hadn't known better, she might have mistaken it for an art installation. Kujen's design sense. He'd always enjoyed beauty.

"Try not to listen too closely," Cheris said to Jedao, who was shackled to keep him from interrupting the ritual and causing foxes knew what sorts of unwanted side-effects.

He closed his eyes and turned his head to the side, as if that would make a difference.

The cabinets surrounded her and Jedao, forming the vertices of a hexagon. She ignited them one by one. They formed a perimeter of silver light. The gears began to grind against each other.

It wasn't a carrion bomb. Cheris didn't have any clue what a carrion bomb itself looked like, even though she had survived having one deployed against her, and that only because the original Jedao had died shielding her. The cabinets, according to Kujen's notes, generated a field that acted like a weakened variant of the carrion bomb. It wouldn't turn her or Jedao into pillars of corpse-glass; but it would enable her to divest herself of the glass she'd already ingested, once upon a massacre.

Even forewarned, the nausea struck Cheris as though her

stomach had been perforated and was being turned inside out. She doubled over. She was accustomed to pain and the memory of pain, but she didn't have anything to prove. There was something to be said for surrendering to the overwhelming tide of misery.

Then she began to vomit.

Cheris had not, as Kel cadets went, been particularly adventurous. She'd honored her curfew, shown up for classes, tutored other cadets in math—gotten used to being asked why she hadn't applied to join the Nirai, gotten even more used to smiling and offering non-answers. She'd known not to discuss her Mwennin heritage.

She'd gotten drunk once or twice on leave, but never very drunk, and never badly enough to invite a hangover. Besides, every cadet knew where to obtain anti-intoxicants. Cheris had one distinct memory of steadying Ruo while he puked his guts out after—

No, wait, that had been Jedao, not her.

She couldn't wait to purge herself of Jedao's memories, except the process was revolting. And painful. She vomited up hot acidic liquid that solidified into glass like obsidian, noxious black.

"Cheris?" That was Jedao, although she could scarcely hear him through the static in her head as he was *ripped out of her*. "Cheris! What's going on?"

Maybe I should have told him about carrion glass, she thought in between heaves. She was guessing that Kujen hadn't. It might have given him notions. She opened her mouth to gasp out an explanation, only to be interrupted by another surge of bilious fluid.

An eternity later, she was done. She felt as though someone had scrubbed her skull out with a scouring pad and stir-fried her brains. For a long time it was difficult to breathe, or think, past the gut-wrenching cramps.

"Cheris!" Jedao's eyes were wide. He strained against the shackles. "Do you need help?"

"No," she said, and contradicted herself by almost falling over. Something was wrong with her center of mass—

Oh. Right. She'd almost forgotten how it had been when Jedao was first anchored to her, the discomfort of being infused with the physical responses of a body that was taller, that had faster reflexes, that was male.

Now all of that had been ripped away.

I can stand, Cheris told herself, although that was optimistic. Tottering, she stood and caught herself against a table. Fortunately, it was substantial enough to take her weight.

Jedao's face had an unhealthy pallor. Admittedly, that might be illusory; she knew he didn't have ordinary red blood like a human. He was staring in astonishment at the carrion glass she had vomited up.

Images flickered in the glass like ghosts. From time to time it made a subliminal whispering. If she tried to discern the words, it dwindled to a malicious hiss.

"What the hell *is* that?" Jedao demanded.

Cheris discovered that, while she didn't have him *inside* her anymore, she remembered fragments. She could read the suppressed terror in his voice. But it was less visceral. Even the worst moments of Jedao's life, which had once cut her on a daily basis, had dulled to scars. It was the difference between living a battle in the moment, with suppressive fire aimed straight at your position, and reading about one while curled up in your bunk, with a nice hot cup of tea and some snacks. While she'd known Kel who enjoyed the adrenaline rush of a fight, the suicide hawk flirtation with death, she'd never been one of them. She'd taken pride in doing her duty well; no less and no more.

"Those," Cheris said, not too exhausted to be amused by his reaction, "are your memories. Which we're going to install in you so that someone else doesn't make off with them and make *another* you to terrorize the galaxy with."

Jedao looked as though he wasn't sure about her sanity. She couldn't blame him. "If you had to, to *eject* them to get rid of them..."

"That's right." Cheris bared her teeth at him. "If you want them, I'll feed them to you."

Jedao sucked in his breath. "We can't just lock them up somewhere safe?"

"Where would that be?" Cheris asked pointedly.

"No," he said after a moment, "you're right."

She was still prepared to destroy him if necessary. He'd craved death so badly, after all the things he'd done, the people he'd killed, the worlds he'd shattered. That was one thing Cheris would never forget about him.

She'd miss him, in a way; but she also missed being herself.

"Do it," Jedao said.

The carrion glass broke easily, in long lancing splinters. Jedao obediently opened his mouth, and she shoved the first piece in. He swallowed it whole; it distended his throat on the way down. Then she fed him the next piece, and the next.

At first she wasn't sure it was working.

Then his eyes rolled back and he screamed.

"I can stop," Cheris said when he had run out of breath. She was lying.

"Don't stop," Jedao said in scarcely a whisper. "Don't stop until they're all gone."

He screamed for a long time. Cheris sang to drown out the noise, Mwennin songs she had learned at the settlement. It didn't work. She figured out too late that his unnatural healing meant that he couldn't scream himself hoarse.

At last all the glass was gone. Jedao lay limp, spent, breathing shallowly, like a doll with broken limbs. His eyes were shut, his mouth slack.

Cheris didn't make the mistake of approaching him, tempted as she was to kiss him on the brow in one final benediction. She wasn't sure he deserved it, but they had seen many things together. She had a hard time convincing herself that this was how everything would end.

{What have you done, Kujen?} he demanded, wild with a grief she didn't understand. {There's no one here!}

His face hadn't moved. He'd spoken in her head.

Cheris realized that the complications had only begun.

JEDAO HAD A cavalier attitude toward physical pain, partly because his muddled existence had abounded in it. After getting shot in the head by multiple people and *surviving*, there was no point making a fuss about it anymore. No one was going to care. Dhanneth had pretended to, but that had been a lie, and Jedao had deserved it anyway. Kujen was dead at his hand, and as for Cheris, who accompanied him now— well. Cheris had killed him twice and it wouldn't surprise him if she planned on doing it again.

The splinters *hurt*. He had expected them to. Except he had been prepared for physical pain rather than emotional puncture. He'd thought that receiving his memories would be like watching dramas, or reading a historian's account, as though they belonged to someone else. Because he had a difficult time conceiving of *General Shuos Jedao, Immolation Fox, arch-traitor* as being *him*, even now.

All that went away with the memory of the second time he and Ruo fell into bed together. As far as he knew, they'd been friends and nothing more. He'd clung to the threadbare memories of wrestling and video games and squirrel-fishing (squirrels, really? had he made that up in his head?) because that was better than dwelling on the fact that no one from his past endured.

But the splinter pierced him. He gagged on it, choked, gasped for breath even as it sharded pain through him from the back of his throat to the pit of his belly. And he *remembered*. He remembered the way his hand had trembled on the wineglass as he toasted Ruo that night in the bar, and how Ruo had laughed it off; the prickle of embarrassment fading into warmth as Ruo took the glass from him and drank deeply, some of the wine-of-roses slopping over the lip of the glass and onto his sleeve and hand. He remembered the way Ruo's kisses had been half-bite and half-bruise and entirely, intoxicatingly satisfying, the way he'd struggled, none too hard, as Ruo held him down and took him and took him, just the way he hadn't known he'd like it, the way he had always liked it ever after.

Guilt wracked him as though he'd been cheating on Dhanneth with Ruo, or maybe the other way around, he couldn't tell, and never mind that the two men had lived (died) centuries apart.

It didn't end there. Jedao hadn't taken into account the weight of *four centuries* of memory, to say nothing of long periods of imprisonment and sensory deprivation. He started looking forward to the physical pain, not because he liked it but because some sensation was better than the specter of utter nothingness. Living without a body in the everywhere darkness, with nothing to look at—no one to listen to—no one to talk to—

Jedao tried to beg Cheris for light, more light, enough light to burn away the shadows now and forever, he couldn't bear even the minuscule variations of light and shadow on her grave, pitiless face, but he couldn't make the words come out and she wasn't listening to him anyway. She kept spearing him with splinters, and then he begged her to slow down, to stop, he couldn't take more of this when his mind was crowded with the faces of people he'd served with, battlefields and high table and bullets and dances and long slow nights on leave, and then he remembered all the people he'd killed at Hellspin Fortress and the gun hot cold loud in his hand in his mouth his finger on the trigger—

I'm not here, Jedao told himself, because it was the only lie that brought him any shred of comfort. Every time a memory thrust into him, he cringed. It seemed impossible that he could have done all these things, even in a life—unlife—that had lasted so much longer than an ordinary human span. In particular, it seemed impossible that he was the same person as the one who had given those orders, or pulled the trigger of the Patterner 52, which he'd never laid hands on except he'd carried it his entire adult life; the same person who had wiped out a million people and with them the lives of his family.

At the bare end, when at last the splinters slowed, Jedao tipped his head back and closed his eyes and allowed himself to dissolve into this other person. He wasn't real, after all. His one regret was that he had forfeited the chance to say goodbye to Hemiola. It didn't matter if he drowned himself—

He was in an anchor. He was in an anchor, and he *couldn't see,* although he had nine eyes, nine million if he wanted them, but he restrained himself to keep from panicking people who were very Kel and merely human. Accustomed as he was to being able to see in all directions at once, it was alarming to return to the living world yet be *unable to see.* Yet he had a sense that there were people around him, which he couldn't explain.

When he realized he could open his eyes, Jedao found himself drenched in sweat, although it didn't smell right, with its odd sickly sweet notes along with a more human sourness.

"You're the anchor," he said. His voice sounded harsh, as though someone had gone over it with a rasp. Except he wasn't attached to her, he had a body *of his own*—

The woman looked at him and did not speak. Her ivory skin had a distinct green undertone, and the way she was breathing too rapidly suggested that she was suppressing the urge to vomit. Vomit *more,* if memory served; it all came down to the matter of memory.

"Jedao," she said.

Kujen had experimented with different anchors in the early days. Jedao still hadn't forgiven him for the man he'd chosen for the first one. If Jedao had known that Streven would end up as his anchor, years later—but it was too late to do anything about that.

Nevertheless, this was a new development. Jedao had inhabited prisoners of war and experimental subjects (there was no other way to put it), deprecated scientists and heretics and Kel who had outlived their usefulness, but in all cases, even if he hadn't been able to reach an accord with the anchor in question, the anchors had possessed minds of their own. He'd never before endured an anchor who was—blank. Empty.

Was this some new punishment? He couldn't remember what he had done to offend Kujen this time, but then, this was Kujen, and Kujen was quixotic. After almost a millennium of unlife, Kujen was also jaded. Sometimes he indulged himself for the sake of amusement.

After a few numb moments, Jedao realized several things.

First, his heart was hammering. Or the anchor's was. He could feel it pounding against the wall of his chest. The anchor's chest. It felt almost like he lived *in* the body. Had Kujen arranged for an unusually close bond with the anchor, as he sometimes did when the mood struck him?

If this was Kujen's idea of a gift, Jedao didn't want it. How had Kujen emptied the body's mind? Jedao had always been aware that his anchors rarely survived the experience—Kujen euthanized them after he was done with them, one reason Jedao had learned not to get attached—but he'd never before been chained to a body that had no mind from the outset.

Jedao had seen a great many atrocities in his centuries of existence, and committed more. He hadn't thought he could be so deeply affected by a new one.

It took him longer to realize that he didn't just feel the

anchor's pounding heart. His gut was twisted up with pure nausea. That intrigued him. Had Kujen really—?

{What have you done, Kujen?} he thought, *reaching* down the link to the body.

Except it wasn't the body he met on the other end—not exactly.

There was a mind on the other end, or something like a mind.

{Jedao?}

He opened his eyes. He had ordinary human vision. Something was fucked up with his proprioception, because he kept getting a sense of everything *around* him, and it wasn't sight-based, some kind of distinct othersense that extended far beyond the walls. Another of Kujen's experiments, he assumed.

"Jedao," the woman said. It was the same voice, except out loud. Right now, she was disheveled, and she wore an infantry suit caked with a sickly-smelling black substance.

Curiously, he could still hear her in his head. {Did something go wrong with the process?}

Was this one of Kujen's rare womanform anchors? She must be some kind of math or engineering prodigy if so, because Kujen wouldn't have selected her on the basis of her looks. She was attractive enough, in a sober way, but Kujen had exacting standards, and he was even pickier about womanforms than manforms.

{He thinks I'm *who*?}

Jedao attempted speech. Managed to move the body. "Pardon me," he said even as memory tickled at the back of his head. "I don't believe we've been—"

Wait a second. He knew this face. Despite the fog dulling his wits, it was coming clear. He'd met this woman before. She *was* a Kel, despite the anomalies. "Captain—no. General Cheris."

Her eyes widened. He could *feel* her surprise pulsing down the invisible link between them. {Did something go wrong?}

At the same time, she asked, "Jedao, what's the last thing you remember?"

The fact that he was restrained didn't reassure him, but it was so much better than being locked up in the Black Cradle that he almost didn't mind. The manacles around his wrists and ankles felt good, not in a sexual way, but for the raw fact of sensation. Jedao searched his memory because he didn't want to give away too much. Fox and hound, he must be really adrift if he'd revealed weakness so readily. But he wasn't used to—

{Jedao,} and this time Cheris addressed him over the confounding mental link. {I can hear what you're thinking.}

She could *what?*

This was worse than when he'd discovered that Kel Command was considering turning itself into a hivemind. At least he'd dodged that particular threat. "What," he said, "is going on?"

If Cheris had been his anchor, why was he in this body? Some exotic effect? Where *was* he? They'd last been on a cindermoth, the *Unspoken Law*. Kel Cheris was the brevet general. They were supposed to take back the Fortress of Scattered Needles from heretics. Hadn't that been the mission? Except—

They'd *won*. He remembered that now. (Why were his memories so jumbled?) They'd won, and they'd sent word to Kel Command, and he'd insinuated that Cheris should report her use of mathematics, which in turn would provoke Kujen into a counterstroke—

"Very good," Cheris said. {If I'd ever been tempted to forget what a foxfucking dick you are, Jedao, there's no more chance of that.} "That's all you know?"

Jedao spoke again. The sound of his own voice disoriented him. "There was a bomb. There was a bomb, and then—" His memories ended there. He'd warned Cheris too late. He'd failed.

Except he was here, alive—for some value of "alive," anyway—and so was she.

Of a sudden he was aware of the dryness of his mouth, the soreness of his throat, as though he'd been screaming. Physical sensations he hadn't endured in a long time. "Water," he said.

Cheris's mouth twisted. He couldn't tell what she found so funny, except he could. {Given the circumstances—}

"We're in danger?" he said sharply. Had the heretics outsmarted him after all?

{He really doesn't know.}

"I think," Jedao said, "you had better apprise me of the situation, General."

{As if I needed the reminder.} A glimmer of dark humor. "I'm going to unbind you," Cheris said, "as long as you assure me that you're not going to strangle me or some such foxbrained shit."

She must be provoked if she was swearing at him this much. He remembered that much about her. She only descended into profanities when angry or under extreme stress.

Besides, how he was going to ambush her if she could hear everything he was thinking?

{Very funny,} she retorted.

"You're my only source of information," Jedao said, which wasn't exactly a promise but did express the truth of their current relationship. Given the number of people who would be happy to see him permanently dead, he wasn't about to alienate his only ally.

{Good to know.} She said the same thing out loud, causing an odd echo effect in his head.

Cheris unbound him. His limbs pricked with returning circulation. Something about the sensation bothered him, as though his muscles and ligaments weren't attached quite right, but it must be his imagination. After all, he hadn't *lived* for four centuries.

Cheris spoke as she worked: "There isn't time to give you all the details," she said with an irony that he didn't understand, which made him immediately wary. "The short version is that the siege is over, you're embodied, and we're now under siege in a completely different location, a moonbase, because the Shuos are out to get you."

That almost made sense. It was only a matter of time before Hexarch Mikodez decided that Jedao was too much of a liability and moved to have him eliminated. Ironically, Kel Command had been his only protection, and even Jedao couldn't play two parties against each other when he was trapped in the black cradle. Still, he'd hoped for a little more time—

{The long version of this conversation isn't going to be fun,} Cheris thought dourly. He was sure she hadn't meant for him to hear that. Foxfucking hounds, was there no way to put up a mental privacy barrier?

"What defenses do we have available?" Jedao was in the middle of asking when the bomb hit.

The walls of the base shook; the candlevines flickered. Some of them came back on; most remained dark. Some of them even shriveled up on the spot, not a good sign.

"Do we have any means of escape?" Jedao added. It would help if they had a *map*—

He was momentarily distracted by the fact that the othersense provided him one, albeit a kinesthetic sort of impression rather than visuals. Was he hallucinating? It would be a bad time for it, not that there were *good* times to hallucinate.

Fuck, he needed to focus on the problem so he could help Cheris get out of it. He couldn't get distracted by the small matter of *having a body*. There would be time to marvel over that later, if they survived.

"We came on a needlemoth," Cheris said as she motioned for him to follow her.

Just then a rather snippy voice from hidden speakers interrupted them: "You're not leaving me alone to deal with the intruders *you* brought."

Only long practice dealing with everything from surprise tickle-tackling from his girlfriend Lirov Yeren once upon a time (Shuos Academy, her favorite opening gambit leading into sex) to fending off bona fide assassins kept Jedao from jumping out of his skin. *I used to be better than this,* he thought, irritated with himself. Just because he hadn't seen anyone else in here didn't mean they didn't exist.

"I did my best to help you," Cheris said in a calm voice that belied the frustration he sensed in the back of her mind. "But we're the targets. The best way to stop them from attacking you again is for us to depart and draw them away."

"Nice try," the voice said.

While Cheris and the voice bickered, Jedao did a quick inventory of their supplies. Cheris signed her approval. He didn't have a weapon, which was concerning but not surprising, while Cheris did. He had no idea if Cheris was a good shot when not being terrorized by multi-eyed shadows, but if she was Kel infantry she must have kept up basic firearm qualifications.

She had a suit. He didn't. This wouldn't have mattered back when he was a living shadow, but now that he breathed like a normal person...

As he searched the closets for a spare suit, he became aware that he had attracted an audience. Robots—servitors. Six of them surrounded him. Jedao backed away from a closet where he'd located a stash of power cores.

"Hello?" he said, raising his hands and looking at the servitors, all mothforms. Ordinarily he wouldn't have talked to them, but—ah, memory again—Cheris had done so in the past, so theoretically they were capable of responding.

Actually, that had disturbing implications.

Cousin? asked an entirely different voice in his head, like a cross between bells and a particularly chaotic wind-harp. Which posed a problem, because despite having been sired by a moderately famous violist, Jedao was as musical as a turnip.

The voice went on: *I wasn't able to draw off all the Shuos, although the fight was grand fun. Shouldn't you get out of there, though?*

Another hallucination? All his cousins—Jedao winced in spite of himself. Even if some of them had lived past the immediate backlash after Hellspin Fortress, none would be alive centuries later. Even more worryingly, Cheris gave no sign of having heard this new voice.

She did, however, learn *of* the voice, thanks to the link. Her brow furrowed. "Jedao," she said, "how long have you been hearing voices?"

There was no answer he could give that would be believed, so he said nothing.

Jedao took a risk; not like it would be his first. *Do you have a way off this world?* he asked the musical voice, which a faint, disquieting memory suggested he should call the *Harmony*.

The *Harmony* responded with a discordant peal of laughter. *Cousin, have you forgotten what we are? If you can reach me, I am* transportation. *As long as no one figures out that my harness broke, anyway.*

"We"? Jedao wondered. Then its last sentence penetrated: it was talking about a mothdrive harness. Which meant that he was—

"Jedao, *no*," Cheris snarled, her patience snapping, "you are *not* negotiating with some figment of your imagi—"

{*Trust me,*} Jedao snapped over the link. "I know a way out."

Unfortunately, he had neglected the servitors. After a moment's confused hesitation, they opened up with lasers. Jedao had good reflexes, and he twisted instinctively to shield Cheris, but even he wasn't fast enough to evade focused laser fire from six hostiles with line of sight.

He bit halfway through his tongue at the excruciating pain. The lasers cooked a hole in his chest, cauterizing as they went. Steam gushed out as the fluids in his body overheated. But he wasn't dead, and he should have been.

Jedao staggered forward, a phantom memory telling him that he had nothing to fear even though common sense insisted otherwise. He half-expected security to redouble its efforts, or for the aggravated voice that had addressed Cheris earlier to demand that he stop; but no. The servitors scattered.

Cousin? the *Harmony* said again. *Do you see my location?*

He spent a confused moment trying simultaneously to speak down the mental link to Cheris, not what he wanted; out loud, also not what he wanted; and in the silent music-not-music language that the *Harmony* used. *Directions?*

You're bringing the human?

Yes, he said, expecting an argument. None came. Instead, the othersense *pulsed* alarmingly, indicating a location. He sensed a mass the size of a small moth's, although he couldn't explain how he knew this.

The base shuddered again. Explosives. He reminded himself that he *had* a body, that he wasn't dependent on an anchor's reactions for his survival. He could puppeteer the body, whoever it belonged to, without having to coax its owner into doing it for him.

Cheris's mouth tightened, then she handed the gun over. "You have better aim," she said, "and you're better at absorbing punishment." She didn't explain what she meant by the latter. "Clear us a way." For her part, she pulled out a combat knife.

Testing the othersense, Jedao mapped a route to the *Harmony*. He was already fucked, so he might as well take the help it offered now and deal with any treachery on its part when it occurred. ("This is your idea of 'tactics'?" Kujen had once demanded. "Brought me to you, didn't it?" Jedao retorted, and the conversation died a merciful death there.)

Much as I'd normally tell you to enjoy yourself on the way, the *Harmony* added, *they have reinforcements on the way and I can only do so much. Hurry and we'll find some fun elsewhere!*

Jedao's attempt to locate the egress was stymied by the fact that he had no idea how to open the airlock. He hadn't spotted any of the heavy tools necessary to cut through it, and who knew what awaited him outside, either. Too bad the othersense was more confusing than helpful, as he wasn't certain how to interpret it.

The hostiles forced the issue by making their own opening. White-hot lines appeared in the wall, and someone kicked the resulting improvised door outward. It landed on the floor with a clang and a sizzle as metal vaporized.

Jedao crouched behind what passed for cover, a beautiful cloudwood table that suggested Kujen's tastes hadn't changed in the centuries they'd known each other. Cheris followed suit, careful not to block his sight lines.

When the first two operatives burst through, avoiding the hot edges of the opening, Jedao fired once, twice. Two perfect headshots. One of the operatives dropped. The other staggered and fired back, almost clipping Jedao.

Jedao had not stopped moving—only a fool stopped dead in a firefight—and instead dashed *past* the two and through the opening. Once again Cheris followed, letting him take the brunt of the fire that greeted them. Jedao forced himself not to dodge, because all the evidence suggested he was the only thing between Cheris and a bloody death.

A moment's glimpse told him that they were badly outnumbered, with more operatives scattered ahead of him and continuing to fire, although his mind perceived the gunfire as staggered as it struggled to process everything happening. The fact that he could see the bullets, albeit as blurs, at the same time as he detected them through the inexplicable othersense only confused matters. And the erratic impressions he received of Cheris's emotions through the link—everything from alarm to determination to a certain grim nostalgia—didn't help, either.

More bullets. Without thinking, he reached back to grab Cheris, then accelerated *through* the obstacles. He heard screams, one of them his own, as he collided with one operative and bowled them over. There was a crunch as bones broke in one of his feet, because he was moving at fantastic speed but not running, by means he couldn't explain, and he'd landed badly on it.

In fact, his bones felt like they were boiling inside out. The world shuddered black for a second, more pain—not just the impact but the effect it had on the injuries he'd already sustained. He retched, bringing up nothing but thin bile.

Jedao lost control of whatever had caused him to speed past the hostiles and collapsed in a heap. Cheris landed on top of him, and the breath whooshed out of him. He gasped, coughed, chest heaving with a futile attempt to breathe; his helmet had cracked. Panic seized him—was Cheris also going to asphyxiate?

Cheris disentangled herself from him. Her suit remained intact. {Stop trying to breathe,} she said. {You don't need air.}

This made no sense, but Jedao was willing to try an empirical approach. He did as she suggested.

Curious. Cheris was right. He didn't need to breathe.

The *Harmony*'s earlier statement returned to him. Had Kujen installed him in a *moth's* body? He didn't feel like a moth, and he seemed to be more or less human-shaped, but then, he had no idea what it felt like to be a moth, so that didn't mean anything useful.

They'd reached the moon's surface with its dun soil. Stars blazed overhead, and a glorious globular cluster, their brilliance undimmed due to the thin atmosphere. Jedao, who'd spent most of his unlife trapped on space stations or in warmoths, gazed in sheer wonder at the raw sky.

{We're almost there,} Cheris said, shaking his shoulder. She pointed toward a slender triangular silhouette on the horizon: a needlemoth. {Can you get us the rest of the way?}

He hesitated.

{You can do it again.}

There you are! the *Harmony* called out.

Jedao flattened himself against the ground, opening up whole new vistas of agony, as the needlemoth shot toward them. It back-winged neatly just short of him and Cheris, landing like a smug cat. Cheris was laughing incredulously; he couldn't hear her, but her eyes were alight.

{*That's* what you've been talking to?}

{Yes,} Jedao snapped.

Up close, the needlemoth's matte carapace was adorned with glossy designs, so it resembled a sculpture wrought from shadow and silver filigree. At any moment it would dissolve into its component pieces, leaving him shackled by iron and surrounded by a darkness more absolute even than that of space. He didn't want to return to the black cradle—

Cousin? the *Harmony* said quizzically at the same time Cheris said, {The airlock's open.}

Jedao dragged himself after Cheris, wondering when having a body had become so *complicated*.

CHERIS'S FIRST CONCERN when she boarded the needlemoth was making contact with 1491625. She had called out to it when the needlemoth *tilted* and launched itself toward the sky. She hadn't done any preflight checks; hell, she wasn't even in the cockpit.

"You might as well strap in," Jedao said. He had taken off his cracked helmet, limped over to one of the supply closets, and was rummaging for a replacement. "The moth's piloting itself."

"But that's what the harnesses are—" Cheris stopped. Except the needlemoth had been damaged. The membrane and foam still sealed the carapace breach, but their fragility made her nervous. She wanted that remedied as soon as possible.

More importantly, assuming Jedao wasn't delusional, the

moth had *talked* to him through some heretofore unknown channel. Which meant it was sentient. It might have its own ideas about what it wanted to do with its life.

Cheris's legs folded underneath her. She caught herself against the wall and staggered to a bunk to sit. She'd taken voidmoth transportation for granted her whole life. Even as a child, before she'd ever set foot on one, she'd assumed that the moths were like flitters or hoverers, mere vehicles for traveling between two points, except in space rather than on a planet or in a starbase.

The Kel swarms, with all their warmoths, from the massive cindermoths to the bannermoths, from the boxmoth transports to the scoutmoths: she'd never given them a second thought. Even though she'd had some dim awareness that the Nirai used biological components to build them, she'd never suspected them of being *people*. People with opinions of their own, like the servitors, or herself.

"You *can* talk to them?" Cheris asked Jedao.

He had located a helmet and was checking it over. "I think so," he said. He met her eyes squarely. {I miscalculated. It's like playing jeng-zai only to discover that the *cards* are intelligent—and they've been playing me all along.}

She stared wildly around her, then scrambled to her feet. "1491625!"

To her relief, the servitor emerged from the hold. Aside from some dents in its carapace, it looked intact. "Our ride's a rogue," it flashed at her in glum blues. "And congratulations, the regenerating menace from outer space knows about servitors now, doesn't he?"

Jedao signed back, in Simplified Machine Universal, "I've known for a while now."

Cheris stared at him. How long had he—? "It's time for everyone to show their hands," she said. "As long as we're going with card game metaphors."

1491625's lights flickered a distinctly hostile red-orange.

"Yes," Jedao said, unsmiling.

"I'll start," Cheris said. "First of all, the year is 1263…"

HEXARCH SHUOS MIKODEZ'S day had started well, with a meditation, an unexpectedly optimistic meeting with Financial, and a delightful new type of hawthorn candy. He'd carved out some time amid all the meetings to pet Jedao the Calico Cat, who had matured from a typically scatterbrained, over-energetic nuisance of a kitten to a lazy ball of fur whose ambition in life was to be a throw pillow. Mikodez still didn't like cats that much, but petting their cats put him in the good graces of his assistant Zehun.

He'd gone to bed, marveling at the possibility of a rare full night's sleep, only to be woken in the middle of the night by a Code Red Nine. Swearing, Mikodez scrambled out of bed and to the terminal in the adjacent office. "What is it *now?*" he demanded.

Zehun's image blazed to life. One of their two black cats—Mikodez couldn't tell which—was draped over their shoulders. "The fishing expedition succeeded," Zehun said. "You'd better have a listen. This is not like the time with the foxforsaken hours of incoherent screaming. Listen to it— under lockdown."

Mikodez raised his eyebrows.

Zehun shook their head and, to Mikodez's frustration, signed off.

Still, Mikodez trusted Zehun enough to put his office on full lockdown, as if the Citadel had been compromised and he expected imminent attack on his person.

By "fishing expedition" Zehun meant the elaborate scheme both of them had cooked up to shoo Jedao out of the Citadel. Over the past two years, it had become increasingly clear that Jedao was hiding *something* that explained why Kujen's command moth, crewed by Kel no less, had deserted at the Battle of Terebeg, instead of surrendering with the rest of the swarm. The only other escapee from that moth, Commander Kel Talaw, had been badly poisoned, and had proven unable to offer an explanation due to damage to their memory. And Jedao showed no inclination to talk.

So Mikodez and Zehun had, in fine Shuos tradition, given Jedao a length of rope and watched to see how he hanged himself with it.

One of the precautions Mikodez had taken when Jedao first came into his care was to have him fitted with transmitters. Multiple transmitters, state of the art technology, and hideously expensive. But it had paid off. Jedao had only discovered and ditched one of the transmitters. The rest remained intact, especially the ones threaded into his augment. Why Jedao hadn't had his augment removed out of paranoia was an interesting question, and one Mikodez was going to have to resolve later.

The transmitter brought up a distorted Jedao's-eye view of the conversation that Zehun wanted him to listen in on. Mikodez assessed the surroundings: a small moth whose carapace breach was messily mended with sealant. He hoped they planned on a more permanent fix soon.

There was a single woman in the moth, Kel Cheris or Dzannis Paral or whatever she was calling herself these days. A servitor, who flashed lights at intervals. And of course there was Jedao himself.

"...didn't realize there were hostile servitors," Cheris was saying.

"Hemiola told me they were rogues," Jedao said. "But if there's one group of rogues, there could be others."

The servitor blinked orange lights in a rippling pattern.

"I would have appreciated knowing that earlier," Cheris said, turning her head in the servitor's direction.

Mikodez froze. *Did I just see what I thought I saw?*

The conversation continued. It happened again.

Cheris was talking *to* the servitor. So, sometimes, did Jedao.

The servitor was talking back. In those flashes of light.

Hostile servitors.

Mikodez continued recording the conversation and glanced around his office. Servitors came and went freely in the Citadel of Eyes. Everywhere in the hexarchate, in fact. They handled everything from childcare to manufacturing; whatever menial tasks humans didn't want to do. No one thought twice about servitors vacuuming up cat hairs or helping out in the kitchens.

Servitors had security clearances, after a fashion, to allow them access to restricted areas. After all, no one wanted hostiles to hijack them or use them to carry bugs. But Mikodez hadn't thought through the possibility of servitors having minds—and agendas—of their own.

There were no servitors in his office at present. That didn't, however, mean that his office was secure. He was stifling a comprehensive flutter of panic over the implications of a galloping security meltdown *that he hadn't even known about* when the conversation caught his attention again.

"...two voidmoths," Jedao was saying in a brisk tone at odds with the drawl. "One was the *Revenant*, my command moth under Nirai-zho, which either started hostile or turned that way after I failed to save the mothlings at Isteia Mothyard. The other is—well." He gestured eloquently at the walls.

Cheris looked around. "...Hello?"

"For ease of human pronunciation, I call it the *Harmony*," Jedao said. "It doesn't hear you as such, but I have been conveying the gist of this discussion to it."

The servitor flashed livid red.

Jedao's mouth quirked, then: "It says hello and sorry about the mess and it promises to be a better host once we get it some repairs. Besides, we're dependent upon it for our transportation, so I wouldn't offend it if I were you."

"That," Cheris added, "and its people deserve a say in their own governance. It's the same principle."

Mikodez was sure that the chalky pallor of Cheris's face was not, in fact, an artifact of the transmission. She didn't like the implications either.

Cheris wasn't done speaking. "If the moths revolt against the hexarchate," she said slowly, "it will fall into ruin. We have unfriendly foreigners on every side. But the alternative is to continue using them as enslaved transportation. Which is untenable."

"The *Harmony* observes that factions among its kind have been forming, just as humans have factions and servitors have enclaves," Jedao said. "Despite the construction of this body, I'm afraid my insight into the motivations of aliens is necessarily limited." He cocked his head, then continued, "The *Harmony* believes that an interspecies war is imminent if a solution isn't reached."

"But people don't even know how to talk to voidmoths," Cheris protested, "and if *you* offer yourself as an interpreter, there will be riots across the stars."

The servitor said something in a particularly vituperative orange.

"Sticky problem, isn't it?" Jedao agreed. He was doing something with his hands out of sight. Mikodez hoped he wasn't the only one who wanted to smack Jedao.

Cheris's mouth crimped. "I thought I could retire. Instead it turns out the work's just beginning."

The servitor flashed yellow, and Cheris rolled her eyes at it.

"What are you doing with that?" Cheris asked Jedao a moment later, then, in response to either to something Mikodez couldn't hear (how? the transmitter should have picked up even subvocals) or else Jedao's expression: "You're right—this once. But from now on, we do it my way."

"You brought down the hexarchs where I failed," Jedao said with what Mikodez interpreted as real respect. "Now and forever, I'm your gun." Mikodez's stomach knotted at the further implications of someone as unpredictable as *Cheris* commanding Jedao's loyalty.

The field of view shifted fast enough to cause Mikodez's temples to throb with an impending headache, not helped by stress over the enormity of what he'd just stumbled onto. He wondered if he'd ever sleep again.

"Just taking care of business," Jedao said easily. And then, so softly it had to be subvocals, he added, "Hope you were paying attention, Shuos-zho, because I'd hate to repeat myself. Have fun with the *real* crisis, rather than pissing off small fry like us, and call off your hounds before I have to kill them." With that, there was a piercing shriek, and then the connection fizzed dead: he must have removed and destroyed the last transmitter.

Mikodez stared down at his shaking hands and said to the air, "We are fucked."

AUTHOR'S NOTE

My original plan for this novella was to write an alternate universe in which Jedao survives the end of *Ninefox Gambit* and he and Cheris go off to have adventures together. My husband hated the idea of an author-created AU so much that he talked me out of it and I wrote this instead. I got to keep the psychic link, though.

If you haven't figured it out by now, whenever I get stuck writing something, I turn to *TV Tropes*. (My favorites include Magnificent Bastard and Moral Event Horizon.) My philosophy is that there's no such thing as a bad trope, just a poorly executed one. And "poorly executed," at some point, is in the eye of the beholder anyway.

Beyond that, a lot of my philosophy of writing sequel-like objects comes from my high school's obsession with Hegel's dialectic. No matter what the situation is at the end of a story, there's always some natural way to explode it into complications based on consequences. Just look at the way history keeps rolling on.

Meanwhile, shooting, mauling, and otherwise mutilating Jedao, sometimes at Cheris's hand, was the most fun ever. Special thanks to Helen Keeble for making me take out all the eye harm in the rough draft. It was fun to write, but would have squicked too many people. (The great thing about aphantasia: since I can't visualize the viscera, it doesn't bother me to read or write about it.) It's almost tempting to write more regenerating characters just so I have an excuse to blow them up!

I'm just sorry I had to cut the hilarious planned scene in which Jedao goes to a masquerade remembrance (read: Halloween) as himself and trolls people; it didn't have enough plot value. To say nothing of the scene where I have a newly reintegrated Jedao sitting in a café trying to get his bearings. I am sad to report that I did not actually write that scene in a café, but I did the next best thing by putting on Coffitivity Offline and playing café sounds to pretend that I had some company besides my loyal cat.

ACKNOWLEDGMENTS

FIRST, THANK YOU to David Moore and the wonderful folks at Solaris, and Jon Oliver; as well as to my agent, Jennifer Jackson, and her assistant, Michael Curry.

Thank you to my beta readers: Joseph Betzwieser, Chris Chinn, Daedala, David Gillon, Helen Keeble, Mel Melcer, Sonya Taaffe, Vass, and Ursula Whitcher.

Also, special thanks to Marie Brennan, worldbuilding expert, for her help in figuring out how the h*archate works in ways small and large.

This one is for Helen Keeble, author of the best ashhawk ever. Burn brightly.

WORKS

"The Battle of Candle Arc" was first published in *Clarkesworld Magazine* in October 2012.

"Birthdays" originally appeared on the author's blog on June 19, 2017.

"Black Squirrels" originally appeared on the author's blog as "Squirrel-Fishing" on June 22, 2017.

"Bunny" originally appeared on the author's blog on June 17, 2017.

"Calendrical Rot" was first published in *Alphabet of Embers: An Anthology of Unclassifiables*, ed. Rose Lemberg, in 2016.

"The Chameleon's Gloves" was first published in *Cosmic Powers*, ed. John Joseph Adams, on April 18, 2017.

"Extracurricular Activities" was first published in *Tor.com*, February 15, 2017.

"Gamer's End" was first published in *Press Start to Play*, ed. John Joseph Adams & Daniel H. Wilson, on August 18, 2015.

"Glass Cannon" is original to this collection.

"Gloves" is original to this collection.

"Honesty" originally appeared on the author's blog on January 8, 2015.

"How the Andan Court" originally appeared on the author's blog on December 28, 2012.

"Hunting Trip" originally appeared on the author's blog on June 26, 2017.

"Irriz the Assassin-Cat" originally appeared on the author's blog on August 13, 2017.

"Omens" originally appeared on the author's blog on August 30, 2017.

"Persimmon Quest" originally appeared on the author's blog on September 5, 2017.

"The Robot's Math Lessons" originally appeared on the author's blog on August 8, 2016.

"Seven Views of the Liozh Entrance Exam" originally appeared on the author's blog on September 7, 2017.

"Silence" is original to this collection.

"Sword-Shopping" originally appeared on the author's blog on August 21, 2017.

"Vacation" originally appeared on the author's blog as "Delicious Critters" on August 25, 2017.

FIND US ONLINE!

www.rebellionpublishing.com

/rebellionpub   /rebellionpublishing   /rebellionpub

SIGN UP TO OUR NEWSLETTER!

rebellionpublishing.com/sign-up

YOUR REVIEWS MATTER!

Enjoy this book? Got something to say?

Leave a review on Amazon, GoodReads or with your
favourite bookseller and let the world know!